Green Thumbs Way Up for
of Ann

THE GARDEN

"A riveting whodunit . . . a   gray days when you can't get into your garden."
—*Chicago Sun-Times*

"A killer serpent among the guests . . . and the extra benefit of good gardening tips."
—*Booknews* from The Poisoned Pen

DEATH OF A POLITICAL PLANT

"The next time your yard calls out for a good weeding, nurture the gardener first. Plop down on the lawn chair, ignore the june bugs, and enjoy the read." —*USA Today*

"[A] well-paced tale . . . peopled with fully dimensional characters . . . her gardening tips are both intelligent and relevant to the story." —*Publishers Weekly*

DEATH OF A GARDEN PEST

"A hybrid of a traditional whodunit and an up-to-the-minute gardening guide." —*The Denver Post*

"Gardening and murder make a fascinating combination in *Death of a Garden Pest*. Gardener-sleuth Eldridge offers an enchanting view of gardens while facing down dauntingly evil opponents." —Carolyn G. Hart

MULCH

"Ann Ripley plants clues in unexpected places, develops a plot with interesting dirt, and seeds her story with colorful characters, including a captivating noxious villain. *Mulch* is not your garden-variety mystery."
—*New York Times* bestselling author Diane Mott Davidson

"*Mulch* is one of those little gems."
—*Mystery Lovers Bookshop News*

The Perennial Killer

Ann Ripley

BANTAM BOOKS
NEW YORK · TORONTO · LONDON · SYDNEY · AUCKLAND

THE PERENNIAL KILLER
A Bantam Book / May 2000

ISBN 0-553-57737-9

Published simultaneously in the United States and Canada

Bantam Books are published by Bantam Books, a division of Random
House, Inc. Its trademark, consisting of the words "Bantam Books"
and the portrayal of a rooster, is Registered in U.S. Patent and
Trademark Office and in other countries. Marca Registrada. Bantam
Books, 1540 Broadway, New York, New York 10036.

PRINTED IN THE UNITED STATES OF AMERICA

OPM 10 9 8 7 6 5 4 3 2 1

TO TONY

Acknowledgments

A FEW DETAILS OF BOULDER COUNTY'S LAND-scape, that is, an occasional hogback, stream, and cliff, had to be altered for this story. And the public officials described herein in no way are meant to resemble the real people holding these jobs. Many thanks to staff members of Boulder County and its Department of Parks and Open Space, with special thanks to Tina Nielson; Rich Koopmann; Michael Sanders; Cindy Owsley; and Nancy Dayton. The chief of the Lyons Sub-Station, Sergeant Pamela Housh, provided valuable details, as did Dr. Anngwynn St. Just and Dr. Peter Levine, experts in post-traumatic stress. The Denver Botanic Garden's librarian, Susan Eubank, was, as always, a tremendous help. Trux Simmons of KRMA-TV, Denver, guided me again through the realities of public television; Richard Romeo, LL.D., through the legal questions. Karen Romeo added her expertise on Colorado ranches. Michael Ogden of Santa Fe, who designs wetlands, generously shared his knowledge. Others who deserve sincere thanks are Judy Visty, park ranger at Rocky Mountain Park; Andy Amalfitano of the Boulder

Rescue League; Bob Tanem; Enid Schantz; Margaret Coel; Sybil Downing; Karen Gilleland; Beverly Carrigan; James Hester; Carol Dow; Dr. Robert A. Sammons, Jr.; Jessie Lew Mahoney; Irene Sinclair; Win and Jane Brunner; Kay Brunner; Allison Sauer; Jim Munson; David Barnes; Rose Linan; and my six perceptive daughters. Particular thanks to my agent Jane Jordan Browne, and my editor at Bantam Books, Stephanie Kip.

Gardening Essays
by Ann Ripley

The Perennial Killer

Chapter 1

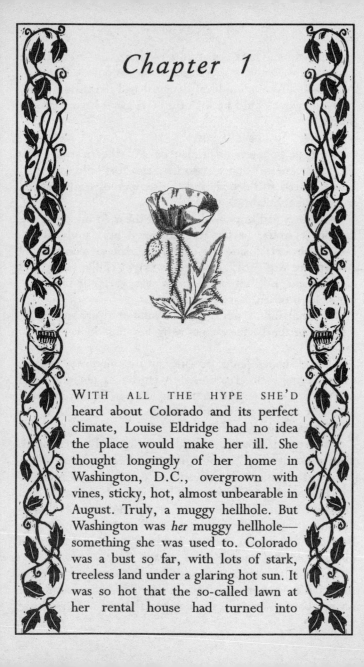

WITH ALL THE HYPE SHE'D heard about Colorado and its perfect climate, Louise Eldridge had no idea the place would make her ill. She thought longingly of her home in Washington, D.C., overgrown with vines, sticky, hot, almost unbearable in August. Truly, a muggy hellhole. But Washington was *her* muggy hellhole—something she was used to. Colorado was a bust so far, with lots of stark, treeless land under a glaring hot sun. It was so hot that the so-called lawn at her rental house had turned into cracked adobe. Three days out here alone, and every single day, she'd wakened with a headache and a queasy stomach. "Altitude sickness," a local druggist had diagnosed airily, "And the heat could be a factor—we *never* have heat like this."

"Never? You have it now."

"It'll all go away in a day or so—the heat *and* the altitude sickness." It was two days ago that he'd said that. Louise's head still ached, and the temperature still ranged around ninety-eight degrees.

But things had improved—or had they? At least she was no longer alone, having just collected her family at the Denver airport. Inside her rental car, the air-conditioned atmosphere was cool, actually downright chilly, as she and her husband, Bill, sat in the front seat, carefully not looking at each other. Barely speaking.

The chill didn't affect their ebullient daughter, Janie, who sat in the back seat enjoying her first look at Colorado.

"Ooh," cooed Janie, peering out the window, "look at those darling little creatures." A cluster of tan, foot-high animals stood together in the field, perched erect as if attending an afternoon kaffeeklatsch.

"Prairie dogs," said Louise.

"Yes, prairie dogs," said Bill, as if he had to reconfirm it to make it true. "And what you have to remember, Janie, is that you can't fool around with them, as much as you like animals. They're not like those baby lambs you used to want to take home with you. They're loaded with bubonic plague. When you go to that wilderness camp, better watch out for rock squirrels, too—I read there's a plague epidemic among them as well."

"Gee, Bill," said Louise shortly, "let's not make everything out here seem terrible for her. Besides, what you're saying about prairie dogs is not exactly true." In preparation for her location shoots for *Gardening With Nature*, Louise had read all there was to read about these little animals, whose unique human qualities of verbal communication were so engaging that they had volunteer groups fighting to save them from extinction. Bill could know only a *fraction* of what she knew.

Her husband looked at her with hurt surprise, and she wished she could take back her words. Suffering from another headache, she knew she was crotchety. Fighting over facts about prairie dogs wasn't the way to treat a husband with whom she had hoped to reconcile. "Sorry," she said. "It's just that when they have plague, they don't last long enough to bother anyone."

He looked at her strangely. Poor man: Everything he had said since he got off the plane with Janie had grated on her nerves.

What a difference from the way she had pictured their time in Colorado. The late-night phone call he received in Washington last week had started it, changing everything, throwing the family's future into doubt. Instead of resigning from the CIA as he had intended, Bill was being suckered in again, persuaded to help with some crisis he hadn't even had time to tell her about before he hustled her onto the early plane to Colorado the next morning.

She had only heard the placating words, "One part of the problem is in Boulder County, right where you're going, so I'll be out there to join you Friday." She bit her lip to keep herself from crying.

Louise couldn't believe it at first: his business was right here where *hers* was. But naturally, his business was much more important than her fledgling broadcast career. He must have told the CIA that she was touring some of the western states, and they had decided to use her trip as a pretext for his assignment. The perfect cover.

But the trip wasn't the whole problem. The next step

her husband would take now that he was not resigning, she thought darkly, would be just what the CIA had wanted for some time: a move to Austria. As CIA station chief in Vienna, she knew, his primary task would be to keep nuclear and biological materials out of the hands of rogue states.

What should she do—trail after him like the loyal wife, or put her foot down and declare her own rights? The whole topic made her feel hollow inside.

By the time Louise had made her way across the arid plains to pick up the two of them at Denver International Airport, she had developed another headache—or was it Bill who made her head ache this time? It flattened her usual jovial spirit, so that even the sight of DIA's jolly white multiple roofs, like an explosion of small white tents up in the sky, failed to cheer her up. And it didn't help when her husband greeted her with averted eyes and only a small peck on the cheek. Now, he continued to be polite but distant in the car, while carrying on a lively conversation with Janie. Plague-ridden prairie dogs, indeed, she thought gloomily.

❦

When they arrived at their rented house north of Boulder, near the little town of Lyons, Louise went straight to bed with codeine-laced Bufferin. That meant Bill still hadn't had the chance to explain himself. She lay with a cool washcloth against one side of her head and brooded. What a passive person she had been over the years. She had leeched onto Bill and lived his life—not her own. Now, she was paying the price. As her job made her more and more independent, she felt the close union with the husband she so dearly loved tearing apart.

It started when she began to work in television—and succeeded at it. And began establishing strong roots in

Washington, where she was making a name for herself. That phone call had made the future clear. Bill would never quit his infuriating job as a spy. He would expect her to continue living in his shadow as he traveled from country to country.

They were two people with careers on a collision course—or was her drug potion making her overdramatic? With this unhappy thought, she lapsed into a restless sleep.

❧

"Feel better?" asked Bill. He sat on the edge of her bed and gently kneaded her shoulder in the spot that usually hurt. He hoped it would work. A massage had helped to clear up little marital storms before.

"Thanks," she murmured. "It's as if someone stuck a knife in there." Bill knew her body almost as well as she knew it herself. As he worked on her back, he felt her relax. He hoped, but wasn't at all sure, that relations between them would soon be back to normal. He felt quite guilty about the recent turn of events in their lives.

His wife smiled at him. "That giant lid that was pressing on my skull has lifted. Maybe I'm over my altitude problems."

"Good. Then how about a little dinner?"

"That sounds great," she said. But when she climbed off the bed, he had to catch her before she fell. He steadied her with a protective arm and gently led her into the comfortable living room.

Janie slouched on the floor, a pile of pillows cradling her blond head, looking supremely bored. She had been ambivalent about this trip. Smitten with hormones, the seventeen-year-old had opted to stay in Washington with Bill the extra few days his job had suddenly required. This had given her more time to say good-bye to her boyfriend

Chris Radebaugh, before an unthinkable separation of two weeks.

"Ma, you've returned from the dead," said the girl, with a big smile. "It's a funky house—I like it. But it's dullsville around here. *Super* quiet. C'mon and give us the skinny—what's there to do?"

Bill chided his daughter. "My dear, you've only been here two hours. Give your mother and me a little time."

Janie slowly got up off the floor and flipped her magazine onto a rustic table near the Taos-style sofa, reaching out with both slim arms in a mighty stretch. "Okay, I get it. You two are still on the outs. You need to talk, so I'll get out of here, maybe take a little walk in the neighborhood, if you can call these fields a neighborhood. See if I can find any human beings, or a dog or a horse, at least."

"Janie," said Louise, "how did you leave Chris?"

"Alone," she shot back, then smiled in spite of herself at the sound of his name. Bill noted she was unusually happy for one who had just said good-bye to her boyfriend in Washington. "He's great. He drove us to Dulles Airport."

Louise sank into an overstuffed chair and smiled weakly at them. "I missed you guys—even my job-obsessed husband." She gave him a challenging look, and he knew things wouldn't be completely back to normal until she got a full explanation for why he had re-upped with the agency. Especially when he had just intimated he was quitting and taking a job offer with the Brookings Institution, a Washington think tank.

He wished their daughter would come through on her promise to give the old folks some needed privacy. But now the girl was clucking over her mother, and in a flash Bill could imagine what a compelling mother Janie would be herself. *"Ma,"* she said, full of sympathy, dipping down and encircling Louise with a surprisingly strong hug. "I can tell what you need—a cup of coffee. Dad figured out how to use the coffeemaker.''

"You've read my mind," Louise called after her, as Janie scampered to the kitchen.

She brought each of them a steaming mug, then left by way of the broad back porch that faced the nearby foothills. Bill sat down at the base of Louise's chair. The light was so strong out here that it was as if he could see Louise more clearly than usual. Her face seemed a little lined, perhaps from the brutal sun—and her skin rough to his touch. Her eyes were tired and bloodshot from the headaches she had been experiencing since she arrived. He felt a pang of guilt for not having shown up earlier.

She seemed just as concerned about him, reaching out a hand and touching his cheek. "You're under a strain, Bill, I can tell. I'm so sorry for being a bear. Forgive me. It's just that I've been so distracted that I haven't even paid much attention to my scripts.''

He bent his head toward her, so that her hand moved across his cheek. "I'm sorry I was delayed—sorry this whole thing came up at the last minute.''

She removed her hand from his face. "Bill, remember the day when you and I first knew we were in love with each other? We sat on the grass on top of the hill at the lake and read love poems?''

"I remember.''

"One of the poems—Shelley, was it?—talked about two souls so close that they were like one.''

"I remember. It was *Epipsychidion*.''

" 'We shall become the same, we shall be one
Spirit within two frames . . .
One hope within two wills, one will beneath
Two overshadowing minds, one life, one death,
One Heaven, one Hell, one immortality,
And one annihilation.' '' She smiled self-consciously. "My

God, Bill, we were melodramatic. We looked in each other's eyes and pledged that this was how close *we* would become."

He put aside his coffee mug and clasped her hand in his. "That was real," he assured her. "We have become that close." His eyes sought hers, but she avoided looking at him.

"But something's happened to us. I feel so apart from you—it's just plain scary. I feel like more of my own person, and that's a good thing, isn't it, for a person to feel strong—independent—not afraid to succeed? But I'm so worried about *us.* It's as if the bottom were falling out of my life." She was on the verge of tears.

He squeezed her shoulder with a gentle hand. "I'm damned proud of you, Louise—and don't you ever forget that." Then he got up from where he was sitting and moved to the windows to stare out at the foothills. Seldom had he been this uncomfortable. His new casual clothes, stiff and strange. This place, Colorado, too bright, too barren of trees. Relations with the wife he loved better than himself, perilously strained. He had better say this right.

"There have been too many changes," he said, "too fast. And I've sent you mixed signals, telling you I wanted to quit my job, then reneging. I apologize." He turned around and his face was grim. He crossed the room in two big strides and crouched in front of her.

"They need me again." He whispered the words. "I just can't walk away when I can help with something that affects all of our futures. Can you understand that?"

"But it will always be like that, Bill. Next, they'll need you back in Europe. I spent twenty years being a foreign service wife while you were leading your double life. Now I have a career of my own; what am I supposed to do, give it up?"

"Let's just take it one step at a time. Louise, the situation out here has to be resolved or there'll be hell to pay. I hate to overemphasize it, but *each* situation we're finding has terrible potential consequences. Think of Chernobyl. As for moving to Vienna, it would not be a covert job. It would be wide open for all the world to see and know about. Working on disarmament, and—"

"Chasing nuclear pirates," she finished.

His eyes pleaded for understanding. "Could we put off talking about that until this emergency is over?"

She reached out and grabbed his hand. "Of course. Just tell me you won't make any more decisions without talking to me first."

He heard Louise's words, but he couldn't quite understand how they'd come to this, and why she was so desperate. It used to be that the exigencies of his job came first, no questions asked. Now, he realized, with some of the same emotion that Louise felt, that the whole equilibrium of their lives had shifted, leaving them both unsettled and anxious about the future.

"Louise, *this* time, I had no choice in the matter." He looked at her, waiting for his words to sink in.

"My God, Bill, I thought we could get out of this . . ."

Then they heard Janie push aside the sliding screen doors and burst into the room, her eyes bright with excitement. "Guys, come outside! We have a real farmer for a neighbor. Horses. Sheep. Even a llama—it spit right in my face! What a cutie! It makes me not want to go off to a wilderness camp in Estes Park. Why, it's wild right here in our backyard."

Then she noticed her parents, huddled together, and she self-consciously brushed her long blond hair back from her face. "What is it, Dad, are you proposing to Ma one more time?"

By the time they went to bed, Louise's headache was gone, and Bill pulled her into his arms. They made love, rapturously, as lovers do when they have had a quarrel and then reconciled—at least for the moment. Afterwards, they lay together in quiet repose in the dark room. Then he turned and talked close to her ear, telling her a little more about his assignment as a peace offering. "We've received information that someone is planning to hijack nuclear materials coming out of the Stony Flats nuclear plant."

"The one near Boulder."

"Yes. It's always been dangerous. It's upwind from Denver, and there's been a release of plutonium at least once, if not more than once, over the years. You know that plutonium is the deadliest substance known to man. A fire they had at the plant in 1969 nearly caused a nuclear criticality situation that could have contaminated the entire population of Denver. Now it's a hot potato, a useless plant with tons of hot material that needs to be dealt with." His arm around her tightened a little.

"How could someone steal materials from it?"

"Right now, stuff from the plant rides its way west to California, to be turned into a less lethal form. We think a high-level person on the inside plans a switch before it gets on the road. What we'll do is open a window of opportunity for the two parties—buyer and seller—so they think they're getting away with it. And then . . ."

"You'll spring the trap?"

"Yes. And that's all you need to know now. Be careful, darling. And while you're remembering poems, recall that old story about Psyche." He hoped she wouldn't take offense at his words. "She was what you might call a prying woman—"

"Are you calling *me* a prying woman?"

"Now, wait—not really. I was just trying to make a little joke about the trouble Psyche got into from prying. . . ." He was silent for a moment. "On second thought, a little prying on your part might not be amiss. . . ."

"What kind of prying?"

"Just keep your eyes and ears open around Boulder, but don't *act*. You already realize it's a pretty sophisticated place—"

She couldn't resist being flip. "You mean it's not Hicksville?"

It was lost on him. "Not by a long shot," he answered. "Boulder has lots of scientists, experts on rockets, weather, time, archaeology. It has high-tech industries, cutting-edge biological labs, that kind of thing, in a corridor between Boulder and Longmont. So there's NIST, NOAA, NCAR, IBM, Ball Aerospace, StorageTek—and the university, of course. People—especially scientists— come here from all over the world. But if you see anything abnormal around here, anyone doing anything that seems out of the ordinary . . ."

"Let's see: I should not be suspicious of people who act normal, only those who skulk around in a suspicious manner."

"Louise, you're making jokes—and I like that. It means you're back to normal. But this is not exactly fun and games."

"I know that. And I'll be happy to help. I'll keep my eyes open, and I'll give you a report when I get home each day."

"Oh." He paused. Her defenses went up again, and she pulled to her side of the bed. "I'm not going to be *here,* because the action isn't only here. It's . . . well, never mind the details. I leave early tomorrow. But I'll call you from my next destination, which I can't tell you about.''

She lay quietly in the bed. He leaned over and brushed her lips with a soft kiss. ''I guess that's as close as you're coming right now.'' Generally, they slept spoon-style, both facing the same way.

''That's as close as I'm coming right now,'' she said in a muffled voice, her head practically buried in her travel pillow.

''I'm sorry if all this is upsetting, Louise. I've probably told you more than I should. Maybe we'd just better go to sleep.'' He turned on his side. ''And one more important thing. Please don't go overboard—you know what I mean? It wouldn't do at all for you to, say, visit the Stony Flats plant, which does allow the public in for tours. You see what I mean?''

''Yes, I see,'' she said, and there was a sad tone in her voice. He knew she was frustrated: his sidekick again, asked to do simple favors, but told very little about what was going on. She tossed and turned beside him for what seemed like hours. Nor could he relax and sleep, with the thoughts tumbling around in his head.

The terrible irony was that Louise had valuable skills— and a peculiar talent for ferreting out criminals. And yet he had no authorization to enlist her help, especially into this current dangerous assignment.

It had felt good to have her back in his arms and to be able to talk about the things that were driving a wedge between them. Too bad there would be little opportunity for romance on this trip. Instead, there was danger ahead for him—but, fortunately, none for Louise.

Open Space
For Plants,
Humans . . .
and Prairie Dogs

IN VARIOUS PARTS OF THE world, it is called open space, open land, nature preserve, greenbelt, wilderness area, greensward, community garden, or park. It's undeveloped land set aside for people's enjoyment. As numbers of the world's least-endangered species—mankind—continue to multiply, open space vanishes. The consequences are great, affecting the psychic and spiritual well-being of people, as well as the very existence of animal and plant species.

Here in the United States, more than 1,200 land trusts make gigantic efforts to preserve land from development. In some communities, voters are asked to foot the bill for open space. (An example: a twenty-five-million-dollar program to save land and farms in Pennsylvania's Pocono Mountains, just ninety miles from New York City and Philadelphia.) Unfortunately, such tax proposals sometimes fail.

Meantime, people fight over existing open space. It may be a pocket park in New York City; a five-acre chunk of space in a fancy Denver suburb that residents thought would remain their private enclave; or historic garden allotments that are being plowed up for housing in a British city. In the booming American West, gargantuan struggles have erupted among municipal officials with different agendas: Some want to buy up all the land they can to keep it out of "development," while others argue that development helps keep the lid on taxes.

The people concerned about this include both the big guns, such as the international group that helped fight a plan to mine gold at the edge of Yellowstone Park, to single individuals with a mission. Environmentalists climb redwoods and make their homes

there to keep the woodcutters away. Environmental terrorists destroy parts of a plush ski resort, allegedly to save the endangered lynx. The U.S. president earns both praise and blame for touting open space, and setting up projects such as the Grand Escalante National Monument, which take vast acreages out of private use.

Is there enough room for animals and plants? Even with these conservation efforts, what is to become of us and our environment as people's need for housing space continues to grow? And what of the plants and animals that must try to exist in skimpier habitats? In the world, one of every eight plant species, ten percent of bird species, and more than twenty-five percent of mammals are threatened with extinction. Speaking for preservation of species and conservation of resources are organizations such as the National Park Service, the Forest Service, the Bureau of Land Management, and the Fish and Wildlife Service; plus the many land trusts, The Nature Conservancy, the National Wildlife Federation, the Sierra Club, and The John Muir Society. Congress, on the one hand, may limit the scope of the Endangered Species and Clean Water acts; and yet it is highly sensitive to public concern for the environmental. In the 104th Congress, it voted more money for the 514 parks in the national wildlife refuge system. Each has a specific mandate to preserve an endangered species or a critical habitat for waterfowl or animals, including certain songbirds, swans, panthers, white-tailed deer, and crocodiles.

The conservator: The Nature Conservancy adds its efforts by purchasing tracts of land in all the fifty states, and certain foreign countries as well, carefully going about its work while avoiding confrontation with private landowners. The Conservancy, with more than 800,000 members, holds three million acres of land, the largest private conservation holding in the U.S. It claims to have protected 9.3 million acres since its foundation in 1951.

In the end, the using up of open space will be at the price of more plant and animal species. Protection has brought some, such as the bald eagle, back from near-extinction. Unprotected, so far, is the prairie dog, and debate over this tan rodent has become a metaphor for the clash between rural and urban value systems. It even made the cover of an issue of *National Geographic*. The animal gives headaches to wildlife experts in western states, as they try to preserve it in the face of growing public objections.

A nice meal for a raptor. The prairie dog is called a "keystone" species, that is, a prey base for many other animals and birds, including the raptor. Some people keep them as pets. Tan, with an unprepossessing countenance, the "dog" has a fetching habit of standing on its hind legs, reaching its tiny paws heavenward, and barking like a puppy. It sends twenty distinct calls to its companions in neighboring burrows. But most astoundingly, scientists have shown that it can recognize people by their clothing. That must be why this rodent has fan clubs of people willing to carry them bodily from the harm of others to new safe havens. (Sometimes they even gently vacuum the little fellows out of their holes.)

Once, prairie dogs proliferated widely in North America, companions to the vanished buffalo. They beat down and smoothed the ground, a good thing for herds of buffalo—though not so good for domestic animals. They now occupy only two percent of their former range, and their numbers and habitat continue to shrink, as they are routinely poisoned, shot, and driven from their homes. En-

emies are not only the bulldozers that come through the fields plowing up their underground homes, but also farmers and ranchers who consider them a pest. Though they enrich the soil, they also eat the ground bare, and are competition for cattle and sheep for grazing grass. Another admitted downside is their penchant for picking up the plague. The disease will rush through a colony, quickly obliterating it, but the idea of "plague-ridden prairie dogs" makes some people think of these innocent creatures as dangerous to the environment.

The prairie dog's place in nature's plan. The people willing to go out with cages and move whole populations of prairie dogs are environmentally aware folks who know this verbose creature is part of nature's plan. Ironically, one of the animals that depends on prairie dogs for food is the endangered black-footed ferret, which is the object of a multimillion-dollar recovery program of the Fish and Wildlife Service. Others besides ferrets and raptors that feed on prairie dogs are coyotes, burrowing owls, and mountain lions. As long as there are these other wild beasts still among us, surely the prairie dog has its place, too.

Chapter 2

LOUISE STARED OUT OF THE window of the covered pickup, praying the man and woman who were her companions on this trip did not expect too much of her until she'd had time to adjust. She'd just packed off her family, Bill in his rental car to parts unknown, Janie off in a van to go to the wilderness camp in Estes Park. As she had watched her beloved husband disappearing down the driveway of their rental house, all she could think about, unfortunately, was the remote possibility of nuclear disaster—and the much more likely prospect of continued marital discord.

Then she was picked up in this giant vehicle, and she had no more time for fretting. The pickup was designed for important male activities such as work, sports—or just showing off. But she wasn't sure it had shocks. They were jouncing up a nightmarish road, a steep washboard of a road that shook her innards, and she wasn't sure what she would do first—throw up, faint from vertigo, or die from lack of oxygen. Then she made the mistake of looking out the side window, and was terrified to see blue sky where there should have been road. Before she had time to scream, the driver saved them from the washout by swerving the vehicle to the left, then violently to the right to avoid colliding with a sandstone cliff on the other side.

"Whoa, there, baby!" he chortled, as if this were just part of the fun of traveling the miserable mountain thoroughfare. "Don't worry, we'll soon be pullin' in t' Porter Ranch."

"Oh, *God*." She felt like Odysseus, with Scylla on one side and Charybdis on the other. She closed her eyes, swallowed hard, and clamped a protective hand over her knotted stomach.

"What's the matter," said the man, "never driven in mountains before?" His blue eyes stared blandly at her.

"Of course I have," Louise said. Her voice trembled with each bump. "The Alps. The Pennines. The Pyrenees . . ."

"Then why do you look like you're gonna blow chunks?"

She sat up straight, and gave him a disgusted look. "That must be your crude way of saying—"

"—you're gonna toss your cookies."

"Well, I don't think so," she said coldly.

He shoved his disreputable hat back on his brown, curly

hair and grinned, his eyes disappearing amid the sunburned wrinkles under his shaggy eyebrows. The only shaggier eyebrows she'd seen were on her neighbor's schnauzer. He said, "You sure *look* like a little gal who's gonna toss her cookies."

She would rather have died than give the man that satisfaction. He was driving this truck like a madman. The only trouble was that she needed him, badly. He was her video cameraman for the Colorado shoots of *Gardening with Nature*. But what rock had her producer found him under? An odd-looking, tall creature, he had folded his lanky legs in their decrepit jeans like an accordion to move his seat forward to make room for the blond young woman in the back seat. Louise's so-called "resource person" for the shoot at Porter Ranch, she was the county's senior land officer and the one who had suggested this reconnaisance trip to see the place. So far, the "resource person" had been useless, not even clever enough to slow down this crazy driver. She just kept her nose buried in paperwork. How she could read anything, Louise couldn't imagine.

Pete Fitzsimmons and Ann Evans. Pete, a joker. Ann, serious as a judge.

"I'm not going to be sick," insisted Louise. "I wouldn't dream of redecorating your upholstery with partially digested strawberries and shredded wheat."

"Aw, no problem," Pete said breezily. "My pickup's seen lots worse than that." The wheels screeched again as the truck went into a tight curve.

"Unnh!" Louise groaned. Her breathing continued to come in irregular bursts. "You *could* slow down, damn it!"

"Oh." He grinned, reducing the pickup's speed. "Sure, I'll slow'er down. S'pose that li'l bite outta the road back there did scare ya a little."

"It's like a bloody Outward Bound experience."

He threw his head back and laughed. But Louise was not finding this trip funny. It was time for her mantra. She relaxed, leaning back in the seat, and her lips began to move.

"Whatcha mumblin'?" asked her lunatic driver.

"Nothing," she said shortly. She wasn't about to share her mantra. He would only laugh. Instead she kept mumbling: *You are a piece of raw liver, you are a piece of raw liver* . . .

After a few minutes, it seemed to work. She cast a careful look at Pete Fitzsimmons. She had to remember to be nice to him, for it was never good for the talent to fight with the cameraman. In fact, what all talent wanted was for the cameraman to *love* them. "The truth is," she said in a sincere voice, "I have two problems." Was that too obvious a play for sympathy?

"Yeah—I'm listenin'."

"One's a certain, uh, aversion to steep bumpy roads like this one. And then there's my altitude sickness—I've had it for days, so I should be getting over it." She swallowed carefully. "Give me a while and I'll be just fine."

"Heights, huh?" he said skeptically. "We're not very high—not more 'n seventy-five hundred feet. This whole road we've been ridin' on is part of Porter Ranch. You're on the crest of a low little mountain ridge, because the Porter who originally laid out the roads had a thing for privacy and insisted on makin' it hard for people to get up here." He gave her another look. "Sure it's heights that ail you? I read it different. Your mind's a million miles away. You're in the dumps."

Great! A complete stranger could tell that she was unhappy. She made an attempt at humor. "If I am, it's because of what's happening to my face." She gave him a fake little smile. "See, each time I smile, the laugh lines cut into my cheeks like a knife, and my lips feel as if they're cracking apart. I arrived Wednesday and in three days I've turned into a wizened old crone." *And I feel like one,* she thought miserably, *now that I'll be hanging out alone again in a rented house and fretting about my husband.*

"Try Bag Balm."

"Never heard of it." But her mind gratefully latched onto this distraction from her dark thoughts. She laughed again. "Bag balm—funny name."

"It's a funny product. It's for cows. If you use it, you'll smell strange, but your skin will love it. Dairy farmers use it to heal sore udders."

"Really?" She thoughtfully stroked her chin and peered over her dark sunglasses at him. He'd already warned her to keep her sunglasses on, lest she burn up her eyeballs. Now, he had a cure for her dry skin.

"Heck," he said, shoving his hat back even further on his curly head, "I'm the kind of man who has solutions for everythin'. Got any female problems y'need advice on?"

She gave him a dirty look.

So much for letting her guard down. The man was certifiably crude. She could either fight with him, or ignore him. She decided to ignore him, but it was hard to do, especially since he kept shooting her looks. He was amused at her outfit—her "location" clothes that she'd unfortunately decided to wear: white cowboy hat covering her long brown hair, scratchy new plaid shirt, western neckerchief, too-tight denim pants with flashy belt and dangling Swiss Army knife, silly-looking tooled cowboy boots that tilted her forward like a butt-thrusting hussy. She was painfully aware of how Nouveau West she must look.

As for him, he was one of those tall, craggy-faced men in worn clothes who blended in out here like a clump of sagebrush—a huge contrast to the men with whom she usually associated in Washington. Louise gave a resigned little sigh. Washington, at the moment, seemed a million miles away. Men in the nation's capital, in their uniform of suits, ties, and leather dress shoes, would appear silly to this ruffian. But they had charm. He had none. They had manners. His were nonexistent. No, Pete was obviously a different sort of person. He would never be a politician, since he seemed to care nothing for the impression he made on people.

She did concede that he could be called handsome, with those incredible eyebrows, the faded blue eyes, and the curly hair—although he badly needed a few extra pounds. With him, faded was definitely in, bright was out. Many washings had reduced the plaid design in his shirt to a shadow. His old-fashioned, many-pocketed fisherman's vest was old enough to have been inherited from his grandfather; it made her think of her own worn, many-pocketed gardening shorts. His filthy felt hat with its ratty sheepskin sweatband around it most likely seldom left his head.

As for the age of this ill-mannered, scrawny cameraman, she guessed early forties, like her. *That'll make for a fair contest,* she decided.

Probably to test whether she'd made progress conquering her acrophobia, he hurled the truck around the corrugated edge of another curve. This time, she rode it out with her eyes closed and said nothing; her pride wouldn't let her.

He gave her an approving look. "Good girl. By the time we wind our way over the top of these foothills, you're gonna be cured of your silly fears." He reached a sinewy arm across her to the glove compartment box and snapped it open. "Look in there," he said, "and grab those soda crackers. They'll help settle your stomach."

She found the little package, unwrapped it, and took a grateful bite of a cracker. Then she shot him a glance. "You think I'm not at home out here in the West, and you're right—I'm not." She quickly gobbled down a second cracker. "It may be hard for you to understand, but I prefer Washington any day. It may be a steam bath, but it's not like this—so hot and dry that it parches your skin. The land there gently undulates; it doesn't leap up at you in big lumps and cliffs."

"Sorry ya feel that way about the West. Maybe you'll change your mind." They bumped along in silence for a few moments, and, despite all odds, her stomach began to feel better. Then Pete drawled, "Y'know, Louise, just the other night I happened to see that TV commercial you're in—the one about a mulching lawn mower. *Man,* was it corny!" He chuckled at the memory of it.

How many times had people laughed at that commercial? For the umpteenth time, Louise explained. "It is a little embarrassing, prancing around that mower and proclaiming its virtues like a circus barker. But you'd be surprised how well they pay me. . . ."

He rattled on as if he hadn't heard her. "You do okay on your gardening show—ya got that edgy, East Coast delivery, but it comes across real well."

Edgy, East Coast delivery. "Thanks, Pete. You're generous with compliments."

"You're welcome. I thought I'd get off on the right foot with you since we're shootin' packages for six *Gardening with Nature* shows." His smile *seemed* sincere. "WTBA-TV must love you—syndicatin' you all over the place. Your family come out with ya?"

Louise ignored the way her stomach clenched again. "Um, almost. My husband has some business out here, but isn't here at the moment. And our daughter Janie is spending some time as a counselor at a wilderness camp in Estes Park."

"So that's the story. Well, for a nice family woman,

you sure have a lurid past. I've heard about those murders you solved."

She remained stubbornly silent; she had no obligation to provide people with gory details.

Pete appeared unfazed. Now he was reaching back into the jump seat, one hand on the wheel, the other rummaging through an open camera bag labeled *Domke*. He explained happily to Louise, "I want to take a few shots. The light's perfect. It just matches your smile." He retrieved a Nikon and held it in one hand, expertly fiddling with it as if subduing a small animal.

"Did I hear the word murder?" It was a soft voice from the back seat. Ann Evans had apparently decided to join the conversation; the senior land officer set aside her papers and leaned forward to catch up, the motion causing a hank of beautiful, straight hair to fall over her sincere face. Louise took her first close look at this woman decked out in tan safari shirt and shorts, and saw surprising lines of care in her face. Ann was older than she had first thought, maybe somewhere in her late thirties. As blond as sunshine, she was wearing no makeup, and had green eyes like a cat's. The world would have considered her a beauty, if only she had thought she were one.

"Oh, just a few situations where I happened to be around," said Louise with a gesture of dismissal. "I didn't do much."

"Those murders up in Connecticut," said Pete. "I know you helped solve them. And when your TV buddy was killed, you caught that guy, too, didn't you—or was it your teenage daughter?" The camera was up to Pete's eye now, whining again and again as the film advanced.

"What are you *doing!*" Louise cried, involuntarily putting a hand up to her face at the same time the car swerved. Pete calmly pulled them back from the edge of disaster and grinned. "Sorry, folks. Can't miss the opportunity to take a picture. That golden backlighting—man, it hit your face just right."

Like every cameraman she had known in her two years in TV, Pete was obsessed with light. Good light meant you turned your attention from anything else you were doing—even driving on a steep road with no sissy side rails—and started shooting pictures.

Louise looked at Ann Evans in dismay. Surely this young county official didn't want to die, either.

"Don't worry," he assured them, "I'm almost done and I won't scare y'all again." This time, Pete simply held the camera in the air and without drawing it to his eye got off a couple more shots. Then he unceremoniously dumped the apparatus back into the carryall. "Now tell us more about those murders, Louise. Was it you, or your family, who caught the killers?"

She gave him a stony glance. "If you keep both hands on the wheel, I'll tell you."

"Promise."

"We did it together," she said shortly, then pressed her lips together, like a stubborn child.

"That's it?"

Ann, the diplomat, stepped in to mend the breach. "Gosh, I'd like to hear about that some time, but maybe not now. Louise, your TV show is doing so well. I'm glad you came out here to do programs. It's terrific publicity for our open space program."

Louise smiled. "Finally, because of support for the idea from the President, people are beginning to understand what 'open space' means."

"And once they see your *Gardening with Nature* program, they'll know all about the tracts of land purchased or donated to the counties, to keep them out of development," Ann enthused. "It's worked beautifully in Boul-

der. Thirty years ago, the city fathers decided they wanted
to keep these foothills untouched, and they succeeded."

Pete chimed in. "Now you have a pretty lil' mountain
town surrounded with enough land to make two more
cities of the same size. Pretty darned luxurious, if y'ask
me. Boulder sits on, say, sixteen thousand acres. But encircling it is over *thirty thousand* acres of parks and open
space. And that's just the *city* of Boulder. The county's out
there, too, buying open space land like there's no tomorrow."

"Darn right," said Ann, her pretty bottom lip stuck
out defensively. "Fifty-four thousand acres."

"That could be three more cities," grumbled Pete.

Louise ignored him. This boorish cameraman sounded
like a developer. She turned to Ann and said, "Marty
Corbin has always wanted to do a show out here. Open
space issues tie in so well with my being a member of the
National Environmental Commission—"

The cameraman chuckled. "Man, that must make you a
pawn of every owl-eyed environmentalist that ever lived."

"Pete." Ann shook her head, as if to intimate that Pete
could not be taken seriously.

Louise went on. "Of course, we'll still talk about flowers and trees, but we want to expand the show a bit to
touch on things like preserving wilderness, saving habitats,
creating wildlife corridors, and finding new ways to purify
water. Boulder County's right in the middle of all that."

"You'll love doing a show at Porter Ranch," gushed
Ann. "It has everything: meadows, valleys, cliffs, special
rock formations, little lakes, even marshes. About the best
assemblage of flora on the Front Range of the Rockies—as
well as some pesky weeds we'll see today while we're up
there. And the animals, we have all sorts of animal and
bird species—elk, deer, raptors, jackrabbits. And, of
course, bears and lions—"

Pete skinned a look back at Ann. "Okay, slow down there, pardner—you're *speedin'*. Are you gonna tell Louise the dark side, how lions've been killin' people?"

Ann made a gesture as if to minimize his statement. "Now, Louise, don't you worry. There have been only three deaths from mountain lions in Colorado in the past several years."

"Yeah," said Pete drily, "*only* three. Includin' a skinny twelve-year-old boy hiking with his parents in Rocky Mountain National Park a month ago. He was only a hundred or so feet from his family when the lion selected him for his dinner. Ripped him apart before they even rounded the bend."

Louise had thought her stomach was settled, but now it rumbled threateningly. Janie—"Surely that was a fluke. . . ."

"Two things are happenin' out here, Louise," he said. "One's the new folks tryin' to meld in with the old settlers who farmed and mined the land. The other is the new folks disturbin' the hell out of the wildlife." He shot a glance back at Ann. "*She* calls what's happened to these animals 'loss of habitat.' Translated, that means the yuppies now share space with wild creatures. So rattlesnakes are biting the kiddies in the backyard, bears are walkin' in people's back doors and stealing their Entenmann cookies off the counters, deer are eating their best landscape bushes, and the occasional lion nabs a dog or a baby—"

The county officer admonished him from the back seat. "*Pete!* Don't make it sound worse than it is! No *babies* have—"

"Baby *dogs,* is what I was gonna say. Hey, look, Ann, I'm only telling Louise the facts—nothing more. Of course, there *is* the trade-off. We may suffer the occasional slaughter by wild animal, but we don't have a helluva lotta drive-by shootings." He paused to let that sink in. "The fact is, the newspapers don't even bother to report the death of *pets* any more. They get eaten by the dozens.''

His face darkened, and Louise realized that suddenly the issue had become personal. ''I tell you, if *my* cat gets eaten, there's going to be hell to pay.''

''Hell to pay?'' said Ann. ''Just what does that mean?''

''I'll sue the city of Boulder for not controlling the wild animals around here, that's what.''

Ann made a skeptical noise. ''How about just blocking the cat door,'' she suggested in a condescending tone.

Pete shook his head. ''Aw, I couldn't do that to him. He's too wild. It would kill his spirit.''

Louise gave Pete a long look, and saw the flashing pale blue eyes, still full of mischief. *Devilish* mischief. Not only would he rejoice if she finally got sick, but he was also trying to scare her witless before she even got started. Well, he wouldn't succeed. She turned back to Ann to talk about more positive things. ''About this Porter Ranch. Are you the one who persuaded the rancher to sell his property to the county?''

Ann blushed and could not help smiling. Louise smiled with her, and even included Pete in the smile, since he was driving more carefully now. ''Yes,'' said the land officer, ''but I was assisted by, well, Cupid. Old Jimmy Porter— he's a darling; I love him myself. There's just something about him. What was I saying? Oh, yes. He fell in love with a schoolteacher he's known for years, and decided to live in town after his wedding. That made selling a lot easier for him.''

She pointed a finger out the window. They had reached one of the highest points on the road. The snow-capped back range of the Rockies had come into sight, while in the foreground, cattle grazed on a downward-slanted meadow. It looked just like a postcard Louise had seen in a Boulder drugstore when she'd bought a value-size bottle of aspirin. "Almost thirteen thousand new acres of open space," Ann was saying in a reverent voice. "There's no question that this is the best thing I've been able to accomplish—to make all this land available to the people, so they can enjoy it, walk it, ride horses or bikes on it . . ."

As Louise gazed out, her own hand relaxed on the handgrip above the door. Her stomach was no longer demanding her attention. How could she not like this beautiful place?

Pete had subsided into silence but was keeping a close eye on Louise. Just why he had to do that, she didn't know. She curbed a sigh and reflected that this wasn't the only weird cameraman she had met since she got into the television business two years ago. And it probably wouldn't be the last.

Then they pulled over the top of the ridge, and she gasped. They were descending into an enclosed mountain valley, skirted by a rapidly running branch of the South St. Vrain River. Amid clusters of pines, lush meadows, and granite outcroppings stood a ranch house in time-stained brown wood. Around it was a scattering of outbuildings, and a few horses grazing in one of many corrals. Beyond the ranch house Louise saw a rock ledge that apparently marked the dropoff to a lower tier of land, and a vast woods that partially obscured a second ranch house.

One might have thought the fierce chaos that accompanied the prehistoric upthrust of the Rocky Mountains had left this wild array of cracked and fissured cliffs, flattened plains, and swift-running stream. But Louise knew millions of years of erosion from wind and water, heat and cold, had played their part in creating this complicated beauty.

Jimmy Porter's great-grandfather had found this place the perfect refuge for his ranch, his cattle, and his family. What she was looking at was a picture of self-sufficiency: she knew all this from the piles of careful research for the program, piles that she had spent the last few days poring over. And now it was here before her. A ranch house with its own barn, toolshed, chicken coop, hayfield, and hay storage shed. An irrigation system of pipes and flumes as intricate as, but more workable than, a Rube Goldberg invention, to bring water to fields, vegetable garden, and house. A nearby abandoned sawmill and blacksmith shop that had enabled the construction of buildings and maintenance of animals. A pioneer family had lived and thrived here with little help from the outside world.

"Told ya," said Pete jubilantly, as the pickup slowly glided down into the valley. "We got here in one piece."

Three weathered wooden poles, two verticals connected by a crossbar, formed the classic ranch entrance. From it hung an old sign that emitted a high squeak as the wind gently pushed it. It read PORTER RANCH, and looked as if it could have been put up a century ago.

Where the fence joined the ranch entrance, the rancher's wife had decided to improve on nature, and succeeded. She'd established a perennial wildflower garden that created a stunning picture. The flowers grew lavishly around an ancient farm wagon, now rusted with age, that was the garden's folksy centerpiece. In the peak of bloom, the brilliant perennials spanned the color spectrum: yarrow for gold, Mexican hat for orange; poppies for red; coneflower, bee balm, and liatris for purple; columbine for blue; wild phlox for lavender.

"Oh," said Pete softly, as the truck passed through the entrance. But it was not the marvelous flowers he was looking at. They all saw the horrible sight at once. The fencing that extended from either side of the gate ran through the open meadow into a cluster of pine trees at each end. Something was sprawled over the fence and hanging above the perennial bed. Something that, at first glance, looked like a bag of bones, or a diminutive scarecrow wearing faded shirt, jeans, and well-worn boots.

As they drove closer, Louise could see blood splattered everywhere—besmirching the perfect perennial garden.

"My God, it's Jimmy!" Ann grabbed for the door and started to open it.

"*Hold* it," growled Pete, twisting around to face her. With a long, muscular arm, he pulled the door shut. "That man's head is blown apart. Who knows where the killer is? Ladies, hit the floor, *now*. We're getting out of here!"

Louise slid down on the floor and braced herself against the door as Pete ducked his head and wheeled the vehicle in a tight circle. As they sped away from the ranch house, she wondered what kind of cruel joke this was—to encounter a murder in the most beautiful landscape she had ever seen. It was almost like a dream. That bag of bones on the fence was a man, granted, but a complete stranger to her. Then she stared up at Pete Fitzsimmons, crouched at the wheel beside her and driving like a madman again, away from danger. The horrid dream became real, and so did the shriveled corpse on the fence. Jimmy Porter had been a real man, probably a rugged, lusty man, like Pete. He had lived and loved, worked, and raised a family, and for his troubles had had his head shot off right there in his own yard.

With her headache gone, Louise found her senses were now hyperalert. Everything looked strange from this low vantage point—Pete, the empty gun rack above his head, the flashes of blue sky outside the window.

In the backseat Ann groaned softly, then said in a trembling voice, "I think you're wrong. We should stay and see if he's still alive. What if he needs CPR?" Firmer now, she went on. "Pete, I *insist*. Let's go back there and *help* him!"

"*Forget* it," said Pete. "Your rancher's dead."

There was a whimper, and then Ann lapsed back into silence. Louise could smell the fear among the three of them. With the fabric of her new jeans scratching painfully against her legs, she struggled back into her seat. She sat, staring ahead, pictures of other deaths returning in vivid color to her mind.

This dead man had looked different, splayed out on the fence. It was totally out of place, unnatural, this death in open space.

Chapter 3

RESPLENDENT IN GRAY UNIFORM, wide-brimmed hat, and dark glasses, standing with one booted leg canted out, Sheriff Earl Tatum could have been a poster boy for western law enforcement. He dominated the swarm of people in the Porter Ranch driveway. He also acted as if Louise and Ann were invisible, though how he could fail to see them under this glaring August sun Louise did not know. Until she realized that the sheriff was the kind of man who, ignoring thirty years of the women's movement, only liked to deal with other men.

"Hi, Pete," he greeted his fellow good old boy. "Looks like they got the old guy with a twelve-gauge. You're a photographer, aren'tcha, in addition to all your other talents?"

"Videographer, primarily," said Pete.

"Videographer, photographer, what's the difference? I betcha ya got a camera on you, like always. We got a little battery trouble with ours, so maybe you could take some pictures for me and the coroner, if I let you on the premises. That agreeable with you?"

"More than happy to help, sheriff," said Pete.

Tatum looked Pete over, as if to make sure he could trust him. "And when you're through shootin', I want you to deliver the film rolls right here to me." He tapped the pocket of his gray shirt, indicating just where that film would reside. "Chain of custody, y'know."

"Sure, Earl," said Pete breezily. Men's business concluded, Tatum turned his attention to Louise and Ann. Louise could see he was cataloging them as potential nuisances. He swaggered over, making no effort to suck in his encroaching belly, which was like a lid of fat on the middle of his body.

Pete introduced them and the sheriff responded with, "You ladies stay well back from the scene. Don't want anyone disturbing things. And especially, don't wander off—one dead body's enough for today."

"Would the killer hang around?" asked Louise in a respectful tone.

Tatum frowned down at her. "Maybe yes, maybe no. We'll never know unless you test it by wanderin' off there somewhere." He waved a hand toward the pine groves in annoyance. "So don't. Stick close to your vehicle here—and that's an order."

The two women gave each other a look, then moved to lean against the front of Pete's pickup. As if with one thought, they both folded their arms across their chests.

When they first sighted the body on the fence, Pete had sped back a mile or so and called the sheriff's office on his cellular phone. Then he had parked the car snugly against a stone cliff. A few minutes later, two sheriff's cars from nearby Lyons responded, and Pete followed them back up to the ranch.

Louise and Ann watched the cameraman walk with the sheriff to where the rancher's body hung on the fence like wash set out to dry. A cluster of technicians and sheriff's deputies now obscured the bloody sight. And yet Louise could picture it all—details of this slaughter in the sunlight were imprinted on the backs of her eyelids.

In a defensive voice Ann said, "I bet you've noticed this sheriff is a throwback."

"Yes, to caveman days." Ann, like her, was not used to being ordered around. Louise noticed her companion's face was pale under her tan. "This must be a terrible loss, Ann, not only for his family, but for you, too."

The younger woman was fighting to keep back tears. "I became very fond of Jimmy during all the on-and-off negotiations. They took more than three years. I can't believe this has happened—and after all my work." Now a few tears were falling.

"You mean, the sale to the county isn't . . ."

Ann shook her head. "It would have become final next Monday. Now there *is* no sale." She snuffled and wiped her eyes with the sleeve of her safari shirt.

Louise tipped her cowboy hat back on her head; it was getting hot standing out here, with her new clothes clinging to her like an unwelcome second skin. "But surely he has family. Doesn't the family want to sell to the county?"

Ann rocked back and forth against the truck's high

fender, like a child trying to handle a hurt that was too big for her. Finally she began to talk. "The family's the problem, Louise. Talk about bickering. The eldest son, Eddie, calls himself the biggest redneck in Boulder county; he seems to think that makes him special. He struts around in what he describes as his 'shit-kicker' boots, and is always on the edge of trouble. He fought like mad with his father over this land deal. Frank is a little younger, but a lot smarter—he's an IBM engineer, but he also operates an andesite quarry down near the highway."

Since Louise looked perplexed, she added, "Andesite's a fine-grained gray volcanic rock; it's used in construction and for driveways. Anyway, Frank's very much on my side. Then there's Jimmy's daughter, Sally. Some people would call her an old maid. She stayed home to take care of her widower father, and she still lives up here, though she works in Boulder. I've gotten to know her pretty well, too."

"And Sally is in favor of the deal with the county?"

"She *seemed* to go along with it," said Ann, "because she's always played the part of the dutiful daughter. But I'm not positive she'll stand up to the bullying Eddie's going to give her, now that he's got a chance to do what he always wanted to with the ranch." For the first time, Louise noticed the tic in Ann Evan's right eye. Was it the shock of seeing the murdered old rancher or had she had it before?

"So whose decision is it?"

The young woman's thick blond brows descended in a frown. "Jimmy did mention he made a new will about eight months ago, after he decided to remarry. I guess he wanted me to know who would be in charge if anything . . . happened to him." Ann paled alarmingly but kept talking. "Oddly enough, he had never announced the impending marriage. But the new will speaks for itself. This fiancée—Grace Prangley—gets an equal share with the three children. Grace knew what she wanted, and Jimmy was softhearted enough to give it to her."

She gave Louise an anguished look. "But I know in my heart that the worst trouble will come from Eddie. He's going to ruin the deal, sure as you please. He's a greedy person, and land in this part of the world is gold-plated. The county pays fair market value for open space. But because of Porter Ranch's particular attractiveness, a developer would pay a premium."

Her mouth turned down in an unsuccessful attempt to fight back a sob. Tears puddled in the corners of her eyes, threatening to spill down her cheeks. "But here I'm talking about Jimmy as if the only important thing about him was that he was going to sell us his ranch. Even if he *hadn't* agreed, I know the two of us would have remained friends."

Louise put an arm around the younger woman's shoulders, and they stood together in silence for a few moments. Louise broke it finally by saying, "We're talking about thirteen thousand acres. That's a huge piece of property."

"Oh, yes. If it were developed, it would be a whole new town."

The tumblers began to move in Louise's mind. "Developers must salivate over this land."

Ann turned her tawny-colored eyes to Louise. "Yes, practically everyone's into land out here. Even Pete."

"*Pete?*" said Louise, incredulously.

"Oh, yes, Pete. What did you think he was—just a good ol' boy cameraman?"

Louise shoved her cowboy hat back and scratched her hairline where the fabric had been digging into her scalp. "With all due respect, Ann, it isn't hard to draw that conclusion. He's very rude, and his speech is so—careless.

He never pronounces his 'ing's. Obviously, he has an aversion to the letter *g*."

Ann broke into a silvery laugh, and Louise was happy that she had some good humor left in her. "Oh, Louise, half the people out here talk like that. It has something to do with western tradition. Maybe echoes of cowboy-and-Indian days, I don't know. But just don't believe Pete's line. It's all, you know——"

"A put-on?"

"Yes. I think he was testing you to see if you were a good sport. Actually, he's a great guy. You'll be friends in no time. He's very big in business around the county, and he owns lots of property. Pete's a real child of the West. He loves to hike and fish and hunt, and he's quite a marksman. But when he grew older he caught on to the value of land in Boulder County. He gave up thoughts of another career—teaching English, can you believe that?—and spent a major part of his time buying devalued properties."

"So this videography——"

"That's just to fulfill his artistic side, that and his 'art' photography. He wins some big prizes for that."

"You don't say." Her eyes were drawn to where Pete was taking pictures of Jimmy Porter's remains from different angles. The tall photographer lithely contorted his body this way and that, totally engrossed in what he was doing, until suddenly he glanced over at Louise. In some confusion, she turned back to Ann and said, "So, there are plenty of people who would do most anything for an interest in this land."

Ann nodded, and her eyes welled up with tears again. "But I don't care about all that. All I want is to know what happened to Jimmy."

"Hmh." Louise retreated into her own thoughts. She was trying to curb her curiosity; she did not intend to get mired down in a murder——not this time. This was supposed to be a fun business trip——her very own business trip——to do location shoots for her PBS program, *Gardening with Nature,* with her very own WTBA-TV producer, Marty Corbin, flying out from Washington to run things. But the schedule was loose——worked around laid-back freelancers like Pete Fitzsimmons——so that she and Bill could take a few field trips. The fact that Bill was not here was the only problem.

But hadn't he said to keep her eyes open. . . ?

The sun bore down on them as if it wanted to press them into the ground, like the dehydrated leaves and bugs lying in the driveway. Louise's new clothes seemed tighter, her sweaty armpits wetter. To distract herself, she bent her long legs in a few deep knee bends, which caused her new boots to cut painfully into her calves. She straightened. Wounded again by things strange and western. That would be her last attempt at deep knee bends. Her gaze wandered back to the crime scene, and she saw that the crowd near the body was dispersing. "Let's go check things out," she said.

"Oh, Louise, thank you." Gratitude shone in Ann's eyes.

Her pulse accelerated by about ten beats. "Wait a minute, Ann. I don't mean I'm going to check this *murder* out."

"Oh, but you must!" Ann, who stood as tall as Louise, fastened her with those extraordinary eyes, ready to overflow again with tears. "You have to help me!"

"Look," Louise said quietly. "I'm not a real detective, if that's what you need——I'm just someone who's been involved in things *in spite of* myself."

Ann persisted. "But you can at least help me find out what's happened here——What if one of the developers is to blame? There's so much money involved . . ."

Louise quickly fantasized and rejected a scenario where she went around Boulder snooping into land deals. She shook her head. No thanks. Surely this was not the kind of eye-opening experience Bill had in mind.

But Ann hadn't given up. "It's not only this, Louise. My whole life is falling to pieces . . ." The young woman started sobbing so hard that, for a moment, Louise wondered if she would ever get her story out. She handed the woman a tissue she found in her jeans pocket, which gave Ann a chance to dab at her eyes and collect herself. She said, "Luke and I—we're having terrible troubles. And now, I've probably lost the biggest land deal that Boulder County has seen in recent history. To think," she said piteously, "that the ranch was going to be signed over to the county in only forty-eight hours!"

Louise was curious about the intrusion of personal affairs into this conversation. "Luke—your boyfriend?"

Ann continued sniffing and shook her head.

"Um, husband?"

When Ann nodded, Louise said, "You mean . . . your marriage is breaking up?"

"Oh, *no*, not breaking up," Ann said mysteriously. "It's much more complicated than that." Louise had known with her first look that things were eating at this young, driven, professional woman. Then Ann surprised her, turning her yellow-green eyes straight on Louise. "But it's losing this deal that's the worst for me."

Nothing like establishing priorities, thought Louise. At least Ann *mentioned* the marital problems.

"All right. I'll help you check out a few things, but I make no promises. Keep in mind, Ann, I'm only here for ten more days, and I'm on location some of those days."

"Louise, how can I thank you?" Ann took another swipe at her eyes with the bedraggled tissue.

"You can thank me by cheering up a bit. Now, let's go see what Pete's doing."

Ann held back. "Would it be all right," she asked, "if I stay here and pull myself together?"

"Of course. See you in a minute, then."

As Louise walked over to where the cameraman stood leaning against the fence, the new boots continued to punish her. It took every muscle in her legs and thighs to walk tall and not pitch forward into the dirt.

Pete's pale eyes squinted as he watched her approach. "Hi," he called. "I'm about done here." Louise could see he was in a grim mood. "It's a damned bloody business, whoever did it to that poor bastard. I'm thinkin' I'd like to look around. Care to join me?" Louise knew that "looking around" to Pete would mean shooting pictures. Together they walked into the ranch yard. Sheriff Tatum was momentarily distracted and didn't seem to notice.

They kept well away from the ranch house, suspecting that they would really be in trouble with Tatum if they went there. Circling the homestead and outbuildings, they wandered out to the edge of the property, where the land sloped down to the edge of a sixty-foot sandstone cliff. Scattered down the hill was a graveyard, all the graves marked with plain white stones. Pete hurried to the base of the hill, took a quick picture of the caprock that marked the edge of the precipitous cliff, then rushed back up.

The graveyard scene threw a pall on Louise. "I guess now Jimmy Porter joins the others in this plot. What an isolated life—they live here; they die here; they're buried here."

But Pete was enthusiastic. He balanced his tall frame precariously on the hill and took closeups of the white stone slabs nearer the top. "Just read this stuff," he said. "It's great. *'Bonnie Porter, Beloved to the Bone, Who Had Her Trial by Fire. Born 1923. Died 1958.'* Man, I wonder what

happened to her. I used to hear things about people dyin'
up here on this ranch—but no one ever could sort it out.
Mountain folks like privacy.''

"Amazing . . .''

"Amazing?''

"Yes,'' said Louise, "all this privacy. Where I live, in
the northern Virginia suburbs, we all get to know each
other's business in a hurry.'' She smiled, thinking of
home. "Of course, it's even easier in our immediate
neighborhood, because we live in a cul-de-sac. It gives you
a bird's-eye view of what's going on.''

He grinned over at her. "You sound like a real nosy
type. Let's get over to this next batch,'' he said, nodding
down the hill toward another cluster of small graves. "This
must be the kiddie graveyard.''

"It looks as if lots of kids died.''

He focused his camera on the first gravestone. "Get
this, Louise— *'Nathaniel, Who Gave Us Three Years of Happi-
ness With Which to Light Our Lives. Born 1946. Died 1949.'*
They may die young, but they get a hell of an inscription.''

A bit callous, Louise thought, but just like a cameraman. He enthused on, "If we still manage to do the show
up here, Louise, we'll use these shots for B-roll material.
We'll be rife with good stuff—that row of old cow skulls
hung on the barn, the abandoned blacksmith shop, the
ramshackle sawmill . . .''

Strong, evocative images were always needed as background to the narration in the script, and the place was
rife with them. Without meaning to join him in his cal-
lousness, Louise thought of some more. "How about that
beat-up Porter Ranch sign? And there are even more
marked graves. Why don't you get them all while you're
at it?''

She looked up and saw that Earl Tatum had spied them.
He started out in a walk, then began loping toward them

at top speed across the huge yard. Louise realized that he was in good condition despite that spare tire around his middle. "Better hurry up," she warned Pete. "The law approaches—and *fast*."

Pete was faster. He quickly photographed the few remaining children's gravestones, and just had time to scramble back up the hill as Tatum arrived. The camera whined as Pete casually exposed a few shots on the end of the roll. With deft hands, he extracted it from the camera and stuck it in one of his vest pockets. Then he turned toward the sheriff, smiled, and straightened his old hat.

Despite the sunglasses, the twitch in Tatum's cheek told Louise that he was angry. Nevertheless, he downplayed the matter, saying casually, "Takin' pictures of graves, huh. Lotta good that'll do you."

"But why would you object, Sheriff Tatum?" Louise asked sweetly. "It's just picturesque old headstones. Pete's the cameraman who will be taping TV programs for me, and we might use these shots for background."

Tatum approached Louise and shoved his face so close that she could smell his breath—garlic mixed with herbs—probably from lunch in some upscale Boulder watering hole. "Look," he said, "that film is *mine*. I think you better mind your own business. This isn't your property, and he's shootin' pictures at my suff'rance, and turnin' 'em over to me when he's done."

She tried to look polite, but she must have failed. "And ma'am, don't look so doubtful at me. I wouldn't want you—bein' from the East and all—to think we're backward. I'm no *hick*. You better believe I know how to enforce the law. Now, I say, he's shot the body and the scene, so he's shot *enough* pictures."

The incident had taken some polish off the man. Hadn't she just told Bill this wasn't Hicksville—in jest? How did this guy ever get elected in Boulder County, which she had heard was one of the most educated communities in America?

Tatum moved away from her, and Louise was grateful. He seemed to want to patch things up with Pete, at least. He said, "Actually, Fitzsimmons, it was just as a courtesy that I came back here t'tell you people what's what. From the look of things, this murder's the work of a poacher. They're dangerous people, and there's big money in poaching these days—twenty grand alone for a single elk, d'ja know that? My guess is Jimmy tried to stop one of 'em."

Pete busied himself covering his camera lens and pulling film rolls out of his vest pockets preparatory to turning them over to the sheriff. Louise looked at Tatum in disbelief.

Silently, Tatum escorted them back to the ranch entrance, then peeled off to issue a few orders to his deputies. Managing things was a tall, competent woman named Sergeant Rafferty. Louise noted he had a more deferential attitude toward the sergeant than he displayed toward Louise and Ann, and she wondered what the woman had done to wring respect from him. She caught the sergeant's eye as they passed, and the woman smiled good-naturedly. Louise gave her a thumbs-up.

They reached the pole fence where Jimmy Porter had died. Blood still festooned the wagon, the fence, the perennials, and the ground. When they joined Ann at the car, Louise sank gratefully into the passenger seat and started pulling off her boots. She turned to Pete, who was observing the boot removal without comment. "If Jimmy Porter wasn't armed, why would he allow a poacher to come so close?"

"Makes no sense," said the cameraman. "That's why I'm findin' it a little hard to agree with the sheriff on that. I have a different take. I grew up around here—don't know if you knew that. In Hygiene, a little community a few miles east of Lyons. My parents were ranchers, and I've known ranchin' since I was little. Ranchers hate things that kill their stock, especially coyotes. Know what they do after they kill a coyote?"

"No."

"They throw the carcass over a fence. Know why? It's to warn other coyotes to stay away." He jerked a thumb in the direction of the ranch. "Someone killed Jimmy Porter and he ended up like a coyote carcass on a fence. I'd say maybe that was a warning."

Chapter 4

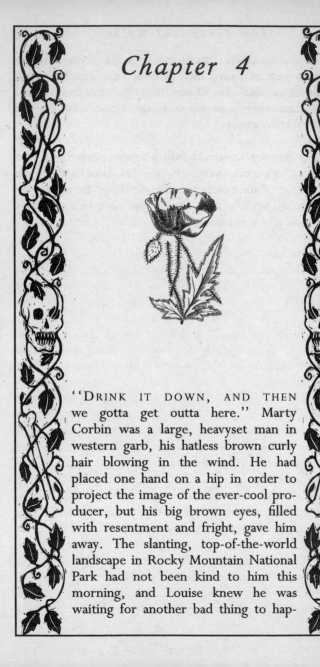

"DRINK IT DOWN, AND THEN we gotta get outta here." Marty Corbin was a large, heavyset man in western garb, his hatless brown curly hair blowing in the wind. He had placed one hand on a hip in order to project the image of the ever-cool producer, but his big brown eyes, filled with resentment and fright, gave him away. The slanting, top-of-the-world landscape in Rocky Mountain National Park had not been kind to him this morning, and Louise knew he was waiting for another bad thing to happen. They had fallen behind schedule in their Monday shoot and were stopping once more to take a coffee break at twelve thousand feet. Louise happily drank her second cup, exhilarated both by the brisk atmosphere and by the caffeine. But Marty had her worried.

It had rained Sunday night, ending the oppressive heat wave and helping Louise feel like a new person, despite Bill's defection—oops, departure—and Janie heading to camp. Her producer, however, who had just flown in yesterday from the East Coast, was the picture of a man out of place—a city guy plunged into a world filled with overpowering mountains staring him down from all sides. Now it would be Marty's turn to get adjusted to this place.

He was standing on the path next to the spongy tundra and was about to place a big foot on a clump of miniature forget-me-nots. "Stop!" Louise cried, rushing over to put a restraining hand on his arm. In a quieter voice she said, "You *have* to watch where you step, Marty. Did you know it could take a hundred years to restore those flowers you nearly stepped on? And I promised Derrell we wouldn't disturb anything."

Derrell, a tall, thin, poker-faced young park ranger, was going to appear in the wildflower segments with Louise and furnish details about the alpine and tundra plants. At the moment, he stood ten paces away and glowered at the clumsy producer. Hawk-eyed and hawk-nosed, he was a botanist and the park's wildflower expert, and Louise could see he wasn't going to permit defenseless plants to be ground under the vulgar boot of this East Coast TV big shot. To Derrell, Marty must seem as crude as a Hun to an ancient Roman. The producer, sensing the ranger's disapproval, glanced crankily at the fellow. "What's he gonna do, throw me in some little jail carved out of a mountain?" As if reverting to his days growing up in a tough Brooklyn neighborhood, he petulantly added, "Anyway, I could take him in a fight—no problem.'' He muttered the hostile words as he wandered off the path again in search of a perfect place to shoot. But now he stepped gingerly, as if he might encounter eggs in his path instead of plants.

Louise smiled indulgently. Before leaving Washington, D.C., Marty had decided a location shoot out West demanded that he look the part. He had arrived wearing new jeans, shirt, and cowboy hat, and now was left with only the jeans and shirt. He had thrown the crew into a panic when he tripped down the wide steps of the steep mountain path. Amidst shouts and laughter, he rolled fifteen feet or so before it ceased to be funny. The sound man ran to his rescue and helped him back onto his unsteady feet, breathless and gasping. It took the entire crew to soothe his nerves and assure him he wasn't hurt.

When he fell, his western designer hat had gone sailing off into the clear mountain air. Louise reflected that it might become a bonus for some passing tourist, or might rest in perpetuity in a crevice between two rocks. Now, Marty reached up often and fruitlessly and tried to smooth his hair. The wind was blowing everything, including the sound, straight east to Nebraska.

More practical after five days in the West, Louise was finally acclimatized. She was also wearing proper clothing; her shirt and jeans were broken in now, and she knew enough to secure her cowboy hat with an under-the-chin rawhide strap. Her hair was imprisoned in a sensible ponytail, so it didn't fly around in the wind like Medusa's. And she had ditched her tooled boots; her feet were now shod in climbing boots with soles that gripped the rocks and gave her a budding sense of being a western woman.

The producer, one eye on the watchful park ranger, returned to the path and swigged down the last of his coffee. "*Jes*us, what a place!"

"Don't you love it, Marty? Above treeline, above almost everything. And look at those mountains." She grabbed his arm and pointed to the white peaks only a few miles from where they were standing. "They just cry out to you, 'Climb me!' "

"Climb me, hell," he grumbled, bending to stuff their coffee cups into a small duffel bag with the thermos. He straightened slowly, panting from the effort, and gave her a weary look. "Gimme a little slack, Louise, a little more time to adjust. How much do I have to suffer for *Gardening with Nature*? Hell, we should call it *Risk-Taking With Nature*. I'll love it here if we ever get any good footage out of today."

Derrell came to the rescue, finding the best display of tundra flowers for the fussy producer to use in the shoot. Pete was whistling contentedly, already happy because he had wandered off by himself and gotten some unexpected shots of bighorn sheep. The sound man was as nervous as Marty. He checked his sound mixer, then looked at the producer and shook his head. "Jeez, what a wind! It's going to be tough getting a good level, even with the wind screen on the shotgun mike."

"We'll do the best we can," said Marty. "Okay, Derrell—heads up. Louise, sweetie, keep the pace even now. This shoot is weird enough as it is, without having a hurry-up, slow-up effect screwin' it up. So let's get started." Pete, walking backward on the perilous incline with the aid of the grip, taped Louise and the young botanist as they approached what looked like a rock garden full of small plants growing out of the tundra. These species favored the environment of a fell field, which was ground covered with small rocks. The high-altitude plants were growing in a climate where a tree could not survive. Never attaining normal size, they sprang up from old roots during a six-week growing season, and received only a few inches of moisture in the form of melted snow.

Derrell's impassive face came alive as he described the qualities of each tough little speciman. He pointed out one of the park visitors' favorites, old-man-on-the-mountain, only a foot high, with protective hairy leaves and showy yellow daisylike flowers. Then he and Louise crouched down to look at the other varieties growing nearby: a cluster of white bistort; the buttercup-flowered avens; the even more diminutive blue forget-me-not; and smallest of all—a mere pink blotch upon the earth—the pink-flowered dwarf clover.

Finally, Marty was satisfied. "Yeah—that's got it!" the producer cried, looking more comfortable now that something seemed to be working. "Good job, Louise, with those dinky little plants. And, Derrell, by golly, you were a real pro. Didn't know you had it in you. I really admire the two of you for not letting your teeth chatter. As for me, I'm freezing my tushy!"

Still hyper, Marty hustled them onward to the next task. "Let's get outta here. We shoot in that wildflower meadow next, and I sure hope a chinook isn't blowing there, too. I gotta confess—they make me edgy." He rubbed his ample stomach. "But first, let's grab lunch. I'm starved. Derrell, how many miles do we have to go to eat?" The park ranger had apparently become Marty's new pal.

"There's a good place near the entrance to the park," Derrell told him, smiling faintly. "It's only an hour away." Groaning, Marty led the way back to the cars, while Pete dropped back to fall in step with Louise. The cameraman gave her a sideways glance. "How're your cheeks?"

"What?"

"Wait," he said, shying back in mock fear. "I know you think I'm being fresh, but don't slap me. All I'm referrin' to is your dried-out face—*those* cheeks. Did you try the Bag Balm?''

"Not yet, Pete." After hearing what Ann Evans said about this guy, she was puzzled. Exactly who was this Pete Fitzsimmons? He strode along, seemingly impervious to the strong wind, his beat-up felt hat jammed on his head without benefit of chin strap. She thought whimsically that this was the test. If those fabulous rugged eyebrows were only glued on, they'd fly away in this gale. They didn't.

"Don't wait too long to grease up," he said with a grin. "Some people come out here to this dry climate and just plain dry up and blow away. I smear that stuff in whenever I'm goin' huntin' or fishin'." Then he rustled around in the canvas bag on his shoulder. "But seriously, Louise, I got somethin' spooky to show you. Look at these. I already hustled a set over to the sheriff's office. I had to do some fast talkin' as to why I hadn't turned this roll over to him. Told'im it got lost in one of my pockets." They stopped on the path, and as tourists streamed by, he drew a packet of pictures from the bag and tried to hand them to her.

Still shaken about encountering a corpse, she was reluctant to look at them. "Pete, I'm not sure—"

He interrupted. "Don't kid me, Louise. How long do I have to stand here in this chinook and convince you? I know darn well you're interested." He shoved the pictures at her, and this time she took them. Then he grinned, as if he had just played an enormous trick on her. "Even with these, I'll bet you ten grand you could never solve Jimmy Porter's murder—it's just not as easy as those lil' mysteries you solved out East."

"I'll do you a favor," she said, "and not take you up on that bet." Then she turned her attention to the photos. They included longer shots of the crime scene. Shots of the ranch, with its rugged rock outcroppings. The blacksmith shop, the old sawmill, the wall of cow skulls. A photo looking down from the top of the steep cliff that backed the ranch property that gave Louise a renewed sense of vertigo. The picturesque gravestones. A glimpse of the back range.

Pete reached over and put his finger on the shot of the piney woods. It appeared to be a landscape shot, and nothing more. "See that white spot? That's why the sheriff had to see this one. There's a face in the pines—someone wearing a dark hat, with a bandanna or something pulled over the bottom of the face."

"The murderer?"

"Who else?" asked the cameraman, challenging her. "Why would someone be standing in the woods when all of us were gathered in the ranch driveway watching the police do their thing? Why didn't that person come over and join us to find out what was going on? Maybe Tatum is right and it was a poacher."

Marty called to them to hurry it up.

"There's no tellin' what Tatum'll do with this—probably nothin'. I'm busy as hell workin' on a couple of specials for Channel Six, but I'll have time pretty soon to make some big prints on fine-grain paper, and we'll see better what we've got."

"But I don't really want to—"

"Yes, you do," said Pete. "You want to know who did it as much as I do. Anyway, how are you goin' to count on our goofy sheriff to find out?"

"Goofy is right. How did a man like that win the sheriff's job in a place like this?"

"You've gotta know the county. It isn't all Boulder sophisticates. There's lots of farmers and down-to-earth working folks who *prefer* a guy like Earl. He campaigns really well. Has big barbecues and invites all the registered voters he figures punched a ballot for him one time or another. And when it comes down to it, he knows how to do the job.''

As if transfixed, Louise continued to stare at the print of the figure in the woods. She didn't need a blown-up picture. She could already see the person in the picture was staring right at her and Pete. Had to have known they'd been snooping and taking pictures.

Marty and the others were already far below them on the path. The producer turned around, gesticulated wildly, and called to them again, but his words blew away in the wind. He looked like an excited actor in a silent film. Louise waved reassuringly. Pete had shoved the pictures back in his bag. He grabbed her hand and they hurried down the mountain path together.

❧

The wind subsided as mysteriously as it had risen, allowing them a less eventful shoot near a streambed in the wildflower meadow. It was so peaceful that Marty said he felt like lying down and taking a nap, like Dorothy in *The Wizard of Oz*. But Pete, arms akimbo, warned him, "It may be peaceful now, but there's your warning." He pointed to the dramatic cigar-shaped clouds floating in the porcelain blue sky. "We'll have more heavy winds tonight."

By practically burrowing into the ground, the cameraman got the clouds, the flowers, and the stream in the frame with Louise. "Streams are good," he told her amiably, "but clouds are even better, better than everything—well, almost everything: old fences, barns, mines, tombstones, and rusting buggies also are good. But clouds, now, they're one of Colorado's endearing attractions. Gotta get 'em, even if you don't get the talent in the picture." A big grin, to assure her he was kidding.

The moist riparian land burgeoned with flower species, each more enchanting to Louise than the next. She and

Derrell walked among masses of rose crown, with its elongated pink flower clusters; eight-inch-tall white marsh marigold; brook saxifrage, whose loose, white flowers and red sepals were as delicate as dancing ladies; and mauve-colored elephant flower, whose curving upper petals resembled tiny, waving elephant's trunks and gave the tall plant a decidedly frivolous air. The fluffy white flower umbels of the hairy-stemmed cow parsnip swayed in the gentle mountain breeze, along with other tall plants, yellow Gray's angelica; and mertensia, with its nodding blue and pink flowers. Louise mentioned that she grew a similar species of mertensia in a totally different environment in her garden in northern Virginia, and Derrell nodded happily. Farther away from the stream they found clumps of paintbrush in rose, yellow, and scarlet; tall, dusky, purple-flowered beardtongue; and drifts of pink pussytoes and avalanche lilies.

When they were done for the day, they said good-bye to Derrell. Marty gave the ranger an effusive slap on the back and the promise of a tape of the program. Then they dispersed, Pete and other crew members to their homes, she supposed, and Marty to the Hotel Boulderado where his wife Steffi awaited him. Steffi Corbin was the other spouse invited on this trip, and unlike Bill, she had shown up. Louise pressed her lips together and tried not to think about it.

She also declined her boss's invitation to join them for dinner, for she knew this was a second honeymoon for Steffi and the workaholic Marty. They had had their share of marital trouble in recent years, none of it helped by an affair he had had with Louise's predecessor at WTBA-TV. They needed time alone, which apparently they didn't find much of while at home in Washington, D.C.

Louise had been left alone in the house in the foothills all weekend, and after finding a dead body, too. Oh, well, it was probably a growing-up experience. She threw her cowboy hat and her backpack into her rental car and headed toward Lyons.

❧

Lyons, population 1,250, had a peculiar charm, with a river running through it, and a welcome sign made of a huge slab of the town's trademark red sandstone. Louise looked up into the foothills lining the approach. She had read that stonecutters had worked in those mountains for one hundred years, bringing out the red rock that was used for New York City's and Chicago's popular brownstone houses, in addition to some of Colorado's most famous buildings. And that included the trendy decor in Coors Field, which was one of the newer jewels in Denver's crown. She smiled. How many cities revered rocks in this way?

Locals liked to call this unassuming town the gateway to the Rockies, for a person almost had to go through it to get to Rocky Mountain National Park, just as she and her TV crew had done today. As they were passing through, Pete had given her the name of a good restaurant. She had to search to find it, but not very hard. It was on High Street, but this High Street barely resembled the Old World atmosphere of High Streets she had become acquainted with when she and Bill lived in England. Lyons's High Street had its own Old West charm. A nineteenth-century red-stone museum, and two turn-of-the-century churches stood in lonesome splendor, with a few desultory trees surrounding them, waving their scraggly tops victoriously in the wind as if to say, "See, we've made it." Trees had a hard time existing in this harsh climate. A string of unassuming red-stone and frame buildings were given over to gift shops and antique stores. Then came a rambling old

blue house with redstone trim and a faded ANTIQUES sign
out front. Finally, there was the Gold Strike Café.

It was only a small log cabin—probably once a miner's
home—now painted dark red, with a peeling white-
lettered sign proclaiming THE NEW HOME OF THE PIE PLACE.
Louise smiled. New, but when?

She went in and found the six or so tables and most of
the counter seats occupied by customers talking a mile a
minute, creating a pleasant babble that made it sound like a
crowd twice as large. It was a mix of tourists in bright
sporty pants and shirts, and locals in faded ones. Every
windowsill and nook burgeoned with geraniums, begonias,
and spider plants—both mature blooming ones, and glass
jars full of new slips with plump white roots. Someone
around here was mad about growing things.

She slid into an empty stool at the counter, and as soon
as she did, a short woman with curly white hair turned
around and gave Louise a big smile. *She must be eighty if
she's a day,* Louise thought. "I guess you must be new
here," the woman said, in a low voice with a golden
twang. "Welcome. I'm Ruthie Dunn."

"I'm Louise Eldridge. Just a visitor to these parts."

"Well, you're plumb welcome no matter how long you
decide to stay," said Ruthie.

As if she were talking to an old friend, Ruthie batted the
conversational ball back and forth with Louise, at the same
time directing the waitresses and flipping meat on the grill.
Louise, while downing the pork special, told her briefly
why she had come to Colorado. Upon hearing this, the
white-haired proprietor said politely, "My gosh, you're
some kind of celebrity, with a TV show of your own."

Louise smiled. "Not too much of a celebrity. And how
about the name of this restaurant? I didn't know they'd
found gold in Lyons."

"Naw," she said, "not here. Jamestown had gold. Gold

Hill. Cripple Creek. But Lyons's gold is *red*"—the "red" could have had three *e*'s in it, the way Ruthie said it. "That red sandstone. That's our main strike."

Ruthie admitted she had never watched Louise's weekly garden show; Louise realized it was because she was too busy doing real-life things like running a café and propagating plants. She got up at four in the morning to start making pies. "Not bad, huh, for an eighty-three-year-old?" she asked with an infectious grin.

The crowd thinned, but Louise lingered, well fed, elbows on the counter now, booted feet slung behind the supports at the bottom of the stool, sipping good coffee and feeling like she used to at her grandmother's house—except Ruthie Dunn was considerably heftier than her skinny little grandmother. As she finally broke down and ordered a slice of butterscotch pie for under two dollars, she smiled and thought of all the pretentious, second-rate desserts she had ordered at Washington restaurants for three times the price.

Ruthie eventually asked the question Louise thought she might. "Doin' any of your programs up at Porter Ranch?" The ranch was a next-door neighbor to the little town of Lyons.

"Not yet—but we hope to, if things settle down after that murder." Louise shuddered.

The woman propped her elbows on the counter and looked across at Louise. She had lively blue eyes that didn't show her age. She didn't even wear glasses. "That's baloney, y'know, that story of the sheriff's. That wasn't any poacher." A small shake of the curly head.

"Oh, no?"

"First off, there aren't any poachers up there. Why, Jimmy Porter would have blown their heads off, and poachers know it." She shook a sturdy finger at Louise. "Porter's ranch, after all, is private property—and there's more than one mountain biker who strayed back there who has the buckshot in his pants to prove it. No, the poachers are up around about Rocky Mountain National Park." Her white eyebrows elevated. "Know what other reason I've got for thinking that?"

Louise shook her head.

"There have been other deaths back on Porter's ranch that've never been explained." She wagged her head just a little, girlishly, and grinned. "So this is just one more, isn't it?"

Ruthie straightened up. Louise could see her rounded back was tired. "Well, I gotta close up now, Louise, but you're welcome to come back tomorrow." Her voice was quiet, but louder than before, as if it would be all right now if someone overheard her. "Life in the mountains is kind of different. It attracts all sorts of people who don't like to do things the way other people do them. What d'you call that, now—non-conformists is what I mean."

"Yes. But Porter Ranch isn't really in the moun-tains—"

"Foothills or mountains, it doesn't matter," said Ruthie. "It's five-six miles back, and that's all it takes to give 'em a mountain mentality. Mountain living is good for people on the edge of the law—course, I wouldn't men-tion names. They're also people who want total privacy." She laughed heartily. "Why, Lyons is *civilized* in compari-son to some of those mountain towns. And in some peo-ple's opinion, Lyons is gettin' way *too* civilized, judging from all the wealthy people movin' in. Why, sometimes you can't park on High Street for the BMW's clogging the spaces."

At that moment, a heavyset man of about forty clumped in the door. He had thinning brown hair with a cowlick at the crown of the head that gave him a faintly comical air, almost like a baby. His scuffed, square-toed boots made a noisy statement as he swaggered to the end of the counter.

"Eddie," said Ruthie patiently, "you know we're closing."

The man seemed distracted. He tapped his fingers impatiently on the counter and cajoled the woman, as if she were his mother. "Gosh darn, Ruthie," he wheedled, "all I want is a couple of quick ham sandwiches and some coffee and chips."

"Oh, well, I can do that much for you. How about some pie?"

"Y'forgot I don't care for sweets."

"People change their minds all the time about things like that," said Ruthie, smiling, as she turned to make the sandwiches.

Eddie's glance took in the remains of the crowd, finally landing on Louise. He didn't smile.

The proprietor brought the food to him in a small paper bag. "Awful sorry, Eddie, about your loss."

"Well, somebody killed'im, and we don't know who," said Eddie, and dropped some bills on the counter. "Anyway, thanks." He slammed the screen door on his way out.

Ruthie smoothed the bills with competent fingers, rang open the cash register, and put them in. She leaned closer so only Louise could hear her next words. "Well, as I was saying, some people are always on the edge of the law." She cocked her head toward the empty door. "Jimmy Porter's boy there, Eddie, for one. Can't help feeling a little sorry for him. The other two kids, Sally and Frank, they're, well, they've had their problems, too. Why, they didn't start socializing with other kids 'til they were way up in their teens. But they're not as *rough* as Eddie. Frank's turned into a fine man. Sally, now, she comes in here now and then, sits right where you're sittin', and has her piece of pie—apple. I think Sally's never had much fun in life, maybe because she doted on her dad too much. Not so unusual, seein' as how her mom died when she was little, but too much of a daddy's girl doesn't get you anywhere. I'm sure she hurts bad right now. I feel sorry for her."

She turned back to the grill and scraped the grill with her spatula, then turned back to Louise to continue her story. "But Eddie, well, what's wrong with Eddie is partly his father's fault. Now, I don't want to talk bad about a dead man, but I can tell you some things from personal experience." Still holding her broad spatula in one hand, Ruthie made a wide gesture with her arms, as if doing the breast stroke. "Jimmy spread out his charm like a big net and captured every lady he ever met. I'm not saying *womanizer,* but don't think he was the paragon of virtue he wanted people to make out he was—and *that's* why he got shot. A flirty man, and a hard man at business to boot." The way Ruthie said it, "hard" had three *r*'s.

"Now, Jimmy's wife, Bonnie," she said, "she died in a fire up there, y'know—maybe forty years ago. She was a honey. Had a wonderful perennial garden there in that mountain valley that Jimmy still maintained, I hear, just out of habit, I guess. But Jimmy had his enemies." She shook a finger again at Louise. "Mark my words: If that lazy sheriff ever finds who did it, it'll turn out to be someone Jimmy wronged some way or other."

❧

Louise was thinking about Ruthie's words and how on earth anyone could pass up a piece of that pie as she headed for home on Route Thirty-Six, so at first she didn't notice the wind. Suddenly, her car started veering left off the road, as if a giant hand were slowly pushing it onto the plains. She took a firmer grip on the steering wheel then and paid attention to her driving. So this was what they meant by a chinook.

When she reached her house, branches of the big cottonwoods surrounding it whipped dangerously back and forth, and she was thankful for the protection of the carport. She unlocked the door, finding it hard to pull open. When she finally got in, she was startled to hear a wail. It took her an instant to realize it was the house wailing, sounding for all the world like a woman in pain. Then the sound broke into several tones, like a choir gone mad, as gusts pushed through every crevice and opening.

For a moment, she thought about fleeing. She could gather up some of her belongings in a suitcase and speed to Boulder and get a room at the Boulderado. Then, she and Marty and Steffi could hang out—maybe in their room, or maybe in one of the hotel's funky but stylish bars.

She put her head between her hands and gave herself a shake. *What am I thinking? It's just the wind!* She went to the windows and pulled the drapes closed. They were heavy, and designed, no doubt, to prevent chinooks from breaking and entering.

She grabbed an old Indian blanket from the couch, and pulled it around her shoulders. Now she knew what it was for. These winds somehow made one feel cold, even in the heat of a summer night. She curled up with a book she had found on the living room table and tried to concentrate, but was distracted. She glanced frequently toward the windows, wondering if they could stand up to the heavy gusts.

Finally, the book grabbed her. It was entitled *Emily: The Diary of a Pioneer Woman*. Emily was an unfortunate woman who lived on her own in the West near the turn of the century, and endured unbelievable drudgery and poverty. Louise was appalled at some of the deprivations Emily suffered. Suddenly she felt spoiled.

Chapter 5

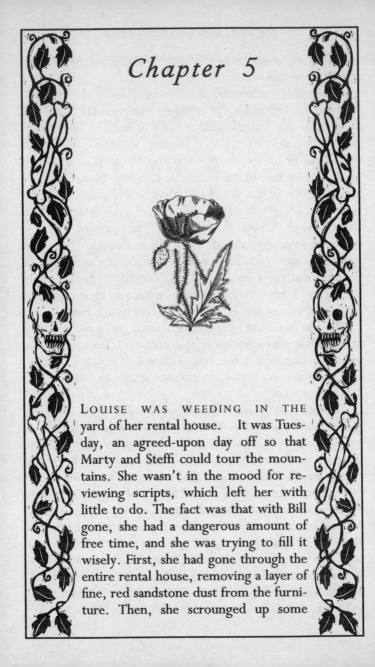

LOUISE WAS WEEDING IN THE
yard of her rental house. It was Tues-
day, an agreed-upon day off so that
Marty and Steffi could tour the mountains. She wasn't in the mood for reviewing scripts, which left her with
little to do. The fact was that with Bill
gone, she had a dangerous amount of
free time, and she was trying to fill it
wisely. First, she had gone through the
entire rental house, removing a layer of
fine, red sandstone dust from the furniture. Then, she scrounged up some

garden gloves and tools in the utility room off the kitchen and went out to do the garden.

She couldn't keep her mind off the murder that happened ten miles up the road, any more than she could keep her hands out of these weeds. If Bill had been around, he would have warned her against getting involved. But he wasn't—so he hadn't.

It was damp in the yard, since she'd turned the sprinkler on for more than an hour. This watering, together with the recent rains, had almost restored life to the adobelike ground and the buffalo grass trying to survive in it—it also made her weeding task considerably easier. This was a pleasant, wild place, she decided, accented with moss rocks, dotted with piñon and ponderosa pines and a few big clumps of ornamental grasses. Here and there were rugged apache plume plants that still held onto a few of their butterflylike white blossoms. The *Nepeta* ''Six Giants'' was in full cry, resembling two dozen delphiniums in bloom, with a cluster of white yarrow another relief from the predominant gray-green colors. Then, against a backdrop of sages and other native plants, was a stand of redhot poker plant, rough-leaved, but with glowing yellow and orange popsicle-shaped blossoms. Quite enough bloom, she thought, for a native garden. She approved. It was a shame the owners had let the weeds get ahead of them. She got down on her hands and knees, the better to confront them.

If only Ann would call, she thought, as she gouged out a bindweed plant, they could discuss the compelling question of Jimmy Porter's death. It was obvious Pete Fitzsimmons and Ann Evans both suspected someone other than a poacher. Even Ruthie, the café owner, was incredulous of Sheriff Tatum's theory. If Louise were to learn anything, she should visit the ranch again. Besides which, she really needed to examine those roadside mountain weeds she and

Ann had talked about, to see if it was worth doing a segment on them for her program.

Like an answer to her prayers, the phone rang, and she rushed indoors. Ann Evans said, "Want to check out weeds?"

Louise rubbed a muscle in her aching back. "I've become quite close to weeds in the past couple of hours—but if you're talking about weeds up at the ranch, I'd love to." It was as if she and Ann were talking in code; both understood they intended to do more than scope out fields of thistle. "But would we bother the Porters? Can we steer clear of the ranch?" She remembered that mysterious figure in the woods that Pete had caught in his photograph, and she knew they had to exercise care.

"We'll go by the back road. It runs right above that house you're renting. It's a little steeper"—Louise's stomach lurched to hear this—"but it's simply wonderful. They have a real weed problem along there."

"Great," said Louise.

"Oh, but wait, my car's in the shop today, and Luke parked the other at the airport when he left town on business. Can you pick me up? I'm not that far away from you." When Louise indicated agreement, she added, "Come any time. I'll just be doing a little practice climbing in my backyard. I live under a cliff, you see."

Louise didn't exactly like the idea of driving that road, but she could hardly say no. Ann Evans, and the world in general, would think she was a wimp. It turned out that the senior land officer lived only a few miles away, up Left Hand Canyon Road. The house was new, large, and stylish; it probably took two professional salaries to pay the mortgage—Ann's, plus her lawyer husband Luke's. As she drove up the long driveway, Louise thought back to that tortured conversation the day Jimmy Porter died and wondered just what was wrong with Ann and Luke's marriage.

At the top of the rise, she could see the gray wall of rock that rose up from the earth on the edge of Ann's property.

When she got out of the car, she could see Ann near the top of the cliff, suspended from ropes. She was rappeling down the precipice as if it were child's play, her long, tanned legs expertly playing against the rock. "Hi," she called. "I'll be right with you."

Louise met her at the base. "How handy to have a cliff in your own backyard."

"It's fantastic," said Ann, flushed and happy, and a little breathless. "This is granite, a lot better than the sandstone around here, which is really trash rock with a lot of vertical and horizontal jointing. Sandstone tends to snap off on you. The cliff is why we bought the house."

"It looks terrifying," said Louise, as they walked back across the big yard to the house. "Of course, I'm not so good with heights."

"Climbing's not hard. It's all in how you put your weight, and friction."

"You mean suction?"

"No. First, you have to have a good boot." She nodded at Louise's footwear. "You could do it in those boots you have. Then you use friction. Dig the tiny nodules of rock into the sole of your boot, then move one limb at a time, and keep three limbs anchored."

"A bit like a crab." Louise laughed. "I still don't think I'd like to try it."

"Oh," said Ann, with a casual flip of her hand, "in the space of half an hour I could have you working that cliff like a pro."

When they reached the patio with its high, latticed walls, Louise knew this was going to be a special house. Sitting on the Mexican-tiled patio floor were a couple of low-slung chairs, and a group of rough terra-cotta pots. One held a brilliant combination of red and orange zinnias and deep purple red orache. In others, Ann and Luke, who apparently both loved flowers, had planted tall, white, lilylike *Datura,* combined with rosy fountain grass and mauve-pink *Diascia,* with its small, intricate blooms cascading over the edges of the containers. A single pure white lotus blossom, just coming into bloom, floated in water in another large vessel.

After seeing Ann's pots, Louise was a little surprised to find the interior of the house was almost stark in its plainness. But it soon captured her. Plain was beautiful here, with a spare amount of comfortable furniture and open-weave natural linen draperies, set against rough-plastered walls painted a light terra-cotta. The floor was flagstone.

Ann, down from her climbing high, was back to her usual sober self. But still she couldn't disguise her pleasure at hearing Louise's praise of her house. "I got the idea from that house they found intact in Pompeii. I liked its earthy feel." She smiled. "And when I pot plants and spill dirt on the floor, I just tell Luke it's a little volcano ash."

Glistening with sweat from her climb, she said, "Time for me to wash up, though since we're roughing it, I won't change." She traded a sober look with Louise. "Just weed research, right?" she said.

Louise nodded. "That's right. Weeds."

※

Louise tightened her hands on the steering wheel, took a deep breath, and confronted her fear: the back road to Porter Ranch. She could feel the sweat forming in her armpits, as she drove up at an angle she was convinced was as steep as the beginning of a roller-coaster ride. Strangely, Trail Ridge Road, which crossed Rocky Mountain National Park, was one of the highest roads on the continent, and yet it hadn't scared her; it was these narrow primitive mountain routes that set her teeth chattering. But just as the second roller-coaster ride wasn't quite as scary as the first, she found today she could handle it. It helped, too, being the driver rather than a helpless passenger.

"This is the old Indian trail into the ranch," Ann explained comfortingly, as if that made it safer. Though she didn't take her eyes from the road for long, Louise could see in fleeting glances that they were passing a valley full of black cattle gently munching grass. Then came an Impressionist vista of mauve fields that caused her to jerk her foot off the accelerator and slow almost to a stop. "How utterly beautiful," she said.

"And treacherous," added her companion. "That's all weeds, acres of them. Musk thistle—it's a scourge out here in the West." On the spot, Louise realized these picturesque but troublesome intruders had to be part of a program.

Though it seemed like suicide to Louise, Ann wanted her to slow down when they reached the next hairpin turn. Louise reluctantly complied. "Uh, is this smart? I mean, couldn't someone come barreling up here?"

"We're all right—we'll hear them coming. I wanted to show you that white smokestack on the horizon. That's Stony Flats. You must have heard about it." Ann shook her blond head in disgust. "Here we have pristine foothills, rich grazing land, and wonderful farmland. Right in the center there is that—*abomination.*"

"I've heard about it, of course," Louise said, picking up speed and pretending to concentrate on her driving. She wanted to be careful not to repeat anything Bill had told her in confidence.

But then Ann came right out with it. "And now they're taking some of the nuclear triggers and sticking them in trucks and moving them to California, where they'll make the stuff less ready to blow."

Louise was amazed. "Is that public information?"

"Of course. It was in the newspaper. A committee of citizens meets all the time, trying to help decide where all this stuff should go—underground, to some other state . . ."

"It's not going away, is it? I've read it takes twenty-four thousand years for only half of it to decay."

"On that happy note," said Ann, giving Louise an ironic smile, "let's get going."

Louise lapsed into thoughts of Bill, and wondered just where he was. Though Stony Flats was central to his mission, she knew he wasn't around, or he would have made contact with her.

"Ah, look," said Ann, "here's someone you might want to meet." Approaching them was a gaunt old woman on a horse, moving slowly down the road. Her figure was erect and motionless. Louise brought the car to a near stop. "It's Jimmy Porter's next-door neighbor, Harriet Bingham. Looks like she's checking out that knapweed on the road. Good thing. It's gotten a big head start on her. Miss Bingham owns the ranch right next to Porter's—a big one, about three thousand acres. And that's after having sold off quite a few parcels over the years."

Ann stuck her head out the car window and said, "Hello, Miss Bingham. It's Ann Evans. How are you today?" The woman, wearing dark culottes and an old plaid shirt, gave forth several robust sneezes. Just a few of many sneezes, obviously, for the woman's eyes were red-rimmed. Louise could see she was allergic to something in the air. She gave Ann a smile of recognition, but since she was riding on the other side of the road, she pulled up near Louise. Ann introduced the two, and Louise saw before her a real evocation of the ranch woman. Harriet Bingham was spare and handsome, with worn hands that were a history of manual work. There was a distant look in the woman's eyes that Louise could not interpret.

Harriet Bingham leaned down and said, "Won't you come in for awhile, Ann, and bring your friend? I could use company. You c'n follow me back to the house." And with a gentle pull of the rein, she turned her big animal around and led them up the steep incline to the driveway to her ranch. It was a good half mile or more from the Porter Ranch entrance.

Once past a small forest of ponderosa pines that fronted the property, Louise noticed at once how rocky the front yard was. It was as if someone had scattered small boulders, and a few larger ones, just for the fun of it. Part of a moraine field, she guessed.

Native grasses of different heights and hues—tan, green, blue-green, and rosy red—grew gracefully between the rocks. Scrub pines and cedars seemed to pop up at precisely the right places to create the finest visual impact. The aesthetic result was better, Louise realized, than the designs of even the most famous designers, such as Oehme and Van Sweden, who had taken the landscape world by storm with their use of native grasses. The wonderful look of Miss Bingham's ranch yard appeared to be, simply, nature left alone.

Harriet slowly dismounted and tethered her horse to the fence, allowing it to feast temporarily on the tall grasses. She beckoned the two visitors onto the front porch of the low gray ranch house. If this ranch had a name, as its neighbor Porter Ranch did, it was not being advertised. Two supporting four-by-four posts stood side by side in the front yard, as if a sign from long ago had fallen down or blown away in the wind, and never been replaced.

Beyond the house were both natural and man-made borders. On one side, an extension of the rock-capped cliff that backed the Porter Ranch. On another, open horse stalls, beyond which a set of cubicles housed rusty farm equipment and old cars, abutted a tall stone outcropping that loomed up like a small monument.

Louise could not believe that much light would reach inside the house with all the trees and rock formations, and sure enough, as Miss Bingham slowly led them into the house, she had to squint in the dim light. The furniture needed dusting, and the lace curtains looked as if they might dissolve at a touch. Louise wrinkled her nose at the smell. It was the odor of an old house that had been kept neat, but lightly cleaned, and probably never polished. Louise remembered Pete's image of how fast things dried up in the West. Someday soon, this house and its owner would turn into a pile of dust and blow away.

The woman invited them to the study, which had slightly more candlepower, since it had a window with a view. "I have some coffee and rolls. Tell me you'll stay and have some."

They nodded.

"I'll help you," said Ann. Miss Bingham's energy seemed to increase inside the house, maybe because it was cooler than the outdoors, or because company was here.

While she waited, Louise took the opportunity to look around. She wandered over to a big library table in the corner that held a number of objects, all with a faint red-dish-tan color from the millions of particles of Colorado red dirt collected on them through the years. A beaded Indian basket. An Indian war shield. A half heart carved of aspen wood, with a jagged edge indicating the heart had been broken. And an old Bible whose limp repose told Louise it had been turned to the same page for years. She wondered what the woman's favorite Biblical verse was. In the center of the mementoes was a 1920's-style photograph of a couple, the man in a dark suit, the woman in a dark polka-dot dress and lacy hat.

"That's a picture of my father and mother when they

were married," said Harriet Bingham when she and Ann returned with the tray. "Henry and Margaret Bingham." Margaret was a beauty, with her head demurely cocked to one side, the man handsome and happy. "My mother died two years after that picture was taken, when I was born. That was seventy-five years ago." There was a flick of emotion in the woman's eyes. "So there was just my father and me for many years."

As they drank coffee and ate savory cinnamon buns, Louise remembered Ruthie Dunn's description of mountain folks. She asked Harriet if she got away from the ranch very often.

The elderly woman laughed nervously. "Of course. What d'ya think, that I'm stranded up here? It's only twenty-one miles to Boulder. I go there once in a while for programs, or the occasional meeting of the county commissioners. Closer to home, I've been known t'help tutor the first graders at Lyons Elementary—the ones that couldn't read well." This bit of spirit was followed by a dulling of her eyes, as if she might be suffering a brief spell.

"Let me tell you about Louise, Miss Bingham," said Ann.

"Please," Louise demurred, but it was too late. When Ann talked about the *Gardening with Nature* program, the woman's interest revived. In fact, when the organic farm shoot was mentioned, the elderly woman turned out to know the operator of the farm. It stood to reason Harriet would know all the large farmers and ranchers in the region, after spending a lifetime here.

The conversation rolled right along until Ann blurted out Louise's "criminal" background, the fact that she was involved in solving several murders. It was as if the room darkened, and the specter of Jimmy Porter was present.

Harriet Bingham's eyes filled with tears, and Louise wished the topic of murder had never been mentioned.

Ann leaped up and went to the woman's side, realizing her faux pas. "I'm so sorry—I didn't mean—"

"Don't mind these snuffles," said the old woman, recovering herself a little. "It's just that Jimmy was my neighbor for my whole life. We grew up together."

"It was so tragic," said Ann, as she returned to her seat in a dark, overstuffed chair. "Both Louise and I wonder about the sheriff's theory that it was a poacher."

A strange thing happened then, as if the woman were physically disintegrating before their eyes. Her face grew flaccid and her whole head trembled, as did her thin hands. "I don't know," she moaned. "Haven't been feelin' so good these days—I was dozing in my chair. I don't even think I heard the shots. Oh, what a loss, what a loss . . ." And her head bowed to her chest, like a wilted flower.

"Oh, Miss Bingham," said Ann, rushing over again, "I didn't mean to alarm you. Whoever did it could have no reason to harm you."

Harriet slowly raised her head again, and Louise and Ann gave each other a relieved glance.

"Maybe we'd better go and let her rest," she told Ann. The woman, as far as she could see, was suffering severe melancholy. No husband, no children, and now, no neighbor. Louise didn't believe the woman still lived the active life she described, and guessed she spent a lot of time alone in that study.

She took the coffee tray to the kitchen. This room was cleaner, and dominated by a blue porcelain stove. It was handsome and old, rather like Harriet, as were the antique canisters for staples. Sharing their space on the counter was a modern microwave oven. Perched in front of the oven was a single frozen plastic-wrapped chicken breast, destined to be tonight's lonely dinner. The leftover buns sat in an ancient baking tray whose decorative striations imprinted the bottom of each bun. Louise couldn't resist examining the bottles neatly lining the window shelf, but they were only multivitamins and iron supplements, and a special vitamin for the eyesight. Surely, the woman had to take other medicine as well, for she appeared to have health problems.

She returned to the study, and found Ann preparing to leave. Unlike Louise, Ann had a schedule to keep, and probably appointments later at her office. "Are you *sure* you're all right?" she asked. "Can't I call someone?"

Harriet Bingham rose out of her chair. In a stronger voice, she said, "I'm perfectly fine, now that you helped me with my pills and my allergy medicine." Louise then noticed the prescription medicine bottles in a metal box with its lid flipped open, sitting on a table beside the woman. "Don't you worry, now, Ann. And please come back again."

They promised they would, and went back out to their car. Harriet seemed a pathetic figure to Louise: obviously a woman of property—valuable property—and yet with no one here to share her suffering. As they climbed in, Ann shook her head and echoed Louise's thoughts, "I feel so sorry for that woman."

But Louise's mind was onto another matter. She didn't know exactly how to tell Ann that she didn't like people to talk about her involvement in murders. She took an oblique approach. "I sure get embarrassed," she said with a big grin, "when someone tries to make me out to be an amateur detective."

The gentle reprimand brought a blush to Ann's tan face. "Oh. Sorry. Well, no harm done, I hope, and I promise you I won't brag you up to anyone else." No sooner had they pulled out of the driveway than a big SUV pulled in.

A blond, sunburned man hopped out in a show of robust athleticism, then stopped for a second to stare at them. Louise noticed a certain masklike quality about his face. In a few great strides he had disappeared through the pines.

"He's going in there as if he lives there."

"I'm not surprised," said Ann. Her voice sounded strained. "That's Mark Payne, a Boulder developer who wanted to buy out Jimmy Porter. He's related to Harriet." She pursed her lips grimly. "He thinks that gives him an inside track to buy Harriet's land."

"Doesn't it?"

"I'm sure *he* thinks so. Let's keep going; I don't want him to come out and talk to us."

"Why would he do that?"

"Oh, just because he knows me," she said shakily. She was trying to sound offhand, but her face had reddened.

Louise drove down the side road. Through a break in the trees, she could see Harriet standing with Payne near a window. They were staring out at them. Payne loomed beside the elderly woman like a north country god. Louise stole a quick look at the woman sitting beside her. Another blond type, the type Payne might choose for his beloved. Suddenly, she realized something had happened between Mark Payne and Ann Evans.

Ann seemed anxious to change the subject. "Why don't we drive back to the Porter Ranch and just give their weeds a quick look?" Louise guided the car past the ponderosa woods and down the road to the entrance with the squeaky old sign.

"There's Sally," said Ann. "Poor thing." Jimmy's daughter was a somber figure in the distance. Wearing a plain housedress, she kept her head down as she swept the sunny front porch of the ranch house. With the light falling on her straight, light hair and stocky figure, she looked like a good subject for a Dutch master. Even from afar, Louise could sense her palpable grief. Here was a woman who, granted, had a career as a teacher, but who otherwise had devoted her life to her widowed father. Something occurred to Louise. She glanced at Ann. "Where was Sally going to go when Jimmy sold this place?"

"Oh, she wanted to get a little condo in Boulder to be near her dad and his new wife. But who knows what she'll do now. . . . What do you say we go out the back way? We'll stop this time to see the weeds."

Louise looked at her with panicked eyes.

"What's the matter?" asked Ann, laughing. "You got in here just fine. Why can't you drive out?"

"Oh, but it's *downhill* this time. You know, steep grade, brakes fail, you fall to your death, end up as a pile of broken bones and seeping blood."

Ann just laughed at her.

"Don't mind me—I'm obsessing. Sure, I'll drive you out the back way."

Louise put the car in gear gingerly, thinking about the lonely Sally, following Jimmy to town and setting up housekeeping right next door. She wondered how the old man had liked the idea. What if he hadn't—or if Sally had hated the idea of leaving this mountain?

Suspicious Interlopers: Weeds in America

WEEDS MAY BE WINNING IN THE West, just as they did in the South some years ago. Nonnative and noxious weeds are invading millions of acres of western land, thus crowding out native species, and clogging waterways. This is another version of the South's experience with the kudzu vine and the *Melaleuca* tree, that have become dominant in parts of Southern states.

These weeds form monocultures that reduce the land's ability to sustain wildlife diversity and livestock grazing.

Leafy spurge, an aggressive sort with roots sometimes twenty feet deep, is actually life-threatening to cattle and elk, because of the habitat degradation it creates. Weed specialists call the result "biological pavement," an enticing-looking scene that to the casual observer resembles a wildflower meadow, but is totally inimical to animals.

Using the simplest method first: grazing. "Integrated weed management" is the expert's answer to getting rid of weeds. Like "integrated pest management," "IWM" calls for using the simplest ecological solution first, and then moving to ever-sterner measures. Grazing is the easiest way to control weeds, and then come mechanical, biological, chemical, and cultural controls. But so far, the efforts to control these weeds are relatively small, as opposition springs up from residents worried about contamination from chemicals. People also complain about manual weed-pulling, fearing its effect on their respiratory systems, and even biological controls, speculating that they might become a problem in themselves.

Some of the worst offenders. Most of what are called weeds were introduced as Europeans colonized the

world. Some were brought purposely, some by accident in ship holds. Some of the toughest in the West are skeleton weed, leafy spurge, knapweed, Medusa's head, purple loosestrife, and Canada thistle. It is thought that these invasive plants have already caused more than seven billion dollars' worth of crop and rangeland losses in the West. Unchecked, the plants affect not only rangeland, but also acreages set aside for wilderness—which are often inaccessible and therefore make it harder to get rid of nonnative pests. Scientists are urgently trying to devise ways to fight them, calling together public and private land managers, commercial nurseries, farmers, ranchers, and foresters.

Is the solution worse than the problem? Herbicide use arouses deep suspicions in communities. An example is Boulder County, Colorado, where people opposed to chemical spraying determined to solve the weed problem another way—with hand-pulling. They gathered an army of volunteers to hand-pull diffuse knapweed and thistle from a certain area of the county. The volunteers obliterated a reported eighty-five percent of the crop, but that was not enough. There was plenty left to reseed the plants. When the county proposed spraying with Transline, a herbicide thought to be reasonably safe, nearby residents objected. It is an ongoing battle in communities throughout the United States.

Objections or not, large governmental efforts will be needed to curb the spread of acres of these noxious plants. But when only smaller tracts are involved, homeowners, not herbicides, can be the best weed control. Pulling weeds seems so old-fashioned, but is marvelously effective. Even dead-heading weeds, thistles and the like, can shrink the problem before it becomes too big for the householder to manage.

Don't buy weeds for your garden. The greatest irony may be that Americans add to the problem by *planting* weeds—even the ones that are sold for $6.95 a pot in our local nursery. An example is purple loosestrife, or *Lythrum,* which crowds out valuable native plants. Some states list it as a noxious weed and prohibit its distribution, while many others unfortunately don't. The naive home gardener can innocently purchase it and worsen the problem. Others that are easy to buy, and hard to get rid of, are Saint-John's-wort and, in seed form, dame's rocket.

The weeds that got a bad rap. Those who have been raised in suburbs where the badge of honor was a weedless lawn may have a tough time ever handling the truth about dandelions: Dandelions are not weeds! They have always been considered weeds by suburban gardeners, and chemical companies cater to their distaste, featuring pictures of droopy, dying dandelions in weed-killer ads. And yet today, as health foods and alternative medicines are no longer a fad but a gigantic and growing industry, the thinking is changing about these charmingly configured yellow-flowered plants. They are nutritional manna spread upon the earth. Enjoy them in salads or soups, harvesting them when young, before the flowers appear. And don't mind the neighbors. Some day they, too, will discover what they're missing, and thank you for providing them with starter seeds.

Chapter 6

IT WAS LESS THAN AN HOUR AF-
ter Louise dropped the land officer off
at her home in Left Hand Canyon that
she received a phone call from Ann.
She had forgotten to ask Louise if she
would be interested in attending the
Boulder County Parks and Open Space
Advisory Committee meeting tonight.

"It's a six-thirty meeting, and
won't last much longer than a couple
of hours because the agenda is short
tonight. It will give you a flavor of the
county's open space program. Everybody will be there, because this is the

night we talk about something that's sort of controversial,
but would be terrific if we can ever get it through. Conservation easements on private land to provide a wildlife corridor system through the whole of Boulder County.''

"And what does all that mean?"

"Well, for wildlife, it would be just great—a swath of
connected paths for animals, many near rivers and streams,
which is high-value wildlife habitat."

"Wouldn't it be extraordinary for people to donate
land in a place where land is so valuable?"

"It's not an easy idea to sell." A tentative quality entered Ann's voice. "But we have to try, and of course,
some people love the idea. Others are mad as hops: They
don't want to relinquish development rights to their land
to the county at any price. It would affect Harriet Bingham
and lots of others, especially developers. Not Jimmy Porter, since it looked as if we were getting the whole Porter
Ranch. But the Porter Ranch will come up in the discussion, because everybody knows the deal is on hold and
they'll want to chew that over for awhile, too. Join Sally
Porter and me for a quick dinner beforehand. Sally's in
Boulder to make her father's funeral arrangements, but she
doesn't want to attend the meeting."

Finally Louise agreed, and Ann told her where they'd
meet.

"The Hogback House—are you kidding? That's the
name of a restaurant?"

"Louise," said Ann, chuckling a little, "get with the
program. Didn't you know you are surrounded by hog-
backs out there in Lyons?"

⁂

The patio of Hogback House, situated on Boulder's
Pearl Street Mall, was packed on this hot August evening.
So were the other outdoor dining rooms in the downtown

area. Lots of people in Boulder, Louise noticed, seemed to prefer eating out so they didn't have to cook. Not only could they get a nice meal, but they also could observe the passing show that Boulder had become: a throng of tourists from all over the country in the usual informal tourist garb; the smartly dressed businessmen and women from the Boulder area's thriving commercial sector; crazily dressed street people who were a decades-long summer tradition in this mellow college town.

Louise sat opposite Sally Porter at the table so she could study her without appearing nosy. Sally was as plain-looking close up as she had been at a distance earlier today. Tonight, she looked uncomfortable in the dark polyester pantsuit she had chosen to wear, just as she had looked totally natural this afternoon: a lonely figure in a cotton housedress, sweeping the porch on which her father would never walk again.

Louise was struck by the woman's impassive face; she probably handled all matters without much emotion. Almost as soon as she sat down, she said to Ann: "I know how you must be worrying about the ranch deal. Frank and Eddie and I are meeting with our lawyer tomorrow. I'll see if they want to sign an agreement to sell to the county, just like Dad was going to do."

Ann reached over and pressed Sally's hand and launched into a little speech about how she would be carrying out her father's fondest wishes if she helped persuade the other heirs that the ranch should become open space. "Your father grew to love the idea of providing people with the beautiful nature experience that his own family had enjoyed for several generations." Louise admired the way the senior land officer discreetly painted a picture of the alternative—the old family homestead becoming the site of thousands of houses. Ann was well into a description of the loss of wildlife that would ensue, when Louise noticed that

Sally was not listening. She was looking past Ann with a worried expression on her unremarkable face.

"Oh, my, I hope this isn't trouble." Sally's brothers were approaching. They caught her eye and came toward their table. When Sally introduced them, Louise said, "I think I've seen you before, Eddie. Last night, at the Gold Strike Café."

"Yeah. You were the best-looking gal in the place." He gave an unpleasant laugh. "Of course, it ain't a very big place."

Sally looked down in embarrassment, and Louise's mouth twisted in an attempt at a smile. Eddie was spiffed up a little to come to Boulder, and didn't wear his shit-kicker boots tonight, but rather a fancy tooled pair in brown and black. He had slicked down his cowlick with hair grease that shone in the fading evening light.

Frank was another matter. He was a slim, dark-haired man in a sporty outfit that quietly stated "professional." He probably wore it to his job at IBM. But right now wasn't a good time to get to know him, because he looked furious. Eddie cocked his head toward his brother. "Me 'n Frank, we been talkin' some things out, Sally, in yonder bar." He pointed back down the mall. "Frank, he got himself all worked up, but he's gettin' over it now. So we aren't about t'talk to *you* until tomorrow morning. It's bad enough between the two of us. Okay?"

Eddie looked at her uncertainly, as if he knew in his heart he shouldn't be treating his grieving sister with such roughness. "Aw, c'mere and let me hug ya, sis," he added, grabbing her out of her chair and pulling her up to her feet. He clasped her in a bear hug, rocking her back and forth like a big toy, all the while whispering things in her ear.

Sally, her stocky body tipped back in the embrace of her eldest brother, seemed to be listening intently to what he was saying. Finally, she raised her head and nodded solemnly at him. Eddie smiled.

Then it was Frank's turn. He came over to Sally and put a gentle hand on her shoulder. She could hardly meet his gaze. "Look, sis," he said softly, "it will be okay no matter how it turns out." He gave her a little kiss on the cheek and turned to catch up with his brother, who was already striding away down the sidewalk.

Sally sat down without looking at Ann and self-consciously stared at the menu. "All of a sudden I'm real hungry," she said simply. Ann stared at her for a moment, then pretended to concentrate on what to order. During the meal, Ann put in an occasional remark, but was not her usual self. Louise felt obliged to carry the conversation with Sally, and asked her about her early life on the ranch. Jimmy Porter's daughter answered Louise's questions in a quiet, halting voice, with no embellishments. It was clear Sally seldom talked about herself. But with persistent questions, Louise learned over the space of twenty-five minutes that, with her mother dead, Sally had become the substitute "mom" at the ranch when still a mere child. She washed and ironed, sewed, churned butter, cleaned, and cooked. Sometimes she traveled to school in Lyons on her horse, more often just riding with her brothers to the county road, then meeting a school bus there.

The way she spoke, it was obvious her father was the center of her universe. But one of Louise's questions had not been welcome: the one about where Sally would go when the ranch was sold. "I had my plans," she said tersely. Louise was now convinced that Jimmy Porter had rebuffed Sally's idea to trail after him and his new bride. What a blow that must have been!

Not once, as they talked, did tears come to the bereaved daughter's eyes for a father who had died just days ago. A frightening thought entered Louise's mind: Was this woman some kind of time bomb ready to go off—or that had already gone off? Another of Sally's answers had also raised little alarms for Louise. "Shoot? Of course I know how to shoot, and to hunt, too. If you live on a ranch, you have to know how; it doesn't matter if you're a girl."

When dinner was finished, Ann Evans gave Sally a polite good-bye and said, "I hope we can talk about this in a few days, when you've thought back on what I said."

Sally stepped forward, extending her hand to Ann. As if it were a requiem for a lost cause, she said, "You were a good friend to my father, I'll say that." Then she turned and walked away.

Ann turned to Louise. "Now we'd better double-time it, or we won't make that meeting on time." They set out for the courthouse at a fast pace. Halfway down the block, Ann revealed what was bothering her. "I am so *pissed*— I'm *royally* pissed!" Louise was a little startled at the strong language coming out of the mouth of this woman. "Did you see that loathsome brother of hers bullying her?"

"You think, right there in front of us, he was trying to change her mind about the sale?"

Ann looked at her in disbelief. "Didn't you *see* it? He not only tried: he succeeded. You could tell by the way he was talking to her, and the way she gave right in and said yes."

"Well, she did nod at him—" said Louise.

"Louise, I've been talking to these people for a year, and I know them. That woman has just transferred all her fatuous adoration of her father to her big, dumb *brother*!"

"But Frank seems pretty darned smart. Why can't he make a case with his sister?"

Ann gave a low moan, and stopped short on the concrete path into the building. Louise could see the tic in her right eye was bothering her again. But she drew herself up straighter and said in a determined voice, "I can't go storming through town venting like this, no matter how angry I am at Sally Porter. People will think I'm nuts. Let's just forget that dinner, okay?" She grabbed Louise's arm and started walking again. "People sometimes call this courthouse Boulder's Art Deco folly," she said, as if the scene with Eddie and Sally and Frank had never happened.

"Ann," interrupted Louise, "hadn't we better talk about this—"

"No," her companion said firmly, then softened a bit at Louise's raised eyebrows. "Later, maybe. Not now." She pointed up at the squarish yellow brick building and continued her history lesson. "Most of the building materials came from the dismantled Switzerland Trail railroad that ran up to Nederland. I like the building. And I like the way Boulder preserves its history. It's no longer a sleepy, unspoiled mountain college town, and everyone complains about that. Bet you wouldn't believe this was once a Republican-dominated, conservative little place where people couldn't even buy an alcoholic drink. The townspeople thought the university people were flaming radicals."

As if swept along by the tide, Louise played along with Ann's mood. "What changed it?"

"The sixties. By then, Boulder was no longer dry, and IBM had moved in with its thousands of employees. And then the hippies came, taking drugs and making love in City Park." She glanced meaningfully at Louise. "I remember my father avoiding that route when we drove through town. That kind of thing certainly helped loosen things up. Now, you have everything here—liberals, conservatives, alternative religions, New Age folks, and the most sophisticated scientists and entrepreneurs. It's totally changed, but it's still a great place to work and live."

As Ann hustled her up the stairs to the third floor, they

encountered another conversational pair on the second floor landing: Sheriff Tatum and Mark Payne. Louise figured the two were engaged in a good ol' boy conversation, which, if it had taken place outside, might have had one of them chewing a hayseed, the other casually spitting in the dust. As it was, Tatum had one arm propped on a high stone windowsill, and Payne was leaning on the stairway wall, one expensively shod foot on a higher stair, done in marble embellished with an Art Deco inset.

Everybody seemed to know everybody else in Boulder. "Hi, Sheriff Tatum," said Ann. Louise nodded politely at the lawman. But Ann sailed past Payne without a word. He didn't change his stance, but his face was transformed when he saw Ann. Suddenly, he looked soft and vulnerable and almost ashamed.

Ann turned her attention firmly back to Louise as they left the men behind. "I'm going to give you a little background that might help you sort things out. There are two tiers of people at these open space meetings—the first being what I call notable locals. People like Tom Spangler, manager of Stony Flats—he'll be here because the land-use people would like river land near that plant for the wildlife passage. Payne, the local developer, because the county is looking at quite a hunk of his properties for the same purpose. Josef Reingold is even bigger. He's with DRB, a German conglomerate that owns a lot of land in the West. He was one of the contenders for Jimmy's land, too. Even Harriet: She'll also be asked to relinquish some acreage for this wildlife plan."

They had reached the big conference room, which had a curved wooden platform on which the open-space committee members were beginning to assemble. "How about the other tier?"

"They're the environmentalists—what Pete Fitzsimmons calls 'bunny huggers.' There're lots of them in Boulder and Boulder County. People are genuinely interested in preserving natural habitats." She smiled. "That's why this place has more designated open space than a lot of others."

Louise thought darkly of Jimmy Porter, splayed over the fence. "Too bad people have to get killed over it."

Louise regretted her words, as Ann shuddered guiltily and bowed her head. "You're confirming my worst fears," she said, in a low voice. "Do you really think that's why Jimmy was killed?"

Louise shrugged. "How can I help thinking that? It just makes sense." She gave a wry smile. "In fact, there's probably a lot of prospective murderers here tonight." She had meant it as a half-joke. But Ann's alarmed face told Louise it was no joke to either one of them.

The senior land officer had her own table at the rear of the room. Louise sat in the row in front of it, realizing now why Ann needed to regain control of herself: She was the puppet-master here. The fourteen illustrious members of the Parks and Open Space Advisory Committee followed her guidance as they decided the fate of undeveloped land in Boulder County. Ann had fastened the buttons on her linen suit jacket, to give herself a more kick-ass appearance, Louise supposed. She'd drawn half-glasses out and perched them on her nose, immediately aging herself by five years. When she arrived, she was handed her notes by her secretary. Only because Louise sat so near could she see the faint trembling of the papers in Ann's slender hands.

The young woman, though totally composed on the surface, was a mass of nerves underneath.

She identified the players for Louise as they came in. Mark Payne, whom Louise recognized, glad-handed everyone in the room as if he were the host at a cocktail party, making a wide, deliberate circle around Ann. Up close,

Louise noted that Payne missed being handsome because of some flaw that was hard to put a finger on. It could have been the overly strong jawline, perhaps, or the hooded eyes, strange in a blue-eyed, blond type. His sandy, almost invisible eyelashes gave the man a faintly sinister look. Maybe this was why he smiled at one and all, but avoided direct eye contact. Except, of course, with people like Sheriff Tatum.

Tom Spangler, a big, confident-looking man, hurried in next. He was heavyset and balding, about fifty, wearing a short-sleeved sport shirt. Louise's heart beat faster: Bill must have something to do with this man, since he ran Stony Flats; was he helping Bill and his team, or could he be in on the plot to steal the plutonium shipment? She turned to Ann. "What kind of a man is he? It must take something special to run a plant like that."

"Tom's a terrific man," said Ann, "a down-to-earth guy, originally from Oklahoma. He's overseeing the dismantling of the plant, and apparently is doing a good job. He's had a little picketing—people complaining about safety—but he hasn't taken the brunt of nuclear protesters: For years, they've been making other plant managers' lives miserable. And he's very supportive of everything the county's doing. Very cooperative on land issues." She tossed her hand in a casual gesture. "Good family man, kids apparently at the top of their classes—and that's good, because he has lots of kids."

Then came Josef Reingold. Slim and no taller than Louise, he looked every inch the urbane European, from his black metal-rimmed glasses down to his loafers, which she suspected were Gucci. As he walked in, she could hear him greeting someone with a slight German accent. A bulge under his expensive jacket had to be a handgun; undoubtedly, some Colorado concealed-weapons law made it legal. "The man carries a gun," said Louise quietly.

"Maybe he needs it," murmured Ann. "Austrian, apparently, and terribly rich—the Wall Street Journal called him one of America's secret land barons."

Reingold made his way through the room with the grace of a seigneur, bowing to the ladies, and shaking each man's hand. He went to a seat right next to Spangler's. *A real meeting of cultures there,* thought Louise. *Austrian and Okie.* They were obviously friends. They put their heads together for a moment of casual conversation, two city figures probably chewing over the latest civic gossip. Then the two got up and wandered to the back of the room to pay their respects to Ann; Louise was pleased to see her new friend had a little clout around town. Ann in turn introduced them to Louise. She immediately turned her attention to the nuclear power plant manager. "You have a challenging job, I hear, Mr. Spangler. Dismantling a major plant from the Cold War days, and then managing all that poisonous waste."

His smile was as practiced as hers: he'd probably turned away much public antinuclear fallout with that down-home smile. "Ms. Eldridge, my job's a delight. I'm a family man who is proud to live safely in a neighborhood not too far from the plant, to raise my six children there, and our horses and dogs—even to own a little chunk 'a land out there as a retirement investment. Yeah, overseeing the dismantling of Stony Flats is the biggest challenge of my life."

"And obviously, it's being done safely, or you wouldn't—"

"Of course not—wouldn't expose my wife and children, or my neighbors. Why, even our little Catholic congregation is out there. We meet in homes, you see. No, everything's going well with Stony Flats, and that includes the citizen's committee that advises us as we go."

The man was utterly convincing. Apple pie, Mother, and—Stony Flats.

"And fine people they are, too, on that advisory committee," continued the plant manager, his eyes lighting up behind his gold-rimmed glasses. "I'm from Oklahoma, a real great place to be from, and I've lived and worked in a lotta places. Yet I find the Boulder area is the most stimulating place I've *ever* had the privilege to live." He cast a glance around the room which included Reingold, standing beside him. Louise could just imagine why Spangler loved Boulder. Besides all the other perks he mentioned, this big, friendly man got to rub elbows with international scientists and businessmen on a daily basis, and he reveled in every minute of it.

Curious, she thought, the way Americans viewed the country and where they came from, and where they wanted to go. Migrating to and fro, in their search for the perfect place to be. Oklahomans yearning to be Californians. Californians, flocking to become Coloradans. And a thousand other cravings and hopes that propelled people back and forth across this big country.

Spangler had ended his quest for the perfect place to live. He wanted to stay in Colorado forever.

During Louise's exchange with the Stony Flats plant manager, the debonair Reingold checked out the people coming into the room, and also discreetly checked out Louise—she did not fail to notice this. But suddenly Reingold's attention was diverted from her to another woman.

Harriet Bingham, with her gray hair swept up in a French knot and wearing a handsome but well-worn purple dress, walked in like the queen mother and took her place in the front row. "Excuse me," said Reingold, with a small bow, and hurried over to sit next to her. Harriet looked the picture of strength tonight, until Reingold came along and spoiled it. As soon as she laid eyes on him, she seemed to shrink into herself.

Louise didn't like to see old Harriet suffer, but mentally

she rubbed her hands together. This potentially boring meeting was becoming downright intriguing!

Then another group caught Louise's eye—the Porter brothers. They were being given a good talking-to by a well-rounded little woman with frizzy gray curls and flashing brown eyes, who looked as if she might reach up and box their ears. What were the brothers doing here, anyway—seeing what kind of a deal they could strike? And who was this little scold? Then she caught on. This must be Grace Prangley, their father's affianced.

When she and Ann first arrived, she had noticed the Porter brothers in the hall, being courted just like congressmen in the outer halls of the Capitol. The courtiers were developers, no doubt. Eddie Porter, cowlick now liberated from the grease and sticking straight up, had looked delighted to be the subject of so much attention.

"Psst." Ann was busy reviewing her papers, but looked up as Louise leaned back to talk. Louise cocked her head toward the solid little woman. "The fiancée?"

"Yes," whispered Ann, "that's Grace Prangley, the one I told you about. The retired schoolteacher."

Louise pressed her hand to her mouth. "Everybody's here," she murmured. "The plot thickens."

Ann looked at the room over her half-glasses. "I wish she were prodding them to go ahead with the land deal." She frowned. "But I have a feeling she isn't. She's very shrewd—you know—regarding—"

"Don't tell me. Land."

Then they heard the gavel, and the meeting started.

There was a solemn mention of the death of Jimmy Porter. But missing from the agenda was the most important question of all. Who would get the biggest and certainly the most beautiful remaining ranch in Boulder County? Obviously, to Reingold and Payne, plus any number of other developers and builders present, Porter Ranch was like a Colorado steak to a hungry man: They wanted it so badly they could taste it. The value of Porter's land only increased when one thought of it in conjunction with the neighboring parcel, the land belonging to Harriet.

But Harriet herself looked as if she would like to evaporate from the chair next to the most predatory-looking one of the bunch. Josef Reingold.

In mid-meeting, the chairman opened the floor to comments from the audience. A parade of citizens went to the podium either to gripe or to commend the county for its actions regarding open-space land.

Louise sat forward with interest when a confident and smiling Grace Prangley came forward. Turning her head from side to side, she unblinkingly eyed the crowd, like a teacher alerting a class to pay attention to something important. Louise whispered to Ann, "She doesn't act like a woman whose beloved fiancé just had his head blown to bits."

Ann, whose glasses had slid down on her burnished nose, rolled her eyes toward Louise and nodded agreement.

Plainly, Grace was not a woman to mince words. "You people sittin' up there, so concerned about animal trails and open space, you're goin' around paying millions so acreage can be held off from development. But do you realize how much money it's goin' to cost to maintain, to say nothing of patrol, that acreage, when y'turn it all into parks? More millions. Otherwise, park hoodlums and weeds are goin' to get the best of you."

With a flashing glance that encompassed them all, she lassoed the open-space board members and figuratively brought them to the ground. "My forebears," she said, "were into development, and that's what's made this county. It's what draws people to the Boulder area: good housing, and enough of it for people t' have a nice selection. You keep on turning this into a no-growth community, and it's all goin' t' go sour on you.''

Grace propped a hand under her chin and gave them a bright smile. "Some people already think Boulder's gone elite, y'know, think it's kind of a joke. Now, I ask you, do you want the whole county to get that reputation, too?"

Then she straightened up, smoothed her dress, and walked confidently back to her seat in her Nike cross-trainers. It was clear now what her sentiments were about the disposition of the ranch. Louise moved Grace in her mental playbill from a bit player to one of the second leads in the Jimmy Porter murder mystery.

What dismayed her most was Grace's lack of grief for her dead fiancé. Why, even Louise liked Jimmy Porter, just from hearing stories about him. This woman couldn't have loved Jimmy without showing traces of a few tears or some sorrow, following his death only three days ago. Or was she in shock, too devastated to grasp what had happened?

But how better to augment the meager retirement package of the schoolteacher than to wangle an elderly man out of a quarter of his valuable property, and then blast him with a shotgun? Startled, Louise realized Grace was the second woman she had pegged as possibly having gunned down Jimmy Porter—the first being Jimmy's own phlegmatic daughter, Sally.

Warming to the idea, Louise decided that little Grace Prangley fit the part better than Sally did. She had a dead-aim, Annie Oakley quality about her. Louise was sure *she* knew how to handle a shotgun. All Grace would have to do now would be to persuade the rest of the Porter clan to back out of the deal.

As discussion ended on the matter of wilderness corridors, people began to leave. The Porter brothers and their almost-stepmother Grace had already gone—probably somewhere where she could continue to cajole Frank into cancelling the county deal.

Payne and most of the other developers had disappeared. Only Josef Reingold remained. He rose from his seat and tried to help a nervous Harriet Bingham from hers, but the woman would not budge; her cheeks were feverish above her purple dress as she resisted his entreaties. He had tried to take her somewhere—to do what? Buy her a cup of coffee? Or twist her thumbs until she agreed to sell her land? Louise was glad the old lady had the strength to say no.

Louise arrived back home feeling restless. She had seen enough people for today, and needed a walk to stretch her legs and give herself some time to sort things out. Although it was not really necessary out here in the country, she locked the house behind her as she took off down the road.

Outside, she looked up at the hogback mountain and gasped. Above it was a sky Tiepolo might have painted, a luminescent moment when the setting sun transformed a poetic cluster of clouds—swirls and twirls and puffs and feathers of clouds—into a pink-and-gold confection that resembled heaven. She would not have been surprised if God had appeared in those clouds.

Pete was right. Clouds were everything in Colorado.

She passed the neighboring farmer's property, and looked over to see if she could see the llama and the horse with which Janie had become acquainted.

That may have been why she didn't notice the rattler, until her foot stepped on its firm body. In utter terror, she let out a screech. Then she backed off the four-foot-long reptile and stared at it from a respectable distance, her heart thumping wildly.

It was some moments before she realized the thing had not moved.

Someone nearby was laughing hard. It was Herb, the farmer, inside his fence, cowboy hat set well back on his head, shotgun cradled under his arm.

Louise tried to regain her composure. And that meant laying blame where it belonged. She pointed a finger accusingly at the snake. "That snake . . ."

Herb laughed uproariously again, and patted his stomach, as if to make himself stop. "Sorry—it's jest real amusin'. I shot that snake out in m' field an hour ago. Then, my cat must of drug it back into th' road. Why, it don't even have its head and rattler on—y'notice that?"

His llama had come up next to him, its alert ears jutting forward, its face twisted in a smirk, as if echoing its master's ridicule of this city slicker who didn't know a live snake from a dead one.

"Dead, huh," she muttered. She peered at the serpent. It was quite headless and tailless. She was so relieved she decided not to be annoyed at Herb for laughing at her. She stepped carefully across the mowed grass to where he stood by the fence.

"Herb—you are Herb, aren't you? I'm Louise."

He gave her a warm handshake and thrust a thumb sideways to indicate the llama, which stood as tall as the barn. "And this here's Daisy."

"Hi, Daisy," said Louise, standing out of range. She didn't know what inspired llamas to spit at people, and wasn't anxious to find out.

"And my wife Ellie's in the house bakin' cookies, so if any time y'want ta try 'em, drop in. She'd love t' meet ya."

"I will, but maybe not tonight." She pointed to Herb's weapon. "That's a shotgun, I guess."

"Yep. Twelve-gauge."

Just like the one used to murder Jimmy Porter, from what Louise had read in the paper. She knew little of guns, and nothing about this kind that was so widely used in the West. "What are you shooting with it now?"

"Mebbe another snake," he said, laughing. "Who knows?" Seeing she was curious, he took a few minutes to acquaint her with the weapon. He showed her how to load two shells and snap the gun back together again. "With a twelve-gauge," explained Herb, "you have ta remember ta hold the stock tight t'yer shoulder." He shoved the wooden end of the gun into the crease between her upper arm and her chest and placed one of her hands at the trigger and the other on the handrest at the base of the barrel.

The gun felt heavy and loathsome in her hands.

"Don't ya wanna fire it?" asked Herb. "It's got the kick of a mule, 'n if ya don't hug it that way, it kin knock y'off your feet and leave ya with a black-and-blue shoulder."

Louise lowered the weapon. "I get the idea. Thanks, Herb, but I doubt I'd ever be comfortable shooting one. I guess I'd rather count on my wits to save myself."

He said, "Suit yerself. But when the chips're down and a *live* rattler's starin' at ya, a gun's a darn sight better."

❧

It took what seemed like hours to fall asleep that night. And when she did, Louise had a dream in which developers' bulldozers climbed up steep mountain roads and she fell off the edge in a pickup, while rattlers lurked menacingly in the tall grass below.

What was particularly strange was that the snakes were

slithering around, not in native Colorado grasses like buffalo grass or blue grama, but rather in clumps of *Miscanthus sinensis* ''Gracillimus.'' Not a native grass, but an ornamental, the kind you had to buy in a nursery. Just as she thought: She continued gardening in her dreams.

Chapter 7

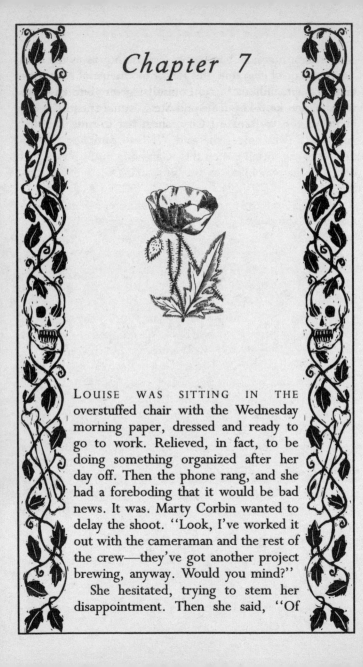

LOUISE WAS SITTING IN THE overstuffed chair with the Wednesday morning paper, dressed and ready to go to work. Relieved, in fact, to be doing something organized after her day off. Then the phone rang, and she had a foreboding that it would be bad news. It was. Marty Corbin wanted to delay the shoot. "Look, I've worked it out with the cameraman and the rest of the crew—they've got another project brewing, anyway. Would you mind?"

She hesitated, trying to stem her disappointment. Then she said, "Of course not, Marty.'' She had no choice but to agree with her producer. That was the deal on this trip—fun came first. Except, unlike Marty, Louise had no one to have fun with. When he told her he and Steffi would spend the day in the casinos of Central City, she tried to hide her distaste. In a light voice, she said, ''I hate gambling, so it's useless to try to sell me on this. Gambling in the city is bad enough. But gambling in the mountains—it's a desecration.''

''Louise,'' said Marty, his enthusiasm put on hold, ''can I tell you something and you won't get insulted?''

''Sure, Marty.''

''You're a hard-ass. Do you *ever* let it go and have a little fun? You, and that Bill of yours? Waddaya do for fun, read *The New York Review of Books,* while you have a quiet cup of herbal tea?''

She laughed. She knew Marty could give as good as he got. ''Look, I know everybody's doing it—so you guys might as well do it, too. Have fun.''

She looked bleakly out the living room window, where a few raindrops had fallen, and dark clouds still threatened. It wouldn't have been a good day for shooting, anyway. But now she faced another twenty-four hours of trying to fill her time.

The phone rang again just as she had stepped out of her jeans to change into shorts. She ran back to the living room and answered it in her underwear, hoping no one spied her through the big windows. The words of the sheriff's deputy were brief and to the point, and sent a chill through her body. She could see the goose bumps on her bare legs. Sally Porter, Jimmy Porter's daughter, had been found dead this morning. Her car had plunged off the Porter Ranch road as she was returning home last evening.

''But who . . .''

The deputy was patient. ''Ma'am, it looks like an accident, according to the sheriff. But a couple of loose ends need to be tied up. Sheriff Tatum wants you to come in this morning and have a nice long talk with him."

Tatum. The aspect of the man, bullying and faintly dishonest, and the smell of him, reeking with garlic, were vivid in her memory. She could not think when she had had a more unwelcome invitation.

"What would he want to talk to me about?"

"You and Ann Evans and the undertaker were the last parties to have talked to the deceased. You may be able to shed light on her mental state." Did they think Sally committed suicide?

Louise was supposed to come in at eleven. That would give her plenty of time to think of what to say, and what not to say, to this unappealing man.

She swooped her long brown hair off her neck and secured it with a big barrette. Then she climbed back into her new jeans. Well, she was involved now—in not just one death, but two.

"Oh, my God," she said softly, "what will I tell Bill?"

Then the phone rang again. This time it was her husband.

❧

"You mean, the daughter of a rancher supposedly shot by a poacher went off a cliff in her car?"

"They think it was an accident."

"*Louise.*" Bill's voice on the other end of the phone line was ominously quiet. "I don't know what's going on around there, but don't believe that story. Damn. I don't have time for this. I don't know how you came to get mixed up in some land deal mess. Now, listen. I'm not that far away. If things get rough, call this number." He gave her a phone number with a Virginia area code: Langley. The CIA would patch the call through to him, if an emergency big enough reared its head.

Now the voice was stern. "I would also like you to stay in close touch with Janie."

"Of course I will. And I have nice neighbors—Herb, and Herb's wife, Ellie, who I hear makes good cookies. Look, I'm so removed from this thing you wouldn't believe it. I'll talk to the sheriff this morning, and that will be the end of it."

"The sheriff? Is that what you call being removed?"

"Ann, the county officer, and I were among the last people to talk to Sally—but neither one of us heard anything that's going to be helpful."

Louise felt guilty. In spite of how preoccupied he was with his own business, Bill was now worried about her. So she was not surprised, just before leaving the house, to receive a phone call from her daughter at the YMCA Camp in Estes Park.

"How's wilderness camp, darling?"

"Ma," the exuberant voice answered, "I love it. The concept, the mountains, the people—especially my fellow counselors." A pause while the teenager arranged some tactful words. "And—how are ya makin' out there on your own?" Her voice seemed to have acquired a twang.

"Janie, I know your father put you up to this phone call. But I'm fine, and I don't need you to worry about me."

"Promise me you'll call if things get weird, Ma?"

"Promise."

"Well, then, I have a little fourteen-thousand-footer to climb, and someone terrific to climb it with."

"Someone?" Louise thought it was probably healthy for Janie to find new male interests at camp; that would relieve the intensity of her friendship with Chris back home. "Who is this terrific person?" she said, and bit her tongue as soon as the words were out. Her relationship with her seventeen-year-old no longer included direct questions like that.

"Well, Ma"—Louise could tell the pause was for some quick thinking—"let's just say that he's the coolest guy I've met since I left Virginia—smart, cute, funny."

"Hmm." Louise was having uncomfortable mental pictures of teenagers making love in log cabins. She could remember being at camp herself, and it had been pretty romantic. Although she hadn't gone that far, that was just *her* generation. Janie's was expected to be much more liberated.

"Well, sweetie, I just hope—"

"What—that I stay out of trouble?" Her daughter's voice dripped with irony. "Hey, get real, Ma. Remember who called whom for what. Compared to you, I am the soul of discretion. Don't *you* do anything rash, and if you do," she added breezily, "give me a call. I'll come down with my friends and try to get ya out of whatever mess you're in. Now I really have to go—he's waiting for me."

It was a little disheartening to realize her family didn't trust her to take care of herself. But she surely didn't need Janie around. It was true the girl had helped her in previous encounters with dangerous people. But even if it turned out Sally had been forced off the road, the killer loose in the county certainly wasn't focusing on Louise.

Chapter 8

LOUISE HADN'T BEEN WAITING long when the door to the secured area of the sheriff's department swung open. In the doorway stood the sheriff with a grinning Mark Payne. Two big men with their heads together, intent as lovers—or deal makers. Since they were almost certainly not talking about love, Louise wondered what the deal was. They didn't notice her.

The sheriff's final words floated out of the office: "It's a question of getting others to do the work for you—" Then, with a start, he saw her waiting in the anteroom. Sending the blond-haired developer forth with a friendly pat on the shoulder, Tatum cocked his head as his desk phone ring. Before turning on his heel, he said to Louise, "Be with you in a second, Miz Eldridge—just let me take this call."

Alone with Mark Payne, Louise found his very size a bit intimidating—among the numerous tall western men she'd met the past few days, he was by far the tallest, perhaps six feet seven. He seemed to realize this, and sat down in the waiting room chair beside her to be closer to her level. He still represented a massive, hulking presence. "Louise Eldridge, right?" He held out a big hand. "I haven't had a chance to meet you, Louise." They solemnly shook hands and he studied her with his pale-lashed, hooded eyes. Her imagination deviated dangerously to a scene where this man was laid on a table and given a whole new face, like a Frankenstein monster—new eyes, new skin, new bones . . .

His words, spoken in a completely normal voice, pulled her back from her fantasy. "I see you're pretty mixed up in this Porter Ranch thing, whether you want to be or not."

"I don't know what you mean, exactly. Do you mean Sally Porter's accident?"

"Yes, and Jimmy Porter's shooting," he continued, in an uninflected voice. "You're all over the place. Up at Harriet Bingham's. At the meeting last night." Sitting this close to him, she could finally see what disturbed her about his face. He had undergone extensive plastic surgery. This, combined with his emotionless delivery, gave her the sense that his feelings were all hidden behind a mask of scars.

"So—you're one of those women who likes to get her hands in things," he concluded.

In spite of the rather hostile words, she forced a smile. "I have all the best intentions, Mr. Payne—"

"Oh, just call me Mark," he said, as if bestowing a gift on her.

"Well, Mark, my producer's out here in Boulder, we've hired a local crew, and we're shooting quite a lot of footage for my *Gardening with Nature* television show. Did you know I have a garden show on PBS?"

"Actually, yes. Harriet told me all about you. She's my great-aunt—now, did you know *that*? I bet any money Ann Evans told you that." Ann Evans: a sore point with this man.

"Let's see," Louise countered sweetly, "it's a little confusing, meeting so many new people at one time. Were you up at Porter Ranch the day Jimmy Porter—"

"Hey!" He laughed. "No way was I up there—not before the shooting, not in all the fuss that went on afterward. No, we leave stuff like that to our talented sheriff. He's got a great record for closing cases." He gave her what he obviously thought was an ingratiating look. "I hear from Harriet you solved some crimes back East."

"Yes." She decided a little self-promotion wouldn't hurt with this man. "Actually, I've been commended on occasion by the Fairfax police for my help." *But more often,* she thought wryly, *I've been chewed out for interfering with their investigations.* She thought fondly of a red-faced Detective Michael Geraghty.

"What kind of crimes were they?"

She looked Mark Payne over for a minute, then leaned forward dramatically and whispered, "Murders. *All* murders."

"Oh." That was enough for him, and he got up from his chair. Somehow, he couldn't fit Louise, a woman who solved murders, into his preconceptions of what womankind should be like. "Well, we sure won't need you on this one. Earl's going to solve Jimmy Porter's death—if he hasn't already done it."

"And what about Sally's accident?"

"Yes, that, too," he assured her. "Earl will get all that figured out. And I'll see you around, Louise."

She watched him saunter out of the room, then turned to see the sheriff standing at the door to the inner offices, staring at her. "Ready, Miz Eldridge?"

He motioned her into a visitor's chair and sat at his desk. In the institutional setting of the Boulder County Justice Center, this oversized mahogany desk stood out as something special. It was free of clutter, containing only a silver-framed picture, an eight-inch-high geode with an intense blue concavity, and a single tan file folder. She looked over its brown expanse at the sheriff. Without sunglasses and with protruding stomach concealed behind desk front, he was an exceptionally handsome man. And sincere: he *looked* like a sheriff, albeit some taxpayers may have thought this desk too fancy for a public servant. Then again, she reflected, he probably brought it from home.

He leaned back in the elegant leather swivel chair and frowned importantly. The only flaw in this picture was his nervous fiddling with his fountain pen. He proceeded to sketch out Sally Porter's accident for Louise. Sally's car had fallen fifty feet or so down a cliff off the back road to Porter Ranch, with both Sally and her car totaled by the impact. Louise tried to stifle a shudder.

"According to our detective team, it looks like she drove right off into space," concluded Tatum. "Car crashed onto the edge of the road below, in a little field of wildflowers. Now, I wanted to talk to you because I hear you had dinner with the deceased last night. Wondered just how she acted, and what you talked about."

Louise shook her head. "There's nothing much to tell, Sheriff. I was meeting the woman for the first time. She didn't talk much, and when she did, she was full of reminiscences of her childhood on the ranch, about how she used to ride a horse down to school in Lyons—things like that."

He said, "I'm waitin' for the team to turn in its report, but I personally am startin' to believe this is suicide."

Louise sat very still in her chair. Finally, she said, "That's entirely your call, Sheriff. All I have to say is, Sally Porter did not sound suicidal. On the contrary, she had a meeting scheduled this morning with her brothers and their family attorney. But draw your own conclusions."

Tatum leaned forward and looked at her as if she had given the wrong answer. "Fine, I will draw my own conclusions. I could conclude, from what you just said, that the lady was sad and nostalgic over her daddy's death." He took a deep breath, as if ready to step into something unpleasant. "Now, Mrs. Eldridge, I know you might feel the need to investigate. I've heard about your *limited* reputation for crime solving. You may have the desire to make this more complicated than it is, like you and Pete did the other day when Jimmy Porter's body was found. I urge you not to do that. I urge you to withhold judgment until this investigation is over. Believe me, I have a whole slew 'a people investigatin' both deaths." He nonchalantly waggled a hand back and forth. "They're checkin' for tire marks on that back road, that sort of thing."

In the back of her mind a question was forming. All those people investigating—why was the sheriff getting so involved in an "accident" case? She said, "I'm glad to hear that, and of course I'll stay out of it—it's none of my business. When will the investigation be over?"

"Could take months, maybe years." He shuffled the papers in the tan folder. Then, as if he had forgotten she were there, he said sourly, "Deaths on Porter Ranch never get resolved."

"Oh? Are you referring to those deaths years ago. . . ?"

Tatum looked at her sharply. "No, ma'am. Actually, I didn't mean Sally's *accident;* I was talkin' about Jimmy's *shootin'.* As for those earlier deaths, they've long been closed matters—not very suspicious, if that's what you're aimin' at. Bonnie Porter, for instance, died in a genuine barn fire. And you wouldn't know just how dangerous fire still is, up there where there isn't hardly a fire truck or organized water supply for miles."

She smiled apologetically at him, as if reluctant to bother him. "There's just a couple of little things, Sheriff, about Sally. Why did she go by the back road? Who else uses that road, besides her brothers and Miss Bingham? And—"

The sheriff put up a hand and half rose out of his chair, as if the interview were over. "Whoa. I'll answer that, just t'getcha off my back. The boys say Sally always used that road t'go back and forth t' town; so did the boys when they lived there. Harriet—Miss Bingham—she goes by the main road because it isn't so steep." He rested his weight on his hands and looked at Louise, as if expecting her to get up, too. "Is that it for questions?"

She looked serenely at the law officer, unmoving.

"Oh, all *right,*" he said impatiently, sitting again. "Since you're so inquisitive, I'll tell ya something in confidence about the Jimmy Porter case. There's just plain *no* evidence in that crime 'cept a couple of spent shells."

"No tire tracks that day, no cars heard or seen leaving the ranch?"

Louise could see he was having trouble curbing his temper. "I told ya, nope to all of that. Nobody heard a car, because who'd hear it? You only have Harriet and a few ranch hands. The hands start early and leave early, so they were done for the day, and Harriet's a little deaf. Jimmy got shot a good hour before you got there. As for tracks, ground's too dry for tire tracks, and poachers like to use little trail vehicles. Fact, there's a real steep mining trail that comes in between the two ranches up there. We figure maybe they coulda walked up that way, even though it doesn't appear t'be big enough for a vehicle."

"Wasn't it odd that the assailant was so close to him? And what about the trajectory of the bullets?"

"The *bullets,* you say?" In exasperation, he flipped his pen into the air and it clattered noisily onto the desk surface, where he subdued it with one hand. Tatum seemed aghast at her ignorance. "There aren't any bullets in a shotgun. There's *shells* in a shotgun." He gave her a jaundiced look. "Well, guess 'twon't hurt to tell you this, since you already saw it. He took a full charge of shot from about ten foot away. It came in at an odd angle—"

She sat forward. "Is that so . . ."

"Even you might be impressed, Miz Eldridge," he interrupted, "by the fact we went back up there and used our laser pointer to get the exact angle so the coroner could make an accurate determination. We figure Jimmy was crouchin' to spring, and therefore, had his head at a much lower angle than the killer."

With this, the sheriff got up and swiped his hands together, as if wiping Louise out of his further considerations. "You see how forthcoming I've been with you? Now, will you let your curiosity go, you and your friend Pete, and let me get on with my work?" He smiled a broad, toothsome smile, and with one hand smoothed back his iron gray hair. She realized Earl Tatum had gotten a lot of political mileage out of those rugged good looks.

She was dismissed. Before she left the office, however, she leaned over to examine the photograph of the youthful woman in the wide silver frame. "Pretty desk. Pretty young woman. Is she . . ." Louise stopped before she said the wrong thing; it might *not* be his daughter.

"That's my wife," he said tersely.

Before she got herself in more trouble, Louise left the office and found Ann Evans sitting in the anteroom, wearing a dark linen pantsuit as if in mourning. She was hunkered forward in the chair, blond hair falling over her red-rimmed eyes. She probably felt guilty for getting so angry last night at Sally's apparent betrayal of her father's wishes. Now that she thought of it, Louise felt a slight twinge of guilt herself about Sally. She hadn't told Ann, but in the back of her mind, she'd thought the emotionless Sally might have been her father's killer. As Louise passed her friend, she put a hand on her shoulder and murmured, "I'll meet you here later."

If Only the Stones Could Talk: Gardening with Rocks

ROCKS ARE BIG IN GARDEN landscapes these days, both in size and importance. Horticultural design has become more daring, to the point where "bold" has become one of the designers' favorite adjectives. These days, huge rocks and boulders are becoming part of the design plan of private homeowners. With a house under construction, it's considered a bonanza to find big rocks in the foundation; once, such large, "found" rocks would have been reburied or hauled

away. Now, they're like a gift from the earth—hosed off, then carefully placed where they fit best. Importing rocks from a stone yard is an expensive business, but in the eyes of many people, well worth the money. They are a permanent, no-care, important structural element of a yard-and-garden plan.

Some stand alone, some don't. Sometimes these massive rocks are set in an array and combined with water accents, such as pools, streams, and waterfalls. Other times, they are used by themselves, or form a simple rock garden. One homeowner bought a cluster of gigantic rocks for his grandchildren to play upon—the idea being to jump from one huge rock to another.

City parks today feature climbing rocks for kids, while other parks treat rocks much more soberly, as objects d'art, much as stone and rock have been treated through the ages, from the gardens of Kyoto to the Alhambra. Today's design artists will group rocks, or scatter rocks on a site, making them into earthworks. Stonehenge, by the way, is also considered an earthwork, though the people who put it together may have had a spiritual, or possibly scientific, motive, and not an artistic one.

Even the British are getting bold. Not only in America is big rock popular: Even the correct and seemly Wisley Garden, in Surrey, England, has "bold new patterns" that include huge blocks of stone in its rock garden. Artful arrays of plants soften their look, as they perch in the crevices and spill down the rock faces.

The use of stone and rock goes far back in the history of man and of gardening. It was used not only for decoration, but also to impart deep spiritual ideas and beliefs. Chinese gardens often have rockeries, which sometimes are whole structures with passageways of mortared rocks, and represent mountains, with nearby water features representing the sea. The Japanese use rocks more sparsely in their gardens, but bring just as much meaning to them; each stone is seen as an individual, whose full character is revealed when its best "face" is put forward. The popular Japanese style has been replicated in many U.S. botanical gardens, and in American backyards. Many an American homeowner is out there raking the gravel areas between rocks.

If you can move it, you can't see it. A landscaper's rule of thumb for using rocks is this: If the rock can

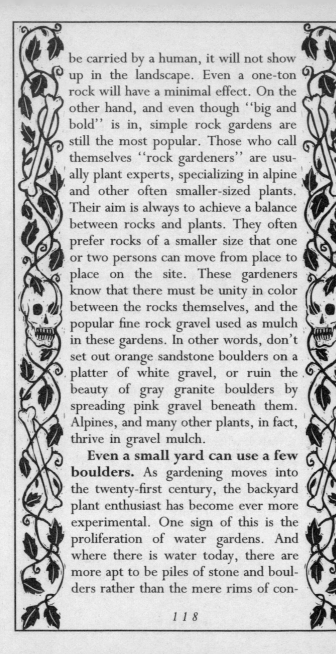

be carried by a human, it will not show up in the landscape. Even a one-ton rock will have a minimal effect. On the other hand, and even though "big and bold" is in, simple rock gardens are still the most popular. Those who call themselves "rock gardeners" are usually plant experts, specializing in alpine and other often smaller-sized plants. Their aim is always to achieve a balance between rocks and plants. They often prefer rocks of a smaller size that one or two persons can move from place to place on the site. These gardeners know that there must be unity in color between the rocks themselves, and the popular fine rock gravel used as mulch in these gardens. In other words, don't set out orange sandstone boulders on a platter of white gravel, or ruin the beauty of gray granite boulders by spreading pink gravel beneath them. Alpines, and many other plants, in fact, thrive in gravel mulch.

Even a small yard can use a few boulders. As gardening moves into the twenty-first century, the backyard plant enthusiast has become ever more experimental. One sign of this is the proliferation of water gardens. And where there is water today, there are more apt to be piles of stone and boulders rather than the mere rims of concrete or tile used in the past. Even a very small, narrow yard can hold a plentiful cluster of medium-sized boulders to surround a pool or waterfall.

As for the suppliers, they are happy at this new trend to punctuate yards and gardens with rocks and boulders. It's a far cry, indeed, from the days when people's ideal was enormous, tidy, but sometimes boring emerald green lawns, and flowers and evergreens all in neat rows.

OR CARVE YOUR OWN ROCKS . . .

During the Renaissance, Duke Vicino Orsini, a wealthy Italian member of the literati and a professional soldier, sculpted one of the most unusual rock gardens of them all. This is the startling Bomarzo garden, outside of Rome, a thirty-year effort of Orsini, who was born in the early 1500's. His huge rock sculptures are now thick with mosses* and the patina of age, the envy of any rock-loving gardener.

The rocky site was a former Etrus-

---

* If mosses grow where you live, then collect a moss-covered stone from a site similar to yours, and position it near your new, mossless stones. Sprinkle the new stones with a mixture of sugar and water, and keep them moist. They, too, will soon grow moss.

can village with neighboring necropolis. Orsini made it into what he called his *sacro bosco,* or "sacred wood." Some thought it blasphemous, with its stone carvings of Cerberus, Persephone, and Demeter, its entrance to Hades, and its sculpted ruins of an Etruscan tomb, all implying this was the underworld. In the garden are enormous stone depictions of hands and feet, bare-breasted harpies, and a general atmosphere of violence and paganism.

The garden was abandoned for years, until a visit by artist Salvador Dali renewed interest in the place in the 1950's. Now it is a popular visiting spot for those who want the ultimate rock garden experience.

Chapter 9

LOUISE WAS RESTLESS, WANDER-ing the halls of the Justice Center to pass the time until Ann emerged from her interview with the sheriff. She passed clumps of worried-looking people caught in the system, but was too distracted with her own thoughts to be very curious. She made her way down-stairs, passing the district attorney's of-fice and then the coroner's office, wondering idly if there was a morgue on the premises. Then she came to a deserted courtroom from which ema-nated familiar voices. Eddie and Frank

Porter, disagreeing as usual. Eddie, even scruffier than usual in his faded clothes and scuffed boots, was dancing around in a boxing stance in front of Frank, as if he might pop his brother on the nose.

The older brother had goaded Frank into losing his temper. As Louise slipped into the room, Frank barked, "I'm not going to do it, and that's that!"

She pulled the door shut behind her. No need for the world to hear this argument. "Hi, Frank. Eddie." She came a little closer, but not too close, in case Eddie let fly a fist. "I want you to know how sorry I am about Sally."

"If you feel so damned bad over our sister," barked Eddie, "then I hope you told the sheriff where I was last night, so I can get clear of his goddamn suspicions." He stopped his jittering about and stood there and glared at her.

Frank looked pleadingly at Louise. "We're here to talk to Tatum again. Did you already see him?"

She nodded.

"I can't remember the exact time we left that open space meeting," said Frank, "and Eddie's pushing me to make up a time. Do you happen to remember? Maybe your recollections will get us off the hook."

"Us!" cried Eddie, and threw his hands out in a gesture of desperation. "Shit! Frank Porter, quarry owner—even if it is just a li'l bitty quarry—and IBM sucky-uppy engineer on his way up. Who's going to think *you* did it? But Eddie Porter, who pleaded nolo contendere to assault and battery, and was also convicted twice for drunk driving? Hell, I'm a prime candidate to have done away with my father and my sister." He looked sweaty and tired, but Louise's heart did not go out to him.

"Why would the sheriff think you killed her?" asked Louise. "He told me he thinks Sally might have lost control of her car—or else decided to kill herself."

"First off," said Eddie, "because I used ta drive stock cars, and there's some paint on the left rear side of Sally's car. They'll think I'm the only one with balls enough to force her off the road. It's sick, damn it!"

"She went off the right-hand cliff?" Louise's mind was constructing the scene. Why hadn't the sheriff mentioned the paint streak?

"Yeah." He frowned, not liking the direction this was taking. "But the paint didn't look fresh ta me—it looked like something Sally mighta done when pullin' out of a parkin' spot months ago. Frankly, I think sis was just carried away with grief last night and went clean over the cliff."

"What color was the paint?" asked Louise.

"White. Not red, like the color of the pickup I'm drivin'. It was white, like about a million cars in the United States."

"Then why would the sheriff think—"

"Because, lady," Eddie said, glaring at Louise, "I'm always a suspect whenever anything goes wrong—the black-sheep brother. And I have *motive*." He pronounced the word with a sneer. "I'm the one who wants to get top dollar for the ranch, and not just give it away to Boulder County. Damned county already has more open space than it can even take care of."

"From what I saw last night, Eddie, Sally was pretty sympathetic to you."

"You're right. But everybody knows Sally was wishy-washy, so they mighta thought I just wanted to get her out of the picture."

She wasn't eager to get in a fight with this redneck, but she had to be honest. "Eddie, as much as we might like to, neither Ann nor I could give you an alibi. I remember distinctly looking around at seven and seeing that you had gone."

"Thanks, Louise—or whatever your name is. I won't forgit this." He stomped away in his old boots.

Frank came over to Louise. "I apologize for Eddie. He's a lot more upset about Dad and Sally than he lets on."

"Sure," she said. "You'd better catch up." Eddie had rushed from the room, apparently to go talk to the sheriff again. The fellow had a lot of bluster and a lot of denials. Was it to cover up murder?

❧

When Ann emerged from her interview with the sheriff, she expressed little surprise to hear that the Porter brothers were still quarreling. But she was distracted by other things. "This inquiry is a sham, Louise, guaranteed to throw people into confusion and get absolutely nowhere. Tatum tells you and me it's an accident, when even *he* knows it's not true. Then, just to add a little eyewash to the investigation, he prods at Eddie Porter." They walked to their cars under still-threatening skies. They were on their way to the mall to talk some more over lunch. "I'll never believe this was an accident—especially not after Jimmy got cut down that way. Something weird is going on."

She turned her pained eyes toward Louise. "You had to know Sally Porter. She was kind of a slow, plodding person who would never speed on that road. And it's a road she certainly ought to have known—why, she must have driven it hundreds of times."

"Did you tell the sheriff that?"

"Yes, though, of course, he already knew it."

"I got to know the sheriff a little better this morning."

"Good," said Ann.

"I talked to Mark Payne, too."

"Oh, *him*." She blushed. He wasn't Ann's favorite

topic; in fact, Louise figured that if the man fell through the earth and disappeared, she'd be more than happy.

But Ann was willing to talk about Tatum. "When Boulder County elected Tatum sheriff, reasonable people were appalled—hip Boulder County going 'retro.' He'll never get reelected."

"It must have been a beauty contest. He's the Marlboro man, with paunch."

Ann smiled at this feeble joke. "He looks the part, doesn't he? And he makes a great speech. More importantly, he's got an organization, including scores of relatives. Tatum was sheriff years ago—something like forty years ago—when he was a young man," she said. "Then he was in real estate for a long time."

"He seems to like developers. Mark Payne is his shadow."

"That's right. They probably have something they're working on together right now."

The two women exchanged a long look. "You couldn't think . . ." Ann started.

Louise shrugged. "When you're looking for suspects, Ann, you have to consider everybody."

They were approaching the first row of cars when she noticed the license plate. "Look." The black Lexus stood in the closest parking spot, the one reserved for the top guy. The vanity plate read 'Sherf-1.' "A sheriff with a forty-thousand-dollar car. And a new wife, too. Sometimes they're expensive."

"Who knows?" Ann agreed, smiling. "A little quiet scandal surrounds him, and a grand jury may get him before his term's up. Good ol' boys aren't as powerful around here as they used to be. People like a more honest, businesslike approach these days."

Louise grinned. "Good ol' boys passé in Boulder

County? Last night in the county courthouse, the good ol' boy network was humming like a high-tension wire.''

"That's natural, Louise. But the boards, the city commission, the people who ultimately make the decisions, are on the up-and-up. They're very professional. They no longer make land decisions, for instance, based on whether it's a buddy of theirs or not.''

"If you say so.'' Louise spotted her shiny red rental up ahead. "What do you say we go to lunch where we can observe some of these characters again—you know, Reingold, and people like that.''

"That means the Rattlesnake Grill,'' said Ann. "It's Boulder's hot new lunch spot. I'll call ahead and get us a res.'' She pulled out her cell phone.

"Rattlesnake?'' muttered Louise, mostly to herself, since Ann was busy cajoling the maître d' into holding a table. She thought dismally of the rubbery feel of the dead snake she had stepped on last night in the road.

"All set, and don't worry,'' said Ann, laughing for the first time since Louise had met her today. "Rattlesnake's not on the menu.''

They didn't have to wait long for their table for two in the upscale restaurant, which featured high-tech, shiny surfaces in silver and black, softened with linen tablecloths and napkins. After studying the food choices, Louise looked up with satisfaction to see Josef Reingold with his coterie, and Mark Payne with another group. "Developers just seem to hover around the county building like vultures.''

"Remember, you wanted to come here—so we could do our sleuthing. I agree with you that after Jimmy Porter's murder, I can't trust these people. But they are a kind of necessary evil, and they provide lots of jobs. I don't want to apologize for them, but they just do what developers do—take advantage of every opportunity, every city and county ordinance and state law, pick up any decent vacant land they can find, then get it annexed to an existing city. Or else build a new town out of it—whatever it takes to promote their business.''

Louise smiled. ''They sound like sweethearts.''

''I see you're putting me on. Okay, they're not sweethearts. They compete with us for the remaining land in the county, which we want kept vacant, and they want to fill with homes.''

Watching Ann carefully, Louise said, ''As I mentioned, I ran into Mark Payne, too.''

Ann tried to sound casual. ''Yes, and I bet he didn't tell you one thing about himself.''

''You're right. He didn't.''

''Well, he's not made it strictly on his own merit. He took over his father's contracting business, and they bought land at the right time—the father in the fifties, the son in the eighties, when Colorado property was seriously devalued. Lots of people with money around here made it that way. But Mark's not very successful in his personal life.'' She made a little moue with her mouth.

Louise held her tongue, hoping Ann would go on. She did. The words came out with difficulty. Ann talked so quietly that Louise had to lean over to hear. ''His wife Carrie left him. It was a terrible divorce. One night, he and Carrie went out for dinner—probably to talk over some kind of business. They were at the Flagstaff House and Mark drank a lot.'' She looked down at her plate self-consciously. ''He *always* has to drink a lot when he confronts a sticky situation with a woman. Anyway, they drove farther up the mountain, and crashed against the side of a cliff. Carrie was killed, and he got all banged up.''

''That's why his face has a masklike quality.''

''He had six operations to restore his face. He's lucky he's alive, I guess. Mark took it so hard that even I felt sorry for him." Ann bowed her head, as if this was a sign of personal weakness. "Don't ask me why, but I started dating him rather seriously."

"He doesn't seem like your type."

She flashed a quick look at Louise. "I was pretty lonely about then, and I thought he was nice. But he wasn't. Thank God I've found a wonderful man—even if we do have our problems."

"Your Luke."

"My Luke." Apparently that was all Louise was going to hear about Luke. Ann continued, "I try to keep my gripes with Mark on a strictly professional basis and put that old stuff out of my mind. Mark tends to cut corners. His houses are attractive, but wherever he puts a development there's trouble. He's underfunded something, he hasn't come through with the services he's promised a given community, he's skirted building codes . . ."

"What about Mr. Reingold?"

"DRB has a great many projects around Longmont, which is nowhere near as built up as Boulder. He's like the others—always working to get his way."

Louise's right eyebrow shot up. "Developers will be developers."

Ann opened her hands. "Look, he's always played square with me when he had anything to do with our office. I know he's in with lots of people who count in Boulder." She smiled ruefully. "I knew you'd call it wheeling and dealing."

As they finished their meal, Mark Payne came and stood near the table, as usual not daring to look at Ann. "I heard you were at the sheriff's this morning, Ann, and I thought I'd tell you why I was there. I'm offering a reward for clues that lead to the killer." He shook his blond head. "I'll be darned if we can let this happen in Boulder County. And Harriet, you know, is all alone up there."

Ann gave him a guarded look and said, "If you want to do it, do it. There's no one who would like to see the person caught more than I would."

They watched in silence as the man made his way out of the restaurant. Then, as Louise decided to yield to the temptation of crème brûlée, and Ann to tiramisu, Josef Reingold walked over.

"Do you mind?" he asked, as he dragged a nearby chair up to their small table. Sophisticated glasses with understated wire frames, expressive hazel eyes, a thin nose, the faint odor of cologne—Louise found it made a rather pleasant impression. He bowed his head toward her. "I deeply regret that I didn't have the chance to talk to you at the open space meeting." Then he, too, went into a lament over the Porter family's double tragedy. "You two were questioned by the sheriff, I hear." His eyes were guileless.

The women exchanged glances. Reingold wanted to find out what they knew. Louise answered. "The sheriff, of course, might want us to keep everything confidential." She leaned forward toward Reingold. "But just between us, Ann and I learned absolutely nothing from Sally, even though we had dinner with her last night." She settled back and took a spoonful of the crème brûlée.

The developer seemed to relax then, and turned the subject to other things, asking her all about her work, where she was renting a house, what her husband did. Reluctantly, Louise told him that Bill worked for the State Department, for somehow she was sure the man would know if she lied.

But she felt flutters in her chest. Was Reingold pumping her? After a minute, she decided that he was merely lusting after her dessert, for, as he talked, he overtly eyed her crème brûlée, with its freshly blowtorched crackling-brown-sugar glaze.

Without thinking, she picked up an auxiliary spoon. "Would you like a bite?"

"Wonderful." His brown eyes lit up. He waited to be served, and she handed him the filled spoon. But he opened his mouth, like a child, and she fed him. It turned out to be a great deal more intimate than she had intended. In fact, she had intended no intimacy at all.

Putting down the empty spoon, she said briskly, "Well, now, Mr. Reingold, tell me about yourself and DRB."

"Yes, I do . . . ." He smiled at his temporary lapse in English usage, then started over again, absolutely unruffled. "I mean to say, yes, I *will* do it. Exactly what do you want to know?"

"When did you come to Boulder?"

"It was five years ago. DRB has had many land holdings in the American West for some time, but by the midnineties, it was necessary for me to be physically present some of the time to manage our projects. It is handy, of course, to travel from DIA to almost anywhere in the world."

"So, your U.S. headquarters are in Denver?"

"Actually, no. Our North American headquarters are south of Juarez. Do you know of northern Mexico? It is another country, a thriving area that almost seems like a part of the United States. We have a number of things going there. Construction supply and prefab plants, as well as the company headquarters."

"How interesting. Are prefab houses the wave of the future?"

He smiled. "Certainly not in Boulder County. We do a great deal of development in this area, notably in Longmont, but people here prefer custom-built homes. Yet there is a fantastic market for the lower-cost, prefabricated housing in the United States. One thing DRB wants to do is provide that kind of housing to Americans."

"How very—"

"Thoughtful? Philanthropic?" He smiled smoothly. "Mrs. Eldridge, I didn't mean to give you a false impression. We are not philanthropists. If it were not profitable, we would not be involved."

The next remark seemed to spill out. "And you deal in other exports and imports?"

He reached over and put his hand on hers for an instant. "I know it would be tedious for you to hear the particulars." Not at all, she thought. She would have liked to get a better sense of the breadth of his business. But as she looked at him, the warm, fuzzy aura faded, and his hazel eyes behind the metal rims examined her a little more critically.

Certainly, that last question was totally innocent. But Reingold hadn't sat down at their table to answer questions, only to ask them.

Chapter 10

AFTER LUNCH, ANN TOOK LOUise to her office, in a turn-of-the-century building of sandstone with granite trim. It was used for the overflow of county offices from the Art Deco county building across the street. They went into the back room so Louise could see a map of both Boulder County's open space, and the Porter and Bingham properties. "The Porter land is the main attraction," said Ann, "though Harriet's stake is a fabulous second prize for someone. If the Porter Ranch becomes open space, think of the field day a builder would have, advertising houses as nestling right next to a thirteen-thousand-acre wilderness."

Louise examined the map. "Look at those cut-out corners on the east side of Harriet's property; it's as if someone cut samples from a piece of fabric."

"Her father sold off some acreage years ago, and she's apparently continued to sell off more land intermittently through the years, as she needs the money."

"To whom?"

"It's hard to know. To development companies, initially, whose owners aren't disclosed. The land isn't far from where you're renting. They're the subdivisions you see running west from Route Thirty-six as you drive to Lyons. Upscale houses, some of them costing millions."

Then she turned her tawny eyes to Louise. "Tell me honestly, do you think Jimmy and Sally Porter died for this?"

Louise wasn't sure what Ann wanted to hear: reassurances, or the truth. In the end, Louise didn't answer and she didn't stay long, because it was obvious from the neat, high piles of papers on her desk that Ann had work to do. Louise promised Ann that she would keep in close touch. She wandered aimlessly back down the Pearl Street Mall, under a lacy canopy of locust trees, past lush beds of tuberous orange and yellow begonias, and magenta impatiens. A little bright for Louise's tastes, but perfect for a public thoroughfare. A thick crowd of tourists, buoyed by the improving weather, mixed happily with the upscale business folks, scattered hippies, and street entertainers.

Her thoughts strayed back to the people in Boulder who might have been involved in Jimmy Porter's murder; she suspended for a moment her suspicion that Sally's death was no accident. There were the men who loved land: Josef Reingold, Mark Payne, Sheriff Tatum. Even her own cameraman, Pete Fitzsimmons, and, for that matter, Tom Spangler. He had his own land stake out near Stony Flats, and a good move it had been, for the area was now under intense development. From nuclear to neighborhoods, she thought with a wry smile.

She wondered why all the suspicion had fallen on *her* today? Her questions to Reingold had been quite innocent, but still the man was on guard. Maybe it was just his European way—some prohibition against women peering into the business of the men. And she hadn't enjoyed her encounter with Mark Payne. He was a person she found hard to like. He, too, seemed suspicious of Louise. As for Sheriff Tatum, the two of them had clashed from the first moment they met, back when Jimmy Porter's body was discovered. Eddie Porter, too, considered her an anathema.

I'm winning lots of friends out here in the West, she thought cynically.

It seemed only reasonable to do some checking at the library. A little guiltily, she realized she should look up Pete Fitzsimmons, too, since he was very much in the mix. She obtained directions from a passerby and started there on foot.

Bill might not like this snooping about, but a little research couldn't hurt anyone, and he *had* said she should keep her eyes open. . . .

It was a scenic walk to the library, with the Flatirons, the almost vertical sandstone mountains that were Boulder's signature, looming heavily over the downtown area. But with the reemergent sun behind them, they lived up to their name: flat, one-dimensional, as if someone had fashioned them of cardboard. Mounding up behind them were big white clouds which would spill the brief daily rain shower on the city at the prescribed hour of four, give or take a few minutes. Louise had learned this by getting wet one day. Now she checked her watch and saw that she had an hour or so before the downpour.

The library yielded some answers. She found a Wall Street Journal article which detailed how Reingold's company had systematically bought out attractive real estate, mostly during the eighties, when the pie-in-the-sky oil shale boom burst in Colorado, and land prices in the West were depressed.

DRB had also made some less attractive moves regarding the transport of American goods over the border. These brought it under the scrutiny of the U.S. Customs Office. Not too unusual, she thought. Big company gets itself into a murky business situation, from which expensive lawyers must extricate it. Fines are paid, and some big shot at the top gets the ax. Louise was interested to read that the debonair Josef Reingold came out of all this on top, as chief of American operations.

She found a few paragraphs about Reingold's international jet-set life and multiple marriages. The accompanying pen sketch showed Reingold smiling enticingly at the world. Hmmm. She didn't feel so bad about the crème brûlée experience any more; she wasn't the first woman to be suckered into something by this provocative fellow.

Next, she checked out Payne. A recent Boulder *Daily Camera* story contained a ten-year retrospective of his career. It talked about him as a former ski bum who eventually settled down and took over the family business when his father died, and made it more successful than his daddy ever had. Louise noticed that land, again, was the answer. The article on Payne was sympathetic, mentioning his parents' tragic death in a plane crash, then carefully alluding to the later accident in which his former wife perished. Ann was right. The rich hometown boy's life had not all been joy and gladness. To Louise, he seemed to be a person who was missing a crucial character trait, for he failed to generate any personal warmth. As Bill would say, a cold fish. Why had a wholesome person like Ann ever become involved with him?

It wasn't hard to find a fresh story on the sheriff, but it only repeated what she'd heard about Tatum's long real estate and business background. The newspaper and the city of Boulder had seemed surprised at his victory in a close sheriff's race; the colorful Boulder good-ol'-boy won by a whisker, despite the scent of scandal that surrounded him.

She encountered only one story about Pete, accompanied by a picture of a youthful man grinning so broadly one could not see his eyes. She smiled. *That's Pete, all right.* It described how this popular former CU lecturer had returned from seven years in California, and instead of resuming teaching English, had chosen to go into "business pursuits." Like so many men around here, the temptation of business—*and for that,* she thought, *read "land,"* was too great to resist.

Seeing that article on the computer screen did something else. It validated Pete as a professional, making it painfully clear that her first impression of him had been way off the mark. Pete Fitzsimmons was both political and savvy, and very much a player here in Boulder County. She thought it only logical that he had had a part in the Porter Ranch land negotiations that preceded Ann Evans's "victory"—not on his own, but possibly as a partner with someone like Payne or Reingold. She would have to pursue this further. Buoyed by her discoveries, Louise decided it was time to go home, after making a little detour to check out Eddie Porter's place.

❧

The Persians, four hundred years before Christ, called beautiful enclosed and irrigated garden refuges *pairidaeza,* or paradise parks. And Eddie Porter lived in one. Irrigated by the South St. Vrain river, which wandered through his land. Backed by cliffs of red Lyons sandstone, shaggy and beautiful, interbedded with limestone and Pierre shale in grays and black. Graced with small forests of mature ponderosas and drifts of fluttery-leaved aspens.

Willows and wildflowers grew rampant on the land near the river, with Eddie's wood-and-sandstone cabin set just a little higher, in case of flood.

It was one of the prettiest pieces of land Louise had seen out here.

The only trouble with this paradise, at least from the aesthetic point of view, was the trash. The property was festooned, as far as the eye could see, with homely out-buildings, decrepit freestanding farm equipment, aging cars, canoes, and fencing—both metal and wood. But that was only the start of it. There were also sloppy piles of bricks, flagstones, cut wood, and gravel, as if Eddie might have wanted to open his own building supply store out here. The net effect was dismal, in Louise's opinion. It dragged "paradise" down to "trash dump."

She had dropped in at the Gold Strike Café, ordered up a piece of pie, and easily extracted from Ruthie Dunn the information about where Eddie lived. When she arrived, Louise parked her car on the road and hiked in. Under no circumstances did she want to meet the man. Once on the property, she had no problem—even though she felt a little silly—hiding behind outbuildings and pieces of junk. She didn't know if she had enough nerve to enter the utility building and the shed she saw, but both had their doors hanging open, so she didn't have to worry about the "breaking" part of breaking and entering.

In search of something of more interest, she made her way to a corner of the property that lay below the looming sandstone cliff. So far, so good: no sign of Eddie. Sitting

behind a pile of old barn wood—which Louise suspected
was now very valuable—was a large, beat-up trailer.
Crouching, she worked her way behind the barn wood to
get a closer look. Behind the trailer, shoved against the
cliff, was an old white pickup.

Louise's heart speeded up as she went over and examined the front fenders. First, she had a feeling of great
elation, but it quickly passed. There were paint marks, all
right, on both the left and right front fenders. It was as if
Eddie had used this car as a battering ram, for there were
streaks in several colors, including blue, the color of Sally
Porter's vehicle.

She shoved her cowboy hat back on her head and stood,
arms akimbo. Eddie was a liar, that much was true, for not
owning up to his possession of a white car. Now, it would
be up to Louise to squeal to somebody in law enforcement
that Eddie Porter, as usual, was not telling the truth.

Had Eddie run his sister off the road to give himself
better odds? Now, it was two against one. He and Grace
Prangley against Frank.

That was when another stray thought nagged at her:
There was someone else who drove a white car—one with
"Boulder County Sheriff" emblazoned on the side.

❧

When Louise went home, she was tired. It was too late
to nap and too early to eat. Cocktail time. But not only
was she alone, she didn't do cocktails well. She thought
glumly of the two-day-old chicken parts in the fridge. She
needed either to cook them, or to throw them away. At
the moment, the thought of raw chicken made her gag.

The events of the day had left her with a sense of discomfort; it was as if she were slogging through a marsh of
dark water, trying vainly to reach the shore—trying to
sort out the developers, the lawman, the bickering and

suspicious family members. If only she could talk the whole thing over with Bill. She took out the emergency number he had given her, thought it over for a moment, and decided not to call.

To heal both her spirits and her complexion, she smoothed some Bag Balm on her face, finally having found some for sale in a Boulder supermarket. The balm made her face tingle, as if something good were happening. Maybe there would be an improvement in the "prune" factor of her skin.

She would set aside her black thoughts and put off drawing conclusions—just as the sheriff had advised. She fetched herself a bottle of spring water out of the refrigerator, grabbed her book about Emily, and went out on the porch to read.

The story of this frontier woman's troubles helped her forget the nagging shadows created by the Porter murders. Because she was convinced of it: Sally Porter had been killed, just like her father.

Dark Water...
and How to Make It
Pure Again

GROWING NUMBERS OF CITIES, businesses, and individuals are constructing plant-filled wetlands to treat industrial or household waste water. Towns and cities in various parts of the country use marshlands as an alternative to traditional treatment plants. They find it costs less to set up than a conventional system, saves them money on chemicals, and creates a beautiful nature preserve for waterfowl and other wildlife.

The technology has been tailored to

140

the needs of homes, businesses, small communities, schools, rest areas, towns and cities, and even Coors Field in Denver. The largest wetlands system is in Orlando, Florida, and treats twenty million gallons of waste water per day. It is used as an open-space park. It is a perfect solution for a homeowner who is building on clay, where an efficient leach field would be difficult.

An idea straight from the marsh. This concept of water treatment comes straight from the marsh, which, like prairies and forests, is a self-organizing, self-maintaining system. Plants and microbes that grow in watery environments remove the contaminants from water by breaking them down into non-toxic forms.

The wetland on a property takes the place of the leach field, which in a conventional system soaks up the outflow from the septic tank. In the leach field, the effluent gradually settles into the soil, like water percolating through coffee grounds. In the wetland, it will take a week to move through a shallow lined bed of plant-filled gravel.

A town develops wetlands. When the little Colorado mountain town of Ouray decided to go to wetland treatment, it first installed a two-

acre wetland plot. Plants such as bull-rushes, reeds, and cattails were allowed to grow for a year before waste water was turned into it. It took another full year to prove the system was working efficiently. Now, the town has excellent water quality, and doesn't even need to chlorinate the final product before it is turned into the Uncompahgre River. This system cost one third less than a traditional one, and saves the town $100,000 a year in operating costs.

Cleansed water from these systems—so-called "gray water"*—can be reused to irrigate gardens, stored in ponds for fire protection purposes, or even piped back into homes or businesses for use. The role of plants in cleansing water is a subject of lively research. Cattails are known to absorb mercury, arsenic, and lead. Roses will remove polychlorinated biphenyls, or PCB's. Cottonwoods are being used to help leach out plutonium at a weapons plant. Wild tomatoes are used to re-

---

* Recirculated "gray" water was a concept promoted by the the Sierra Club years ago, when there was little technical knowledge surrounding the idea. More than one devoted householder would simply run a pipe from the upstairs bathtub, out the window, down the side of the house, across the yard, and into the garden, so that this precious commodity was reused.

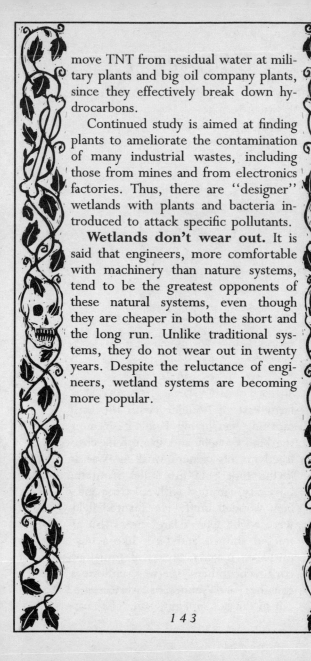

move TNT from residual water at military plants and big oil company plants, since they effectively break down hydrocarbons.

Continued study is aimed at finding plants to ameliorate the contamination of many industrial wastes, including those from mines and from electronics factories. Thus, there are "designer" wetlands with plants and bacteria introduced to attack specific pollutants.

Wetlands don't wear out. It is said that engineers, more comfortable with machinery than nature systems, tend to be the greatest opponents of these natural systems, even though they are cheaper in both the short and the long run. Unlike traditional systems, they do not wear out in twenty years. Despite the reluctance of engineers, wetland systems are becoming more popular.

Chapter 11

They were on an organic farm east of Boulder, with the early morning sun giving Pete Fitzsimmons the kind of light and shadow he cherished for his camera work. It was an idyllic spot only five miles from the busy city, rimmed with tall trees and a high wooded bluff. The planted fields were edged with a large pond that attracted animals and birds like a blue-mirrored magnet. Acres of tomatoes, corn, cucumbers, herbs, sunflowers, squashes and pumpkins were spread out in the hot morning sun. The crops grew without chemicals. Only chicken dung and cow manure touched them.

But it had been an early start, because it was Thursday now, and they were running out of time. Marty Corbin's extra days off had succeeded in condensing the shoots into four days, and they had a lot of work to do.

Louise had made a major mistake. She had overslept and not had time to eat breakfast. Now, she was famished, and had a fantasy of reaching down to scrabble for roots, like Scarlett O'Hara in *Gone With the Wind*. For more than an hour, she and Marty and the crew had stumbled after the farmer through the furrows, with their agrarian informant yelling, "Take care, folks, not to step on those tomatoes." They followed this tiller of the soil over ditches, up hill and down dale, and across a rickety two-by-twelve plank spanning a roaring stream.

When Pete greeted her today, he looked grim and had none of his usual quips. He told her, "I've been thinkin' real hard about Sally Porter's murder."

"Pete, they're not even sure yet—"

"Aw, c'mon, Louise, face it. She was just plain run off that cliff. If that isn't murder, I don't know what is. Sally Porter wasn't one of those flatlanders who are always falling to their deaths because they're too dumb to know that a mountain is up in the air."

"I agree with you—I was just trying to tell you what Tatum said."

"Tatum." He rolled his eyes. "I've done my best for Earl. I gave him a blowup of the picture of the person in the woods."

"And?"

The cameraman's chin jutted out defensively. " 'Inconclusive,' the dumb jerk tells me." Louise could tell it was more of an insult to his photographic abilities than to any detecting skills he might have; he had probably nurtured the hope that his photo, as in the movie *Blowup,* would disclose the killer. He told her, "Stop by my studio in town. You can see what you think. Whoever it is probably killed both those people."

She looked at him and wondered: Were she, Pete, and Ann the only ones who suspected that the deaths were a sinister, connected plot?

They had taped at two locations in the fields, and were now doubling back to the pumpkins, huge, orange-red spheres that looked as though they came out of an illustration of a Mother Goose rhyme. The farmer dropped back in step with Louise, who could feel her body sagging in the heat. He was lean, handsome, and sunburned, and she thought he could have been a movie star, or a model, had he not dedicated his life to something infinitely more worthwhile: growing healthy food for people to eat.

He looked down from his handsome heights at her sad-sack appearance. "Hungry?"

"Famished. No breakfast."

He reached down, plucked a tomato off a vine and thrust it in her hand, then strode over to a nearby row of corn, grabbed an ear, ripped the leaves down, and brought it back to her. "There. They'll keep you for awhile."

"Eat raw corn?"

"Hell, we eat it all through the corn season, Louise. Believe me, you'll like it."

She took a bite out of the pearly white rows, and it tasted delicious. Next, she chomped into the warm flesh of the tomato, and realized this was one of the best breakfasts she had ever eaten.

Following the line of the furrow, she lagged behind the group, slurping down the last of the tomato. It took some doing to keep the juice off her shirt.

Suddenly, sharp noises rang out and she realized her hat had blown off.

She was surprised to see the farmer and her crew running toward her. Transferring the tomato to the hand that held the corn, she walked over and picked up the hat. There were two neat holes in the crown that went in one side and came out the other.

The hand holding the hat began to shake, as the message about what had just happened was transmitted from brain to nervous system. There seemed to be nothing better to do than slump down between two rows of tomatoes. Their tendrilled arms seemed to reach out to protect her, their pungent scent like a comforting anesthesia. As if turning off a switch, Louise let her muscles relax and simply lay there. She began to feel a part of the earth, this good-smelling earth, so crumbly and rich to the touch. She picked up a handful of it and ran it through her fingers.

At least it prevented her from thinking about the fact that someone had just tried to shoot her head off.

※

Louise's producer and her cameraman were crouching over her. The farmer stood by looking agonized, and she realized they were trampling his crops. He would have yelled, "Mind those tomatoes!" had not a murderer just tried to finish the location shooting for the day.

Pete's face was tense. "I tell you, Louise, you've got to get some protection. This has gotta have somethin' to do with the Porter murders."

"Look, pal," said Marty, "don't scare the kid any worse than she's already scared." And he pulled Louise up from the ground, putting an arm around her to guide her back toward the trucks. "We're gettin' outta here," said the producer.

She halted and pushed a mass of tangled brown hair back from her face. "Marty, no. Whoever did it has probably gone." She strained to think of a solution. "I know—

a kid. It's probably a teenager with a gun who's bored and ready to go back to school. What do you think?''

The farmer had limited the wooded bluff to see if he could catch sight of the shooter. He came back shaking his head. ''I think the person drove right onto that bluff. He disappeared by the time I got over that fence and up the hill. I caught the tail end of a car leaving the drive.''

''What kind of car?'' asked Marty.

''An old white pickup—the kind kids might drive, actually.''

''Oh, no,'' moaned Louise, ''not a white truck!''

They put in a call to the sheriff's office. Twenty minutes later the sheriff's vehicle arrived and drove imperiously into the farmer's field, bumping over the crop rows and coming to a stop close to where Louise waited in the tomato patch. She was surprised to see Earl Tatum himself step out.

He looked grim as he walked around the area with Marty and Louise. ''Could a been kids,'' he agreed. ''Now, I told you, and I'll tell your producer here, too, Mrs. Eldridge, you have to be careful, and not get into things. This coulda been a prank, and coulda been something else. Just try to—''

Her voice was ironic. ''Mind my own business? What if I said I'd been doing that?''

He threw his hand out in an exasperated gesture. ''Well, then, that's the best you can do.'' Just then Louise looked down and saw that the front quarter panel of the sheriff's car was scratched and dented. And was that blue paint, the color of Sally Porter's car? With thumping heart, she watched him climb in the driver's seat, and reflected on how hard it would be to implicate this lawman even if he had murdered Sally. But what was she thinking? Surely her recent brush with death was behind these rampant suspicions.

When Tatum had departed, leaving a team of deputies behind to complete the investigation, Marty wanted to call off the day's shooting. His cowboy hat was shoved back, revealing a mass of worry wrinkles on his forehead. The producer's new western outfit was broken in like hers, but he had guessed wrong in size, so he looked like a potbellied cowboy who had almost grown out of his clothes. "Damn it, I'm scared for you, Louise, and that half-baked sheriff doesn't seem to want to help. What's Bill going to think of you being in danger?"

She looked around at the rich farm fields, and then up at a cloud-flecked sky that reminded her of a blue-and-white spatterware bowl. It was hard to think that a killer had just been here in this beautiful place. Nevertheless, the last thing she wanted the producer to do was hover around her; she could take care of herself. "I doubt I'm in danger. I think the person picked a target and tried to have a little fun."

That sounded plausible, didn't it?

"And Marty," she continued, "I don't want Bill to know about this. He'll be back in a few days, and I'll tell him then." She finally persuaded him to continue the day's camera work in the pumpkin patch. Then, they broke for lunch and drove to a water treatment plant in the city of Louisville, east of Boulder.

Watching the swirling brown residue floating and foaming in the sluiceway at the plant, Louise was overcome with a gut sense of how primitive life really was, with its cycle of birth and death, and the functional activities in between.

She had to struggle to focus on the words she had learned in her script. She looked into Pete's camera, telling her audience that the biosolids that remained after purifying human waste were like gold in the garden. Except for the caveat about how some could contain injurious metals. Did everything have a catch?

"It's a wrap!" called a jubilant Marty.

During the shoot, Louise had forbidden her mind to wander off to the universal questions, such as, "What is life all about, really?" And, "Who wants to kill me?" Now that the shoot was finished, she gave way to her emotions.

Turning to her producer, she said, "Being shot at really pisses me off."

"Now, Louise," warned Marty, taking her arm and lowering his dark brows in a worried manner, "I wouldn't want you to do anything . . ."

"I promise you, Marty, I won't do anything rash." Not unless, Louise thought to herself, it helps me catch this open space murderer.

❧

As a safety measure, Marty wanted Louise to stay and have dinner with him and Steffi and spend at least one night with them at the Hotel Boulderado. She assured him that her rented house was safe, especially since it had an alarm system. She finally extricated herself from her fussy producer and drove north on Route Thirty-Six, past the turnoff to her house, straight to Lyons. She would get a bite of dinner at the Gold Strike Café and then go home and get a good night's sleep.

Despite Ruthie Dunn's warm welcome when she entered the little log cabin restaurant, she immediately regretted not going straight home. There, straddling a stool at the counter, was Eddie Porter, eating his meat and potatoes. He saw her as soon as she walked in and gave her a disgusted look. To her dismay, her only choice of seats was a stool next to him, or the table behind him. She chose the table. On it sat a bud vase with a pale pink rose, which gave her some solace. She called out her dinner preference to Ruthie, and was quickly served the roast chicken special. She'd only eaten a few mouthfuls when Eddie stirred, turning on his stool to fix her with unfriendly eyes.

"Done anybody any more favors lately, Mrs. Eldridge?"

Louise felt put upon. Here she was, a lonely woman in a strange community, tangled once again in murder, and possibly the target of the murderer herself. A murderer who could, in fact, be this turkey.

She said, "I've had a hard day, Eddie."

"Hard day out on location at that farm, huh—you television people have it real hard, I bet. How about me? I got lots a' pressure—from all sides. I mean, who could be feelin' more pressure than me, losin' my dad, and then my sister . . ."

Louise went cold. How could Eddie Porter know the crew's shooting schedule?

Ruthie, white hair straggling a bit tonight in the heat, knew when an umpire was needed. Wiping her hands on a towel, she said, "I see you two, uh, know one another." Then she reached over and put her hand on Eddie's rough one. "This boy is suffering. But even so, Eddie, don't take your grief out on this nice lady."

He pulled his hand away and forked up the last bite of his dinner. "Don't tell me how to live, Ruthie." He threw some money on the counter and stomped out. Louise looked out the plant-filled window and saw him slam himself into his red pickup truck, gunning the motor until the restaurant was filled with noise and fumes. Then he drove away in classic redneck style, the squealing tires raising the sandstone dust on Lyons' High Street. His departure reminded Louise that she had forgotten to tell the police about the white truck on his property.

The elderly proprietor heaved a big sigh. "Sorry, Louise. I'm afraid Eddie's just plain rude. When you're done, why don't you and I talk." She cocked her head toward the tiny kitchen. Louise couldn't finish the heavy meal; the encounter with Eddie had probably turned her stomach for a week. She got up, and Ruthie, with her clientele properly cared for, ushered her into the clean space where food was prepared. "Let's go straight out back," said Ruthie, in her rich twang. "It's too darned hot in here."

They sat out on the back stoop of the restaurant, on springy metal lawn chairs that had been new in the 1930's. Beyond the porch, lit by the antique store's tall floodlights, was a casual profusion of plants, vegetables, and trees, including some heavy with fruit. In a far corner on a rise was a graceful clump of aspen trees with round chartreuse leaves and pale trunks, looking like a corps de ballet ready for action once the main players went offstage. Ruthie's garden was rimmed with dill, rosemary, and parsley, and overlaid with a sprawling bower of the pink roses. "What a classy garden. Do you grow some of the food for the restaurant there?"

"Yes. Know how that started? It used to be little more than a junkyard, years ago, when we bought it. We covered the junk with dirt to make that aspen hill. Then, I threw out some cherry pits and got me some cherry trees out of it. That's where our pie cherries come from. Course, there's boysenberries out there, too—that waterfall of green over there." She pointed a pudgy finger to a mass of plantings. "Then, I decided we needed a few rosebushes, so there they are, growin' over everything. Next, I thought, we ought to be able to harvest our own peppers"—she indicated a lush growth of green, yellow, and red—"and there they are. Hot, not so hot, mild. Then I always have a little patch of garden for peas, broccoli, zucchini, whatever I feel like doin' of a given year."

Immediately a program came to Louise's mind. She

would call it, "The Spontaneous Garden," perhaps, or "Gardens Can Sprout Up Anywhere." She would propose it to Marty tomorrow.

They sat there in companionable silence for a moment. "You like Eddie Porter, don't you, Ruthie?"

"Oh, yeah, I like Eddie."

"You treat him sort of like a son."

Ruthie dismissed this with a gesture of her hand. "Well, you know, I treat everybody that way, no matter how hinky they act sometimes. Sally Porter ate here, too, sometimes, and I treated her like I do you"—her face broke into a fond smile—"kinda like a daughter. I feel real bad about how Sally fell off that road up there. And for that matter, about Jimmy getting his head shot off."

The old woman shook her head hopelessly. "But Louise, I'm so *unfussy* about people. I mean, I never expect people're going to be perfect. I just withhold judgment— leave that to the sheriff, or the Lord. Eddie? I don't know if he'll ever make it in life. Eddie's always messin'up."

"I've met a lot of people in the last few days," said Louise, "and it's interesting and sort of spooky how they all fit together. Eddie's right there with them."

Ruthie pulled a pair of glasses out of her apron pocket, put them on, and looked over at Louise. "Now, my dear, you're a nice person. There's two people died up on that ranch now. I sure hope you're not gettin' involved."

Sorry, Ruthie, Louise thought. Too late.

But she said, "Trying not to," with a shake of her head that bordered on a shudder. "Tell me, can you remember any more about the things that happened up at Porter Ranch years ago?"

Ruthie rocked a little faster. "As I recall, Jimmy Porter's wife died suddenly. Then, that baby died—such a tragedy. But Bonnie Porter lost several children." She took her glasses off and rubbed her tired eyes. "I tell you, Louise, I've been in business here for sixty years. I'm used to speakin' no evil—and anyway, I'm gettin' so I don't remember things so good."

Louise could see that discretion was bred into this woman's bones. Like other folks around Lyons, she had a philosophy of forgive and forget.

That was very Christian indeed, but it didn't help Louise demystify the Porter murders, of which she now felt uncomfortably a part. She was sure that no amount of Gold Strike Café comfort food was going to cure the queasy feeling in the pit of her stomach.

As she left Ruthie and headed for her car, Louise recognized Sergeant Rafferty as she pulled up in a sheriff's department cruiser. She slowed her steps. This was the woman who handled things so well the day Jimmy Porter's body was found slung over the fence.

The sergeant, holding an armful of outgoing mail, approached quickly, and when she saw Louise, gave her a big smile of remembrance. She was tall and athletic, with brown hair bundled back in a no-nonsense ponytail. But little tendrils had escaped around her face, and these and her big brown eyes softened her severity. In a staccato voice, she said, "Hello. You're the woman with the TV show. Louise, is it? How're you doin'?"

"Great—"

"I won't shake. My hands are full, and I have a load of work at the station. Ruthie Dunn's told me all about you. Foreign service wife. Two daughters. Lives in northern Virginia. Is a real nice gal."

"That's awfully nice of Ruthie. I'm doing—okay," said Louise, figuring she'd better leave out such details as having been abandoned by her husband, intimidated by a dead rattlesnake, and shot at with a high-powered rifle. She knew she had to get to the point. "So, you're stationed in Lyons?"

"Chief of the Lyons substation, yes."

"Any news on the Porter, uh, deaths?"

With the sergeant cradling the mail like a baby, they stood on the sidewalk and surveyed each other. "I'm afraid not." The sergeant talked lightning fast, but with lots of expression. "But I couldn't share peak attention information with you, anyway—I'm sure you realize that—peak information being that information known only to the perpetrator and the police. What about you?" she said. "Learned anything? I heard you visited the ranch a couple of days ago."

Word traveled fast around here, Louise noticed. "Just to, uh, survey the weed population." It was high time to tell someone this, and she'd rather tell this woman than Sheriff Tatum. "By the way, I happen to know Eddie Porter has a white truck, in case that's of use to the sheriff's department."

"Oh, he does, huh?" The sergeant looked sober and surprised. "I'll certainly follow up on that."

"And if I go up to that ranch again, I'll be happy to keep an eye out for you."

"Do that," Rafferty urged. "Call me any time. I hear that out East, you've done some crime fightin'—in between your TV career, that is." She grinned at Louise with a mixture of admiration and amusement. "Some kind of a wonder woman, huh?"

"Oh, please. You know how it goes. It was mostly luck. Tell me about yourself, Sergeant Rafferty. How did you get into law enforcement?"

"Oh, easy," said the sergeant. "I graduated from high school in a little Nebraska town. There were two ads in the paper—one for a dispatcher, and one for a dishwasher.

I looked up 'dispatcher' in the dictionary, and it said, 'one who dispatches.' Sounded good enough for me. I've been doin' police work ever since. Although I don't know how different the two jobs really are, since I get my hands into plenty of hot water.''

Like Clues,
Gardens Can
Spring Up Anywhere

A NEW HOME PRESENTS A BLANK
canvas on which a builder's landscaper
usually lays the yard-and-garden design. Buyers of used homes often are
on their own, and can have a world of
challenge before them. In spite of what
seem to be impediments, a garden can
sprout up anywhere they want it in
their newly acquired yard—even in the
middle of a monolithic sea of green
grass. Home owners must ignore the
surface, and look with a true gar-

dener's eye at the endless opportunities that lie before them.

A trash heap can become a treasure. True, these used homes can come with eyesores—genteel trash heaps in the corner of the backyard, abandoned dog runs, weed-filled alleys, and little ugly spaces at the house corners which no one ever spent a moment thinking about. Sometimes the mortgage also paid for outbuildings such as extra garages or metal storage sheds.

Far from griping, the new home owner should rejoice: the more trash, the better, for one man's trash pile can be another man's Garden of Eden. Literally, the trash pile is an opportunity to start a hilled garden. First, cover the pile generously with good planting soil. (In the case of one householder with a huge hill filled with farm "trash," this meant bringing in five truckloads of soil to cover the debris of years.) On a little hill, start with an accent plant, perhaps an arborvitae or a juniper, placing it off center. Embellish it with a few other evergreen shrubs, then use the angle of the incline to display flowers, an assortment of ornamental grasses, or perhaps a cascade of vines. Mulch it attractively and well, because it will become a standout feature of your yard.

Beautify the desultory dog run. A ten-foot-wide dog run can be transformed into an exciting avenue with curved walk, flanked by delightful shrubs, trees, and flowers. Some intrepid home owners would even manage to fill the area with rocks, and let a stream meander through its length, with a small recirculating pool or waterfall at one end.

The entrance to the basement door, or the side of the house that holds the gas meter, is often ugly and ignored. Tiny corner spaces that others neglected over the years can be made into small garden oases. Even a space four feet square can be used cleverly, to hold vines, plants, and flowers. In the background, place several flue tiles of different heights and place a plant in each one. Train vines up the back wall, and in the foreground place a slow-growing shrub and some groundcover. Or, alternatively, place a couple of interesting rocks in the area, tuck in an evergreen shrub and a hardy perennial such as yarrow. The tinier the area, the smaller-scale the plants should be.

Don't tear down that decrepit outbuilding. Neglected or even abandoned outbuildings are like a gift from heaven. The British know how wonderful they are: They paint them

1 5 9

delightful shades of robin's egg blue or dove gray. They nail on charming windowboxes trailing with lantana, hang the walls abundantly with vines, and grace the front with old roses, delphiniums, and verbascum. Any building, ruined or not, is wonderful background for a garden.

It is a major challenge to transform an ugly outbuilding that claims a major part of the view of the house, for instance, a metal workshop of the sort that hobbyists buy. Since all these workshops seem to be cumbersome and ill-styled, and painted in a mustard yellow color, the first step is to paint them a neutral tan-brown, to help them disappear into nature's kind arms. No amount of vines or roses will take the onus off such a hideous structure, so the thing to do is distract——by erecting as much stockade fencing as one can afford, and planting generous clumps of disguising evergreen trees. Your next objective should be to clothe the (newly painted) walls, and especially the front wall, with sturdy plants such as trumpet vines. Eventually, its basic ugliness will be disguised. This same ''plant and conquer'' philosophy should apply to homely garages. Paint them, and plant them. No homely garage should be left to glare out at you, when you can make it the site of another charming garden.

Boring expanses of worn-out lawn: Probably more common than inheriting a junk pile is inheriting a yard with nothing in it except lawn, and often tired, shabby lawn at that. The new owner looks on this expanse with a sinking heart, for how can it ever be transformed into something interesting?

That is when our gardening imagination should come into play, seeking out the creative solution to the use of this open ground. Envision where trees or rocks will go: Then start out slowly, piece by piece, building the garden as you have time and money. The more tentative gardener might take the approach of starting with a garden that hugs the house, like a timid child clinging to his mama's skirts. This is not necessary, and not nearly as much fun as starting at the most dramatic focal point of the yard.

Prepare the earth in this area, digging up and removing turf, and enriching the soil, and then set in place one significant garden accent—a large boulder, a sculpture, an evergreen bush or tree, or a small deciduous tree. Don't skimp with this feature—that is, make it big enough. It will capture at-

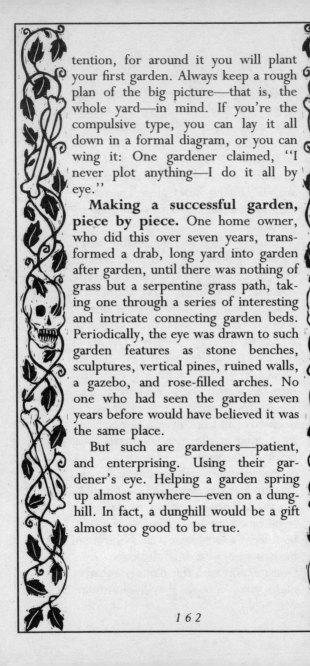

tention, for around it you will plant your first garden. Always keep a rough plan of the big picture—that is, the whole yard—in mind. If you're the compulsive type, you can lay it all down in a formal diagram, or you can wing it: One gardener claimed, "I never plot anything—I do it all by eye."

Making a successful garden, piece by piece. One home owner, who did this over seven years, transformed a drab, long yard into garden after garden, until there was nothing of grass but a serpentine grass path, taking one through a series of interesting and intricate connecting garden beds. Periodically, the eye was drawn to such garden features as stone benches, sculptures, vertical pines, ruined walls, a gazebo, and rose-filled arches. No one who had seen the garden seven years before would have believed it was the same place.

But such are gardeners—patient, and enterprising. Using their gardener's eye. Helping a garden spring up almost anywhere—even on a dunghill. In fact, a dunghill would be a gift almost too good to be true.

Chapter 12

RETURNING HOME IN THE DIM-
ming evening, Louise drove slowly
around the circular driveway, to see if
there was anything amiss. Her car
crossed from the shadows of the
ponderosa pines and cottonwoods into
a patch of dying sunlight. Beyond her
property, toward the foothills, she
could see a figure outlined in the twilight. It was her neighbor, Herb, leaning against his fence.

Herb looked like the type who
might talk about the things that went
on in this rural neighborhood. She

parked the car, and walked down to visit with the old farmer. His eyes were on the West.

Mindful of snakes, she stepped gingerly over the rough grass parkway.

"Jest eyin' the last rays of the sun," the farmer explained. His straw hat was pushed well back on his head, and his face was a map of browned old wrinkles, with bright, friendly eyes showing through.

Louise stepped on the other side of the fence. "I swear," she said, "this has to be one of the prettiest places in the world."

He gave her a warm smile. "Indeed, I think so. And there's lotsa new folks think so, too. They're buying up the farms and the old homesteads and makin' 'em pretty fancy. Jes' hope they watch out for critters. It's dry in the hills, so we got our lion and our bear around here."

She'd heard this kind of warning from Pete, and had a hard time taking it seriously. As she saw it, it was a problem associated with those who lived farther into the mountains. She put it down to something the old-timers liked to scare newcomers with. "So who are these new people?" she asked him.

"Got quite a bunch of 'em," he said. "A computer guru, a couple of scientists, some mighty well-heeled retired folks. We even got our very own expert on some syndrome or other." Herb pushed his hat back to scratch the front of his bald head, possibly to aid his recall. "Believe it's called . . . post-traumatics."

Louise was puzzled. "Post-traumatic stress disorder?" she guessed.

He snapped gnarled fingers. "Yep. That's it. Stress. That's it, exactly. Doctor Gary Rostov—I jes' call him Gary—master of post-traumatics . . . stress. He explained it all t'me. Folks get all fussed up when they have a big shock—like maybe their ma dies, or they shot down so many people in the *Vi*-etnam War that it made 'em disgusted with themselves. This keeps comin' back to haunt 'em like a bad dream.''

"So he's an authority on that."

"Yep. Sez he knows how to snap 'em out of it. He lives back in that green house next t'the stream. Told 'im it was flood plain, and the house there's had some problems. But he likes that spot. Bet he'll have some stress hisself when we get another hundred-year flood in a few years.''

Louise laughed. "So hundred-year floods aren't reliable."

"Sure ain't. They don't keep a calendar. Our expert'll just have t'head for higher ground is all."

She didn't have time to mention what was on her mind before Herb got around to his concerns. "Got somethin' important t'tell ya, Louise, kinda off-puttin'. Wanna come in? Ellie'll give us a fresh cookie, so it won't smart so much."

As they walked to the house, she saw that someone liked roses. The house was fronted with them, each one growing in its own separate wire cage.

"Ellie loves them roses," the farmer said unnecessarily, "and course, we gotta protect 'em against those deer, 'cuz they love 'em, too."

"Beautiful." She wasn't just being nice. They were impressive and healthy plants, if dwarfed by their protective cages. Louise sighed. Gardens all across America were being treated in this clumsy fashion because of the scourge of deer.

They entered the plain, elderly farmhouse, and Louise could tell a fastidious housekeeper reigned here—there was no red dust in this home. Dominating the living room were two plush recliners, their backs and arms prudently covered with crocheted antimacassars. They sat facing a large-screen television, and Louise could imagine the farmer and his wife sitting in cozy comfort in front of the big box when the day's work was done. The place smelled of sugar cookies and coffee, and Louise, who loved coffee, gladly homed in on the kitchen to meet Herb's short, plump wife.

After introductions, Ellie didn't waste time giving her the news. "Herb saw someone suspicious snoopin' around your house today—'cept they didn't get a chance t' break in, because he went right down there. You didn't appear to be home."

"I wasn't home the whole day. So someone was—hanging around?"

Herb answered her. "It was somebody in an old white car. Noticed he wore a wide-brimmed hat. Wondered if y'knew 'em or not. Kind of lingered there in your driveway, drove around once, and then took off fast."

"Toward where?"

"Toward Boulder."

Took off fast, and hurried to Boulder to the organic farm to shoot her? She ran down a little mental list: Eddie Porter? Tatum, Payne, or Reingold? One of their accomplices? Or hired gunmen? This was getting absurd.

Louise was an eager customer for Ellie's cookies, and as she ate, she gave the couple a glimpse into her work in television. When she told them that she had been up at Porter Ranch when Jimmy Porter's body was found, Ellie's eyes lit up with excitement.

"Um, we live about as close to the Porters as a body can get," she said, primping nervously at a bouffant hairdo already immobilized with hairspray. " 'Cept for old Harriet, of course. I reckon I know as much about those ranch folks as *anybody*."

At last, thought Louise, she'd found a real source of Porter family history. But as Ellie began to pour out her story, it soon became apparent it was not the clear history

Louise had sought, but a confused, emotional recounting of events. "Bonnie Porter suffered *terrible* up there on that ranch. Three of her little kids died there before she died herself. 'Course, she grieved the *hardest* over the boy who had the fits. Why, can you imagine holdin' your lil' son in your arms while he shook to death in a crazy fit?" The farm wife shook her head in disbelief. "And it sure didn't help that family. Why, I know it affected Eddie—riled him up somethin' awful. And maybe Sally, too. She was always such a depressed lil' girl. Then, as if all this wasn't bad enough, the *de*formed baby died, and Harriet's *father* passed on—no one knew why. I wasn't that surprised when Bonnie was caught in that fire. She was so low—it was like she *wanted* ta die herself, just ta get away from the pain . . ."

Louise set down an uneaten half of cookie, her appetite failing her. "How terrible," she said, "and how good of you to have shared it with me." After a moment, she changed the subject, feeling there had been enough talk of tragic family events. "While we're talking history here, would you know who bought that stretch of land on Route Thirty-Six from Harriet Bingham?"

Herb sat up straighter in his chair. "I kin help ya there." He gave Louise a shrewd look. He had probably subdivided all the land around this farm and made a bundle at it. "Harriet sold that land off, over time, to Earl Tatum and his friends. Yessir, Earl has always had the inside track with Harriet, and I wouldn't be surprised if him and some buddy—say, that Payne fellow—didn't buy her whole ranch off her mighty soon. After all, what's an old lady like that gonna do up on that mountain all by herself?"

"Why, she might not even be safe up there," chimed in Ellie. "After all, why's everybody dying up there? If I was Harriet, I wouldn't want to stick around with not hardly a soul ta talk to."

Louise was becoming overwhelmed with fatigue and a surfeit of family history that was interesting, but of doubtful significance. What was important was the fact that Tatum had bought all those prime patches of land from Harriet Bingham. She thanked Ellie and Herb, and insisted she was quite safe walking the quarter of a mile home by herself, since there was still a little light in the sky.

Back at her rented house, she pulled the draperies and shades down and rooted around in the living room to find paper and pen. She had to start keeping notes on everything that was happening; right now, it was a confused mass of details. She found no paper, but her hand came upon a can of pepper spray, around which a scrawled note was fastened with a rubber band. She read:

"This is useful for when you walk the mountain trail. We hear there are lots of mountain lions this year. Two is better than one when meeting a lion. Stand tall, put hands above head to make yourself look taller. Bark like a dog or make another kind of racket, since this upsets mountain lions. DON'T TURN YOUR BACK ON THE LION! Also, avoid eye contact. If all else fails, pepper spray might help."

Next, there was a paragraph on bears.

EITHER talk softly to a bear so it knows you mean it no harm, OR ELSE (some people think this is better) chew the bear out by yelling "bad bear, bad bear." DON'T make eye contact with the animal. Whatever you decide to say, back slowly away from the bear, but do NOT run. Don't get between mama bear and baby bears!! If the bear attacks, you will have to use a stick, the pepper spray, or your bare hands to beat it off.

Bare hands? Louise shuddered. She certainly wouldn't walk those mountain trails until Bill returned. Pepper spray might help with wild animals, but she realized it was a pitiful match for a rifle—like the one used to shoot holes in her cowboy hat today. Maybe she should have asked Herb if she could borrow a real weapon, a shotgun, perhaps. It could ride in the trunk of her car. Meantime, she would carry the pepper spray in her purse.

She tried the kitchen in her continuing search for paper, but was overcome with the sickening smell in the room. It made her wonder if someone had stashed a dead body under the sink. Then she realized she had forgotten to remove the trash from the wastebasket, and the odor was from the unused chicken parts she had thrown away.

After shoving the garbage down into the plastic bag and tying it, Louise went out the back door to deposit the trash in the Dumpster by the road. Once outside, it was a magic world, with clouds scudding across a full moon as if propelled by giant winds—and yet, it seemed there was no wind at all on the surface of the earth.

Lost in the beauty of the scene, she picked her way across the yard, past a decrepit greenhouse, and down the garden path. She was thirty feet from the Dumpster when she saw two almond-shaped yellow eyes staring at her. The eyes of a puma.

"Unnh," she moaned, feeling a terrible disconnect from the civilized life she had led for the past forty-three years. Wondering if, after all her recent brushes with disaster, her death would be delivered by lion's teeth.

In the light of the moon and Herb's distant yard light, the sight was surreal. The two eyes slowly sank toward the ground as the lion crouched in a defensive pose, much like a big house cat. As if the huge animal were metamorphosing back and forth between its molecular structure of bones, muscle, and blood, and thin air, Louise caught only momentary glimpses of it: the powerful line of the shoulder, the gaunt flank, those terrible eyes, and the ominous swishing of its enormous tail.

Although she had just read the renter's instructions upon meeting bears and lions, her mind went blank. What was it she had to do with a lion, slink away—or scold? Look it in the eye, or look away? The cat then did something that sent terror into her heart. It blew air out of its nostrils in a series of high-pitched snorts, and then got up from its crouch and began to move, slowly circling to her left. She realized that in a matter of seconds the question of what to do would be moot. She would be outflanked and done for.

The answer came from her gut. She raised both arms high, one still holding the aromatic trash. "Owwwrrh!" she cried. A deep guttural sound came out of her throat and she began to growl and then yell at the beast. "Owwrrh! Owwrrh! Go home! Go home! This is *my* home! Get out!"

The cat stopped dead in its tracks. Knowing she had nothing to lose now, she sprinted a few feet toward it, and the mighty beast sprang back. With surprise, Louise realized she was just as much an unknown quantity to this lion as the lion was to her. Having closed the distance a bit, she sent the white plastic-clad garbage of putrid chicken parts toward the animal with a mighty underhand pitch. Disappointingly, the cat did not pounce upon it, as she hoped it would. Instead, it slunk back into the shrubbery near the Dumpster, perhaps to see if the bag was going to move.

Still growling, Louise backed away. She stumbled over an apache plume bush, but did not fall. The growls had sent her adrenaline raging; she was determined to survive. Upon reaching the carport, she sprinted into the house and slammed the door.

Inside, she gave a frightened look at the big curtained windows. Thank God she had not heard stories of wild animals breaking through glass, or she would never sleep again. She flung herself on the living room couch. For a few moments, she just lay there, until her shuddering gasps turned into normal breathing. She felt a complete sense of oneness with the pioneer woman, Emily. She now *believed*, like St. Thomas after he placed his hand in the wound in Jesus's side. Then, overwhelmed with a great fatigue, she closed her eyes for just an instant. To her surprise, she did not wake until morning.

Chapter 13

BEING A PERSON WHO ATE OR-
ganic shredded wheat for breakfast,
Louise didn't care much for brunches.
But Marty had insisted that he and
Steffi meet her for one this morning,
since he had begged off again on
work—despite the tightening schedule—and had another proposal for the
day instead. They sat in the restaurant
of the Hotel Boulderado, plates heaped
with intricate omelets sided with fruit
wedges and chunky fried potatoes set
before them. Marty was running down

the details of the remaining shoots, while Louise picked at her omelet.

As much as she wanted to, she wasn't going to tell them about the mountain lion. Marty would not allow her to stay alone in her house if he knew both humans and wildlife were after her. It would be a good story to tell people later—if they would believe her.

"Pete and the sound man are okay on taking today off," said Marty. "Steff and I want you to go with us to Aspen for the weekend."

Louise let that one ride for a minute, and launched into her idea for a program on spontaneous gardens, describing what a great interview Ruthie Dunn would make. He liked it, and said they could work on a script together in Aspen.

"Do come with us, Louise," urged Steffi, "and we'll take Aspen by storm." She was a large woman with dark curly hair, who looked so much like her husband that they could have been sister and brother. She looked thinner and more sparkly of eye than she had when she arrived, and was full of praise for Colorado. "I'm telling you, we're having more fun than we've had since our honeymoon." She turned to her husband, and apparently reached under the table to squeeze a part of him. His brown eyes lit up, as if she had turned on a lightbulb.

"Steffi, I can't. I just don't have a trip in me today. I decided I had to kick back and relax, and I even dressed for it, to get me in the proper mood." Louise was in a casual summer dress with sandals and a big straw hat. She looked across at Steffi, who was wearing a joyously loud black-and-white-checked cowgirl dress and a squash-blossom silver necklace that must have weighed twenty pounds.

"Well, no relaxation for me," said Steffi. "I'm ready to roll."

Louise tried to soften her refusal. "How's this—I'll do

the weekend chores for you, Marty. Make a couple calls and firm up details for shooting on Monday at Porter Ranch. I'm sure I can work it out with Frank Porter. He's a reasonable person, and knows we're here only a few more days. Also, I want to get Harriet Bingham to take part in the program on weeds—she's perfect, since she not only owns a lot of weeds, it turns out she's allergic to them. And it will help take that old woman's mind off what's happened to the Porters.''

Marty pointed a finger at her. ''That's what I mean about havin' fun—sometimes I don't think you know how, Louise. Furthermore, I don't like to leave you here in town alone. I don't *trust* Boulder any more.'' The producer paused to shovel in the last of his omelet. ''We'd have fun together, drivin' over the mountains, then eatin' in some nice restaurants once we get there.''

''I'm perfectly safe. Anyway, Marty, you were forty feet away in that farmer's field, and that didn't stop someone from taking a potshot at me. Nothing's happened since yesterday morning. If someone really wanted to kill me, don't you think they would have done it by now? I sincerely believe it was kids.''

''Louise.'' Marty sat back, black eyebrows raised skeptically, looking like an uncle who had taken over the care of a rambunctious child in the absence of a parent.

''I want to believe it.''

Steffi had checked her enthusiasm for the West for a moment, and was eyeing Louise with a sharp woman's eye. ''Louise, honey, you look a little strung out. Are you sure you're okay?''

She looked down at the table, sorely tempted. How many people get in a showdown with a lion? How many lived, unscathed, to tell about it?

She finally raised her eyes and gave Steffi a guarded look. ''I'm going to be just fine. But you're right—I need rest, and the extra day off will be just the thing to set me right.''

❧

Louise had been nervous about meeting Pete at his studio. For some reason, this man threw her off her stride. Therefore, she was relieved that from the moment she arrived, Pete's attitude was all business. No jokes or jibes. Looking a little different today, in a new blue plaid shirt that complemented his pale blue eyes. No hat.

She looked at the bare space, as clean as a computer chip factory, the only decoration the large, dramatic photos of animals and landscapes on the wall. She wandered around the room's periphery, admiring them. Pete set out cans of cold soda and they sat elbow to elbow at a little Formica counter and drank them, like two old chums.

She told him about the encounter with the lion, laughing, if also shuddering a little, as she described how she growled at the beast. He looked at her and shook his head. ''Louise, you've got to take this place seriously. It's not downtown D.C., where the only predators are two-legged. That was probably a young male who got kicked out of the nest and hasn't learned how to hunt very skillfully yet. It sounds like you handled it well—I'm proud of you. But I'm a little worried, too, about those people with guns—no growling's gonna keep *them* away. You're gonna have to watch your rear end.''

''I just had breakfast with Marty Corbin, and he would agree with you. I tried to convince him that the person who shot at me was some wild and crazy teenager.''

''Oh, yeah,'' he drawled, ''lookin' for a little homicide before returning to Boulder High School next month? Get real, Louise. That was a thirty-ought-six—a rifle with a two-hundred-yard killing range, not a BB gun.'' He casually shoved his hand through his brown curls, as if looking for a hat to shove back on his head. But his eyes showed his concern.

"Okay, then, explain this. You must know Eddie Porter—I ran into him last night, and it seemed a little suspicious that he knew we'd been on location."

Pete sniffed. "I know the answer to that. He was by here yesterday, and my assistant told him we were out on a shoot. Probably even mentioned the places we were going."

She looked at the cameraman more closely. "You mean he's a friend of yours?"

He gestured as if to say it was not important. "Louise, everybody knows Eddie. Everybody knows Eddie's a screwup—a real bad screwup. You mean, you're thinkin' Eddie shot at you, that he's the killer?" Pete scratched his head. "I know the guy's heavily in debt. He runs up gambling tabs in Central City when he doesn't even have a steady job. Always got bailed out by his old man, until recently I heard Jimmy put his foot down. . . ." He looked at her with a frown.

"So he turned to a moneylender."

"Yes. Josef Reingold's got his ass in a sling—sorry. I mean, he's in debt to the man for a lot of money—and his only collateral seems to be his piece of property, and his share of the ranch."

"And of course you know Reingold, because you know everybody around Boulder County—don't you?"

His eyes crinkled in a grin. "With a few exceptions, yeah. You're not lookin' at some kid; you're lookin' at a middle-aged guy. I'm forty-three. My dad and mom were local schoolteachers, and I grew up on a little old ranch in Hygiene, where we kept cattle. But I've had a home and a studio in Boulder for fourteen years. I wasn't stupid or blind—I cashed in on the 80's real estate bust. Picked up as much property as I could here in town and in the county. Turned some of it around, held some of it. So, horror of all horrors, Louise, I, too, am in real estate— I'm even rung in on the occasional big deal."

Louise felt a bit naive. She and Bill, a supposedly sophisticated State Department couple who had lived in six foreign countries, had, at the same age as Pete, only recently bought their first piece of American real estate.

Pete looked at her carefully. "You won't hate me, now, will ya? I'm afraid you'd class me as another one of the good old boys around here. But that has its advantages. Ask me anything about this part of the world—I'll know it."

"What do you think of Josef Reingold?"

"Big operator. But it's funny. He always makes himself available to do favors for people around here, gives lots of money to local charities. I think that's why it's so easy for him to cut deals that lots of others don't get to cut. You know, like with the town councils of these little burgs that are becoming bigger burgs by annexing his projects. It was easy for Eddie Porter to get acquainted with a guy like him"—Pete smiled, thinking of it—"though it's a bit of a mismatch. Eddie needs money. Reingold has it to spare. So, now it's like Josef more or less owns Eddie."

Louise thought about that for a long moment. "Could Eddie have killed his own father?" She remembered how she had briefly suspected Sally Porter, who was a much less suspicious person than Eddie.

Pete shrugged. "Hey, look, I'm not a shrink. The guy's hot-tempered and impetuous. But he's also one hell of a hunter and fisherman, and pretty good company when you go out with him. Knows his home territory around that ranch like the back of his hand."

"He could be the one in the picture." Her heart was hardening against Eddie, thinking of all the unpleasant contact she'd had with the man—and the white truck hidden away in a corner of his property.

"I can't tell *who* that is in that picture. Come judge for yourself." Pete got up from the stool and led her into the darkroom.

She walked into the narrow space and stared. Staring back out of a twenty-four-by-thirty-six-inch photographic enlargement propped against the steel counter was an intense face. The person was hunkering down in the woods as if trying to avoid the camera, wearing an oversized coat, a crushed cowboy hat, and a dark scarf tied around the lower face.

She tried to joke about it. "Looks pretty anonymous to me."

Pete looked down at her. "No human being on earth can ID the person in that picture. The sheriff's right—the photo is useless."

"But it's proof that the person didn't leave the scene. The question is, why not?"

"I'd say because they hadn't had the opportunity. The guy looks like an outdoorsman, not afraid to make his way back to his land vehicle hidden somewhere down the mountain, maybe on that real steep mining road back there. Someone used to eluding the police." He looked disgusted. "Damn. I'm describing a poacher."

She touched the face in the blowup lightly, as if to remove a hex. "How about the pictures of the gravestones?"

He showed her his enlargements. "I love these photos; I'll work them into the program when we tape it." He stood with his shoulder touching hers as she examined them. "The writing's easy to read now," he said. "Dig these. They belong to Harriet's family. That must have been a common graveyard. '*Henry Bingham, Beloved Father*.'

Pretty terse, that one—he croaked forty years ago. Actually, there was lots of action forty years ago up on those ranches.''

There was another gravestone for Harriet's mother, who died seventy-five years ago. Louise leaned closer to read the inscription. '' '*The dearest woman in the world.*' He certainly cherished his wife, didn't he? Harriet told me about her mother. She was a very beautiful woman, and she died giving birth to Harriet. Somehow I think the woman still feels guilty about it.''

''Pretty stupid to carry around that kind of baggage,'' Pete said. ''I sure wouldn't.''

''Look, there's Bonnie's stone again. '*Bonnie Porter, Beloved to the Bone, Who Had Her Trial by Fire.*' Barn fire, I heard from the sheriff. And the children's graveyard. Nathaniel, Mary, Jacob, and baby Henry.'' She let her finger pause on each one, then read aloud, '*Jacob, Whom We Cherished in Life, and Whose Passing Leaves Us Bereft.*' Oh, gosh . . . what a kid that must have been. He was about eight when he died.''

He passed her another photo. ''This one will really grab you, Louise.'' On the small stone was the inscription, *''Dear Baby Henry, Who Could Not Cry.''* Henry had lived a few days, then died, forty years ago.

For some reason this inscription moved her as the others had not. As if removing a speck from one of her eyes, Louise wiped away the moisture. Pete put a hand on her arm, and for a moment she was afraid he might feel he had to comfort her with a hug. But he didn't.

''Nothin' to be ashamed of, crying,'' he said, brusquely. ''It's pretty sad stuff.''

Pete put the pictures in an orderly pile. Here was a man who was cool and emotionless, busying himself with equipment, photographing life with as much truth as he could summon. Living from moment to moment and not lingering long on the ones that had passed. She wondered if he were married, or had ever been close.

She quickly pushed *those* thoughts aside. "It might be interesting to know more about these deaths."

"It might, though it will probably be a big waste of time. But I forgot—you have some time to waste, don't you? Now, before you run off on me, how about a couple more pictures?"

"For what? Publicity stills?"

"Maybe. Maybe they'll win me a prize in a national photography contest."

"Well, okay." Louise was reluctantly falling victim to his rough charm. "Where do you want me to go?"

Back in the big room he perched her on a stool and then painstakingly arranged the lighting. He photographed her with her long bare legs crossed one way and then another; wearing, holding, and fingering her straw gardener's hat; smiling big smiles, little smiles, and half-smiles; with hand on face, behind her head, in lap. "Those great hazel eyes," he murmured to the studio at large, as he tipped her chin up so her face caught the proper light.

Finally she called it quits. She was sure he would get some good pictures, but wondered if he had any other motive. Of course, she was a happily married woman. Or if not exactly *happy,* certainly married.

❦

She left Pete's studio and strolled lazily down Boulder's Pearl Street Mall again, shielded from the full force of Colorado's sun by her big hat and sunglasses. She was feeling strangely detached from her normal life. That was what being away from her family did to her—or maybe it was the surfeit of sun.

Pete was not married, she'd discovered. She made sure

of this before she agreed to the dinner date with him. Zeeno's Pizza Palace, which he assured her was the best greasy spoon in town, was going to be an improvement over spending another evening alone in her rented house.

"I have no wife, Louise," he had told her. "Once I was married, but no more." It seemed strange to her that such an attractive man of property wouldn't even have a girlfriend. But then he hadn't *said* he didn't have a girlfriend. He probably did.

Since Pete's studio was near the courthouse, she stopped there first, grateful to enter its air-conditioned gloom. She wanted to check on the deaths of Baby Henry and Beloved Bonnie, but was told both birth and death records were available only to relatives. The Carnegie Historical Library had records from the *Daily Camera* that would probably help her, the clerk told her cheerfully. The library was an old building in classic style, only a few blocks away. Inside, the huge, south-facing windows turned it into a huge, golden oasis of information. A motherly, gray-haired librarian sat Louise down at an oak table and pointed out the large old books that held obituaries of yesteryear.

She told the woman she needed help in another area, too. The script for her Porter Ranch program had a little detail on the ranch's beginnings, but not as much as she would have liked. "Do you have any books that describe how the big ranchers around here came into such large tracts of land?"

"Some families wrote down their history," said the librarian, "and often in glowing terms. I'll get you some of those books." She smiled. "But there's others that liked to keep their business to themselves, and they'd no sooner write a family history than they'd fly. Who are you interested in?"

"The Porter Ranch—and the Bingham Ranch, right next to it. I assume it was the great-grandparents that did the homesteading."

The woman readjusted her wire-rimmed glasses, and nodded. "I know a bit about them—*private* types. They settled up there before 1876, which was when Colorado became a state. The Homestead Act of 1862 provided each farm family living west of the Mississippi with one hundred and sixty acres of land that would be theirs if they could work it for five years."

"That's how Jeremiah Porter—Jimmy Porter's great-grandfather—got started, isn't it?"

"Yes, it is. The cost for these settlers was next to nothing—one dollar and twenty-five cents an acre. Jeremiah Porter probably began his ranching on a small scale, then began to pick up homestead acreages around him from less successful ranchers and farmers. Some sold for profit, and others couldn't take the hard life. Some were disappointed when they found the land wasn't good for agriculture. But it was perfect for cattle ranching. Once he acquired a larger holding, Jimmy Porter's great-grandfather, if he was like the others, would have turned around and sold some—"

"Maybe to Bingham?"

"Probably. Then he would have been able to retire his own debt and keep himself afloat. Yep, that's how the big ranches came into being—and Jimmy Porter's forebears were darned good at it."

"And the Indians didn't claim the land around here?"

"No, but they used it. The Arapaho used to do their summer hunting near Lyons. By 1870, there were only renegade bands of Utes roaming the area, as well as some very tough white outlaws. Settlers had to deal with them with nobody's help. You can see when you get inside some of those ranch houses what the families faced. They even built special passages as escape routes.''

Louise thanked the librarian, then dove into the obits, and soon understood the diversity of Boulder County's residents. Some were country folks, some mountain dwellers, some city dwellers.

But she caught her breath when she came to Bonnie Porter's obituary, remembering that she had *seen* this woman's simple grave. Bonnie's death was dramatic, in a class with the more grotesque stories: the miner impaled by a support beam, the farmer pierced through with a pickax, the Boulder father of five who smashed himself to bits in his car on a locally historic cottonwood tree, and the ranch hand who died of pneumonic plague after cleaning mouse droppings from a barn. Bonnie died in a barn.

Mrs. Porter died of burns covering the entire body, as a result of being unable to escape from a burning barn on Porter Ranch west of Lyons. An accompanying, one-inch-long news story said the sheriff's office was investigating the possibility that the fire was arson.

Louise read on, about the deaths of the children Jimmy and Bonnie Porter lost. Mary Porter, the firstborn, died at the age of four from diphtheria. Nathaniel Porter, the second-born, succumbed to whooping cough a year after Mary, at the age of three. Louise stared with dismay at the story of the third child, Jacob, born the same year Nathaniel died. He lived the longest, but died at the age of eight from lockjaw. She remembered what Herb's wife, Ellie, had said: *Why, can you imagine holdin' your lil' son in your arms while he shook to death in a crazy fit?* She shuddered.

The significance of the three deaths finally sank in, and her heart thumped harder in her breast. Diphtheria, lockjaw, whooping cough: DTP. Three scourges of childhood before the advent of vaccines. Why on earth, at the midpoint of the twentieth century, hadn't Bonnie Porter seen that these children received DTP shots?

Louise flipped through the *P* section of the worn book to find the details about Baby Henry. Nothing was recorded. She was disappointed, having acquired an empathy for the baby who "couldn't cry." She decided to go on to the Bingham obituaries.

But here she found the answer, in a forty-year-old death notice. *Henry Bingham, son of Harriet Bingham, born July 9, 1958, died July 14, 1958, of oxygen insufficiency. Father, unknown. Other survivors: Henry Bingham, Sr., grandfather.* Disbelieving at first, Louise read the words again. The death notice of the grandfather, Henry Bingham, Sr., was on the next page. He passed away just months after his grandson, of "unknown causes."

The mountain's secrets were being unlocked. The lines were fuzzy, indeed, between the Porter and the Bingham clans. In their cozy little mountain cemetery, they had not wanted to make distinctions between the two families, even about whose baby was whose. Deaths, births, and tragedies such as fires seemed to belong to them in common. Private matters, that needn't come to the attention of the rest of the world.

Louise thought about old Harriet Bingham. Incredible that the spinster had given birth. And then to have her father perish so soon afterward in a mysterious way. Could there have been incest up in that mountain safeness?

But why hadn't Ellie remembered that Harriet Bingham had had a child? After the original printing of that obituary, Louise guessed the matter was swallowed up among the other secrets on that mountain.

Louise sat in the glow of the golden room and stared out the immense library window. Funny: The Porter and Bingham ranches were disappearing, after these families had inhabited them for one hundred thirty years. How would these beautiful lands be described from now on? As a new town? An annexation to Lyons? Or an enormous public park? And somewhere in this maze of land owner-ship and family history, could there be an answer to the deaths at Porter Ranch?

Chapter 14

Louise had fifteen more minutes to kill before she met Pete for dinner. She wandered slowly back to the mall, where large crowds streamed back and forth on the wide sidewalks. The stores filled with clothes, gifts, and art didn't attract her. It was when she turned onto a side street that a sign caught her eye: HERBAL REMEDIES FOR ALL AILMENTS. She wondered if there were one for loneliness, for all at once she sorely missed Bill.

She ducked into the shop, and into another world. The walls were painted pale mossy green with mauve trim, and hung with abstract watercolors in pastel tones. There was a strange smell in the air—herbs, no doubt—that was quite pleasant to the nose.

Signs on each basket of delicately bottled substances told of their use: A shampoo guaranteed to increase health of not only the hair, but the entire body. Flower derivatives—echinacea, goldenseal—that mended sore throats, and which Louise had tried on occasion. Powders in various subtle hues said to encourage sleep, energy, and even "sensitivity."

But her attention was soon drawn to the pair at the cashier's counter. The proprietor was a woman with no makeup, long, dull red hair drawn back in a ponytail, braless body encased in a tan sack dress that bagged at the derriere. She looked at the world through a pair of concerned brown eyes. She was talking to an excited blond woman in a tennis outfit who held a cat in her arms.

The cat, fat and white, seemed somnambulistic to Louise, and she wondered if it were drugged. No, the conversation revealed, but it was on the verge of being drugged.

"So my neighbor lets *his* cat out of the house," complained the blond customer, "and it immediately comes over to my yard and attacks my Freddie. I can't tell you how many vet bills I've had."

The proprietor's voice was low and remedial. "Your Freddie does not defend himself, I gather."

"Look at him," cried the woman, and grasped Freddie's impassive cat face to show her the scratches.

The proprietor peered at the cat through half-glasses, then floated over to a mauve-colored counter and pulled out a big drawer underneath it. "The solution is right here." Louise, fascinated now, could not tear herself away from the scene. The proprietor was pouring liquid from two bottles into two smaller vials. She returned with the vials and set them on the counter before the woman and her cat.

"You must give Freddie three drops daily from *this* container. It will make him into more of a man——"

"Oh, please, no!"

The woman was apparently afraid Freddie might take on unpleasant manly habits, such as spraying the family furniture.

"Not to worry. Freddie is fixed, and in no way will he become unfixed. This potion will make him just a tiny bit more dominant." She held out the second vial. "Then, you must give this to your neighbor and persuade him to administer three drops daily to *his* cat, whatever its name is——"

"He calls it Toughy," said the woman in a disgusted tone, "and believe me, the name fits. So what is this stuff, a tranquilizer?"

The woman in the tan sack dress smiled. "So to speak. It's vervain mixed with vine and beech root. It will make Toughy less dominant. Isn't that nice? You see, you'll be meeting in the middle."

"Both cats, meeting in the middle?" The customer was straining to understand.

The proprietor smiled, a magician's smile. Louise suspected alchemists used to smile like that back in the fourteenth century. "Both cats, my dear, are having their behavior modified, so that they can come together in peace and love."

Louise was stifling a great urge to laugh, and her mouth had already broken into a silly grin. The proprietor looked over at her, a challenge in her eyes. Louise tried to pull herself together and stuttered, "I—I couldn't help overhearing. That's a—a splendid solution."

It was as if the shop owner had paralyzed her with her

earthy, brown-eyed gaze. "You sound a little skeptical. But that's how we do things here in Boulder."

That put Louise in her place. The only thing left was a speedy retreat. Forget buying that powder that increased sensitivity—though God knows she needed it. She waved weakly at the two women and said, "Well, 'bye, now," and hurried from the shop.

Chuckling as she hurried down the street to the pizza parlor, she did not go unnoticed by the mixture of locals and tourists she passed. They probably thought that this middle-aged, middle-class woman had gone loco. And between secretive mountain people, snipers, and roving pumas, maybe she had.

Pete Fitzsimmons was standing with his tall frame draped against the wall near Zeeno's front door. "Well, Louise, what's so darn funny?"

"How can you tell something was funny?"

He smiled. "You're like Pooh-Bear—as if you've found a pot of humor. It's all over your face. So, shall we eat in or out?"

It was a beautiful, balmy night, which meant anyone in their right mind would choose an outdoor table. Yet she and Pete had serious things to talk about—after all, why else were they having dinner?

"Maybe, under the circumstances, in."

They found a booth in back. Nervous suddenly to be alone with him, she launched into the story of the lady and her timid cat, and the mysterious potions that were to make everything right. "So whoever owns this Toughy is going to be under a lot of pressure to reform his villainous soul."

"Wait," growled Pete. "The cat's name was Toughy? Shit! That's *my* cat's name." He slapped a hand against his forehead. His pale blue eyes sparked with outrage. "Of course. It's that dingbat next door, Jenny Drexler, with that half-dead cat of hers. Well, if she thinks I'm feeding weird medicine to Toughy, she's just plain wrong."

Louise was having a hard time keeping a serious look on her face. "Pete, it's really natural stuff. Just eye of newt, and toe of frog, wool of bat, and tongue of dog . . ."

Pete nodded distractedly. "The *nerve* of the woman . . ."

"Hey, I was just kidding. You must know about eye of newt and toe of frog. From *Macbeth.*"

He winced and leaned forward. "You mean, '*Adder's fork, and blind-worm's sting,*
Lizard's leg, and howlet's wing;—
For a charm of pow'rful trouble,
Like a hell-broth boil and bubble.' "

Together they chanted, " '*Double, double toil and trouble; Fire burn; and cauldron, bubble,*' " then sat back, laughing.

"Ann Evans told me. I should have remembered."

"Told you what?"

"That you're an intellectual under that good-old-boy pose."

He grinned. "I figured Ann told you somethin'. But she might not have told you I earned a master's in English, and was goin' for a Ph.D. when I realized land was a better bet."

"A Ph.D.?"

"I did all but the dissertation," he said offhandedly.

She sat there, refiguring things again about this raucous man. "So why do you pretend to be someone different?"

He leaned back, tall even while sitting, and looked wise. "You'd be surprised how much mileage there is in just acting down to earth, like an ordinary guy. Remember, a lot of the folks around here are just plain folks, especially the ones with the land to sell." He couldn't resist a grin. "You might say, there are no rocket scientists on ranches. It's more apt to be a poorly educated sucker who's worked his ass off for half a century or so herdin' cows, birthin' calves, and sloppin' barns."

"Like Eddie Porter."

"Like Eddie Porter. I mean, you've been around to Lyons. Can't you see the collision of cultures? The old-timers and the newcomers, like oil and water. They'll mix, but it takes a bit of shakin'."

She looked at him. It was hard to get to know the real Pete Fitzsimmons. She switched the subject. "Now the alchemist—I mean, the proprietor said this substance was made of vervain, whatever that is, and vine and beech root. Just herbs, apparently. And it does sound like Toughy could use a little softening up, if you don't mind my saying so."

"He is a tough little bugger, I'll concede that." Pete's brow was still creased in a heavy frown.

"I'm sure you'll handle it with your neighbor. As for me"—she grinned widely—"I caught the essence of Boulder in that herbal shop."

"Hold on, pardner," he said, frowning. "Holistic cures are part of it, but it's harder than you think to capture the essence of Boulder. You just glommed onto one part of the city's murky mix."

"I know," she said softly. "But Pete, you're taking everything—even Toughy's future—so seriously. Toughy's going to be all right, but how about you? It's as if you've become terminally serious since Sally's death. Where's the old lighthearted cameraman I used to know?"

"I can't help it, Louise. Part of it is because I'm worried about you since that bullet ripped through your hat. It could just as easily have torn the back of your head off, just like President Kennedy's."

She gazed down at the table, not enjoying that familiar

image of death. "Well, then, I guess you've been more worried about me than I have."

"Aw, nuts," he said, smiling, "I'll stop being so heavy. But what are friends for, if not to worry about each other? I admire you for your sense of fun. You get a kick out of life, even when things aren't going well, don't you?"

"I guess I do." She shook her head. "While my producer accuses me of being too serious, our daughter, Janie, accuses me of caring for nothing. She told me, 'Ma, all you care about now that you have a job is your work, and having fun.' I said to her, 'Good. That way, I'll keep my nose out of your business.' "

She felt a twinge, talking about Janie, and realized how much she missed the girl, how much more comfortable she would feel with her around. She turned her attention back to her companion. "Tell me more, Pete, about Boulder."

He smiled. "Like I was startin' to tell you, it's a strange town. You think you know it and its people, and then you get thrown a curve. You think it's liberal, and then you run into a pack of hidebound conservatives. You think it's forward-looking, and it does some damn fool thing that shows its head is still back in the nineteenth century. Take those murders. They have something to do with Boulder— something that even Ann Evans can't figure out, and she's right in the middle of all that land use stuff."

Louise ordered a small designer pizza, and Pete, a mid-size one. She went along when he suggested not only salads, but also a bottle of red wine. When he heard she wasn't much of a drinker, he promised to consume the lion's share himself.

As they settled in with their first glass, Louise said, "I found out something really exciting this afternoon. About Baby Henry, and who his mother was." She told him, but Pete was not that surprised about the news that the sedate-appearing Harriet Bingham had given birth to an illegitimate child. Even the details of Bonnie Porter's death in the burning barn didn't faze him.

"That's mountain life, Louise. No doctors. No fire trucks. It was all volunteer firefighters, and it still is in the mountains. Even though those ranches are only six miles from the highway, the people living there feel like they're in a separate world."

"I wonder who the father of Harriet's baby was . . ."

"How about Harriet's dad? Father and daughter alone in the same house for years and years—think about it."

"Oh, dear," said Louise, even though she *had* thought about it. "It's depressing."

Pete shook his curly head and refilled her glass. "Now, Louise, don't get all delicate on me. Incest's been goin' on since the beginning of time. Anyway, I only said the father *could* have done the deed. All that family stuff you've investigated today probably doesn't mean a thing."

"Well, there has to be some reason that two members of the Porter family are dead. Now, only Eddie and Frank are left . . ." Then Louise remembered what Pete had said earlier today, and she nearly choked on a mouthful of her Pizza Quattro Stagioni.

"Hey," he said, reaching over to pat her between the shoulderblades, "take it easy there."

She took a deep breath. "Do you remember saying that Reingold owns a piece of Eddie?"

"Sure do. A big piece."

"And where does this leave Frank? Look at it from Eddie's point of view. His whole future may rest on whether he can arrange a deal for Reingold to buy the ranch."

Pete stared off into space, then set his glass down with a sharp click. "I think you've got something there, Louise. And it leaves Frank in a good deal of danger."

Louise leaned forward. "That's what I was thinking, too."

"I hate to think Eddie's involved in these deaths, or Josef Reingold either. But obviously, Eddie's in a bind, and maybe this was his primitive way of gettin' out of it." He put a hand on hers and said, "What do you think we should do—call the sheriff?"

She gently slid her hand free. "I don't trust that sheriff much, and besides, I doubt he'll put a bodyguard on Frank."

"Frank's pretty smart," said Pete, seeming to take the removal of her hand in stride. "I hope he can take care of himself." He paid the bill, but Louise insisted on leaving the tip. Then he suggested they discuss things further at his house, of which he obviously was very proud. She agreed without thinking twice.

❧

Louise fairly floated along as they made their way through the packed crowd. The wine had gone to her head—and not for the first time in her life. Oh, well, since nothing special was planned for Saturday morning, she could afford a small hangover. They left the crowd behind at Tenth Street, turned north, then walked two blocks down Spruce.

"Second house," he said proudly. It was a low-slung sandstone-and-frame home with a prime view of the Flatirons. Inside, Louise could see evidence of the craftsman style: quarter-sawn oak beams in the ceiling, and intricate built-in cupboards in each room. "It was built in 1900 by a Boulder doctor," said Pete. "I picked it up for a song in the mid-eighties. That was the depth of the market here. The walls are solid stone, three foot thick, so it's cool in summer and warm in winter."

At some point, Pete had flipped a switch on a remote

control, causing quiet Chopin preludes to play. The music immediately made her feel good, maybe too good. It spread an ambience she should have recognized as dangerous. On the other hand, was there anything wrong with the fact that she felt relaxed and happy, for the first time in days?

She was surprised by his taste. Again. Sparse, modern furniture rested on Oriental throw rugs. Built-in bookshelves from the original house were augmented by freestanding ones, and seemed to be everywhere. The walls held a collection of art that was mostly western in theme, with the exception of a couple of modern pieces. One instantly attracted her: a bright painting with an abstract feel, of a swimming pool and a figure sitting beside it. The figure radiated silence and solitude. Louise went over to examine it, doubting it could be a David Hockney—but it was. She smiled. "Hockney. I *am* impressed."

"Thank you, ma'am," he said, refusing to give up his corny western facade. "I was fortunate to pick that up in my California period, back in the late seventies. Couldn't touch it now, that's for sure."

She couldn't help but be drawn to the books, the central feature of the room. There were rows of classics and a big collection of poetry. "Shelley," she said, slipping out a volume from a shelf, and flipping through until she found *Epipsychidion*. She wanted to see if she had remembered it right when she quoted it to her husband a week ago.

"Interesting poet," said Pete. "Do you think he drowned himself, or were the waves of the Mediterranean just too much for his little craft?"

"He had a lot to live for, didn't he? Mary Shelley, good friends, work he loved. I'd hate to think he killed himself."

"Who knows?" said Pete. "Poets live on the edge."

He came over to see what she was reading, and looked at her inquisitively.

She said simply, "Bill and I always liked this one," and closed the book.

"It's nice to have someone who appreciates literature." He grinned. Their eyes met for an instant, and then he said, "C'mon, I'll show you the rest of the place."

She trailed behind him as he showed off the modernized kitchen, softened with Mexican tiles he had ordered specially made in a French blue. He and Louise drifted through the rest of the house, finally reaching the master bedroom. It was so understated that at first Louise didn't realize how beautiful it was—until an evening breeze caused the long taupe curtains to swell at the wide window. The rest of the room was done in off-white, with a puffy off-white comforter tucked primly around the mattress of the bed, and voluminous deep red pillows strewn near the antique headboard.

The room definitely had a nice atmosphere. And the bed looked lovely; they were standing right next to it.

But this couldn't go on. She knew this with every fiber of her slightly inebriated body, because every fiber of her body had somehow been activated. Was it the paintings, the books, his familiarity with poetry, his pristine and innocent-looking comforter? Whatever it was, she had the sense she had already lost control. Maybe the problems with Bill were deeper than she realized. Maybe he had been away too long for her to remain faithful. . . .

It had started on the mall, when Pete bent his head solicitously toward her so he could hear her better as they forged through the noisy crowd. Even then she could discern a softening look in his pale eyes. It was the first time she had admitted to herself that she was attracted to him. And now here they were in this bedroom with its supreme good taste and its promise of earthly delights, to be shared in that bed with its deceptively innocent look.

The whole house had defined and illuminated Pete Fitzsimmons, the man. A man with a soul and spirit. In no sense a good old boy—except when he wanted to play the part—but, instead, a deeply sensitive and artistic human being. One who loved art, literature, and—cats.

Pete had put his hand on her shoulder, the part not covered by her little sleeveless dress. A ripple of feeling went through her that threatened to obliterate twenty-one years of a happy marriage.

"Louise," he said, and turned her around to him so they were facing each other and she could not avoid what was happening. Tall, warm, and comforting, he put his arms around her in an embrace that made her feel safe from all earthly harm. With a gentle but not intrusive touch, almost as if he were posing her for another picture, he raised her chin. She felt dizzy, helpless, mesmerized by those searching eyes, the soft, parted lips, the pressing body—

Then, something happened. A warm object thudded into the back of her bare calves, and then leaped onto the bed beside them. She yelped and jumped. "What the—"

Pete jerked back, too, and cried "Toughy! You little son of a gun!"

Thank heavens for Toughy, Louise thought. She sighed gratefully and leaned down to greet the feline. "So this is Toughy. How d'you do, Toughy. You really know how to make an entrance."

❧

"Gosh, I miss Bill. Did you know that this is the longest separation we've had in years?"

"Keeps you by his side, does he? That's what I'd do, if I

were married to you. Otherwise—girl like you—couldn't tell what trouble she might get into.''

Pete was jaunty and full of jokes, as if their romantic moment had never happened. Louise was sitting on a stool at the kitchen counter watching him open a can of premier cat food for the slightly-worse-for-wear orange tabby who prowled the counter's length. Toughy nudged Pete affectionately each time he went by, stopped politely for Louise to scratch him behind the ears, then restlessly pursued the remainder of the countertop.

"See," said Pete, "male, unfixed, and hungry. That's my Toughy. How can I ask him to stay home all day and sit on the living room windowsill like a wuss?"

"So it's his destiny to go out and get in fights that send the gentler neighborhood cats to the vet."

"Yep, until I block that cat door. With the mountain lion situation like it is, I may come to that." He shot her a halfway serious look from under the reckless eyebrows. "So, back to Bill. I kind of figured you were the loyal wife—even when I was puttin' the moves on you." Louise felt herself blushing in embarrassment. As far as this man was concerned, it was just a trial balloon—putting the moves on her to see how far he could get. He had no guilt, and he didn't expect her to have any, either. But did she? She wouldn't carry this as a secret the rest of her life. But on the other hand, she didn't intend to tell Bill, at least not right away.

Then Pete surprised her. He leaned both arms on the counter and said, "Look, Louise. If you didn't miss your husband—I'd think less of you. You're not only awfully pretty, you're better than that. You're like an old shoe. And that's the very best thing I can say about a woman."

With that, he dumped the cat food in a clean cat dish and set it on the floor, causing Toughy to jump lithely down from the counter and stick his nose into it. "Now that we've got that straight, d'you want to catch the art movie with me? I promise I won't even try to hold your hand. For sure, it's too early for you to go home to that lonely house."

"Thanks for likening me to an old shoe. I can't remember when I've had a compliment just like that."

Fleetingly, she wondered what it would be like to have love affairs with other men, which would have been easy to do on a number of occasions during her marriage. Here she was tonight, with an especially attractive, intelligent, naturalistic man who, to read from his eyes, had great depths of passion.

Pete wouldn't have "taken" her—they would have taken each other in an egalitarian kind of way, in his beautiful, shadowy bedroom. But when the cat pounced, the little sexual pang inside her evaporated like a drop of dew in the western sun. And, of course, it helped that the wine was wearing off. Although he was a lovable man, she didn't need or want Pete. She wanted no arms around her except her darling Bill's.

"So hold on for a minute," he was saying, and disappeared to retrieve his cell phone. She wandered into the dining room and over to a big rolltop desk. She couldn't help seeing the set of papers in the upper corner. Leaning over, she looked at the name on the top. Reingold. It was a business proposal, handily—for her—prepared in a graphic, easy-to-read style. It named Pete, Josef Reingold, and two others in a one-thousand-unit housing project on land proposed to be annexed to the city of Longmont. Pete had attached a Post-It note to the front. "Josef—What do you say we call it the Twin Peaks Mountain Shadows Development?"

She smiled at how ridiculous the name was. Even she knew that if you could see the twin peaks of the Rockies, you were on the plains, not in the mountains' shadows.

But Pete had created a name that would appeal to home buyers, whether or not it made any sense.

Such a skilled marketer. Once again, she realized she was in the presence of a real mover and shaker, fully as competent as the movers and shakers she met and sometimes had to deal with in Washington, D.C. Pete Fitzsimmons was skilled in everything: capital acquisition, marketing, and especially, a flair for people management that would be the envy of many a Washington pol.

She heard footsteps, and barely had time to scamper away from the desk.

"Ready?" he asked.

Louise looked at him, and her suspicions mounted as quickly as one of those piles of afternoon thunderheads over the Flatirons. He'd called her an "old shoe," which somehow had felt good—but was that to assuage whatever shame she might have felt at nearly being persuaded onto that big white bed?

And Pete *pretended* to be concerned about the Porter murders, and about Frank Porter's short-range future on this earth. Yet here he was, deeply involved with Josef Reingold, the key figure in any Eddie Porter plot to murder his family. Not only that, but Pete himself had just as much motive as anyone else to get rid of the two "knee-jerk" Porters who were going to sell the ranch for open space.

As she looked up at his smiling face, however, her suspicions dissatisfied, like those clouds that dropped their brief rains on the Front Range and sailed on eastward to Kansas.

Chapter 15

A FEW MINUTES LATER, THEY were standing in front of the movie house, and Louise was having second thoughts. Pete said, "Look, pardner, I promised—no hanky-panky. I want to be your friend. Remember that old shoe business? Let's just be old shoes together. Anyway, what're ya gonna do, go home and fight with lions again?"

A shiver ran through her. "No, thanks. I just have a lot of free-floating worry."

"About what?"

"Well, Frank Porter, for one. What's Eddie Porter up to? I'm even worried about Bill. I haven't heard from him in days."

"Aw, c'mon. Better to worry with me than alone in that house with lions prowling around it."

She nodded reluctantly and they went in.

It was dark inside the theater itself, for the feature had begun. "Gives new meaning to film noir," she said, giggling. They stumbled down the aisle and felt their way into two seats. After awhile, she could see a little, and noticed two men come down the aisle and sit far to the front of the theater. She and Pete exchanged glances; he had seen them, too.

Since the movie was not compelling—the agonized French heroine was too self-engrossed for her taste—Louise found herself focusing on the late arrivals. Finally, as the story was moving toward a predictable conclusion, she had an idea. Plucking Pete's sleeve, she whispered, "Those two . . ."

"Yeah, I know. You've been watching them instead of the movie. I'm beginning to read your mind. Let's just duck out the front door." They hurried down the side aisle and opened the exit door near the stage, throwing illumination from a streetlight onto the couple. Josef Reingold, again, this time with Tom Spangler. They were so busy talking in their isolated theater seats that they didn't appear to notice Louise and Pete's departure.

But they looked back, as they started down the street, to see the theater door had been shoved open right after them. Out came Reingold and Spangler. The nuclear plant manager, jovial as ever, caught up with them and said, "We decided to join the artsy crowd tonight, like you. But what a dismal film!"

Josef Reingold, who had paused to light a cigarette, sauntered up to join them. He eyed Louise and Pete, nodding politely to her. "Mrs. Eldridge, hello. And Pete, my friend."

"So, you two are just out for a little Friday night fun," said Pete. He appeared to be a little nervous in the presence of Josef Reingold, while Louise was busy trying to figure out what linked the developer to the plant manager. Was Reingold lusting after Spangler's prime piece of undeveloped property near the plant?

Then Tom Spangler took the mystery out of it. "Josef invited me out for the evening, because my wife and family are back visiting in Oklahoma. Not often do I get a night out with the boys." His eyes shone—evidence he enjoyed palling around with the debonair Reingold? Or the effort of keeping up this aw, shucks facade? He studied his watch. "Heck, it's ten, and I don't know about you folks, but it's gettin' to be my bedtime."

They bid good night to each other, and Louise and Pete went to the parking garage where she had left her car earlier in the day. "Reingold keeps interesting company," she said. Pete looked at her strangely, as if she'd gone a step too far. "Louise, you're getting a little paranoid, aren'tcha? Did you ever think that Tom Spangler is just one of the guys? Next, it might be *me* Josef is talkin' to. As for your investigating habits, if I were your husband, I would worry about you—because you put *everybody* on your shit list."

They stood awkwardly next to her car. Pete seemed to realize the reason for her silence. His criticism had made her embarrassed and uncomfortable. He said, "Some people are not as bad as you think, if you only knew them on a day-to-day basis. How can I say this? Land is fair game. Anyone can buy land . . . and make a ton of money. Land is destiny. It's my destiny. Don't think of me as a ruthless fellow. I'm just a guy who likes land." His eyes widened. "Hey, wait. You couldn't think that *I*—"

"No, of course not," she protested. But she remembered the papers she'd peeked at on his desk.

He reached over and took her hand. "You don't look convinced, but I'll take your word on it. Louise, look, we're just beginning to become real good friends. Why, we've gotten through the hostilities stage—sparring with words, and that sort of silly stuff. And through the romantic stage—when I foolishly, but not unnaturally, tried to seduce you. And now you're aiming to make me into a suspect." He shook his curly head. "I sure wish you wouldn't do it. I think you should just go home, lock your doors, and go to bed."

She didn't know what to say. Actually, Pete was beginning to sound just like Bill, constantly asking her to quell her natural curiosity. But unlike Bill, Pete had his own selfish motives.

"Thanks for the warning, Pete. And thanks for the evening." Her voice was remote. So much for a budding friendship.

For some reason, she felt tears coming to her eyes. She turned away from him and let them roll down her cheeks. Probably the wine.

Anxious to get home now, Louise pulled into the downtown traffic, a residue of tears still on her cheeks. A bumper sticker on a passing sports car provided a welcome distraction. HONK IF YOU'VE BEEN DIVORCED FROM DANA, it read. Irrationally, her tears began to turn to laughter.

Mood swings, she thought. *Don't tell me I'm in that stage of life. Oh well, maybe veering from crying jags to fits of laughing goes with fooling around with other men, getting shot at, and facing down a mountain lion.*

Louise speedily maneuvered past a couple of cars to catch a look at the driver. It was a lush-looking female with a mass of long, dark hair. Dana herself. What an egocentric she must be, but an egocentric with a sense of humor. Dana must have felt the stare from the neighboring car, for she flung her long mane aside and turned big, flashing eyes on Louise, then broke into a grin. She stepped on the gas, and her car fairly leaped down the road.

Louise was still chuckling when she spied a gray Jaguar pulling into the next lane. It was Reingold. As the stream of cars hurried north through town, her thoughts churned. He was going to his house, and she simply would continue the twelve miles north to her house. This was what Pete, Bill, and Marty—all the current men in her life—would suggest.

They were in north Boulder, with its desultory factories and abbreviated strip malls, homeless shelter, and topless bar. Reingold's car gracefully swerved left at the street next to the bar, and Louise realized he must live in Boulder Heights, a subdivision of close-in but exclusive mountain homes that Ann had described to her.

It was almost a reflexive action. When she reached the road, she turned left, proceeded slowly for a half block past the garish nightclub, then followed the gray Jaguar up into the mountains. If she didn't find out about this man, who else would? Since the moon was shining, and Reingold was leading, she had no trouble following. She saw other headlights on the road above Reingold, so it was obviously a well-trafficked route. She should be perfectly safe.

Following the road's steep twists and turns, she saw the Jaguar pull into a driveway and disappear around the back of a big modern house set in a forest of ponderosa and Douglas fir. While the other houses she had passed were wood and stone, Reingold's was like a concrete fortress. It was girded by a tall fence with a red sign that warned of high voltage. Through the trees she could see that a high aerial, proclaiming the ham radio operator inside, rose above his roof.

How strange, she thought. Most people in the Boulder area—including her neighbor, Herb—used electrical fences to keep livestock from straying. Residents of this expensive mountain community must all own some expensive furniture, art, and possibly jewels, but they did not feel obliged to erect high-voltage fences. What did Reingold have in that house that merited one?

His car had disappeared, probably into an under-the-house garage. Louise stopped her own car and quietly got out, creeping along the fence to get a closer view of the house. Inside, lights were being turned on. Draperies covered most windows, but one set had an enticing slit, through which she saw what appeared to be an array of equipment banked against a wall. From this distance, she wasn't sure.

When she was just about to give up and drive home, she saw Reingold's figure on the porch. He had removed his suit jacket, and stood there, white shirt gleaming in the moonlight.

The man looked around slowly until he was facing her. Her footsteps in the soft pine mulch had been as quiet as a cat burglar's. Nervous now, she realized something else was at work. Did he have a motion detector on the boundaries of his property?

Forgetting caution, she ran to her car, started the engine, and quickly wheeled it around in a U-turn. Almost a mile down the mountain, she calmed down a little and began to feel safe. Then headlights appeared in the side mirror. She realized the man was following her. She increased her speed, frantically trying to avoid the deep gullies on either side of the road. Reingold's car was catching up!

Louise veered sharply into the parking lot of the topless

bar and cast a quick look at the assemblage of vintage pickups and robust vans. Bad move. Her shiny red rental car would stand out in this funky group. Now she had no time left to escape him by going south on Broadway back to town. Desperate, she wheeled around the big building, her eyes searching out a hiding place. Hope returned when she saw an overhung roof near the rickety back door. She drove her car into the niche and turned out the lights.

From this hidden place, she could not tell where Reingold had gone. She waited several moments, and felt a flood of relief. Just as she turned her motor back on with a noise that seemed to reverberate in the quiet night, the Jaguar silently appeared in the lot like a cruising shark. He must have heard her engine start.

The driver slowly surveyed each car in the far row. Louise flipped the ignition off again and slouched down in the seat, her heart thumping, realizing it would take little time for him to turn the corner, exhaust the next row, and then come to check her car out, too.

At that moment, she heard the back door of the bar open. A greasy-bodied young man, who at first glance appeared to be nude, danced down the steps and cavorted over to her car. Now she could see that a g-string covered his private parts in a minimal way. "Wow, I've found me a woman!" he chortled.

She sat up and put her finger to her lips to shush him. She pointed to the cruising Jag, which was just turning into the last row. She whispered, "Can you get rid of him?"

The dancer had more wisdom in his eyes than his age merited. He gave her a wink, then twirled around and headed for Reingold's car, which was slowly making its way down the outer column of autos. To Louise's amazement, the young man pulled a pack of cigarettes and lighter out of his g-string; so *that's* what the extra lump

was. He was casually smoking by the time he reached
Reingold's car, which had come to a halt on seeing this
scantily clad person.

The dancer bent over and put his greasy forearms on
the window, slowly waggling his bottom back and forth,
and exhaled a puff of smoke into the car. Then, in a
suggestive voice loud enough for Louise to hear, he asked
Reingold if he could do anything for him.

The dancer leapt backward to safety as Reingold pushed
the car's accelerator to the floor and zoomed out of the
lot. Victoriously, the young man danced back to Louise's
car, adding a series of bumps and grinds for her pleasure.
She quietly chuckled and pulled a twenty-dollar bill out of
her wallet.

"You may have saved my life," she told him. "What's
your name?"

"Jeremy. And what's yours?"

"Louise." They shook hands through the window.

He shoved a thumb in the direction Reingold had gone.
"Fancy dude there, but one hell of a nasty expression on
his puss."

"You are a friend in need, Jeremy," she said warmly,
and offered him the twenty. He arched his hip so she could
reach it more easily, but she demurred. "No, I
don't . . ."

"Tuck money in a fellow's g-string? That's okay with
me," he said. "I'll take it anyway." He grabbed the bill,
pausing long enough to kiss her hand before he ran toward
the back door.

Stopping in mid-stride, he struck a hand to his head, as
if a great idea had just come to him. He called back to her.
"You're a babe, Louise. But I gotta warn ya. Watch out
for guys like him. He looks like he enjoys messing with
women."

Still another admonition from a man in her life.

A Deer in
the Headlights

DEER HAVE BECOME AMERICA'S
biggest gardening pest. (To some people, "damndeer" has become one
word.) They have moved from the
woods, mountains, and empty spaces
into the yards of the suburbs and sometimes even the city. They eat and destroy millions of dollars of trees,
flowers, and shrubs each year, but control of this pest is fraught with both
tactical and political problems.

When they see *any* deer, small or
large, moth-eaten or sleek, most peo-

ple can only coo and think of Bambi. And it is true, even as they stand there eating the buds off your roses, or remove their horn fuzz by demolishing your young tree trunk, they are just plain winsome. Long-legged, perky-eared innocents that we might like to keep around as pets if they weren't so voracious.

Controlling Bambi is hard. In some states, controlling their over-population is a political impossibility. But the state of Virginia is meeting the problem head-on, Al Capone style. Designated sharpshooters have been authorized to enter suburban neighborhoods where deer are troublesome and assassinate them quietly and tastefully with guns with silencers.

Fences, double, single, electrical, triangular, and up to ten feet high, are talked about a lot as remedies, but can be costly and sometimes troublesome. Homeowners can find deer trapped, squeezed, and sometimes impaled on these elaborate fences. Lightweight Dacron deer-net fencing—which comes in handy seven-foot-by-one-hundred-foot sizes—also is effective, especially if one has avenues of trees or high bushes against which to prop it. But one homeowner who tried this found that the only critter it caught was her dog—who could not see the flimsy stuff, and tangled himself into it as he brought the entire fencing off its moorings.

The "prison" solution. Individual plant cages made of wire or netting are the old-fashioned remedy, and though not attractive, they are totally reliable. They can be erected around each bush—with the Dacron netting cage being much less obtrusive than wire. Individual tree trunks can be protected by using tree wrapping tape, or by encircling the trunk with pig wire, being careful that as the tree grows, its circulation is not constricted by the wire. This kind of solution is labor-intensive and annoying, especially if one has fifty or so trees and shrubs to protect. It looks as if you've imprisoned your plants so they won't run away.

There are the off-beat remedies, the most picturesque being suspended slivers of Irish Spring soap from the branches of one's bushes and trees. Or one can try red pepper, bone meal, a radio left on at night, water cannons, human hair, mothballs, Driconure, or even lion scent from the zoo. Many experts are skeptical of these remedies, and they do not yet seem to have caught on with the public. Wily crea-

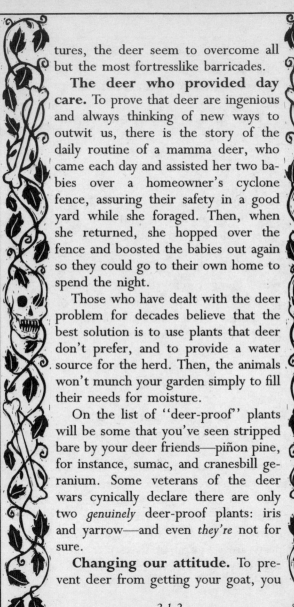

tures, the deer seem to overcome all but the most fortresslike barricades.

The deer who provided day care. To prove that deer are ingenious and always thinking of new ways to outwit us, there is the story of the daily routine of a mamma deer, who came each day and assisted her two babies over a homeowner's cyclone fence, assuring their safety in a good yard while she foraged. Then, when she returned, she hopped over the fence and boosted the babies out again so they could go to their own home to spend the night.

Those who have dealt with the deer problem for decades believe that the best solution is to use plants that deer don't prefer, and to provide a water source for the herd. Then, the animals won't munch your garden simply to fill their needs for moisture.

On the list of "deer-proof" plants will be some that you've seen stripped bare by your deer friends—piñon pine, for instance, sumac, and cranesbill geranium. Some veterans of the deer wars cynically declare there are only two *genuinely* deer-proof plants: iris and yarrow—and even *they're* not for sure.

Changing our attitude. To prevent deer from getting your goat, you

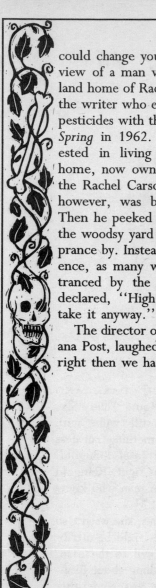

could change your attitude. Adopt the view of a man who visited the Maryland home of Rachel Carson. Carson is the writer who exposed the dangers of pesticides with the publication of *Silent Spring* in 1962. This man was interested in living in Carson's former home, now owned and rented out by the Rachel Carson Council. The rent, however, was beyond his resources. Then he peeked out of a window into the woodsy yard and saw a young deer prance by. Instead of scorning its presence, as many would do, he was entranced by the pretty creature, and declared, "High rent be darned. I'll take it anyway."

The director of the Council, Dr. Diana Post, laughed and said, "We knew right then we had the right person."

Chapter 16

As she drove the dark and dangerous curves of Route Thirty-Six, Louise's eyes were still wide with fright. There was something ruthless and insinuating about Josef Reingold. Jeremy the dancer was right. Reingold looked like the type of man who knew how to hurt people.

Yet, after a few miles, she wasn't so sure. She realized she could be attributing way too much evil to the man. She knew next to nothing about Reingold, except that he was sometimes charming and sometimes not, a local philanthropist but out for the big profit, very debonair at all times, horizontally integrated, and hellishly rich.

With relief, she spied a rocky outcropping, a baby hogback, that was a splendid highway marker for her when she first arrived in this strange place. She now knew she was only a few miles from the turn-in to her rented house. Then a car pulled up alongside her. It was Reingold.

She felt the fool. This crafty man had used the same tricks that her spy husband, Bill, had employed, and actually taught her when she had occasionally helped him on stakeouts. Reingold had played "possum" back in that parking lot, pretending to leave, but actually hunkering down and waiting until his adversary was dumb enough to shoot out of the lot.

Now, she was in trouble, for they were cruising side by side at fifty miles per hour, and he was edging his Jaguar into her lane. "Oh, God!" she yelled, and swerved to the right. There was a deep gully, and he was forcing her into it. Her heart leapt. This was the very reason Pete called Route Thirty-Six "Death Highway," for many had lost their lives in these picturesque roadside ravines. She'd be damned if her name would be added to the list of those who'd died here.

Surely, this man would not want to crease the side of his expensive vehicle! Louise refused to give way, but then the road narrowed even further, and a series of highway reflectors limited her ability to maneuver. She checked Reingold—the man was going to smash her right over into the deep gulch, dented car or not. Ahead on the right a driveway appeared, and she skidded into the turn and drove in. In the distance she saw the lights of a ranch house.

Would she be safer there, trying to roust out a frightened country family, or was she safer simply confronting the man? In the end, there was no contest, because she hesitated. Like a small tank the Jaguar bumped past her and cut across her bow, leaving a swirl of dust to rise in the moonlit night. She swerved to a halt.

Groping quickly in her purse, Louise found the pepper spray, then locked the car doors and let down the driver's side window four inches. Now she was ready.

Reingold walked slowly to her car. The bulge under his dark suit told her his handgun was still strapped to his shoulder under his suit coat. "Louise Eldridge, my dear." It was as if they were meeting after a long absence.

She looked at him and didn't speak. If he wanted to shoot her, he could. He could have done that on the highway, and he could do it here. No glass window would keep her from dying on the spot.

He leaned both hands against her door and examined the car as if seeing it for the first time. "You hid from me in the parking lot of that cheap bistro." He stared down at her through his black metal glasses, and she saw eyes that were not kind.

She smiled coolly. "Did you like Jeremy?"

"That creature," he sneered. "Part of America's trash. But, Louise"—his voice was like a cat's purr—"you act so suspicious of me. You come to my house to snoop, then you flee like a criminal down the mountain and into the arms of sleazy people. What am I to conclude? If you had just announced yourself, you could have come in and had a drink."

"I was merely curious about where you lived. I meant no harm."

In the bright moonlight, she could see he was giving her one of his debonair smiles. A bit of a waste, she thought. "Then why didn't you stop, instead of fleeing? You acted like a spy in a cheap thriller."

She dared to look at him, so close to her beyond the

glass window. "It's because you scared me. As if it were a crime, or something, to pass your house."

Emboldened because he had not threatened her, she added with a shake of her long hair, "And it must be a special house, to be guarded with a high-voltage fence."

That was going too far. He grabbed the handle of the car door and would have opened it if it hadn't been locked. And done what—pulled her out and shaken her like a rag doll? Throttled her?

"I could—" he warned.

"I wish you wouldn't," she said, and raised the pepper spray. He stepped well back from the window, aware of how painful the spray could be. His hands on his hips now, he swiveled his head and scanned the area, as if deciding what to do next. Here they were, two cars with headlights on, only thirty feet or so from a nearly deserted highway. A little suspicious on the face of it, provided anyone noticed. Hope sprang in her breast.

He raised a warning hand. "Don't try to release that spray at me. Stay out of my affairs, Louise. My house is my castle, as Colorado law provides. It is very private, and I have quite a collection there."

She couldn't believe it. This was like something out of a thirties movie. Reingold pulled a slim gold cigarette case from his breast pocket, opened it, and offered her one. Long cigarettes of some kind. When she declined, he selected one for himself and lit it with a lighter that shot the flame out sideways, defying the frisky little zephyrs that otherwise would have made lighting a cigarette a major undertaking.

"First," he said, in his smooth voice, "I see you with Pete in the theater. Were you watching me as if I were doing something outside the bounds of the law? That, my dear, is nonsense." Big exhale, and pause. Cigarette smoking seemed to turn people into actors.

"Next, you follow me to my house—which is clearly marked *No Trespassing*. I must warn you I cherish my privacy. I am not the only wealthy man to do so."

Louise had been keeping an eye on the rearview mirror, watching the desultory traffic coming north on Route 36. A car had slowed; it was a white van with red lights on top. A sheriff's department vehicle. She put her hand on her car horn and kept it there, until the van turned around and drove into the rutted dirt driveway.

Reingold hissed at her, "All right, here's the sheriff's car, but this is my last warning, Louise. If you spy on me again, or if you try to bring charges against one of the most respected businessmen in Boulder County, you will regret it."

She realized that he was quite right. He held every advantage. She opened her window further and kept her hand on the horn, giving Reingold the dirtiest look she could muster. "If you're lucky, I'll tell the deputy how you were trying to help me with my stuck horn."

By the time the sheriff's department car was parked behind them and a figure had emerged with gun drawn, Reingold had on the million-dollar smile that had brought him so far in life already.

It was worse than she thought. The deputy knew Reingold. He gave only one suspicious look at the way the Jaguar blocked her smaller car on the dirt road, and then believed the logistical story the man cooked up. He also swallowed the story of the car horn, and offered to follow her home to see that the horn didn't repeat its malfunction. Louise declined his offer, and thanked both of them, treating Reingold like a helpful stranger who had merely stopped on the highway to assist her.

❧

The woman was *eindringlich*. Reingold liked the long swing of her hair, to say nothing of the muscular movement of her hips and legs. But all that aside—she could be terrible trouble, he thought, with that inflated ego she developed from having helped solve a couple of petty crimes. It was inconceivable that a woman like her could seriously affect what he had worked so hard to achieve.

Still, he had to find out everything he could about Mr. and Mrs. Louise Eldridge. He sped the Jaguar up the mountain road, taking the tight switchbacks like a race car at Indianapolis. Soon he pulled into the underground garage of his Boulder Heights home and raised a hand to check his wristwatch. Nine minutes. That was nearly a record.

He went into the house, took a chilled bottle of 1993 Ratzenberger Beerenauslese from the steel refrigerator, and opened it. With his glass of wine in hand, he walked back out to his porch with its fantastic view of the mountains, and looked to the north. All that beautiful land up there would soon belong to him. When it did, he intended to build a new house, on the highest and the best site on those thirteen thousand acres.

❧

By the time Louise was settled in her own house, she was exhausted. She didn't know what to make of Josef Reingold. Was he a killer or not? He could be involved in the Porter murders—perhaps putting Eddie up to it, with little or no trouble—and still not have wanted to kill her on a public roadway. After all, if she had been found dead, Jeremy the stripper easily could have fingered Reingold as the killer.

For the first time since arriving in Boulder County, she had to admit to herself that she was in too deep—with no family and no neighborhood full of friends to help. It was a little like teasing a mountain lion, or bear, and expecting nothing bad to happen. And it appeared that she had teased both a mountain lion *and* a bear.

She wished she could talk to Bill. She missed him, and felt guilty that she had even *leaned* into Pete Fitzsimmons with romantic intent. And she desperately wanted to tell him that she was seriously over her head in the Porter Ranch affair.

Tonight, she took no chances against intruders of either the two-footed or the four-footed variety. She went into the bedroom and placed the pepper spray beside her bed. Fearing that was inadequate, she went through the house and jammed a wooden kitchen chair under each door. Knowing Reingold, and having seen some of the electronic contrivances at his house, she was sure he knew how to disarm a simple thing like a house alarm system. Dislodging the chairs would at least make enough noise to waken her.

Tomorrow, she would borrow that shotgun from Herb. A gun would be a great equalizer if Reingold, or anyone else, tried to attack her. As her daughter Janie might say, a gun ruled.

Chapter 17

LOUISE ROSE SATURDAY MORN-
ing with the sun. And when she did,
she rued the fact that she had missed all
the Colorado sunrises up until now by
sleeping too late. Sunrise was a spec-
tacular show in a place surrounded by
foothills on three sides. Dramatic
bands of deep rose clouds, like magma
from an erupting volcano, filled a
notch between the hills to the east,
while a milder rose—the color of a
Betty Pryor hybrid tea—was reflected
onto the filigree clouds that floated in
the West. She wondered how she could

go home to northern Virginia and live without these glorious skies.

With a jolt, she realized her stay in Colorado was coming to a close. As she looked out into the bright day, nothing seemed as desperate as it had last night. There was no need for her to borrow Herb's shotgun after all, for within a few days she would be out of here, and the Porter murders would be left for someone else to fret over.

And there was Janie to think about. Louise had nearly forgotten she had to collect the girl tomorrow, the closing day of the wilderness camp. She called the YMCA Center in Estes Park, but was told by some person in the know that Janie and her campers were out climbing Long's Peak. Long's Peak—the very one in whose shadow they had taped one of the programs, and which had cried out to Louise, "Climb me." She was glad somebody in the family was answering the challenge.

The person in the know—youth, or woman, she couldn't tell from the high voice—had more to say. "Oh, yes, Janie Eldridge. A fine young woman. She knows a lot about the environment for her age. Quite a lecturer on the subject. She has made great contributions here at camp."

"Well," said Louise, her heart swelling with pride, "I'm glad to hear—"

"And," said the youthful but authoritative voice, "she's—well, she's developing very strong personal relationships as well. And of course, that's usually good."

Usually? What did that mean? Was the girl caught up in another love affair? "Well, good," she responded slowly. Strong personal relationships with whom was the question. She never thought she would prefer to have Chris with Janie, teetering on the brink of serious romance as they were. But now she did. And Chris Radebaugh was back in Washington, D.C.

Louise hung up the phone. While her daughter was

impressing wilderness camp staff with her intellectual and social strides, and Bill was out getting his man, what the heck was she doing? Nothing, except being lonely and dodging both bullets and wild game. Unable to help her husband in any way and flummoxed in her efforts to unravel the Porter Ranch affair, she brought a cup of coffee into the living room and slumped into the overstuffed chair. It was as if a black Colorado raincloud were hanging over her. But surely coffee would help.

She had few responsibilities for the next two days: Clean up the house for departure, do a little wash, review scripts, contact a couple of people up at Porter Ranch about the Monday shoot. And she would call Ann. She wanted to tell her about the complicated events of Friday night. It was quite evident she couldn't confide in Pete. Though she hated herself for it, as soon as she was away from his compelling presence, she had serious doubts about him. The big Longmont annexation deal tied him and Reingold together like Siamese twins.

She reached for the phone and dialed Ann's home number. They agreed to meet in Boulder for a late lunch at the Rattlesnake Grill.

Once that was settled, Louise stood in the living room, as restless as before, staring out at the hovering foothills of the Rockies and gathering her thoughts. There were things related to the Porter murders that she hadn't pinned down, facts she hadn't gathered, because other people— had it been Pete?—had discounted them. Questions about the circumstances surrounding both Jimmy and Sally Porter's deaths.

Then, an inspiration hit her. There was an oral historian who might clear up the picture, if she only put her mind to it: Ruthie Dunn. She might be able to tell Louise things that no county records could reveal. Or she could have learned something from Sally Porter in the days before

Sally's death, as the unfortunate younger woman sat at a restaurant stool and quietly talked to the elderly proprietor while eating her piece of cherry pie.

Louise tried phoning both Frank Porter and Harriet Bingham, without success. A wave of nervousness passed through her. Harriet was probably out pulling weeds and sneezing her head off, on the verge of collapse. And Frank—she hoped he was safe. She closed up the house, drove to Lyons and parked in front of the Gold Strike Café. At the kitchen entrance, Ruthie, perspiring in the heat of the morning, answered her knock on the screen door.

"Louise! It's good to see you. C'mon in." She opened the door, pushing curly white hair away from her forehead. "It's just plum hot today, isn't it?"

Louise held the door open but didn't enter. "Ruthie, I need to talk . . ." She peered in the kitchen, bustling with Ruthie's helpers, aromatic with the smell of peach and apple pies.

"Good grief, Louise, I'd like to but I really can't, not right now. I've got my hands full with the late breakfast and early lunch crowd. Tourists are comin' out of the woodwork. Sure you don't want to come in and have a bite and wait for the crowd to leave?"

"Thanks, but I can't. What if I stop back later in the afternoon? Would that be good for you?"

"Sure would," said the old woman, closing the door. "See you then. I'm liable to be dozin' in a chair, but you just go ahead and shake me, hear?"

Chapter 18

LOUISE DROVE UP THE STEEP back road to Porter Ranch with one hand loosely on the wheel, the other resting casually on the window, her cowboy hat tilted back on her head but not falling off. If it threatened to, she knew just the right muscles in her scalp to flex to restore its equilibrium. She smiled, for in the matter of wearing hats, she had learned to defy the laws of physics just like Pete.

Braless this morning, in what she thought of as the Boulder way, and wearing comfortable clothes that, granted, needed a wash, she felt free and unfettered. And it felt good to be unafraid of heights for a change. She sped up the perilous road at fifty miles per hour—slowing, of course, for the curves.

Hank Williams, Sr., blared from the radio. She hoped it would help restore her inner peace. She blushed to remember her romantic encounter with Pete, and she felt a stab of discomfort again as she thought of Josef Reingold on that isolated road. All this had taken a toll on her nerves, and a little down-home music would surely help.

She smiled. Her "edgy, East Coast chick" image was fading. She'd become westernized.

In her side-view mirror, she caught a flash of light from a car following her up the road. She forced herself to stay calm. She should be safe up here. There would be people around—at the very least, Harriet. Since she hadn't been able to reach either Frank or Harriet by phone, she'd decided to drive up and settle business directly. Marty Corbin would be furious if she blew it.

And besides, this was one last opportunity to check things out.

As she approached the ranch, she could see Harriet at the roadside pulling weeds. One down, one to go, though she knew it might be harder to locate Frank.

She pulled the car to the side of the road and hopped out. Harriet was an engaging picture, there on her knees. Louise would have to persuade her to do it again it for the Monday shoot—wear the same clothes, bend over the dry ground in the same resolute manner. She was a portrait of a western pioneer woman with her wide-brimmed black hat, aged denim shirt, and long gray skirt. Old leather gloves covered her hands as she pulled out blooming knap-weed plants.

"Miss Bingham," Louise said enthusiastically, "hello. I came up to ask you a favor." As she squatted alongside

Harriet and pitched her proposal for the program, she took hold of a weed herself. Grasping it firmly near its base and trying to ignore the fact that it had the prickles of a baby porcupine, she gave it a sharp tug. It didn't budge. It was as if this recalcitrant weed with its cunning white flowers was pulling back toward the center of the earth with all its might. Her fingers were raw from the effort. She looked at the woman kneeling beside her with increased respect for her strength.

Harriet's face was engraved with sadness. It was as if this weed-pulling was a spiritual moment that Louise shouldn't have interrupted. Finally she answered. "Yes, I'll allow you to photograph me, but . . . I don't want to do any talkin'."

"Well . . ." Louise would have loved the woman's terse, to-the-point commentary on western weeds, but she could see in her face that she was getting prepared to scotch the whole deal. "No, no talking on camera if you don't want to."

Harriet, still kneeling, was phasing out again, staring beyond Louise out into blue space, her hands shaking slightly. Maybe the weeds had got to her, too. "I don't have much talk left in me these days."

Louise thanked her and said good-bye. As she slowly drove onward up the isolated road, she felt a twinge of guilt, as if she had somehow taken advantage of the old woman.

Then came the traffic. First, a UPS truck passed her, apparently looking for Porter Ranch. Close behind it was a white four-wheel-drive vehicle that pulled to the side of the road so she couldn't see the driver; it must have stopped near Harriet. She frowned. More people came and went on this mountain than she ever realized.

She continued the short distance to the ranch, passing the delivery truck again on its way back down. She drove into the yard, and Frank came out of the ranch house to greet her. "Louise, good to see you."

She was inordinately grateful to see this slim dark-haired man, whom she hardly knew. Grateful to see he was safe and sound. His life was in danger, but she was in no position to blurt it out to him. She realized he probably knew his brother was perfidious enough to kill him, too.

"It's beautiful up here, Frank," she said, as they strolled toward the house.

"I remember it when I was a child, before Mom died, and before Jacob died. It was like a perfect childhood dream of a happy family. Why, even Eddie and Sally were happy then."

"I'm so sorry about your mother . . ."

He shook his head. "Actually, everything changed before that. It was after Jacob passed away. He was eight when I was four, and everyone, *everyone* loved Jacob. Although they wouldn't admit it, he was the favorite of Dad and Mom, and Harriet and her father, too,—even the ranch hands and the kids at Lyons Elementary. When he died, I only *heard* him screaming. They closed the bedroom door and wouldn't let me see him once he got real sick."

Louise looked at him, afraid to ask too much, wishing she knew how to offer some comfort to smooth over the long-ago trauma.

"Everyone died a little when Jacob died," Frank continued, in a sad voice. "These days they'd call it 'freaking out.' Dad started drinking. We kids were kind of shooed away. But Mom was hit the worst, I remember. For that year between when Jacob died and she died, she never read us another bedtime story."

"It must have been terrible."

"Yes. I think that's why, when Dad finally found another woman that he loved, he didn't want the world to know he'd decided to marry again. I thought it was great, as long as he loved Grace."

"He kept that engagement quiet, then?"

Frank scratched his head. His tone was sympathetic, as if he identified closely with his dead father. "You see, he was a private man. And I know he didn't want to hurt our neighbor, Harriet, either. She's being left all alone up here when Porter Ranch gets sold."

"Now there's this problem of who to sell it to."

"Yeah. And speak of the devil, here comes Eddie. We can't quite agree on it, as you well know." She had heard a car pull up; and turned to see Eddie jump out of his red pickup. He hustled onto the porch and stared at Louise, self-consciously trying to smooth down the stubborn cowlick in his hair. "Hi," he grunted. "Let's get in the house—I need coffee."

It was dim inside the old ranch house. The front hall had several doors, all of which were slightly crooked, as if the house had settled. One led to a formal parlor in which Louise could spy an old organ and faded flowered wallpaper. Another led to a well-lit kitchen with white-painted, oilcloth-covered walls. There were creases in the corners where the heavy cloth didn't fit quite right. Gingham curtains moved slightly in the breeze.

Here, Jimmy Porter had knocked out an old wall and installed a large picture window that gave one of those postcard views of the ponderosa forest with back range behind it. A strange little window on the inner wall of the kitchen drew her attention. "Is that part of the double walls?" she asked.

"Yes. That's all that's left of the Indian escape routes," said Frank. "When this house was built in 1870, there were double walls all through the house, so you could slip down those narrow spaces away from an Indian attack and get out a back door or window. Dad kept that one window just for history's sake. It opens into the stairwell.''

Turning away from the little window, Louise could see that the Porter kitchen was an interesting room, with one corner devoted to crude, built-in shelves that Sally had carefully edged in two-inch-deep brown cotton cutwork edging. At first, Louise'd thought it was a dropped carved edge. The shelves held well-dusted, framed family photos of children grouped around Jimmy and Bonnie Porter in their earlier, happier days. In a glass-front antique cabinet stood a collection of distinctive carved figures—primitive and homemade. When she inquired, Frank said they were sculpted by his father long ago. Little Hummel statues sat upon most of the other flat surfaces, including a Victorian sewing cabinet with a neat basket of undone sewing still resting on its top. Sally's touch remained.

"Sit down and get comfortable," said Frank, indicating a chair at the very long, old pine table. She guessed this table had seated not only the family, but many ranch hands in its day.

She took a seat deliberately near a pile of papers. Quickly, her eyes sought out meaning in the upside-down letters before an alert Eddie swept them into a tan envelope. Raising an eyebrow at her, he shoved the envelope into a blue-green painted sideboard that would have made an antique dealer want to deal.

She smiled disingenuously at both brothers and told Frank that yes, she would have that cup of coffee.

When the brothers settled in their chairs, Louise knew from their demeanor that there had been good times and bad at this weathered table, the good times sufficient to draw them back here again to try to talk things out. It helped reduce her gut fear that Frank Porter was somehow in danger from his cantankerous brother—or his creditors. She sipped the coffee, and the cup nearly jumped from her hands as she took the first surprisingly hot mouthful. Slightly embarassed, she wiped away the spots with a dishcloth Frank offered her.

Frank said, "Sorry—didn't know it was that hot. I'm glad you drove up, Louise. Eddie and I are talking about the disposal of the ranch. Since you're doing this program, you understand what open space really means to this country, and that we can't keep plundering our resources."

"Oh, come on, Frank," said Eddie, "you've already plundered some of this land. You plumb wore out that land near the river."

"You mean the andesite quarry?" asked Louise.

Frank nodded. "It's true, we've about run that out—"

Eddie said, "So all the more reason for you to want to sell to a private party. Simple fact, you get more money. When this land is gone, my knee-jerk friend, that's the end of your inheritance!" He sat with the chair cocked back on two legs, his cowlick sticking up as if in defiance, his beer belly pushing his faded plaid shirt out into a rounded shape. He turned toward Louise. "I may become a murder suspect because I feel this way, but that sure as hell ain't gonna stop me from sayin' my piece." He flapped a hand in the direction of the sideboard where he had stashed the papers. "I even got us an offer for this property that would make us both rich." He stared at his brother. "*Rich,* hear me?"

Louise could picture the little boy who learned to become first a bully, and then a braggart, to overcome a shaky ego. Wasn't that one of the ways that murderers were made? She guessed that Eddie emulated his father every chance he had, probably even down to the country way he talked, but never had his father's acumen. So he retreated to being a bully, and bully his brother he surely would, with that contract in hand.

Louise decided she had been brought in here to play

devil's advocate, so she stepped right into the role. "It makes sense what Eddie says, doesn't it, Frank? You have every right to make top dollar off this land."

Eddie looked at her, surprised and pleased at her remark. Frank seemed upset, his eyes downcast. "It's true my quarry's played out. But I'm going to turn those holes into pools surrounded by marshes, and deed the property over to the county for park land. I guess you could question whether or not I'm a hypocrite—profiting from the quarrying, but not wanting Eddie and me to make the biggest profit by selling to someone who'll build twenty-six hundred homes out here."

"Good grief," said Louise. She had never heard the number of houses this property could hold, and it sounded enormous.

"Yes," said Frank. "The place was platted, years ago, into five- and ten-acre plots." He smiled ruefully. "My dad always hedged his bets. Now those small sites are like a time bomb. Developing them would be like introducing a new town with eight thousand people in it. That's five times as big as Lyons. It would swamp Lyons's schools and facilities. I don't want to do it, Louise. I know thousands more homes will be built on the Front Range of the Rockies. There's no stopping it. But Eddie and I can halt the development of this place, and we should. It's one of the best remaining nature preserves in Colorado." He shook his head wearily. "I just want to see the land left to the animals and the birds, and let the people in to see how great it is."

"The same old song," bellowed Eddie, banging his feet down on the floor and righting his chair. He got up and lit himself a cigarette, pacing the big kitchen like one of the mountain lions pacing the foothills. "If I hear that old song again, I'm gonna puke." He went to the sideboard and grabbed the envelope, throwing it down in the middle of the table. Then he turned watery eyes to his brother. "There it is, a golden deal from Reingold. Have a heart, Frank. I'm a guy with a no-good education, a two-bit job in a lumberyard, who's had a miserable time these past ten years. I just don't have the earning power you do. I'm up to my ears in debt. I need that money, and bad, for right now and for the rest of my life."

Frank looked at his brother sympathetically. Louise could see that Eddie had hit pay dirt. His brother knew full well how unsuccessful he had been at supporting himself. Eddie's life was like a dark pool that needed cleansing.

Frank slumped in his chair and stared at the envelope, while Eddie continued his harangue. "People got a right, Frank, to live on a nice place like this ranch. And as for animals, hell, there's plenty of land around here for the animals to go and live. The park, if nowhere else."

Frank sighed. "Eddie, you know as well as I do, it's a question of limited resources . . ."

Louise had had enough. This wasn't the time to ask Frank if they could bring the crew up Monday to tape a couple of programs, and she began to wonder if there would ever be a right time. She raised both hands, as if she were a referee halting a fight. "I hope the two of you can continue to talk this out, but I have to go." She looked at each of them. "I wish you well, whatever happens."

And what would happen? If Eddie wanted to do his brother harm—and she had a suspicion that he did—he had plenty of opportunity. Neither she, nor Pete, nor the sheriff could do much about it.

Footsteps sounded on the porch. Frank stood and let Harriet Bingham in. Like a tall ghost, she stood near the door and asked the brothers the time of the wake this evening. Louise realized it was a memorial for both father and daughter.

Frank gave her the details of the seven o'clock affair,

which was being held at Frank's house. The old mountain woman took it all in, then told him she'd bring some fresh sweet buns by.

Eddie put an arm around the old woman's shoulders and said, "I'm bringin' my famous enchiladas over to Frank's, and I bet you'll like 'em, Harriet." Apparently having said all he wanted to say, he clumped off somewhere into the interior of the house.

Frank turned to Louise. "Maybe you would like to come, too."

"I would. Thanks for asking me." Perhaps, afterward, peace would be restored between the feuding brothers, and they would settle on a date for the TV crew to visit the ranch.

Frank started some small talk with Harriet about his father's and sister's gravestones, and how the graves were now being dug back on the hill. The woman nodded approval. She was clearly accustomed to being a friendly advisor to the Porter children, ignoring Louise as if she were an interloper.

This was a strange back-country neighborhood, indeed, and she didn't feel comfortable here. Not only because of Harriet's coolness, but also in the face of the intractable hostility of Eddie Porter, who was like a snapping dog.

As she left the kitchen, Louise paused to examine the wood sculptures. They included several renditions of a steer—after all, cows were Jimmy's business. A couple of dog figures. The figure of a very old man, as if Jimmy were presaging his own antiquity, an antiquity he never reached. Casually perched in a corner was a half heart with the bottom half of an arrow through it.

She nearly said something right then. Harriet and Frank stood watching her. Surely this was the other half of the heart she'd seen in Harriet's living room. Was this a sentimental remembrance of the beloved Jacob, or something else?

A short time later Harriet left the house and Louise followed her out, saying her good-byes to Frank. She was thoroughly exhausted, and sensed Harriet was, too.

Another car pulled into the drive, and both of them hesitated. A small chesty woman with tight gray curls, wearing jeans and a bright shirt, sprang out. She was carrying a covered plastic bowl. It was Jimmy's fiancée, whom Louise had seen at a distance at the open space meeting. She hurried up to the ranch house, a determined expression on her face.

"Hello, there," the woman called out to Louise and Harriet. "I'm Grace Prangley." She looked up at them and added in a girlish way, "I know *one* of you, but not the other." Harriet and Louise were almost a foot taller than this diminutive woman. Transferring the bowl to one hand, she shook Louise's hand, solemnly blinking her blue eyes. She reminded Louise of an animal trying to demonstrate its amicable intentions toward another.

"And here's Harriet," Grace acknowledged briskly, "I haven't seen you in ages, Harriet. Last time was when I asked you to serve on a county-wide citizens' committee, wasn't it? The one to get support for a new school tax." Waspishly, she added, "As I recall, you turned me down."

"Seemed pretty silly to me," said Harriet, "seein' as how I didn't have any kids." Louise felt a tug of sympathy for the ranch woman. If only little baby Henry had lived, Harriet would have sent a son—no matter who the father was—through the school system, and had him by her side today, a man of about forty.

Grace was chatting on, and Louise realized nothing was casual with Grace. Each remark was intended for something. "Well, Harriet, it won't be the last we see of each other, either, will it, with me so involved in the Porter family? Jimmy and I had kept our wedding plans very much to ourselves, but of course, after what happened to poor Jimmy, and then to poor Sally, the boys need me, and I'm going to be here for them. In fact, I brought some potato salad for the wake tonight."

The implied intimacy of this didn't go over well with Harriet. Louise couldn't say she blamed her. This petite woman was pushy. With hardly a pause, she turned to Louise and said, "And you're the lady with the public television garden show, and that strange mower ad."

Louise just barely caught Harriet's eye. Grace Prangley knew how to stick in the shiv. "The very one," she said, with forced joviality. "And you're just the little lady *I* wanted to meet."

The curly gray head cocked to the side, and the unyielding eyes stared at Louise. "Oh. How so? What could you possibly want with me?"

Next to her, Harriet Bingham had frozen in place, her glazed eyes peering suspiciously at Grace.

Carefully, Louise said, "I was clearing up some business before taping a couple of shows here at Porter Ranch. Now, I hear things have changed, and maybe it's *you* I should be talking to."

This rattled Grace a little; she had obviously not been in on the details when her now-deceased fiancé gave permission for *Gardening with Nature* to use the ranch as a location shoot. "Well, not really, not yet . . ." It took only a moment for her to come up with an answer. "Whatever Eddie—he's the oldest, you know—whatever Eddie says, I would consider the final word."

"Really?" said Louise, smiling.

Grace gave Louise a closer look, her eyes cataloguing her lack of a bra, her less-than-neat hair, the spots on her well-worn jeans, the dribble on her shirt front from her coffee spill. She cocked her elbow out and put a solid little hand upon her waist. "Just exactly what are these programs going to be about?"

"The ranch, a bit of its history, but mostly"—Louise spread her hand out to indicate the wildflower garden— "the late Bonnie Porter's beautiful and historic garden. The unusual topography of the land. And, of course, the ranch's future here in the crowded West."

"Hmmh," said Grace. "I certainly hope you do a decent job. Turning this great big piece of land into an open space park has its problems, you know, whether anyone has spoken of 'em or not."

Louise said, "Harriet, here, has kindly agreed to be featured in another segment on weeds in the West—"

Grace turned from brisk to brusque. Kind words about Harriet didn't seem to agree with her. "That, of course, is your business. I must go. I have to talk to my boys now." Grace bounced off, her Nikes pattering against the steps of the ranch house.

Louise had learned more than she ever thought she could from one brief encounter with Grace Prangley. The woman was not only bossy and opinionated, but as she had suspected from the first moment Louise saw her at the Parks and Open Space meeting, she was on Eddie's side. She intended that the ranch be sold privately. Louise had no doubt this woman would be around when she and her crew came up Monday to tape the show.

Noting how droopy Harriet appeared, she doubted the older woman had caught those nuances—but who knew? One thing was sure, Harriet didn't like Grace much; it was quite clear in her sour facial expression as she went to re-mount her horse.

Louise decided it was time to go. She was not anxious to stay in this strange neighborhood, where yet another person had come to intrude in the affairs at Porter Ranch.

Chapter 19

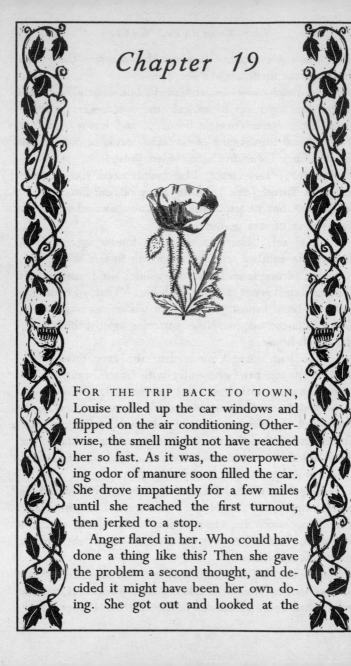

FOR THE TRIP BACK TO TOWN, Louise rolled up the car windows and flipped on the air conditioning. Otherwise, the smell might not have reached her so fast. As it was, the overpowering odor of manure soon filled the car. She drove impatiently for a few miles until she reached the first turnout, then jerked to a stop.

Anger flared in her. Who could have done a thing like this? Then she gave the problem a second thought, and decided it might have been her own doing. She got out and looked at the wheels of her car to see if she could have driven through this excrement. But when she opened the back door she discovered the smell was coming from a plastic bag filled with manure. An open bag, set neatly on the floor just in back of the driver's seat.

Of all the infantile tricks she had ever seen, this was the worst. Was it a warning from the angry Eddie, to mind her own business? Or could it have been someone else? After all, the traffic up here had been heavy this morning. Who, for instance, had been at the wheel of that four-by-four?

It was probably no more than a silly joke. After all, someone making a serious threat would surely have thrown the stuff around the car, ruining its interior and her day.

As it was, it was manageable. Turning her nose carefully away, she lifted the bag out and set it aside while she opened the trunk of her car. She had to think of this differently. Someone had given her a gift of natural fertilizer, and she would not spurn it. She would throw it on the compost pile in the garden at her rented house.

Closing the bag of offal as best she could, she tucked it in her trunk, got back in the car, and resumed her speedy ride over the ridges of the foothills. By the time she reached her rental house, her mind was on other things, and she completely forgot her smelly little present.

❧

Louise had taken a long, hot shower, and come into the bedroom still toweling herself. "Damn," she muttered when she saw the message button flashing. She pushed the replay button and heard her husband's voice for the first time in days.

"*Hi, honey. We're pullin' outta here—and I reckon I'll be home by tomorrow.*" Was this really Bill, or someone trying to pull her leg? "*I hope y'all're doin' real good,*" he continued. *"Sure was great t'hear your voice on the answerin' machine."*

Y'all? Reckon? Real good? The voice was definitely Bill's. But her husband's devotion to the Queen's English seldom slipped; now he seemed to be wallowing in a quagmire of southwestern colloquialisms. She wondered who he was hanging out with to make his language change so dramatically. He sounded distinctly—Texan. *"I hope somebody's fixin' t' solve those murders, and I hope you're stayin' out of it. Honey, I want you ta watch out for people, now—and you know what I mean."*

Fixin' to? The answer came to her. He was associating with a bunch of southwest government agents, and their speech habits were rubbing off on him.

Next came a message from Pete. *"Maybe I'll see ya this evenin',"* the cameraman said. *"Eddie was by earlier and told me about the wake. If you're comin', I'll be right there to try to protect you"*—was that gentle taunting?—*"though I'm sure you're insulted to hear me suggest you need protection."*

Pete Fitzsimmons. She wished she weren't so suspicious of the man.

"And one more thing," he continued, *"my great cat, Toughy. This mornin' I talked to Jenny next door, and just on account of you I held my tongue, for awhile, anyway. And she gave me this little bottle of drops. Just for fun I think I'll try 'em on Toughy. But I blew it with the woman. Couldn't resist tellin' her that her cat ought to get some balls."* He chuckled. *"Course, that's impossible because the critter's been deballed. Jenny's the kind of woman that can't tolerate a real male cat around th' house, much less a real man. Well, I'll see ya, Louise."*

She smiled, and then immediately sobered. It was a mistake to fall for this man's considerable charms. Why couldn't he be in league with Reingold in an attempt to get Porter's ranch? He could have shot Jimmy Porter and driven to her rental house in time to rendezvous with her and Ann Evans. Then, he only had to drive the three of them up the road again and innocently discover the body . . .

With a little shock of remembrance, she could picture that empty shotgun rack above his head in the truck. *Where had his gun gone?* Men like Pete always had their gun handy.

If Pete was the murderer, he had done it with his customary aplomb. It was a superb job of acting—showing her photos of the murder scene and the Porter Ranch and speculating darkly on the figure in the woods. Was all that just to finesse her, to throw her totally off track? It gave her a pang. Her old-shoe buddy, part of a murder plot . . .

Unfortunately, Pete fit the profile of a killer. He was more physically competent than most other men, and an excellent marksman. A man who knew Boulder inside out, who played different roles for different people, and played them smoothly. A man with no close family to know exactly what he was doing. A man with a modern, laissez-faire outlook on both the world and on sex—for he would have happily bedded her down in his National Landmark home had she given him the nod.

She shuddered and pulled her towel more tightly about her. She was getting scared.

She needed to talk to Bill and quit playing the tough guy, airily dismissing the fact that someone had tried to kill her. Hurriedly, she looked up the Langley, Virginia, emergency number Bill had given her. She told the operator her message was urgent. As she sat on the side of the bed and waited for the call to go through, she grabbed one of her scripts. She turned it over and on the pack she wrote down some names, then connected them with lines. Eddie Porter, connected to Josef Reingold, and to Grace Prangley. Frank Porter, his name standing alone. Pete Fitzsimmons, with a line drawn to Reingold. Mark Payne and Sheriff Tatum connected with another line, with Harriet's name linked with both Payne's and Tatum's. Tom Spangler, with a dotted line connecting him to Reingold. Ann Evans, just for the record—but when Louise thought about it, with links to all of the other people. She drew the lines in. As she'd told Ann, everyone—no matter how unlikely—had to be considered when investigating a murder. She placed the script back on the bedside table.

The operator suddenly broke the silence. "Ma'am," she said, "you say this is urgent? Maybe you should contact someone closer to you if you're in an emergency situation."

"Well," huffed Louise, "I'm not in immediate danger. I just need to speak to my husband!"

"We can't get through right now, Mrs. Eldridge, but we'll try our best," was all the aloof message-taker would say. Louise slumped down on the edge of the bed, disappointed. She felt as if she might never see her family again.

Cover-Up:
What's New
in Mulch, Manure,
and Compost

IS THERE ANYTHING TRULY NEW in compost, manure, and mulch? Yes and no. Various entrepreneurs think so, and market new products all the time. Meantime, home gardeners can be assured that bacteria, fungi, and worms are unfussy: They will go to work on anything they find in the pile, gourmet or not. The action of these microorganisms and small creatures magically transforms "green" nitrogen-rich stuff (plant tops, kitchen vegetable matter, a little horse manure, etc.) and "brown" carbon-rich material (dried leaves, and sticks, hay, or straw) into nutritious, well-balanced meals for our plants.

One can hardly do it wrong: Even the most amateur compost pile, mixed and seasoned a bit, may not look like a brown, rich cake mix, but it still will do the job as well as a mix that does. And magically, it will turn out to have a well-balanced chemical content that is perfect for the garden, a pH of around seven; this is somewhat acidic and good for most plants. The gradual addition of compost, by the way, is the best means for improving alkaline soils.

Worms in the *kitchen*? Vermiculture is the art of persuading red worms to eat your garbage. Some gardeners even keep their setups—about the size of a backyard grill—in their kitchens, cozy and warm. They feed the worms once a week, and the results are rich dark compost. Do worms smell? Apparently not; the whole process is supposed to be odorless. However, some people's antipathy to worms might make it worthwhile to place their work station in the garage—or maybe the basement.

No kidding, soil is a science. They say soil is a science, and urban planners are beginning to realize they need to listen to the experts on the subject. Now, they get specific plant "recipes," a special one for a steep roadside berm that is quite different than the one for a city park. Custom-made topsoil might be laced with sand, compost, and the barley mulch that is the residual of beer making. Sludge, carefully selected to assure it contains no heavy metals, is also a popular soil ingredient. The homeowner might take a leaf from the experts' book: When laying sod, for instance, nothing is more important for making a success-ful lawn than that rich layer of soil un-derneath it. When enriching our garden soil, our eye will tell us some things, but a soil test will tell us even more, about the chemical content, and what it might need to support a thriv-ing batch of plants.

Designer compost—from Seat-tle, of course. Gourmet compost, aimed, perhaps, at the latte crowd, is produced by a Seattle company, which calls it smoother, better-smell-ing, and more effective than regular compost. Its cost is almost a third higher. It is a mocha color, surely in tune with the city itself. A crucial in-gredient is coffee grounds. Quick-drying and cooling fans to air out the compost are part of its avant-garde

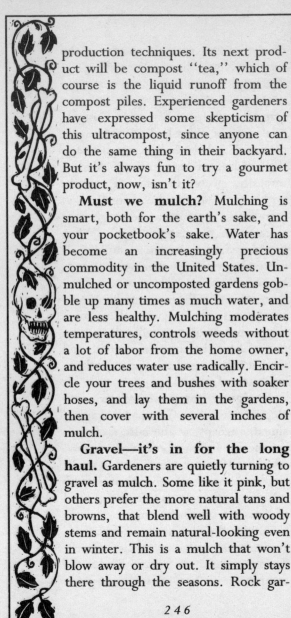

production techniques. Its next product will be compost "tea," which of course is the liquid runoff from the compost piles. Experienced gardeners have expressed some skepticism of this ultracompost, since anyone can do the same thing in their backyard. But it's always fun to try a gourmet product, now, isn't it?

Must we mulch? Mulching is smart, both for the earth's sake, and your pocketbook's sake. Water has become an increasingly precious commodity in the United States. Unmulched or uncomposted gardens gobble up many times as much water, and are less healthy. Mulching moderates temperatures, controls weeds without a lot of labor from the home owner, and reduces water use radically. Encircle your trees and bushes with soaker hoses, and lay them in the gardens, then cover with several inches of mulch.

Gravel—it's in for the long haul. Gardeners are quietly turning to gravel as mulch. Some like it pink, but others prefer the more natural tans and browns, that blend well with woody stems and remain natural-looking even in winter. This is a mulch that won't blow away or dry out. It simply stays there through the seasons. Rock gardeners and xeriscape gardeners have long been its advocates.

The animal parade. One gardener, who lives in the wilds of western New Jersey, shares his compost pile with the animals, with the crows, possums, and then raccoons taking their turn, tearing apart the kitchen scraps he puts in the pile, and leaving him with a nicely shredded mixture. Because of bear and lion foraging, many western gardeners have quit digging *any* kitchen scraps into an open compost pile—and that's where vermiculture can help.

A caveat for composters: Mulch and compost both contain bacteria and fungi—and in fact, that's what makes them operate. But they can get into the respiratory tract, allegedly causing breathing difficulties and even more serious symptoms such as fever. The condition is called "organic dust toxic syndrome." To prevent it, gardeners are advised to keep mulch and compost damp, so that it doesn't shed so many in-air particles. Applying mulch or compost with a gentle hand also reduces the problem.

Notes from the manure pile: Some gardeners, and lots of organic farmers, swear by poultry manure, feeling it is the best encouragement for

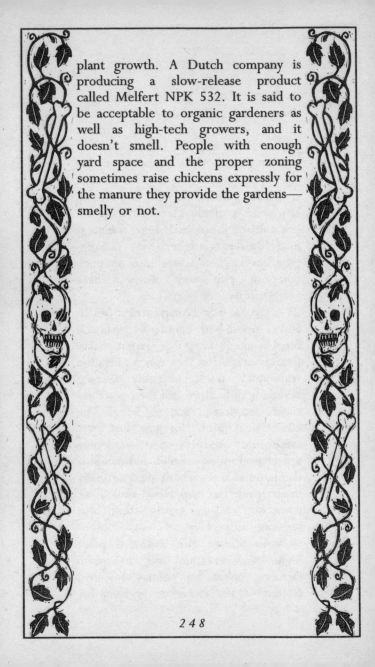

plant growth. A Dutch company is producing a slow-release product called Melfert NPK 532. It is said to be acceptable to organic gardeners as well as high-tech growers, and it doesn't smell. People with enough yard space and the proper zoning sometimes raise chickens expressly for the manure they provide the gardens—smelly or not.

Chapter 20

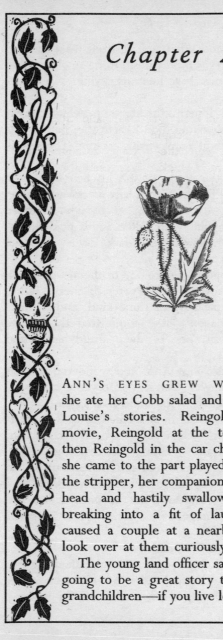

ANN'S EYES GREW WIDER, AS she ate her Cobb salad and listened to Louise's stories. Reingold at the movie, Reingold at the topless bar, then Reingold in the car chase. When she came to the part played by Jeremy the stripper, her companion bowed her head and hastily swallowed before breaking into a fit of laughter that caused a couple at a nearby table to look over at them curiously.

The young land officer said, "That's going to be a great story to tell your grandchildren—if you live long enough to have any." Then, mortified, she realized what she had said. "Oh, I'm so sorry. I didn't mean to be so glib. Being chased on that road must have been terrifying. You take a lot of chances."

Louise had lost her appetite for her soup, which constituted lunch today. "Reingold didn't harm me, but he was absolutely furious to think I was spying on him. The man is a mystery."

Next she related the scene in the kitchen of Porter Ranch with Eddie and Frank. "I still have an uneasy feeling about Frank's safety. It's a toss-up as to who is more suspicious, Josef Reingold, with Eddie as his possible accomplice, or the combination of Mark Payne and Earl Tatum."

Ann said, "Developers—every one of them—profit no matter *who* killed Jimmy and Sally Porter. If Sheriff Tatum and Mark Payne are partners of some kind, and it looks like they are, they needn't have committed the crimes themselves. In fact, any one of them could have hired someone else to do it."

Louise looked carefully at Ann, and wondered if what she said next would be going too far. "Do you want to tell me what happened between you and Mark Payne?"

Ann bit her lips together, then seemed to make a decision. "I was wondering when you'd ask. We're not on, well, good terms. It wasn't too long after his wife died in the accident. He came around and softened me up so I'd go out with him. It was fun for a while—we skied and hiked, and that part was good. But he does drink, and that's when things got impossible. So I told him I wanted to end our relationship."

"How long had you been dating?"

"Oh, six months. And, you know, sleeping together . . ." Her face turned red. "After I broke it off, he came over one night when I was all ready for bed and insisted on coming in. To 'talk.' I let him, not knowing how loaded he was. And then we had a terrible fight and . . ."

"He . . . forced you?"

Ann leaned forward, her lips trembling, but in the end she couldn't say the words. She only nodded.

"Oh, Ann!" Louise reached over and gripped her friend's hand. "Did you . . . what did you do?"

Ann pulled her hand away and sat back. After a moment she said, "It's what I didn't do. I didn't bring charges. I couldn't. There I was, recently promoted to senior land officer for Boulder Parks and Open Space—"

Her voice shook. "How could I bring charges against my lover, when he was the biggest builder in the county? The terrible thing is, I've always regretted it, even though I know it would have injured my career. I would have been that raging, illogical female who 'consented' for six months, and then changed her mind." Her breaths came heavy and uneven, her chest heaving.

"Ann, I'm so sorry," said Louise. "I shouldn't have brought it up. But I did it for a reason."

Her companion nodded, silent for a moment as she tried to regain her composure. Finally, she said, "I know why. You wonder if Mark Payne is a man who could kill in cold blood. Louise, I've never forgiven him. I *do* think he could. After what happened to me, I even wonder about that accident that killed his wife . . ."

"You mean, he could have set it up?"

"When he's drunk and high, he has this monster inside of him—and I think it's still there."

They fell silent as they turned back to their food. Louise realized there were now four strong suspects in the Porter family murders. Josef Reingold, Earl Tatum, Eddie Porter, and Mark Payne. A moment later, she acknowledged that she must add a fifth. Pete Fitzsimmons.

She smiled sadly at her companion. "You realize I won't be around when all this is finally cleared up. I leave the middle of next week."

Ann's face fell, as if she were going to cry. "I know. I'm going to miss you."

"I'll miss you, too. I'm off to my next stop on the West Coast, and then home to confront real life. Our older daughter, Martha, will be home from her latest internship, but just briefly. Then her college term begins. Bill will be back from his latest assignment—" Her brow furrowed as she thought of her unresolved problems with her husband.

The tawny eyes were examining her closely. "I'm having difficulties in my personal life, too."

"I'm sorry to hear that," replied Louise, in a voice with as little emotion as if Ann had just disclosed she had a rip in her jeans. She patted her lips with her napkin and reached for the check. She had known Ann had some kind of trouble in her marriage, but she had no desire to hear intimate details, any more than she would have shared such details with another woman herself. Furthermore, how did this woman know that she and Bill were having problems?

Ann said coolly, "We'll split that bill, okay? And don't you worry, Louise—I'm not about to dump more details of my sex life on you."

She had seen right through Louise and her up-tight Presbyterian background. Louise realized what a hypocrite she was, encouraging Ann to spill her guts to her—about everything but her marriage. *No sex talk, please: I'm a prude.* "Look, I didn't mean—"

Ann interrupted. "It's okay. Actually, it does have to do with sex—but it's strictly clinical. Luke wants me to quit work to undergo in vitro fertilization again."

There was relief in Louise's voice—this was indeed clinical, and wouldn't involve strange positions, practices, or partners. "Oh, I see. That's unfortunate. I've read that low sperm count is a problem in all the developed nations. But you—you don't want to try it—again?''

"No. You may not know how traumatic it is. You and Bill were lucky. You just went ahead and had children in your early twenties. But if you're like me, with the biological clock ticking, it's totally—''

"Unrelaxing?''

"More than that. It's tyrannical, trying to get pregnant. When to do it, when to hold off. Fertility pills. We've tried in vitro a couple of times. We could spend fifty thousand or more and still not have a baby. I have several friends who've failed at it, too.'' Ann's anguished eyes sought some answer in the ceiling. "Now he wants me to quit my job so I can make a total commitment to the process.'' Tears sprang to her eyes.

Louise knew well how Ann loved her job. "Oh, Ann.''

The waiter, observing that their conversation had a new lease on life, wandered over and refilled their water glasses. When he left, Ann continued. "There's more to it than just the anxiety,'' she said. "I think even childless people can have a purpose. I adore my job, and I know it helps thousands of people, including children. What I really hate is what happens to some of these women. Acquiring a baby is *everything* to them. They've labored so hard to come by a baby that it's as if the baby is a mirror of themselves—you should hear them.''

She looked around, to be sure that no one at a nearby table fit this category. "One in particular I know. She talks to her baby in this low voice, telling the child all these things that relate to the mother, as if she's inoculating that baby with her ideas. So that the little creature can grow up and be just as wonderful as the parent!''

"In other words, she's very proud of her new possession.''

"Exactly,'' said Ann, delighted that Louise seemed to

understand. "Now, my dad and mom were great. I remember them for what they *didn't* do. They held me on a loose rein, although, on the other hand, they wouldn't have let me crash and burn . . ."

Louise looked across the table into the intense, yellow-green eyes, and could not imagine Ann crashing and burning, for this woman was tough as nails. Beyond that, she didn't know Ann Evans any better than she knew the other principal players out here. Why was *Ann* totally free from suspicion? Louise sensed that, under the right conditions, the woman could be quite ruthless. And why not now? She had just lost an opportunity to provide the public with a wilderness park almost as large as the city of Boulder!

A quick scenario played through her mind: *Jimmy Porter is gunned down. Frustrated by the loss of her multimillion-dollar open space deal, senior land officer systematically kills, first, Jimmy's turncoat daughter Sally . . . next, the reckless son Eddie, and finally, Jimmy's wrong-thinking fiancée, Grace . . . leaving good son Frank to do the right thing.*

Louise pulled herself from her reverie, feeling cheap. The fact that she suspected Ann indicated the pathetic quality of her investigation. Unable to get the dirt on genuine suspects in the case, she'd reached out frantically to find a new one. Next she'd think Harriet Bingham was tottering around with a shotgun, offing people just for pleasure.

Ann was saying, "My parents stayed out of my business, and that's all I asked, even when I did things like climb the toughest rock face at Eldorado Springs. They were silent, and silence, to me, meant support. My dad, who's a lawyer, could have told me how disappointed he was when I went into environmental studies, but he kept mum."

She gave Louise a radiant smile. "And my career has worked out so well."

"But now, Luke wants the two of you to have your own child."

"Yes. I'm thirty-eight, and if we don't do it now, I'll be too old. What's worst of all about this is that I don't agree with the original premise that we must have children of our own to be a perfect family. We can adopt."

Louise admired Ann, but the woman certainly had odd taste in men. First, she got mixed up with the violence-prone Mark Payne. Then, she married a man who insisted on a child of *his* blood, just like a European monarch. Yet Luke couldn't be that intractable. After all, he did like gardening and flowers. He'd probably come around to the idea of adoption.

"What will you do?"

"I don't know. I don't know what more to say to him. He's off on a long business trip"—she blushed—"and I'm hoping maybe the reunion when he comes back will be the time something happens. Then I'll be off the hook. Otherwise . . ."

"I know what you mean. I have a problem I can't make up my mind about. It's just like yours."

"How could it possibly be?"

"Your argument is not about a baby. It's whether you or your spouse is going to determine your future."

Ann sighed. "You're right."

"It's the same with Bill and me. I love him about as much as a woman can." She pushed a strand of long chestnut hair back from her face and gave Ann a glance, wondering if she were revealing too much to a person she didn't know very well. Yet she could hardly stop in midstory. "It's about his taking a job overseas. If he does, my career suffers just when it's going so well. I don't know if I'd . . . ever feel quite the same way about him again."

"I wonder if there's a happy solution for either one of us," said Ann. Then, she tried to lighten the conversation.

"But it may not be so serious for you—you don't pay much attention to what your husband says, anyway."

The words crowded in on her. *You don't pay much attention to what your husband says* . . . "What do you mean by that?"

"The Porter murders. You've gone right ahead and investigated them, even though you told me Bill didn't want you to . . ."

Louise frowned, for what Ann said held at least a kernel of truth. She needed a rapprochement with Bill. Suddenly one came to mind. Maybe she could work out a deal with WTBA-TV to spend part of the time in the States, and the greater share with Bill in Vienna. Maybe her cohost John Batchelder could step up and shoulder half the program. That way, she would not have to give up her job or her marriage. Of course, Bill might not like this plan, either. . . .

These interior thoughts completely occupied her, until her companion brought her back to the present.

"Louise, are you all right? I didn't mean to upset you by anything I said. . . ."

Louise moved onto a safer topic. "What were we talking about—investigations? You know, this hasn't been much of an investigation, Ann, just visiting the ranch with you, doing a little searching through records . . . Maybe I should have done more."

"What did you do to help solve those other murders?"

"Not that much. Sometimes Bill and Janie and I did a little surveillance. Without physical evidence to check out—and the police have to do that, usually—you just kind of wait, and maybe nudge a little, and something happens."

"*Nudge*—and then something happens? And then what?"

"You can try to stay out of the way, but if you find

yourself deep into it, you have to use all your wits. It becomes a question of who survives the final battle.''

Ann shuddered. ''Good grief, Louise, that sounds awful! A final battle?''

''Believe me, Ann, nothing like that's going to happen. I'm talking about a couple of situations that got out of hand. What happened then could never happen again.''

As they left the Rattlesnake Grill, she and Ann made arrangements to go to the wake together. Ann would pick Louise up; that way, the land officer would have a chance to talk to the Porter brothers and do a little persuading. And Louise might be able to get in a private word with Frank Porter about using the ranch for location shooting.

Ann said, ''Maybe we can get Pete Fitzsimmons to drive with us tonight. You know, just to have a little moral support . . .''

''You mean, if we have a man around we'll be safer?'' twitted Louise.

The other woman smiled. ''Something like that. It's probably fallout from our luncheon conversation about final battles, and about Josef Reingold chasing you. I've never been exposed to the treacherous side of the man. I see him only in public settings.''

''It's true Pete seems safe. He's nice and big, and he carries a shotgun in his truck. But something bothers me.'' She looked at Ann, who was brushing her blond hair back in a gesture that reminded Louise of her teenage daughter Janie. She didn't want to disillusion this woman, any more than she would have wanted to disillusion her young daughter.

Yet she had to go ahead now, or Ann would wonder what she was concealing. ''It was strange that Pete had an empty gun rack the day we went up and found Jimmy Porter's body.''

"Oh, not strange," Ann replied. She didn't even recognize the suspicion in Louise's remark, so trusting was she of the beguiling Pete Fitzsimmons. "He probably had it home cleaning it—he cleans it all the time. He's an equipment freak who keeps stuff in tip-top condition. So he's always prepared if he needs to use it.''

Chapter 21

LOUISE KNEW WHAT SHE WAS
doing was a bit foolish, but she was
sure there would be plenty of people at
the Justice Center, even on a Saturday.
She came to see Earl Tatum, for he
now seemed as central to the Porter
murders as Mark Payne, Josef Reingold, Eddie Porter——or her buddy,
Pete. If he asked her why she had come
to see him, however, Louise intended
to say she was concerned about the
safety of Frank Porter——which she
was.

Once at the Justice Center, she

found she had guessed wrong about one thing. The place was deserted. She felt a moment of panic as she saw the sheriff's official white car in the parking lot near the entrance, its engine running. Then the man himself trotted out the double doors toward her. It was now too late to run away without looking foolish.

"Miz Eldridge," he said in a booming voice. He was out of uniform today, wearing jeans and an expensive-looking plaid shirt instead. And a big cowboy hat in black—a good choice for the man, she thought. The usual big dark sunglasses, so no one could read his soul through his eyes. Provided that he had one.

"Hi, Sheriff Tatum. I just dropped by . . ." She didn't like the look of him today and wished she'd left when she had the chance. "But I see you're leaving, so I'll go on my way."

His chin was elevated, as if he wanted to look down on the world more than even his six foot-two frame allowed. Or was this some vain mannerism that he hoped stretched the wrinkles out of his mid-sixties neck and made him more attractive to the opposite sex?

"No *way*, Miz Eldridge, I won't let ya go. Hop in, and whatever you want to say to me, you can say on the way ta Boulder Falls. Rescue's goin' on there and I gotta check it out."

She looked him over from behind her own dark shades. He was five inches taller than she, outweighed her by fifty pounds, and was not in top physical condition because he probably didn't exercise. The red veins in his face suggested he was a drinker. So, was she safe with this man? Not completely. But curiosity won the day.

"Okay, Sheriff." As she went to the passenger side of the vehicle, she again noted the scratches on the front fender area. What irony if Tatum himself had engineered these murders, bumping poor Sally Porter into the great beyond with his sheriff's cruiser. She settled herself in the seat and vainly tried to pull down the skirt of her rather short summer dress, uneasy now. Curiosity *did* kill the cat. . . .

"Now, fasten your seat belt," he admonished her, casting a free glance at her long legs. As they drove speedily up Boulder Canyon, they passed clusters of funky old green- and brown-painted houses, lodges, and restaurants that clung to the canyon edges close to town. Soon there were only granite cliffs, bereft of humans. She, and Tatum, alone on a canyon road, but with lots of tourist travelers. If all else failed, she could throw herself out of the car door into the path of some unsuspecting Texan.

He seemed amused at the concern in her face. "Relax, ma'am. All we're doin' is talkin', and you're the one that came to me. I got somethin' to say t'you, too. But first, look at those granite walls." The sheriff was feeling chatty. "Aren't they somethin'? I been travelin' up this canyon since I was a kid, and I always thought those rocks was like old men makin' faces at me. Didja know I was born in Boulder? Yep, I'm one of the natives."

Her heart lifted. This was the very opportunity she had sought, to get his story right from his own lips. "I bet you and your family own quite a bit of land around here."

"Quite a bit was in the family, y'know, handed down over the generations."

"And then you were in real estate, so you must have picked up a lot more during the eighties."

He waved a casual hand at her. "Oh, all through the years I've picked up properties. That's one reason"—he gave an unpleasant laugh—"I can afford both alimony and a new wife."

"Yes. I saw the picture. A nice young wife." Louise said the words amiably, as if pronouncing the judgment of the whole world.

"Yep, I married a young woman the second time around. I've accumulated some property. Doin' well. No law against havin' an elected sheriff do well in his personal affairs."

"Are you in business with Mark Payne?"

He didn't look at her, but she could tell the remark was not welcome. "Ma'am," he said, distancing himself about twenty miles in two seconds, "I'm in business with a lotta people. My business affairs are no concern of yours. I'm sure you'd find them much too complicated to understand."

"The little woman just can't understand, huh?" She couldn't resist the barb, but he didn't even consider it an insult, so low was his sensitivity.

"That's right," he said. "I truly find women do *not* understand land deals the way men do." Well, Louise thought, that was probably the end of his self-revelations.

Up ahead, the canyon road was clogged with sheriff's and fire department vehicles, and vans from two Denver television stations. "Here we are," he said, pulling into a spot across the road from the falls. They walked together across the busy highway. "Funny," he said, as he swept an arm out to encompass the canyon's rock walls, "you'd be surprised at how many people fall from here."

"And die?"

"Lotta the time, yeah," he said matter-of-factly, guiding her down the stone steps to the tourist outlook for the falls. "Some of the rocks are slipperier than a seal's coat. They hardly ever survive. If they do, they're vegetables, and their families take 'em back to Michigan or Indiana, or whatever flatland they come from, and have to tend 'em the rest of their lives in bed. This one here's a water rescue. Not promisin'."

On the narrow trail, they passed a stricken-looking blond woman with a sunburned face who was being shepherded up to the road along with her two young sun-burned children. With a jolt, Louise realized it was her husband who was churning about in that cold water.

"That's the family, with a victim advocate," verified the sheriff. They descended the stone steps to the tourist outlook.

"You mean," said Louise, "he fell into the falls?"

"Worse'n that. He got stuck *under* the falls. That rescue team is tryin' to find him." To Louise, it looked like a modern ballet, with men on the shore holding out ropes to support men in the water in wetsuits and red vests and helmets. They tumbled about with flailing, muscular arms, trying to win the victim from the grip of the ferocious river, as cameras onshore recorded the struggle.

"He went off up there," said Tatum, pointing out a high cliff over the falls.

As they watched, a deputy sheriff came up to Tatum to give him a report. It produced first a nod of affirmation from the sheriff, then a few crisp orders. Louise was impressed with his take-charge manner. All tourists had been shooed away during the rescue. Suddenly, the rescue workers' heads shot up in unison, and they were yelling excitedly to the people on the shore.

Louise stared, open-mouthed, as she saw a body come floundering toward them through the surging waters of North Boulder Creek, looking like a very large, dead fish. The men on the bank plunged into the water and intercepted it in front of where she and Tatum were standing. She wrapped her arms around herself in a reflexive gesture of self-protection.

Guiding the pale body to a quiet eddy behind a large rock, they called for the litter. After carefully strapping the victim to it, they immediately began CPR. Other rescue workers covered him with blankets.

"So there he is," muttered the sheriff. "Hope he has a

chance." The remaining members of the rescue team wearily maneuvered themselves out of the punishing stream, took off their flippers and their hats, and solemnly passed by on their way back to their vehicles, giving the sheriff a thumbs-up.

"Good job, men," said the sheriff. They acknowledged him with solemn nods. "They think he's gonna make it. That's what that means. But as I was sayin', people pay a high price for a little showin' off. Most folks aren't as lucky as that fellow."

Louise walked a little farther from the stream and settled herself down on a flat rock. Tatum crouched near her on his haunches and lit up an unfiltered cigarette. She rather expected a flask to appear from his back pocket, but guessed he wouldn't do that for fear the public might throw him out of office sooner than he would like.

He expelled some smoke, then gave her a big smile, as if to assure her of his friendly intentions. "Now, I'd like to use all this as sort of a parable, Miz Eldridge. We don't like tourists getting their brains jellied for just goin' some place they shouldn't have gone. And you"—he pointed a nicotine-stained finger at her as if it were a small pistol— "you're doin' the same kind of dangerous thing—goin' where you shouldn't."

"What exactly do you mean?"

His chin jutted out. "You're comin' too close ta things. I hear you were up at that ranch agin this mornin'."

"Now, why would you have heard about that so quickly?"

"I got my ways," said the sheriff. "Now, it's one thing to have locals killed by poachers, or whatever we finally determine happened up there to Jimmy Porter, and then Sally."

"Those were murders, Sheriff."

"Whoa." He sniffed in annoyance. "Murders? We're

thinkin' Sally's death was an accident—and we still have grounds for thinkin' Jimmy took that shotgun charge from a poacher—"

"If that's what happened, then why are you warning me to be careful?"

"Because I could be wrong, that's why. And that's how come I have a sheriff's car makin' an occasional round up there, t'see that Harriet Bingham's safe." So that explained the white four-by-four she'd seen up there this morning.

But Harriet was pretty much alone up at her ranch. What if Earl Tatum had an alternative scenario—not of protecting Harriet, but snuffing out her life? Since she'd already favored him by selling him prize sections of her land, maybe she had also given him some advantage in her will, such as first option to buy Bingham Ranch.

Louise tried to pull her mind back to what Tatum was saying. "We don't want *anyone* killed, including you. Remember—you already got shot at. What would people think if you—a TV personality—got murdered out here in Boulder County?"

"It would be embarrassing for you. It would attract a lot more publicity than the two murders on Porter Ranch, right?"

"You're exactly right. We're busy trying to close those two cases. Don't need any more."

"Did it ever occur to you that I had business up at Porter Ranch? I'm in business, Sheriff Tatum, just like you." She spread her hands. "You're in the law business. I'm in the media business. This morning, I had two business matters about location shoots. That's the only reason I was up there."

"Oh. I guess I see." His mouth twisted in a grimace, and he thought this over for a few seconds. "Even so, Miz Eldridge, can I ask you a favor?"

"Sure."

"Stay clear of Porter Ranch unless you're shootin' up there, or whatever you say your TV crew intends to do." He shook his head with its big black hat. "It's not safe, I'm tellin' ya."

Louise stared at the rushing falls. What did this man fear, and from whom? Was she interfering with some large plan to exterminate Porter family members who were sympathetic to the county—or was it something else, something to do with Harriet? Whatever it was, it wasn't recorded on paper, only in Tatum's head. And that, she thought, was exactly why these insiders were so annoying. Why, they could commit grand larceny every day with their land-deal shenanigans. Who would ever know? The word "cover-up" kept springing to her mind. She guessed that Sheriff Tatum would be the master at it, if anyone was.

"Sheriff," she said, "I won't be up at that ranch alone again. The whole crew, my producer, the sound man, the location chief, the cameraman, Pete Fitzsimmons, will all be there with me. Is that good enough for you?"

He looked relieved. " 'Atta girl."

"And then, I'm pullin' out of here Wednesday morning, and I must say that I'll be glad to be going."

Chapter 22

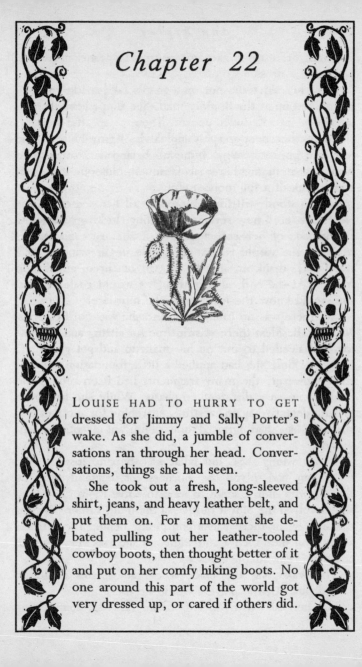

LOUISE HAD TO HURRY TO GET dressed for Jimmy and Sally Porter's wake. As she did, a jumble of conversations ran through her head. Conversations, things she had seen.

She took out a fresh, long-sleeved shirt, jeans, and heavy leather belt, and put them on. For a moment she debated pulling out her leather-tooled cowboy boots, then thought better of it and put on her comfy hiking boots. No one around this part of the world got very dressed up, or cared if others did.

And tonight, at this wake, was no time to prance around in heels and a dress.

Over her shirt she put on a man's fake suede vest she had picked up at the Boulder mall. She slipped Bill's cellular phone into its inner pocket. Then, as an afterthought, she stuck her pepper spray and Swiss Army knife in the opposite pocket. Bulgy, but well balanced. Not even as heavy as Steffi Corbin's silver squash-blossom necklace, and a heck of a lot more useful.

Louise stood still for a moment, all her senses on the alert. She felt a new revelation coming, lurking just below the surface of her consciousness. If she were Simenon's Maigret, she would retreat to a table in the window of a small café, drink an aperitif or two or three, and brood heavily. At the end, all her thoughts would coalesce, and she would know the identity of the murderer!

But there was no café handy, and she was not Inspector Maigret. Besides, there wasn't time for sitting and cogitating. She needed to put on her makeup and get going.

By the time she had applied a little foundation and lipstick, however, the many fragments had been refiled and resorted, with a different emphasis. While she had been playing detective again, zestfully searching for motives and suspects, she had ignored one significant avenue of approach.

It was a long shot, but what was there to lose?

No one had solved the murders yet, certainly not the sheriff, who didn't seem to *want* to solve them. The long shot involved the oldest motive of them all. Either that was the answer, or there was a conspiracy behind the ruthless killings on the ranch—and someone she was very fond of could be right in the thick of it.

The wake was the place where all of this could be sorted out. All the players would be there.

But her talk with Sheriff Tatum had left her feeling

defenseless. Tatum had warned her to stay out of the Porter matter. She was afraid that if she did get into trouble tonight, she couldn't count on the sheriff to help. Then she remembered there was help at hand. Sergeant Rafferty in Lyons.

She called the Lyons substation, and her mood lifted when a woman's voice answered. "Sheriff's Department, Sergeant Rafferty."

"This is Louise Eldridge. I need to talk to you about a touchy situation. I know Sheriff Tatum is your boss, but— is there any way you could help me?"

They talked about the wake that night, and Louise's suspicions. Sergeant Rafferty asked a few questions, pausing as if she were writing something down.

"Let me think about this for a minute." Louise waited in silence for what seemed like an eternity before the woman spoke again. Her words came out slowly and carefully. "I think it's only right that the sheriff's department be represented at the wake. So, why don't I plan to meet you there?"

"Thanks, Sergeant."

It was the lull between the lunch and dinner shifts. Louise knew she had to be quick, or Ann would be sitting in her driveway waiting. She leaned close to the screen door of the Gold Strike Café, and only then could she see Ruthie Dunn in her faded flowery cotton dress, sitting to one side of the kitchen, her stockinged feet propped up on a three-step folding ladder. Her glasses were resting in her lap and she was staring into space, while a blatting radio voice emanated from the restaurant proper. It was a conservative talk show that Ruthie disliked, but left on for her customers. The woman herself claimed to be a liberal Democrat, which Louise teased her about, saying it made her part of a vanishing species. The show had at least one good point. It had effectively put the old woman into a relaxing daydream.

"Ruthie," she called softly, not wanting to startle her. The white-curled head shook a little, as if the old woman were waking from sleep. She put on her glasses and peered at the door. "Louise, come in. No, better still, I'll come out and we'll sit in the afternoon cool."

She slipped on her tennis shoes and carefully tied them before joining Louise on the porch. The woman looked tired, and still faced a hectic evening shift of tourists and locals who depended on her for the evening's sustenance. Louise wondered how much longer she could keep up this very full-time job as restaurant owner, manager, and chief cook.

"Ooh," Ruthie said suddenly, in a tone that indicated a moral failure on her part, "I didn't get us anything to drink."

"I don't need it," Louise assured her, "unless you need something." She urged Ruthie to sit in the metal lawn chair. "I've come to bother you only for a minute—and, incidentally, thank you for putting in a good word for me with Sergeant Rafferty."

"Oh? Did you need the sergeant?"

"You never know when you might need the law to help you," Louise said, and let it go at that. "Ruthie, do you recall saying that you couldn't remember much about the past?"

"Yeah, and that's God's truth. I put bad things out of my mind."

"Ruthie, suppose I told you that your brain is like a computer, and that it stores millions of bits of information—sort of files them away. Things Sally Porter might have mentioned to you recently. Things from years ago."

Ruthie chuckled. "I've heard that, but it doesn't help me remember things I've forgotten."

"Let's assume that you have more stored in your head about Porter Ranch than you think," said Louise, and smiled engagingly; she was giving Ruthie her strongest sales pitch.

"Well, I guess I probably do, but how to get it out?"

"First of all, are you comfortable?"

"Sure am," said Ruthie, rocking a little in the old metal chair.

"Why don't you take off your glasses? You don't have to see, you just have to remember." She looked at the tennis shoes. "Want me to loosen your shoes?"

The woman chuckled. "You sure are a determined one, Louise—like a dog with a bone. Naw, my feet are just fine the way they are." But she took off the plastic-framed glasses and laid them in her lap, then put her hands on the arms of the chair and tipped her head back a little. "Next you'll be telling me to close my eyes."

"Good idea—close your eyes and relax, like a limp dish towel."

There was a smile on the old woman's lips, but she closed her eyes and looked completely at ease. "Now, just exactly what do you want me to *retrieve*?" she asked in her friendly twang. "What are these things filed under?"

❧

When she returned home, Louise paused only to put her purse in the house and note that she still had half an hour before Ann arrived before heading down the road toward the creek. Daisy the llama and Herb's horse stared at her curiously as she passed. "Hi, Daisy, hi, Horse," she called self-consciously. The horse whinnied.

No one answered Dr. Gary Rostov's bell, but Louise would not be thwarted so easily. She went around the low-slung green house to find him. He was sitting on an old bench with his half-glasses perched on his bald forehead, sipping something from a mug and staring into the fast-moving stream. He seemed oblivious to all around him, the cliff above which two eagles soared, looking for prey. The tumult of butterflies gliding back and forth with the skill of aviators. The congregation of clouds that would have sent artists rushing to their easels. In his lap was a pile of periodicals, all opened, as if he had sampled them all at the same time. Nearby was a weathered little table with a celadon teapot.

Dr. Rostov had not yet detected Louise's presence, and she was reluctant to break into this moment of unusual peace. Finally, she said, "I hate to interrupt you—it's so utterly peaceful here."

He turned slowly to observe her. He did not seem startled. "Hello," he called. "I would venture that you're the woman Herb told me about—the television personality." She recognized a Boston accent.

He stood up and stretched to his full height of more than six feet, extending a slim hand. They introduced themselves. "I was just sitting here, enjoying my licorice-root tea. Will you join me?"

She did, and with very little encouragement, Dr. Rostov gave her a thumbnail sketch of his background. How he had become interested in the field of post-traumatic stress thirty years ago, when the term was not even formulated, and his current research on survivor guilt.

"It's Greek to me, I must admit," said Louise. "All I have is a pop view of the subject, which could be quite inaccurate. But I have some candidates for post-traumatic stress disorder—actually, several of them. I wanted to test them on you—you know, give you a set of life circumstances, and ask you if these people could be suffering from this problem."

"And just what do they have to do with you, Louise—if I may call you Louise. Is it something work-related, or something to do with your family?"

"Neither, I'm afraid. Actually, it could have something to do with the Porter murders."

His eyes behind his glasses were confused, and he looked very much the absentminded professor. "I—I'm terribly sorry. I just flew back to Colorado after a six-week teaching stint in Los Angeles. Have there been *murders* around here? My word! And that name is faintly familiar. Why? Porter. I *know* I've missed something. But do tell me all the particulars, and then maybe I can give you some clue as to whether or not your candidates fit the profile of one who is suffering post-traumatic stress."

And so they sat by the river, dark and beautiful as it tumbled over the rock rubble from the nearby mountains, watching butterflies and talking about the somber side of human behavior.

A Butterfly's
View of Life

FOSSILS SHOW US BUTTERFLIES
have been around a lot longer than humans. We love them, as one of our
most cherished insects, and deplore the
fact that some species are disappearing
from the earth. Fortunately, home gardeners can help preserve these beauties
by maintaining "natural" yards, and
planting the right flowers in their gardens.

It is well to know the ways of butterflies, if we are to become garden
buddies. Some hibernate as adults,

tucked away in loose tree bark, in eaves, and in woodpiles. When temperatures rise, they unfold their wings and take flight. Species such as the sulphurs and the whites appear in early spring. The insect becomes more noticeable when the summer flowers open. This is the time to observe the gyrating dance of the female white butterfly as it tries to discourage unwanted suitors, and the brilliant blue of the spring azure and the tailed blue.

The monarch arrives from Mexico. The tiger swallowtails come, with their yellow-and-black-striped wings, along with an array of butterflies in many colors. They soon are joined by the monarch, probably the best known of the butterflies. It has closed up its winter home in Mexico, and is back north to enjoy the clovers and milkweed.

The activity of butterflies begins to wane at the end of July. They have had a full season of gathering nectar and pollinating plants. At season's end, some monarchs are easy to see, as they cling to flowers, storing energy for the return voyage south. As fall sets in, chrysalises and cocoons, many butterflies' winter headquarters, are set deftly into place under leaves, attached to branches, in evergreens, and in the crevices of trees.

The life cycle of the butterfly progresses quite simply. A female mates within a few days of emerging from her chrysalis. She then seeks a tender, succulent host plant on which to house her eggs. In a few days, a caterpillar emerges from each egg, with this state lasting from one to twelve weeks. As gardeners, we have encountered these voracious little creatures, and—think of it!—destroyed many a potential butterfly in the process. The surviving caterpillars build themselves a chrysalis (moths build a cocoon). Some butterflies emerge from the chrysalis in a week, while others take much longer.

Butterfly houses for the addicted. Today, there are butterfly houses and pavilions throughout the United States, with many people addicted to them as heavily as the Victorians, who housed them in atriums and conservatories. But there is an alternative: a butterfly garden of one's own.

We often get our best view of butterflies in the garden while they are basking. They need these sunbaths so they can warm up their muscles to fly. They also have a great need for water. We can fulfill both needs by providing them stony, shallow pools to hang around. A birdbath set with some larger stone or stones will do nicely. A salt block is welcome, since it helps male butterflies develop sperm.

Meadows are a favorite of butterflies, but few of us have turned our premises into a meadowland. Nevertheless, the more trees, shrubs, and tall grasses, the better. The objective is to have the butterfly spend its entire life in your garden.

Don't murder butterflies in the woodpile. If you want to be really kind to butterflies, provide them with a windbreak against the cruel north wind. Also, check to see that you aren't murdering butterflies before throwing a log on your winter fire: a log is a favorite spot for a chrysalis. It is even possible to relieve the butterfly's work by purchasing a hibernating box, where the guys can overwinter when they're in the adult stage. Put it out in the fall: That's when they need it.

When we plant a garden to attract butterflies, we must realize they see color through complex eyes. According to the experts, they prefer purple, pink, yellow, white, blue, and red, in that order. Try to have a steady supply of bloomers, which means constant

nectar for them. Tuck insect-deterring plants among the others as pest controls.

Flowers that butterflies like: Butterfly bush is the best attracter of these insects. An expert's list also includes: butterfly weed, coreopsis, hollyhock, lantana, New England aster, phlox, purple coneflower, verbena, violet, yarrow, cosmos, heliotrope, impatiens, marigold, Mexican sunflower, nasturtium, and zinnia.

Trees and grasses are important to butterflies for many reasons: the nectar of their flowers; their rotting fruit, a delicacy in the eyes of the comma, mourning cloak, and viceroy; their sap, favored by satyrs, admirals, and question marks; and their leaves, useful both for laying eggs, and later, for caterpillar lunches.

Find room in your garden for butterfly "hotels," or host plants. Among these are sweet fennel, caraway, and dill. The black swallowtail, a knockout of a butterfly, can't resist dill or caraway. Actually, you can't go wrong by popping herbs of all kinds into your garden, even less well-known ones such as burdock, nettle, hyssop, and vervain, for there's a butterfly that's a pushover for each one of them.

Find out what's endangered:

Prominent on the butterfly endangered list is the regal fritillary, with its extraordinary panels of gold and purple. Sightings have become fewer and fewer of this beauty in the wild, but it is being reintroduced to certain areas to reverse this trend. The Palos Verde blue was a beautiful bright-blue-colored variety, but now extinct. Still another special butterfly is the Schaus's swallowtail, once found in Florida, now only raised in captivity.

Gardeners should do what they can to help butterflies. The endangered Karner blue, for instance, uses only one host plant for its larvae: the blue wild lupine, *Lupinus perennis*. If we can establish this dry-soil prairie plant on our properties, we can help save this insect. The more natural and diverse our yards are, the more butterfly species will be attracted, to live and propagate, and create a new generation.

Chapter 23

EACH NERVE IN LOUISE'S BODY jangled, from the realization that tonight at this western wake she was bound to find out something conclusive about the Porter murders. Ann, sitting beside her, was a picture of relaxation and beauty in a pale blue print lawn dress. The younger woman was dressed more formally than usual, and she had even curled her hair a little. Louise realized this was all in the name of Ann's imminent reunion with Luke, who was due back at DIA on a late plane, rather than a reflection of the solemn occasion.

A lot was at stake in that reunion—probably as much as would be hanging on her own reunion with Bill tomorrow. "The whole megillah," she muttered.

"Excuse me?" said Ann.

"Oh, nothing," said Louise, "just thinking out loud."

She was suddenly glad they had decided not to invite Pete to ride with them.

The sign at the highway turn clued them in that they were coming to a very special house. Upscale rustic, she guessed one would call it, the sign had Frank's name burnt into the wood, and a string of little mountains carved across the top, painted pale purple with white tops. Frank Porter's house turned out to be a ranch house with two-story glass windows, rough wood beams, granite rock trim, and landscaped gardens. It was light years away from his father's simple, ancient ranch house, and from his brother Eddie's ramshackle log cabin a few miles down the road. This architectural model perched quietly on a rock cliff that overlooked the South St. Vrain River and the Porter Ranch acres of wild Colorado land.

The house was approached by way of a road steeper than most people would have been comfortable with, but which was no longer a challenge to Louise. She had insisted to Ann that they take her car, since she had found she liked mountain driving and would have few more opportunities beyond this weekend.

In deference to others who might be closer to the family than they were, they parked at a distance from the house and walked up. Louise, on her caffeine high, had to slow her pace for the laid-back Ann, strolling gracefully beside her.

The broad front porch had steps on either end. They went up the nearest set and knocked but no one answered the door, so they walked in, imagining Frank and Eddie to be busy with last-minute preparations. Before them was an imposing living room with tall peaked windows, beige carpeting, and spare, bleached oak furniture, but bereft of plants, pictures, and decorations.

Ann touched Louise's arm and said in a low voice, "It's a little bland, isn't it? Maybe Frank could use a decorator."

"Not even sister Sally's been here, with her Hummel figures or folksy touches."

Ann nodded and called, "Helloo!" There was no answer.

They wandered into the dining room, expecting Frank to walk out of the kitchen at any moment. On a big, glass-topped dining room table sat a now-departed caterer's work: trays of carefully arranged meat, cheese, vegetables, breads, and sweets.

"Oh, yum," said Louise. Set around the trays were the jewels of the culinary crown, the very best donated dishes from the kitchens of good cooks, offered in condolence for the Porter brothers' loss. Among them were a glazed cake with strawberry and kiwi on top, cheese-topped au gratin potatoes with a curl of steam coming out of the edge of the casserole lid, sprightly pasta salad with shrimps poking out, a rich yellow potato salad—the dish Grace Prangley had delivered to the brothers earlier—a small mountain of home-cooked sweet buns, and Eddie's own enchiladas.

People had already helped themselves. "Frank and Eddie must be around here somewhere," Louise said, "having an early snack before the crowd comes." She eyed the pastries. Suddenly, her stomach growled and she realized it had been six hours since her meager lunch. "Ann, let's eat *something* . . ." She reached for the plate, grabbing a sugar cookie and a frosted bun. She got frosting on her fingers and was about to lick it off when they heard an unearthly moan.

❧

Louise dropped the pastry and rushed through a swinging door into the big kitchen, leaving frosting fingerprints behind her in her haste. Beyond it was a large patio with a table and chairs, and lying on the wood deck was a writhing figure with another bent over it. Frank Porter, trying to regurgitate the poison that had entered his system, and Eddie kneeling beside him.

Louise assessed the situation in a glance and said, "Stay with them. I'll call an ambulance." She grabbed her cell phone and made the call, but was at a loss to give an address. "It's that big pointy-roofed house on top of a cliff on Route Seven. There's a steep gravel access road, and you can't miss it. It's marked by a new sign with mountains carved on it that says 'Porter.' "

She joined Ann, who knelt next to Eddie. Frank looked at them through slitted eyes and hoarsely whispered a single word: "Poison." He was fast losing consciousness. Eddie was crying inconsolably. "Frank—God, Frank, don't *leave* me!" he cried. Louise ran down a hall off the kitchen in search of the bedrooms, and finding one snatched several blankets from the big bed. She ran back to the porch to cover the afflicted man. Unfortunately, she had seen a poison victim before, writhing in her death throes, and the very least she had done then was what she was doing now. Keeping the victim warm.

Ann stood up, and the women looked at each other. "God, we have to do something," said the land officer. "He ate one of those foods . . ."

Louise knew what she had to do. "Will you be sure that no one eats anything more? And keep an eye on Eddie to see that he's all right. I have to go check on Harriet."

Before Ann could ask any more questions, Louise turned on her booted heel and ran back through the house. On the front porch, she came to another quick stop. Pulling up into the turnabout was Josef Reingold's gray Jaguar. A shudder ran through her. She instinctively shrank down behind the porch railing, where he could not see her. Reingold was here to get his contract signed.

Louise heard sirens coming up the canyon. Help was coming for Ann. Crouching down, she moved rapidly toward the stairs on the far end of the porch. Like a child playing capture the flag, she scuttled down just as Reingold came up the near side. She hovered behind a ponderosa pine and watched him go through the knock-on-the-door routine. There was a grim expression on his face, and the usual bulge of his handgun under his suit jacket.

Confident that he wasn't paying attention to her, Louise hurried down the driveway to her car, but paused with her hand on the door. She sensed she had left something undone. Reingold had disappeared inside now. She walked back up the hill to his gray car, expecting him to re-appear on the porch above her at any moment. He had left the car door unlocked, so she cautiously pulled it open. That's when she saw the shotgun on the car floor, clad loosely in a piece of new chamois. Next to it was a small suitcase.

Reingold was getting out of town—and in a hurry. Louise knew just how bold her next move was. Without thinking about it further, she crouched down, unclasped her Swiss Army knife from her belt, looked at the little menu of weapons, and plunged the sharp awl in the side of the nearest tire, then repeated the process on the other three. Each time she was rewarded with a steady hiss of released air. The expensive vehicle now sat there, looking cumbersome and useless in the slanting rays of the setting sun.

She opened the car door again and lifted out the loaded shotgun. She had slashed, after all; she might as well steal. For a moment she pointed the gun straight at Frank Porter's front door, just in case Reingold returned. He wouldn't like her stealing his armaments. Then she ran back down the hill to her car, knowing that at any moment the man could plug her in the back.

Placing the purloined gun on the seat, she drove down the steep driveway, then west on the highway until she reached the back road to Porter Ranch.

🙟

Louise made the trip to Harriet's in record time. She parked the car a little beyond the entrance to the gray house, turned off the ignition, and sat quietly in the driver's seat, taking a few deep breaths to compose herself. It was time to confront the demons of this mountain, and make sure everyone who lived here was safe.

Grabbing the borrowed shotgun on the outside chance she would need it, Louise climbed out of the car. She held the weapon flush against her leg, the way she had seen Herb do it. Coming to the break in the ponderosa pines, her gaze was attracted by the open horse stalls and the old shed that lined the edge of the yard. She wandered toward the stalls, which now held only a few horses, plus the rusting machinery that had replaced animals. It was reminiscent of Eddie's place, only much neater. She noticed the rusty tractor, a pickup from the 1920's, a more recent truck, a dark 1980's-vintage sedan, and finally, in the last stall, a car covered with a tarpaulin. Louise pulled up a corner of the cloth. It was an old Chevy covered pickup, four-wheel drive, white, with a floodlight attached to the front, and fresh scratches on the right front fender.

Just then, Harriet strode out of her house. The woman

looked powerful, her black hat tipped at a distinctive angle. There was no pioneer skirt today to impede her progress, but rather trim jeans tucked into boots that made it easy for her to move rapidly toward Louise at the same time she slowly raised her shotgun.

Chapter 24

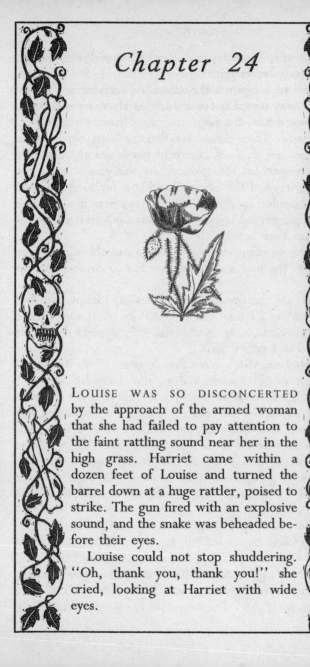

LOUISE WAS SO DISCONCERTED by the approach of the armed woman that she had failed to pay attention to the faint rattling sound near her in the high grass. Harriet came within a dozen feet of Louise and turned the barrel down at a huge rattler, poised to strike. The gun fired with an explosive sound, and the snake was beheaded before their eyes.

Louise could not stop shuddering. "Oh, thank you, thank you!" she cried, looking at Harriet with wide eyes.

In a flat voice, Harriet said, "Put the gun down, Louise, and put your hands up."

Louise had forgotten she was even carrying a gun, although it was aimed unconsciously in Harriet's direction. For a few seconds, the two women confronted each other, guns pointed. Then Louise recalled the speed with which Harriet got her shot off. She bent her knees and carefully placed the gun on the ground. As she gazed up at the woman in front of her, she realized how foolhardy she had been to blunder up here alone. Harriet was not the frail thing she purported to be. She was as dangerous a killer as Louise had ever faced.

And the woman seemed to sense exactly why Louise had come. She had no choice now but to come right out with it.

Slowly, she straightened up. "Harriet, I know you shot Jimmy Porter. I know you forced Sally off the back road with your white Chevy. And Frank is dying right now from your poisoned sweet buns."

The western voice was calm as ever. "You'll have to prove that an old woman like me did things like that."

Louise could picture a jury not believing her for one minute. All Harriet had to do was bring on the shakes, that vacant stare, and those flat, convincing words. Even Louise was halfway convinced she was wrong about the old lady.

"But when they bring an honest investigator into this case, they're going to be able to check the paint on your Chevy; it's old, so it will be easy to identify on Sally's fender."

"I don't think you'll be around to tell anyone that."

Louise knew it was foolish, but she couldn't back down until she knew the truth. "That isn't all I know, Harriet." She lowered her arms a little, since they were getting tired, but Harriet signaled with her gunbarrel that they should go up higher. Then she told the woman what she'd learned from Ruthie Dunn earlier that day. "Ruthie recalled the story that county folks gossiped about for years. It was about how you got pregnant, and shortly before the baby was born, Jimmy's wife died in that barn fire. Ruthie remembers Jimmy Porter coming down to the restaurant. You won't like this much, Harriet . . ."

She could see the old woman was engrossed in the story, as if she had waited decades for someone to recite it to her.

". . . but Jimmy wasn't true to you, or any woman, ever. He tried to take up with Ruthie then, but she wouldn't have him."

Louise took a half step forward. Harriet tightened her hand on the shotgun.

"You killed Bonnie Porter so you could be Jimmy's wife, didn't you?"

Harriet seemed to wake up from the trance into which Louise's narrative had taken her. "First I hit her on the head," she muttered. "Then I set the barn on fire. That took care of her. That meant I could be with Jimmy, and my little baby would have a father." She drew the gun to her face and pointed it right at Louise's head.

As sweat emanated from Louise's every pore, she could hear the click of the shell going into the chamber. An outright confession, and now she'll shoot me, Louise thought. Dear God, she hadn't had a chance to make her peace with Bill, and now she was going to die. She suddenly felt very weary. She thought about that snake, with its head blown off. This would be the fate of *her* head any moment now.

Desperately, she hurried on. "And then your baby was born, and he died quickly, isn't that right?"

The gun dropped slightly, and Louise's hopes rose. "How do you know that?" asked Harriet.

" 'Lack of oxygen,' " Louise continued. "That baby didn't die naturally, did it?"

Harriet's calm finally shattered, and a gentle rain of tears fell down the weathered cheeks. Louise watched with relief as she lowered the shotgun to her side. She wiped away the tears with a shaking hand.

Louise stepped forward, hands out, hoping the woman would give her the gun. Harriet instinctively stepped back. She could take the gun by force now, while Harriet was crying—or could she? The bony old hand on the stock was still firm, and despite her tears, the woman's eyes scared Louise.

They were within three feet of each other. "Why didn't your baby cry, Harriet? The gravestone reads *'Baby Henry, Who Could Not Cry.'* Was he deformed?"

Harriet nodded, the tears still falling. In a dull voice she said, "He just lay there and stared at me. His throat and breathing were so bad. I smothered him with a pillow when I found out he wasn't right. And since then"—her eyes raised up as if she were an ancient prophet—" *'The voice of the innocent's blood cries to me from the ground,'* just like the Bible tells me."

Louise remembered the dusty Bible on the library table, turned to what appeared to be Harriet's favorite passage. But it had not been her favorite passage at all. It was an eternal indictment for killing her own baby. Louise repressed a shudder.

Then Harriet began to spill out in a trembling voice, a story that sounded like a recurring nightmare: *"The baby is coming. It's insisting on being born, shoving apart the mother's bones. But something isn't right. The mother's body is in shock. The mother is dying. Can't breathe, losing too much blood. Then it's born—held up in the air, healthy, crying . . ."*

Harriet stared into the distance, and Louise realized that *she* was the baby, telling the story. *"Baby's eyes are staring at the mother in the bed. They're the eyes of a killer. And the father wailing at the bedside, cursing the crying infant . . . cursing her forever after . . ."*

"Oh, my God," said Louise.

"My father knew what I'd done," Harriet continued, her eyes focusing again. "He detested me for killing my mother, then he detested me for killing my babe. He detested me because Jimmy still wasn't about t' marry me."

This seemed to ignite Harriet's anger again. Before Louise could make a move to stop her, Harriet had stepped back and pointed the weapon straight at her forehead.

She put up her hands. "Wait, now, Harriet. Put the gun down—"

"Move back, Louise. Neither you nor anyone else can prove anything."

She had been a fool. Momentary compassion for an elderly woman who seemed on the verge of collapse! Louise carefully maneuvered herself backward, conscious that the rattler Harriet shot might not be the only one making its home in her yard.

"Harriet, those old deaths up on this ranch didn't cause you to kill Jimmy and Sally. It was that fresh insult, wasn't it?"

"What do you mean by that?"

"I saw evidence with my own eyes that Jimmy loved you—that half heart that's lying on your library table, and the other half I saw today on the Porter's kitchen shelf. Jimmy just told you—what, a week ago?—about Grace Prangley, right? Did he tell you on the day you killed him? He decided he would marry a younger woman, sell his ranch, and leave here forever."

The old eyes blazed briefly. "That man was my lover off 'n on for forty years. It was *Bonnie's* fault. He came to my bed when Bonnie wouldn't be a wife to him, she was so busy sorrowin' over the boy that died of lockjaw. He fathered my child. And he kept coming back to my bed. And now he was running off with another woman.''

"You mean, you and Jimmy still . . .''

Harriet sniffed contemptuously; the shotgun wavered but did not falter. "Huh, a lot you know 'bout things. Yes, Jimmy and I still were lovers. And that's enough talk. You're standing out here like a sore thumb—get goin' to the backyard.''

Louise slowly walked down the row of sheds toward the backyard, still talking as she went. "It seems to me," she said in a casual voice, "that killing Jimmy was a crime of passion. But why kill Sally?'' She took a chance and turned to look at the woman, who had slowed and was staring at the shrouded white truck under the rusted tin roof.

"That Sally, she *would* be that stubborn. Just like her dad, in wantin' to sell the ranch. And she was a scairdy-cat driver. It only took a little push to get her over the edge of that cliff.''

The woman took one hand off the gun and wiped her brow with the back of her hand—or was she crying? It was tears, Louise thought, and Harriet's head trembled a little as she cried. "I was sorry about Sally, real sorry. I weep over her every night, along with Baby Henry. But the bad people just keep comin' and comin' . . . why, today that woman drove up here, and I know, she was only tryin' to boss those boys around.'' Louise had sensed how Harriet resented Grace Prangley invading her mountain neighborhood. "But there'll be no more Frank or Eddie to boss around.''

Harriet sighed and nodded her head, as if poisoning the boys had been the only reasonable thing to do. The old woman came right up to Louise and prodded her forward. "You're too clever by half. You remind me of Jimmy's wife, Bonnie. Get goin' and stop trying' to distract me.''

Louise didn't need to be told twice. She stumbled along the rocky outcropping, the image of Eddie bending over his brother's body fresh in her mind. Suddenly another memory of Eddie crowded in—Eddie picking up dinner at the Gold Strike Café, Ruthie Dunn offering him a piece of her marvelous pie—and she realized Harriet didn't know the truth. Maybe there was still a chance to get through to this woman. "So you poisoned Frank. Such a nice guy, Frank. But Eddie doesn't eat sweets. He's just fine, and he's still going to sell the ranch."

Harriet let out a wild howl of—rage? Frustration? Then she seemed to calm herself. "It don't matter. With those others gone, Eddie will listen to me. He's a good boy, Eddie is. He's just like his father used to be . . ."

Louise looked at the woman curiously. Like his father used to be before he threatened to run off with a new wife? No, there was no getting through to Harriet. Back to stalling for time. "You're the one who shot me out at that farm, weren't you?"

"Well, I missed. I drove right out onto that bluff and watched you while you stumbled around in that field like someone who'd never set foot on a farm before in her life. Knew you from your hat, even at a distance. Knew you were a nosy one that would figure things out. Just like that nephew of mine, Mark, only he's scared of me, so he minded his tongue. The worst one of all was that Josef Reingold."

Louise tossed the words over her shoulder. "You know, Harriet, I thought Mark Payne or Josef Reingold killed the Porters for their land."

"I right did them a favor, didn't I?" the old woman said. "Them and Earl Tatum, who's thick as thieves with Mark. Reingold kept pokin' around up here." Her voice rose querulously. "But I'll show him. I'm going to kill *him* next time he sets foot up here."

As they reached the end of the enormous back yard, Louise realized what was in store for her. The land dropped off at the steep sandstone cliff which rimmed both Harriet's and the Porter ranches.

"My God!" Louise cried, and rage overcame her. "Do you think you're going to run me off that cliff, like a buffalo?" Caution cast aside, she dived toward Harriet. But amazingly the woman eluded the attack, leaving Louise to stumble to the ground, her palms stopping a complete fall onto the rugged terrain. This gave Harriet time to reposition her shotgun. "Stop," she ordered.

But Louise was not about to stop. She scrabbled to her feet and ran as fast as she could over the stony yard, dodging and crouching to make herself a smaller target. A charge of buckshot missed her, but by that time she had reached the back corner of the house. She raced along its clapboard perimeter and collided with an ancient pitchfork, which crashed painfully against her shins. Gasping, she rounded the house and flew toward the waiting shelter of the thick band of ponderosas at the front of the property. But even they were no defense. Another burst of shot tore a hole through the bark of one of the pines, and she could feel a tingling sensation in her upper arm. Whimpering quietly now, Louise crouched lower, still moving. If she could make it to her car, she might live! There it was, shiny red and welcoming. She slipped the ignition key out of her jeans pocket, and sprinted toward it.

Just Like Plants, Detectives Must Show Their Mettle: Perennials That Know How to Survive

MANY A GARDEN HAS BEEN NE-glected, and is waiting for a good gar-dener to return and bring it back to life. If you resurrected a garden after years of neglect, what would you find still surviving? Certainly not the del-phiniums, and probably not the hybrid teas, or the verbascum.

A recent garden restoration near Washington, D.C., involved removing masses of seven-foot pokeweed and yards of ropy poison ivy. Underneath this mass of intrusive weeds were the

ultimate survivors: peonies, generic orange daylilies, phlox, rudbeckia, hollyhocks, and old shrub roses. Today, regenerated with the digging-in of rich compost, all these plants are again flourishing without competition from bully weeds.

Design a garden for survivability. If you're working too hard at your job, or have a family and little time to be in the yard, designing your garden for its survivability makes sense. You have to measure the amount of neglect you will give your plants—or, conversely, the time you can afford to give them. Even a modicum of care will enable you to lengthen that "ultimate survivor" list by many plants.

First, check out plants with gardeners in your area. Others that are good and dependable are asters—seas of blue, pink, or fuchsia blooms; hybrid lilies in brilliant and pale hues, sometimes spotted, sometimes striped; *Polygonum bistorta* hybrids, with their bright, poky blossoms; plume poppies, tall, with many-lobed leaves and frilly peach flower bunches; heleniums; joe-pye weed; veronicas, with their worthwhile icicle-shaped flowers; frilly-flowered thalictrums; sedums, with their geometric excellence; *Anemone japonica,* with tall pink or white blossoms waving in the wind, but don't expose it to too much sun; clematis, in many hues and flower sizes; shasta daisies; coneflowers, with their rose daisy look; ligularias, bringing height and bright yellow into the late summer garden; nepetas, providing a mass of bright blue, hardy flower spikes; and Oriental poppies. Iris are beautiful, but short-bloomed and rampant spreaders.

A xeriscape combination. The gardener with low-water requirements will be captivated by this combination of long-blooming, late-summer perennials: clumps of pale yellow hollyhocks as a centerpiece, combined with a series of mostly yellow flowering plants, and gray foliage accents. *Artemisia frigida* is in the foreground, with lacy gray foliage and tiny, yellow flowers. *Baptisia tinctoria* is a three- or four-foot-high clump standing alongside the hollyhocks, with ovate leaves and yellow pealike flowers. *Penstemon perfoliatus,* a forty-inch-high serrated-leaf species with soft lilac flowers, adds another color to the planting picture. The cup plant, *Silphium perfoliatum,* with its three-inch yellow flower heads, and coarse, whorled leaves that catch water, soars above the other plants. The last part of the picture is a repeat

of the gray tones, in the three-foot-tall prairie sage, *Artemisia ludoviciana*.

Tuck a few evergreens into the mix. To make the garden even easier and more permanent, intersperse these "tough" perennials with slow-growing evergreens and specimen bushes—variegated leaves are good here—that will look attractive even when the perennials have passed their prime. And don't forget yuccas, for they, plus a few clumps of the slower-spreading Siberian or Japanese iris, will provide the garden with needed vertical lines.

The peony needs a special word. It is one plant that is as good in flower as it is afterwards. It is tough, and its beautiful foliage remains intact through the hardest northern frost. Two exceptional variations of the plant are the delicate-leaved dwarf variety with red flowers; and the tree peony, about which too much cannot be said. It has flowers like pale colored tissue paper, that are nevertheless strong and fairly long-lasting. Its cut foliage rises out of the garden on three- or four-foot stems, to make any garden look as if Gertrude Jekyll had been there, planning things. Delicate, beautiful—but also very tough.

Chapter 25

LOUISE SHOVED THE KEY IN THE ignition and turned it. Silence greeted her, and she felt a moment of utter panic.

What kind of horrible luck was this? Her eye was caught by something— someone—outside the car. Standing there in the fading light was Sheriff Earl Tatum, stomach protruding insolently, but otherwise looking neat as a bandbox in a fresh outfit and his trademark black hat. He was holding a pistol in his hand, which he didn't even

bother to aim at her. This was the final ignominy. He
didn't even respect her ability to save herself.

"*Miz* Eldridge." It was that same slightly sneering
voice, one she had hoped she never had to hear again.
"Went to Frank Porter's, and figured out where you must
have gone. I thought I told you it wasn't safe to come up
here."

Louise bowed her head onto the steering wheel; she
could hear the violent thumping of her overworked heart.
If the man wanted to shoot her, let him. She was too tired
to care.

Then a new wave of strength slowly moved through her,
and she raised her head. "The thing about you, Sheriff, is
that you can't afford to let people know you've covered up
at least four murders up here on Porter Ranch. It would
send you to jail for life. Manipulating a crazy old woman,
who has handily killed the people in the way of your big
land deals. Why, I can even believe you put the idea in her
head. What kind of a lawman are you? How many people
do you blackmail, besides her?"

"Whoa, there," he protested.

She leaned out the window and kept up her diatribe.
"And you've practically stolen her most valuable land—"

He was shuffling anxiously from foot to foot, but the
gun was still steady in his hand. "She *sold* me that land,
damn it!"

"For a pittance, I'll bet," retorted Louise. "And in
return, you kept her dark secrets. How does it feel to
become rich by bilking a sick woman?"

He tried to laugh. "Harriet, sick? You just don't
know—"

"And now *this*," she scolded, giving the steering wheel
a good whack with the palm of her hand. She decided it
was time to stage a hysterical scene, which would fit right
into this man's stereotypical view of women. "What did

you do, take off my distributor cap?'' She opened the car door, jumped out, and shoved him in the stomach so that he stumbled back a step.

The son of a bitch was laughing. "This car don't have a distributor cap, dimwit."

She poked a finger in his chest and screamed, "Don't you know this is a rental car and I am responsible? Do you know they charge for this kind of thing? So what the hell *did* you do to it?"

"Are you crazy?" he snarled, and looked around to see who might be listening as his good-old-boy dignity melted in the face of her temper. "What do you care about a few loose wires? This car's goin' t' be your casket, so don't worry about it, or anything else. We're going t' arrange a little accident."

Her hands were on her hips. "Who, you and Harriet?"

Then, out of the darkness came what seemed like an apparition—a figure on horseback with a dark hat, galloping up the road toward them. Harriet, shotgun at the ready, like an avenging angel. This was her chance! Louise bolted for the woods, reached the stony yard, then ran to the side of Harriet's house and grabbed the old pitchfork. While she dodged behind the back corner of the house, she could hear the sheriff's noisy approach. He rushed by, breathing roughly. In the distance, she heard horse's hooves as Harriet searched for her on the other side of the yard.

The sheriff stopped and bellowed at Harriet, who hardly could have heard him over the horse's hoofbeats. Nor could he hear Louise sneaking up behind him. "Jesus, you old crow, did you have to get us fouled up like this? You've blown it!"

Then he did hear something and turned around, gun drawn. He only had time to say "Whoa!" before she slammed the fork down against his head, and he tripped backward as his gun discharged.

The sound brought Harriet at a gallop. Tatum appeared to be unconscious. Quickly, Louise stooped down and took the gun from the ground next to his body. It was heavy in her hand. Harriet was not going to kill again, not if she could help it.

Louise shouted, "I have you now, Harriet." She felt like a gunslinger in a bad western. But the tremble in her voice belied her tough words.

Harriet stopped her horse. Louise saw with wonder that she sat as tall in her saddle as the day she had first met her. What was keeping this woman going? It must be adrenaline alone, for Louise believed Harriet was truly very frail. It was adrenaline or the powerful urge to destroy her latest enemy—Louise.

Then the woman laughed, and Louise's courage failed. She would not shoot Harriet. Instead, she would be shot dead herself. In terror, she made a run around Harriet's flank toward the edge of the yard. A grave mistake. Louise was trapped on the outside, with Harriet holding the inside position. To the left was the long car shed. On the right were those snaggly barbed-wire fences guarding the family graveyards. Otherwise, she might have used the tombstones of dear Baby Henry or the other dead mountainfolk to deflect Harriet's shots.

The only way out was down—down the rock cliff. Louise shoved Tatum's pistol into the waistband of her jeans. She counted on the heavy leather belt to hold it in place, and hoped it didn't fire and shoot off any of her body parts. The image of Ann Evans climbing her backyard cliff fresh in her mind, Louise swung her legs over the caprock and began to climb down. It only took a moment for her to learn why Ann called this "trash" rock, as she dislodged stones with each clumsy move she made. Terror began to grip her as the rock seemed to dissolve under her feet, and the heavy gun weighed down her backside, pulling her weight perilously away from the safety of the rock face.

Panicking, she saved herself by thrusting either hand into a fissure in the rock, as if her limbs were pitons. Her feet had no purchase, hanging in the air fifty feet above solid ground. Death by falling. It would be just another story of a flatlander who had ventured too boldly—and a handy solution for the woman who was trying to kill her.

She closed her eyes and leaned her forehead against the Permian sandstone. It was cool and comforting. To think this stone had stood in this place for almost three hundred million years, silent witness to the affairs of mankind. Louise allowed herself to slide down another inch or two, and gratefully found rock on which to place her feet. Her left arm hurt again, but she couldn't afford to stop and investigate.

In the gathering darkness, Louise had to go by the feel as well as the look of the rock; her hands searched and found the cracks, knobs, and ridges she needed to make her journey. She had descended almost fifteen feet when Harriet discovered where she had gone. She announced her find with a raucous laugh. "So there y'are. This is gonna be about as easy as shootin' fish in a barrel." The words dropped down on Louise like shotgun pellets. Helpless now, she stared upward as the old woman brought the gun to her shoulder and pointed it straight at her.

Louise let go. Her fingers and booted feet scuttled over the outward-bellied cliff as she fell. It worked—Harriet was too stunned to shoot. But now Louise was falling to her death. To herself, she whispered Ann's dictum: *"Dig the tiny nodules of the rock into the sole of your boot . . ."*

Her heart rejoiced when her feet were brought up hard against a narrow, flat surface. Almost directly in front of

her was a small mine opening. She pitched forward into it,
just as a load of shot splattered on the rock ledge behind
her.

The cave was actually a dark little room where some
hopeful miner had once scooped out rock to a depth of
about ten feet, then found it worthless and quit digging.
Louise ran her hands carefully over the rough walls, but
there was no magic passage to lead her away from the
danger outside. And yet she blessed that miner for his
efforts, for this little gouge in the rock had saved her life.
She returned to the entrance and stood for several moments in complete silence, gazing out at the overlaid sil-
houettes of distant mountains fading in the dusk. She
listened for a sound, any sound. Crazy laughter, shots,
horse's hooves.

What had happened to Sergeant Rafferty? She longed to
hear police sirens, but she was beginning to doubt she ever
would. Carefully, she stuck her head out of the mine and
looked up. There was no one there. Then she peered
down. Below her was a rubbly wall of trash rock. She shut
her eyes momentarily, to blot out the reality of the problem. She would never make it down that treacherous pile
of sandstone.

Suddenly, it occurred to her that she wasn't the first
one to be stuck on this cliff. How on earth had the miner
gotten down? She stuck her head out of the opening and
looked to her right, sobbing in relief. A century or so ago,
that hardscrabble dreamer had carved a narrow, gently
ascending path across the cliff face to carry his ore back up
to the top. It was badly eroded now, but still passable. She
had not seen it at first, because of the bulge in the cliff
wall. Now she traversed it slowly, hugging the rock so
closely that it scratched her face. Relief swept over her as
she realized she might make it after all.

The protruding rock at body level was an encumbrance,

but a defense against more shots from above. Every few feet, she stopped to listen, and was heartened by the silence. Either Harriet was holding her fire until Louise reached the top, or else she had given up the fight.

Louise realized she was going to end up far from her point of origin, somewhere on the Porter Ranch property. When she was near the top, she raised her head cautiously over the caprock, almost able to feel a shot whining her way. When she saw no one, she scrambled onto solid ground and lay there for a minute to regain her breath. She was in the cemetery, surrounded by ghostly white gravestones gleaming at her in the darkening twilight. Nearby were mounds of dirt encircling the freshly-dug graves that soon would receive the bodies of the rancher and his daughter.

The sight might have frightened her, but did not. Instead, it put fire in her heart. For she was about to bring Harriet to justice for killing two of the innocents lying beneath those headstones, and the two more soon to join them.

Louise withdrew the pistol from her waistband and held it in front of her. After what she had been through, the weapon no longer seemed formidable or even heavy. Nor did it seem out of the question to shoot Harriet.

It took a moment for her eyes to adjust to the light and shadows. She clambered over the fence that bounded the Porter Ranch and walked cautiously onto Harriet's property, squinting to make out the forms of the trees and the ranch house. With a jolt, she picked out a large, motionless object in the center of the backyard. It was Harriet, still sitting on her horse. Because of the falling darkness, Louise could not see her face, but there was still the pioneer-woman look in her dark silhouette—a pioneer woman with a slumped, weary back and bent head. Fleetingly, Louise was reminded of a Remington statue of a tired cowboy in the saddle.

"Harriet," said Louise in a resigned voice, "I'm not frightened of you any more. I'll shoot you if you damned well don't get down off that horse."

The shape did not move. "Get *down*, Harriet," she insisted loudly, *"right now!"*

Harriet still did not obey. Instead, there was the leathery sound of the old woman's boots kicking her horse, and the silhouette suddenly whirled about and moved past Louise. Straight toward the cliff.

"Stop!" Louise yelled, and ran after her. Though Harriet urged the beast forward with rapid kicks to its flanks, the horse balked. Harriet sailed off and over the sandstone cliff, down into the valley below.

The horse danced on the edge of the cliff, snorting and confused. What did its rider want from it next? Louise stared over the edge of the precipice. She could barely make out the figure lying far below. She watched it for a few minutes to be quite sure Harriet did not get up, and finally lowered her gun.

Chapter 26

LOUISE WAS TOO TIRED TO move. After a time, she heard the sirens. Then a car door slammed. Pete and Ann were calling to her from the front of the ranch house, but she couldn't seem to call back. Eventually they followed the sound of the whinnying horse to Harriet's backyard. They found Louise standing at the edge of the cliff, looking stunned.

"Ann," she said, "friction saved me. I pressed the tiny nodules of rock into the soles of my boots." And then she sank to the ground in a faint.

❧

Louise woke Sunday morning feeling euphoric and light-hearted. She put on simple, loose clothing—a big rough shirt to cover her bandaged arm, comfortable Japanese farmer pants, and sandals, and she wandered from room to room in the empty house, appreciating the way the sun painted patterns on the furniture and floor, savoring the look and even the dry, clean smell of her borrowed western home. It was delightful to be alive.

Before she had a chance to eat, her neighbors, Dr. Rostov and Herb, called on her, the farmer bearing a plate of his wife's cookies. He had been concerned when cars and trucks kept driving up to her place in the early morning hours, "especially since I knew you'd had a spotta trouble." She explained that two of the cars had been Pete and Ann in separate vehicles, for her two friends had gone to the hospital with her and then accompanied her home. Sheriff Tatum had also been at the hospital, but he would recover from his head injury, and leave under a much different escort. Louise had also confessed her vandalism and theft to Sergeant Rafferty, who'd pardoned her after retrieving Reingold's gun from Harriet's yard.

After discovering that she was all right, Herb left, still urging Louise to borrow one of his shotguns for her last days in Boulder County. Gary Rostov stayed to talk, and willingly accepted her offer of tea.

Listening to Louise recap last night's events, he nodded vigorously. In a careful, professorial way, as if everything were now clear to him, he said, "It seems quite likely that Harriet Bingham was experiencing survivor guilt. And survivor guilt can lead to madness of sorts—an unconscious madness. The woman undoubtedly functioned day to day, and thought of herself as quite sane, and so did others. Yet, when your existence causes the death of someone else, you feel tremendous guilt. Harriet may have believed that she killed her own mother—and didn't her father's dislike of her affirm that? Kill or be killed became her road to survival.''

Louise remembered Harriet's terrible, nightmarish story of the killer baby being born, and shuddered. She said, ''Harriet couldn't have understood what was happening to her.''

''I'm certain neither parent nor child understood,'' he said. ''That generation didn't understand birth trauma. There was no help for that father or that little girl.''

''And that's why it made sense to Harriet to kill Bonnie Porter. Bonnie stood in the way of Harriet's plan to get Jimmy Porter to marry her and be a father to her child.''

He nodded again. ''Quite likely.'' This man never gave a simple ''yes'' to any question. Now, in a classic, absent-minded professor gesture, he scratched his head. ''Now, refresh my memory, Louise—did you say that she also killed her own baby?''

''Oh, yes. She told me straight out that she smothered the child with a pillow.''

''Ah,'' said the professor, and his eyes lit up over his half-glasses, as if he'd discovered a new wrinkle in the case. ''Harriet viewed this as a *choice* to be made. In her troubled mind, if both she and the baby were in trouble, only one could survive. That, then, was a reverse position. Not mother dying and baby living, but just the opposite. Then, recently, she was threatened again. And doesn't it make sense that when Jimmy Porter told her he was abandoning her, that she would act?''

''Yes. Then Sally Porter . . .''

''Ah, Sally. Another cherished neighbor was leaving her.''

''She was a very dangerous woman, Dr. Rostov.''

''Indeed she was. It is important to understand that

survivor guilt is one of the most lethal products of our society. And it has been with us since the dawn of time. It's rampant in war zones.''

Although wilting by the minute, Louise was fascinated with the unraveling of Harriet's soul.

"Now, Louise," he said, "what of that other case you mentioned—the man who is violent with women, and who actually may have killed his ex-wife? I wonder if this man, too, isn't suffering from the unresolved issues that surround trauma. From the story you told me of last night's events, I understand he turned out *not* to be involved in these murders?"

"I don't know for sure," she said. "Sheriff Tatum could still implicate him. Mark was close to his great-aunt Harriet, because he wanted her land. But these murders may have been a dirty secret just between her and the sheriff."

Rostov looked at his watch and said, "I must go, Louise. I hope someone is coming soon to take care of you—and that you can relieve yourself of the trauma of this experience."

She smiled faintly, thinking of other wounds she had suffered, and how she had worked through the trauma by spilling it all out to Bill, sometimes not in a day, but over weeks. As she bid the professor good-bye, she wondered when her husband would finally show up. She hoped the criminals he had been chasing were not still loose upon the world.

※

Laboriously, Louise pushed down the trash and tied the white plastic bag tightly. She had taken it as far as the carport when the phone rang. She left the bag where it was and hurried inside to answer it. It was Ann Evans, calling to find out how she was.

"I'm doing all right," Louise said, so her friend wouldn't worry. Actually, she was ready to take one of the pain pills in her pants pocket and crawl into bed. Then Ann inadvertently gave her a clue as to Bill's whereabouts. It set Louise's heart pounding faster. She told her about big doings south of Boulder late last night. "There were so many police cars and army trucks, you could hardly believe it. *Something* was up. I told Luke it must have involved Stony Flats, but of course there was nothing on the news or in the paper this morning."

Louise's heartbeat quickened. Bill and his team. She wondered if they had caught the hijackers in the act, according to plan. It sounded as if they had, and she wondered if Tom Spangler was part of the scheme. From being relaxed, she now felt all her nerves tingle. Too bad she couldn't share this with Ann. So she changed the subject, finding out that Frank Porter was doing well at Boulder Community and was expected to get out today. And the police had taken in all of Harriet's canisters, as well as the buns, for testing. One canister held a substance they suspected was arsenic.

"Great," said Louise. "There's one detail, Ann. Thanks for all you and Pete did last night. And, uh, I wondered what happened to that bag in the trunk of my car . . ."

"The manure, you mean." Ann laughed. "You were out of it last night when you got home. But you mumbled about something smelling terrible in your car. It didn't take long to discover that bag—I can't believe I didn't smell it when we drove to the wake. Anyway, I just dumped it in your garden. It's good compost. It was in a bag from the lumberyard, so it was obvious—well let's just say I took the liberty of giving Eddie your number. He wants to call you. He feels bad about his little trick. And he has some news—I'll let *him* tell you."

"Okay. Now, to more important things. How is Luke?"

"He's wonderful," said Ann, in a voice guaranteed to patch up any divisions between the couple. Maybe Louise could take a cue from the younger woman. Though tough as nails on principle, Ann had great faith in the survivability of her marriage. The two women promised they would stay in touch with each other. When she hung up, Louise felt a strange sense of loss and wondered if she would ever see Ann again.

Then she propped herself up in the chair and waited for Eddie's call. It was worth waiting for.

"Uh, about the horsesh—, uh, manure . . ." mumbled Eddie, "I'm awful sorry. It was a kid's trick, but I tell ya, I've grown up since last night, Louise. Hell, I've lived a whole lifetime, seein' Frank on the floor there, maybe dyin' and leavin' me with absolutely no family."

"But it's terrific that he's going to be all right."

"Yeah—Ann called ya, right? Well, last night I told her I was gonna swing this decision about the ranch right back ta where it was before my dad passed on."

Louise smiled to herself. "So you'll go along with Frank on the decision to have the ranch become open space."

"I sure will. The two of us have the controllin' votes, so t' speak, and we'll get Grace won over. I screw up everythin' that has anything ta do with money, but I realize money wouldn't't'a mattered if Frank had died. So, that's all I had t'say, Louise. Now, d'ya think you'll show up at Ruthie's café before you leave for the East?"

"My husband's due back, Eddie, and I bet we'll be at Ruthie's Monday night, for dinner."

"Then I'll make it a point ta be there, and—we'll hit it off better this time, right?"

"Sure, Eddie."

Louise was completely out when Bill phoned. Fighting dizziness, she said, "I'm so glad to hear from you, darling. Is everything all right?"

His voice was tired and strained, and he spoke in his usual shorthand, not bothering to impress her by using the good-natured Texas lingo he'd picked up this past week. "The project was successful. We still have to make contact with one man, though." His way of saying one of the principals escaped their net.

"Bill, I met someone here who could be involved—"

She could hear someone at his end calling him. "Honey," he interrupted, "as long as you're safe, let's talk about that later. We've got a briefing right now. I'll call again, and I'll be there soon. I can't wait to see you."

She had been too punchy—too slow on the draw—to protest. And then he had rung off. Well, she was probably just being paranoid anyway.

She struggled to a sitting position and looked around the sunny living room, feeling dizzy. She got to her feet and slowly went out through the wide-open porch doors to get some air. Her wounded arm now felt as if it were a gigantic log. As she stood, admiring the weeding job she had done in the yard, she heard excited chattering. A family of chipmunks was threshing in crunchy leaves from an early leaf fall off a cottonwood tree. She saw that the door to the old greenhouse was ajar; the little creatures were debating whether or not to go in. She went to close it, then wondered why it was open in the first place. Pulling it all the way open, she peeked in and gasped.

Chapter 27

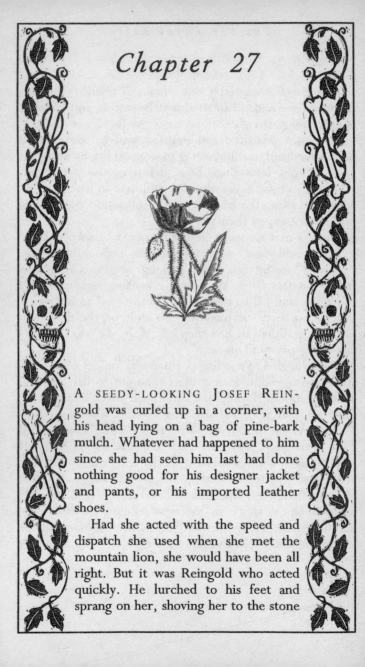

A SEEDY-LOOKING JOSEF REIN-
gold was curled up in a corner, with
his head lying on a bag of pine-bark
mulch. Whatever had happened to him
since she had seen him last had done
nothing good for his designer jacket
and pants, or his imported leather
shoes.

Had she acted with the speed and
dispatch she used when she met the
mountain lion, she would have been all
right. But it was Reingold who acted
quickly. He lurched to his feet and
sprang on her, shoving her to the stone

floor. Why her head didn't crack open like a melon she didn't know. "Ow!" she yelled. "Watch it—my arm's already hurt."

With one hand on either side of her body, he straddled her. A dark beard grew on his face, and his hazel eyes were wide behind his stylish black-rimmed glasses, now sitting a little crookedly on his nose. His breath caused her to turn her face away. For a moment, she strained to push him away, then realized she was totally at his mercy.

His voice was calm. "I need food badly. We're going inside, and you're going to cook it for me," he said. He clambered off her and pulled her to her feet, stumbling as he regained his balance, but keeping a grip on her arm.

Good. He wouldn't kill her until the meal was done. If she played dumb, maybe he wouldn't kill her at all.

With his other hand, he pulled a gun out of his pocket. The nonchalance of his movements scared her more than any words could have. He shoved the weapon in her side and marched her slowly across the garden, as if he were a houseguest getting a little glimpse of the late harvest. Once in the house, he checked the doors and locked all but one, then sat down at the breakfast table, pulled out his gold case and a lighter, and lit up a cigarette. His eyes lazily checked out the room, noting everything in sight. "An ashtray, please," he commanded.

"We don't smoke here," she said. She was way too calm, practically floating on her feet because of that last codeine pill. She needed something to pull her to earth.

"I know. I'm sorry, I must. Anyway," he said slyly, "your husband Bill and your underage Janie are not here anyway, to be affected by second-hand smoke."

She knew then that Reingold had investigated her family, probably right down to the size of their mortgage. Maybe he suspected that by this time, Bill had told her everything about him. Glumly, she realized her life wasn't worth much right now. If she only had a plan . . .

He ordered breakfast as if he were in a restaurant, and she played his game, listening and frowning slightly, like a dense waitress. "I must have eggs," he said, "several eggs in a light omelet with cheese. And meat, if you have any. Bacon, sausage, ham, something of that sort. Toast with butter, please, *not* margarine. And coffee, very strong, with cream."

The hazel eyes focused on her. "After I eat, my dear, we will take off in your car."

"Take off for where?"

"As you Americans say, 'for parts south.' "

"Where's your car?" she asked, turning to get things from the refrigerator so that he couldn't see her face.

"I think you know. I had to leave it up at Frank Porter's yesterday evening."

She remembered the papers he'd wanted Eddie to sign—at his father's wake. *A real estate deal one minute,* she thought, *and hijacking plutonium warheads the next. Was that part of his horizontal integration?* "I'm sorry if that put a damper on your deal."

He tapped his cigarette ashes into a saucer she had skidded across the table toward him, and flicked her a worldly-wise look. "If you were to call me a Renaissance man, Louise, you would be right on the mark—as you gun-happy Americans are wont to say. I handle a vast array of business deals, all over the world. But *no* deal—even for the best parcel of open land left in Colorado—is worth getting involved in a murder. And a messy one, at that."

He was getting chattier and chattier, and she was getting wider awake. On the counter, she had assembled ingredients for a very good breakfast. She put on the coffee and began grating the sharp cheddar cheese.

Reingold took a deep draught on his cigarette, as if

preparing himself to talk about something distasteful. "The scene at Frank Porter's house was quite unnecessary. Anyone who watches American movies knows it is much easier to kill than that. But instead, here was a grown man writhing on the floor, retching his guts out and dying as I watched."

Louise popped six pieces of low-fat bacon into a frying pan and turned a gentle heat on underneath them, playing for time.

And then the phone rang. "Please—do not answer," commanded Reingold. She turned back to the stove and let it ring. A sense of desperation filled her when the caller broke the connection without leaving a message. No one knew she was here alone with this villain. Her hands shook as she broke six eggs into a bowl and began whisking them.

Reingold had lapsed into silence, his back bent as he slumped down in the chair like a ruined member of the aristocracy. He looked as tired as she felt. Turning her back squarely to him, Louise carefully added ingredients to the omelet mix, ending with the cheese. She wanted this to taste good, so that her guest would eat up the whole thing.

"Matters were made much worse, of course, when a parade of sheriff's deputies arrived."

She smiled at him over her shoulder. "What's the matter," she asked innocently, "didn't you want to talk with them?"

He gave her a sour look. "I had to take to the ground to get out of there, though of course the foothills of the Rockies are nothing to me. I'm a proficient skier, and quite at home in the back country. I decided that you must help me escape. It was no trouble to get to Lyons, though I was somewhat conspicuous in my Armani jacket, especially in view of the fact that the town was having a 'good old boy' celebration." He exhaled smoke through his nose haughtily, and Louise wondered if he ever lost his composure.

"I arranged to borrow a young lad's truck, but it ran very poorly. In fact, it gave out on the way here and I had to walk a distance. I saw your greenhouse and decided to wait until morning rather than trip your silly alarm system. Without the proper tools these things can be quite a nuisance."

Having drunk the orange juice she gave him, he had mustered up enough energy to produce one of his famous smiles. "So we will go away together. I presume that's agreeable to you?"

"As long as you let me drive."

"*No,*" he said firmly, "You'll be tied up—I think that should suffice. I want you immobile, and unable to use your ice pick, or whatever you employed to ruin my expensive tires—Christ . . ."

She realized a less wealthy man would have sworn with more feeling. But wealthy as he was, he still sat there at her kitchen table, out of resources. He sighed, and looked over at the sizzling frying pan where Louise was doing her best to create the perfect omelet. "When will that food be done?"

Don't press a hungry man too hard, she thought philosophically, pulling the golden-brown toast from the toaster and buttering it. She drained the bacon carefully and placed it on the plate along with the puffy omelet. On a smaller plate she put the toast, and even found a jar of black raspberry jam to serve with it. She delivered the meal to the table, along with a cup of strong Colombian coffee. She watched him wolf the food down, realizing he must have gone without dinner last night. Too bad he hadn't come earlier to Frank Porter's and snacked on poisoned buns. She poured more coffee in his cup.

"This is *quite* good," he said.

She didn't reply, because she was thinking so hard of what she should do next.

The phone rang again, and again she let it ring. This time it was Pete. He wondered where she had gone, and wanted her to phone and let him know she was all right.

Reingold listened carefully to the message, fork paused in midair. He smiled. "A popular lady," he said.

She didn't smile back.

"And you're my insurance." His voice had developed an insinuating quality. "You'll make a pretty companion, especially when you clean up a bit."

A wave of pain moved through her head, somehow leaving it feeling clearer. She thought to herself, *Companion, indeed. He means to make me his hostage.* Suddenly, she was completely awake, the codeine effect gone. As she puttered about the sink, cleaning up, she eyed the collection of knives in a wooden case on the counter. The big iron frying pan hanging from a rack. The square Chinese chopping knife she knew was in the drawer only inches from her left hand. As her eyes scanned the kitchen shelf, she spied another weapon, lying in a decorative garden basket. A broken pair of heavy-duty pruning shears with jagged, formidable edges, that the lady of the house apparently couldn't bring herself to throw away. While Reingold concentrated on the food, she stuck them in the waistband of her gardening pants. They were so uncomfortable that they made her feel like a *penitente,* one who deliberately tortures the body to cleanse the soul.

Wanted: A Bold Solution

(The Jungle Look, Revisited)

MAYBE IT IS A RESPONSE TO years of exposure to pink-and-blue English cottage gardens. "Bold" and "tropical" gardens have taken hold in the public's fancy, and continue to be the favorite trend of designers. This flies in the face of the realities of temperature zones: Most Americans, for instance, live in climates too cold for tender plants. Clever gardeners achieve these effects with hardier varieties, while always tempted to cave in and buy a tree fern* —or the nonhardy banana plant, which can be a good deal of trouble.

Acknowledging that exotics like these may make or break our tropical garden, let's look at a few hardy plants that provide bulk and/or bold color, and thus make the job easier.

The hot end of the color spectrum: Red is the first color people think of when they plan bold gardens, and it will go far in helping you believe you've created a jungle. Second favorite is probably yellow, with orange a close third. (Don't forget, one has to balance these with such shy additions as gray, blue, and purple.) Many hardy plants come in this bright color range.

Crocosmia was almost designed for a bold garden: Colors range from pale yellow to deep red. It is not only fiery, it is sturdy. Its lines are graceful, and the flowers fall in little fans, providing blooms from July to September. This plant likes a rich, moist, sunny, or partially shady environment, and wants to

---

* Sir David Attenborough wintered his Mexican tree fern on his London stoop, with some browned foliage the only result. If you're zone five or above, maybe you can keep yours alive in a cubbyhole on your own front porch. *Dicksonia antarctica* is hardy to −18 degrees Celsius. If you succumb to a sumptuous banana plant, it's best to winter it over in that prize spot in your south window.

be divided before too crowded. The newest hybrids have larger, showier flowers. Even its spiky foliage is a relief from all the other full-leafed plants around it. There is no better wild, tropical accent than this in our bold garden.

We're talking *really* **bold here:** For a double-whammy of primary colors, plant a clump of bicolor yellow-and-orange "red-hot poker" plant (*Kniphophia uvaria*) behind the crocosmia. (The more restrained gardener may prefer to save the magic of *Kniphophia* for a more subtle spot—say, as the focal point in an herb-filled all-green garden. *But,* we're talking bold here, so why not a little overkill?)

At the feet of the graceful crocosmia, try the hosta. Although it has insignificant flowers, this specimen is one of the best ways to introduce rich green tones to our garden—from blue-green to chartreuse, and many shades in between. Variegated-leaved hosta is one of the most valued plants in existence. It's hardy even in cold climes, and may even outlive the gardener. In spring, the plant unfolds its large leaves and adds unbelievable class to almost any planting.

Bergenia, like hosta, is useful simply for its foliage. Its main attraction is its fat, satisfying, leathery leaves, that add a strong base note to the lower plant story. It goes well in combination with the brilliant *Liatrus spicata*.

The impact of the daylily: One can never underestimate the contribution of the daylily, whether designing a dramatic tropics or an old-fashioned garden. It comes in enough shades to please everyone, and has generous-sized flowers. A vibrant red or orange clump will light up the garden, and its color impact only increases over the years as the plant spreads.

White is a necessity in this garden, relieving our eye and adding drama. Introduce it by way of clouds of tiny white blossoms of baby's breath, spikes of white verbascum, or big white buttons on the tall *Achillea ptarmica* ''Boule de Neige.'' This *achillea* is the perfect coda for dramatic displays of hotter plants.

The hollyhock can be underrated. It is an old-fashioned stem that some people might not think of as a quality flower, much less bold. Yet one gardener's use of apricot hollyhocks, *Alcea rosea,* teamed with the flaming orange double flowers of a daylily, *Hemerocallis fulva* ''Flore Pleno,'' and a flutter of white *achillea,* could have won a design prize.

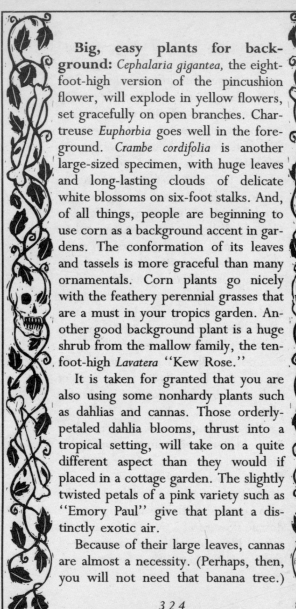

Big, easy plants for background: *Cephalaria gigantea,* the eight-foot-high version of the pincushion flower, will explode in yellow flowers, set gracefully on open branches. Chartreuse *Euphorbia* goes well in the foreground. *Crambe cordifolia* is another large-sized specimen, with huge leaves and long-lasting clouds of delicate white blossoms on six-foot stalks. And, of all things, people are beginning to use corn as a background accent in gardens. The conformation of its leaves and tassels is more graceful than many ornamentals. Corn plants go nicely with the feathery perennial grasses that are a must in your tropics garden. Another good background plant is a huge shrub from the mallow family, the ten-foot-high *Lavatera* ''Kew Rose.''

It is taken for granted that you are also using some nonhardy plants such as dahlias and cannas. Those orderly-petaled dahlia blooms, thrust into a tropical setting, will take on a quite different aspect than they would if placed in a cottage garden. The slightly twisted petals of a pink variety such as ''Emory Paul'' give that plant a distinctly exotic air.

Because of their large leaves, cannas are almost a necessity. (Perhaps, then, you will not need that banana tree.)

Use them in clusters of five or more to create the greatest impact.

Adding a few pots: Endless variations can be achieved by adding specialty plants grown in pots—ginger, cyperus—even water plants. Tuck a trough or barrel of water in the border, and grow in it the beautiful, tall, hardy, white-flowering lotus *Nelumbo nucifera*. The lotus will remain attractive through the season, producing distinctive flat seedheads of exquisite beauty that can be dried for bouquets.

Hardy favorites such as verbena, the big, bulbous allium, monkshood (*Aconitum*), and a clump of spiny *Eryngium*, may have filled all your needs for the color blue. (Delphinium, somehow, won't do; though beautiful, it's too prissy for jungles.) But bold gardens can hardly do without one nonhardy plant, the agapanthus. Pot up some, insert them in the garden, and let their tall, swaying, deep blue flower heads cool off your tropical Eden.

Chapter 28

BILL THREW HIS CLOTHES INTO the suitcase helter-skelter, then went into the bathroom and desperately scooped up his toilet articles. Never had he packed in such a sloppy fashion, but he couldn't care less. This morning, he had come down quickly off the high he had experienced—in fact, that they'd *all* experienced—when they knew their strike force was going to succeed. An end to the good-natured badinage with his able and witty Texas colleagues, an end to the mutual self-congratulations.

It would be small consolation to foil the plan of high-tech nuclear burglars if in the process he had put his own wife in danger.

He had phoned Louise again, to tell her he was coming, and was worried when she didn't answer. The person she spoke of meeting couldn't be Josef Reingold. Surely, in the space of a few days, Louise couldn't have gotten mixed up with that man, told him where she lived, and put herself in jeopardy.

And yet, for some reason, he was uncomfortable about her being alone in that house. She might be outside with Herb and his wife, petting the llama, or taking a tour of Herb's farm—but that didn't make sense, because she'd told him she was tired and needed sleep.

It would be overkill to request a sheriff's deputy to go visit her—he'd do it himself. He left a quick phone message with his associates, grabbed his suitcase, and ran for his car.

Pete Fitzsimmons had planned to go fishing this morning, but decided it would be better, as a strictly business thing, to pay a visit to Louise Eldridge. So he had taken a little jog around the neighborhood and then hung out on the patio reading a book until he thought she would be up and about.

He had tried to contact Marty Corbin at the Boulderado this morning, but the producer and his wife were not back from their trip yet. Marty should be told that Louise had been injured, and the chances that she could go on camera Monday morning were slim. Of course, he needed to see for himself how Louise felt—and looked.

Besides that, he missed her. He'd tried to get over his attraction to Louise, but he realized he hadn't, not yet. He'd known from the moment he first saw her in those

silly new western clothes that she was a sweetheart. He'd
tried to keep her away by acting like an asshole, but it
hadn't helped much—which in a way was a comfort, because she could see right through him to the fact that he
wasn't an asshole.

It might help if he met Bill. That would give some
reality to the fact that the lady was already taken.

He put on his hat and climbed in his truck. She couldn't
have gone far, because she'd had that buckshot taken out of
her arm last night and he knew darned well that this morning it would feel like a hot poker. Most likely she was out
walking, or maybe just sitting in the garden. Or in bed,
drugged to kill the pain.

He zigzagged through town and then charged north on
Broadway, but took care to go only seven miles over the
speed limit. There was a lady judge in Boulder these days
who threw the book at people who sped. And if they went
to court to protest the ticket, they got slapped with an
additional twenty-five dollars in court costs, just for the
pleasure of listening to the smart-mouthed babe's little
jokes.

❧

Reingold dabbed at his mouth with his napkin. "I commend you. Everything was *quite* good."

"Yes, you said that already." Moving like an old lady
now with the pruners in her waistband, Louise took his
plate over to the sink and rinsed it.

He shoved the chair back and stood up. "Now it's time
to go. But I need to find something in this house, and I
want you with me while I look for it. Tape of some kind,
preferably what you call duct tape."

"Duct tape?" A twinge of fear ran through her, but she
tried to pass it off with a joke. Lightly, she said, "I could

tell you stories about the effectiveness of duct tape that you wouldn't believe . . ."

"Never mind being facetious, Louise."

He pulled her to his side, and she gasped as she got a good jab from the shears. He began walking with her toward the utility room.

"Are you going to put it over my mouth?"

He didn't answer. "Will we find it in here?"

"I have no idea."

"That's all right," he said, tightening his hold on her arm. "We'll substitute rope—or even rags, my dear." At least she could be thankful that the man lacked personal animosity toward her. And yet who knew what he would do if he did find tape? Her left arm ached in anticipation; if he bound her up, the pain would be excruciating.

She only hoped her little ploy would get her out of this mess.

Then, they heard the crunching of tires on the driveway, a door slam, and someone whistling. It was a light, birdlike whistle. Pete. Her heart gave a happy thump. But then she realized the danger Pete was in. To Reingold, a man like Pete was a challenge—unlike her, an already-wounded woman. She had to warn him, whether or not she was punished by Reingold.

"Pete, heads *up*! He has a gun!"

"Bad move, Louise," said Reingold. He slid behind her and with strong fingers squeezed the wounded arm so that her whole body shuddered with the pain.

"Ohhh," she moaned.

He pulled out the gun again, and whispered, "Shut up. Come with me, and no more tricks." He prodded her forward through the house, and she cooperated dumbly, the pain in her body overwhelming.

He stumbled once, over a couple of pillows Janie had

thrown on the floor a week ago and Louise had never removed. A good sign, she thought.

Outside, she heard scuttling across the ground. Chipmunks—or Pete?

Reingold was thinking out loud. "The car is in the carport. Your friend is on the other side of the house, from the sound of it." His eyes glazed over for a moment, and he swayed. Then he heaved a big sigh and said, "We have to get out of here and head south. You're my companion, Louise. Get the car keys and let's be off."

She retrieved the keys from the hall table, and he ordered her to open the door that led to the carport. She tried to delay by fumbling with it for a moment, but, catching a glimpse of his dark face, quickly turned the bolt and pushed the door open. He shoved her out in front of him, and told her, "You'll drive after all. Get in." He waited until she was settled with her seat belt on, looking down at her with remote eyes. She knew he would kill her or Pete if either of them got in the way of his departure.

Reingold moved quickly around the car, gun clutched in his right hand. She turned her head to watch him, hoping for an opening to get away.

Suddenly, he disappeared from view, and she heard a curse in German. He had stumbled over the trash bag she had dropped earlier to answer Ann's call. With nervous hands, she loosened her seat belt, pulled the pruners out of her waistband, and opened the car door. Crawling carefully along the driveway, she spotted Reingold, drawing his gun and ready to get up. At the same time as she raised the heavy shears over her head, two voices shouted out simultaneously: *"Drop it or I'll shoot!"*

Bill had come up the driveway and had his handgun trained on Reingold. Pete Fitzsimmons had cut through the patio and come in from the other side, his shotgun at his shoulder.

Josef Reingold slumped back onto the floor of the car-port. His gun fell to one side, his legs splayed out in front of him, and he raised his hands listlessly above his head. Bill came over and kicked the gun out of the suspect's reach.

"What's wrong with him?" asked Bill. She couldn't help grinning. Her husband looked like an unshaven dere-lict in a low-crowned felt cowboy hat and disreputable clothes that hadn't been washed in a week. "Is he snakebit?"

"I drugged his breakfast," she said. "And now, honey, meet my cameraman. This is Pete. Pete, this is Bill."

Pete took one hand off his weapon and tipped his sweat-stained fisherman's hat.

Bill nodded in return and said to him, "Hold your gun on him while I get some rope?" To which Pete nodded again.

She grinned. "I can't believe you two are finally meet-ing."

Bill shook his head. "And I can't believe that you caught my man."

❧

Louise felt sorry for Pete Fitzsimmons. Little was ex-plained to him, as Josef Reingold was taken away under maximum security by members of the strike team. Louise, Bill, and Pete sat and talked awhile, but it was awkward, for the cameraman was obviously filled with questions that Bill couldn't answer. He must realize the arrest had some-thing to do with the commotion at Stony Flats. All he said to Bill was, "I guess I have a little clearer idea of what you do for a living." Bill smiled and said nothing.

"I know you don't want to talk about that," said the cameraman. "But something we *ought* to talk about is what your wife did last night. It was pretty impressive." He turned to Louise and grinned. "And by the way, I guess I owe ya ten grand. I never thought you'd solve this thing."

When Bill heard about the drama up at the ranch, he exchanged a long look with Louise. "Catching a two-time killer—what a gal. I was afraid those ranch murders would end up right on your doorstep."

"Pete took a picture of the murderer on the day that the old rancher was shot." She smiled at her friend. "The mysterious figure standing in the ponderosas. But no one could recognize who it was."

"Yeah," said Pete. "It was a little hard to figure that an old lady killed Jimmy Porter." He got up and said, "I'll be shovin' off. But I'll see you tomorrow up at that ranch, Louise. I see your bruises don't show—that's good. Are you gonna make it?"

"I think so. Would you call Marty and make it an hour later?"

"Deal," he said, and stuck out his hand as if he and Louise were the kind of buddies that did a lot of handshaking. Then he reached out to shake Bill's hand. "Will I see you—or maybe not—"

"You'll see me," said Bill. "I'm going on location with you tomorrow, and the next day, too."

"Good," said Pete. "We could always use another grip." There was faint sarcasm in his voice. Both he and Louise knew a grip was the low man on the totem pole, and nobody would want the job if he didn't need it badly.

"Sure," said Bill, escorting him to the door. "I do grip real good, don't I, honey?"

She smiled. "He sure does." It sounded so chummy for the three of them to be on location together up at the ranch. She hoped Bill and Pete would learn to like each other.

Once the cameraman had left, Bill came over and gently took her in his arms. Tipping her chin up to kiss her, he paused in surprise, and smoothed his hand over her cheek. "Louise—your face—it's soft again."

She smiled. "I know. I've worked on it." Despite his rough whiskers, she gave him a lingering kiss, then nestled her head on his shoulder while he continued to hold her. "Honey, do you know what I need right now?"

"Anything, baby."

"Food." She looked up at him.

"This may not be romantic, but I'm starved. I haven't even had breakfast, and it must be noon. I only made breakfast for your pal Reingold, and then watched him eat."

"And you slipped him those codeines."

"You thought he was snakebit? I must say, Bill, I'm impressed with your western idioms. Never seen anybody pick them up so fast."

He grinned at her. "It's Texas. The idioms stick to you like flies on flypaper. A very funny place. Did you know why Texas cowboys wear pointed boots?"

"No, why?" she said, realizing he was feeling very good about himself.

He crinkled his blue eyes into a premature smile. "That's to kill the roaches in the corners." Then he straightened his face into a mock-grave expression. "A sample of Texas humor—though it isn't too far from the truth, since roaches grow to the size of rats down there. Now, to get a little more serious, Louise. My part of this task force effort was on the receiving end, where they had a very intricate scheme planned to get the plutonium warheads across the border to Mexico—"

"Which is where Reingold's plant is."

"Hmm," he said, surprised at how much she knew. "That's right. Reingold had this scheme rigged all the way from Colorado to a getaway by sea to the Middle East. He did it right under the nose of the Stony Flats plant manager—"

"You mean Spangler wasn't involved?"

Bill pursed his lips, "I might have known you would have met Spangler. No—his assistant manager was the link with Reingold's outfit. Spangler must feel damn lucky the thing didn't come off. They had their plan in place, right down to paying off the man who runs the traffic light in the truck yard at the El Paso-Juarez border. That system is supposed to make a random determination of which trucks will be searched. But Reingold paid plenty to assure that the light was going to go green for *his* truck full of warheads." He shook his head. "I have a lot to tell you, but let's eat while we talk."

"I know just the place. You'll get a great piece of pie, and you'll meet Ruthie Dunn. She was probably the first one to make me see that the old ranch woman could be a murderer."

"How?" he asked.

"Ruthie helped me visualize the scene up there in that closed-in mountain community. The pregnant spinster. The young rancher next door, who charmed every lady he ever met. The rancher's morose wife whose child had just died horribly of lockjaw. Then the mysterious deaths that followed. It made a kind of insane sense. Later, this hypothesis—as crazy as it was—was all corroborated by our neighbor down the road. He's an expert on post-traumatic stress . . ."

Her husband looked confused. She caressed his whiskered cheek. "It's complicated."

They heard the sound of tires on the dirt driveway. A car door slammed, and footsteps sounded in the gravel. The voices were familiar—their daughter Janie, and her boyfriend, Chris Radebaugh. The glowing, sunburnt couple walked in, in shorts and hiking boots, carrying a load of baggage—and looking, as far as Louise was concerned, much too comfortable with each other. Louise and Bill stood open-mouthed.

Janie said, "Aren't you going to say hello to us?"

"Of course," said Louise, and came over and embraced them. She looked up at the young man who was her daughter's boyfriend; he seemed taller, blonder, and more virile than when she saw him last. "But how did *you* get here?"

"Well, Mrs. Eldridge, we might have seemed to deceive you a little, though we didn't mean to," said the tall young man, shoving a shock of hair away from his eyes. "You see, as soon as Janie left, I called the camp, and they just happened to have a vacancy on the counselor roster."

Janie had one hand on his shoulder and was leaning against him, smiling. "Chris took over as a counselor."

"You mean you've spent the whole time together up there in Estes Park—"

"Don't worry, Ma," said Janie, flipping back her blond hair, "we not only had chaperones, we *were* the chaperones."

"Oh," said Bill matter-of-factly, "no problem. So, what do you say the four of us go out and eat? Your ma and I have some exciting things to tell you young people. Of course, I can't reveal too much, but some of it's going to be public, anyway." Louise hoped this assignment signaled the end of Bill's covert work with the CIA—but it was a very small hope.

Janie came over to her father and put her slender arms around his neck. "Dad, you think *you* have stories to tell? Wait 'til Chris and I tell you what happened when we climbed Long's Peak in a snowstorm!"

Louise smiled, basking in the comfort of having her family with her, even though she knew she wouldn't get a word in edgewise. Too many exciting stories to tell—a perilous climb on a fourteen-thousand-footer, a thwarted hijacking of nuclear warheads. How could she possibly top those? After all, what was so exciting about a double murder? But maybe . . .

"Want to hear a story about a *lion*?"

ABOUT THE AUTHOR

ANN RIPLEY writes mystery books and short stories in her home in Lyons, Colorado, where she lives with her husband, Tony. A former newspaperwoman, she also is an organic gardener.

ANN RIPLEY'S

Gardening Mysteries

"This hybrid of traditional whodunit and up-to-the-minute gardening guide is certain to appeal to mystery readers with a green thumb."

—*The Denver Post*

Mulch
___57734-4 $5.99/$7.99

Death of a Garden Pest
___57730-1 $5.99/$7.99

Death of a Political Plant
___57735-2 $5.99/$7.99

The Garden Tour Affair
___57736-0 $5.99/$8.99

The Perennial Killer
___57737-9 $5.99/$8.99

- -